THE OTHERWORLD

ALSO BY KATHERINE GENET

The Wilde Grove Series

The Gathering

The Belonging

The Rising

The Singing

Wilde Grove Series 2: Selena Wilde

Follow The Wind

The Otherworld

Non-Fiction

Ground & Centre

The Dreamer's Way (coming soon)

The Otherworld

KATHERINE GENET

Wych Elm Books

Wych Elm Books

Otago, NZ

www.wychelmbooks.com

contact@wychelmbooks.com

ISBN: 978-0-473- 64799-5

For Barbara, my mother, who told me to focus, and tell the truth.

1

IT WAS STILL SUMMER, WHEN EVERYTHING INSIDE SELENA SAID it should still be winter. There should be a cold wind coming down from the hills, a crust of snow underfoot, and if she lifted her head, she should hear the distant crash and roar of the sea churned to cold fury.

She lifted her head. The air was warm, soft and fragrant against her cheeks, as though she'd stepped into some exotic eastern market, all spices and silk.

A bird called out from the tree above her, a series of clucking and throat clearing before it sang three clear notes then fell silent, apparently satisfied. Selena took a breath, straightened her shoulders and walked, following the path through the Botanic Garden as it wended its way downhill, then back up. She passed a sloping lawn, blinked at the groups of young people lying supine in the sunlight, their laughter floating lazily on the air above them. Selena dived back into the shade again, turned right onto a narrower path, then turned right again onto a path that was barely more than a deer track.

Except of course, this was a garden, and there were no deer.

Still, this track wove its way through forest, full mostly of beech trees, their leaves small and precious, little green coins. Selena breathed deeply, tasting the thick mulch of the forest floor and ducked her head under a low branch, smiling as the twiggy finger lifted a strand of her hair. She tugged it gently away and continued, letting herself relax.

It was February, not much past Lughnasagh and Rue was back at school. Teresa had gone home in the new year, leaving behind plans for their garden and strict instructions for the planting. Selena smiled slightly. Teresa had been a whirlwind, touring all the plant nurseries, spending hours talking to gardeners, learning all about the native flora and fauna.

She'd left behind – pointedly, Selena thought – a book on the native trees.

Selena broke out of the small patch of forest and crossed the path to walk along a grassy bank towards the stand of oaks. The garden was divided into great sections, each with plants and trees from different areas of the world, and it was a marvellous place, Selena had decided. She was fortunate to live right on its doorstep, and she came walking in it whenever she could get away, learning her way around, seeing where she was drawn.

Reaching out, she touched her fingers to one of the oaks. The first acorns were dropping to cover the ground around the tree's roots, and she stooped down to pick one up, holding it loosely in curled fingers, her other hand still pressed against the tree's trunk. Selena closed her eyes.

Her spirit kin Hind flashed across her vision, tail flicking as she disappeared again. Selena opened her eyes.

How she missed her home.

There. She'd admitted it.

'I miss my home,' she murmured, unsure if she was talking to the tree or herself, and did it matter? The words had been on her tongue for the last week, now that the excitement of the move and entertaining two children over the summer had quietened, and she had time to herself again.

To be herself.

Except who, Selena wondered, was she, when she was here and not Lady of the Grove?

'I miss the woods at Wellsford,' she said, and now she was talking to the tree. Her fingers tightened around the acorn. 'I miss the Fae Folk of those woods.' She closed her eyes again and leaned against the sturdy trunk of the oak, sighing.

Something feather-light landed on her shoulder, and she stilled a moment, feeling the soft weight of it. A bird.

When Selena opened her eyes, there was no bird, and yet there was - she could still feel it there. Straightening slowly, Selena slowed her breath, not wanting to frighten the small spirit creature away.

'Where did you come from?' she asked.

The youngster – barely bigger than her hand – shifted its weight, then spread its spirit wings and took off.

Selena touched her shoulder where it had sat and

couldn't help the smile that bloomed on her face. She looked off into the air.

'Thank you,' she called. 'I am blessed by your visit.'

She was. The bird had come to her, greeted her, acknowledging her presence in its land. Selena shook her head.

What an honour.

The oak rustled his leaves in a quick breeze, and she nodded. 'Yes,' she said, as though in answer. 'Yes, you are right.'

She'd been loath to go bumbling across the spirit borders of this land that was so far from her home, so new to her. The Fae Folk of this land would have different customs to those she was used to.

One did not go barging into their world.

But now, she thought, now a bird had come and greeted her briefly, and she knew that her presence was being acknowledged.

Contact had been made.

The knowledge renewed her. Selena stood, touched the oak once more.

'Thank you, my new friend,' she said.

She slipped the acorn into her pocket and nodded. 'It's time, isn't it?'

The tree agreed with her. It was time.

Selena patted his fine trunk, then stepped back onto the path, following it in the direction that would lead to the edge of the huge garden and out onto the road across from her new home.

Where her new friends would be waiting for her.

It was time to find the place and space to go travelling

between the worlds again. She felt almost as though she would have to learn a new pathway through the worlds – a thought that might have been tiring, a weight upon her, but she touched her shoulder now, where the small bird had rested, and felt the warmth of its feathers, its large, slow-blinking eyes, its curved beak.

The task could also be a joy, if she chose it to be.

She'd been given an invitation. Perhaps she could find a welcome in this new world after all.

2

'Goodness,' Selena said. 'That smells wonderful.'

Tara looked up from the book on the kitchen counter and smiled. There was a touch of flour on her cheek.

'I never really did much baking,' Tara said, glancing back down at her book. 'But I'm trying out some biscuits for when the children get home.'

'Well,' Selena said, looking around the kitchen, where if there weren't cooking utensils, Tara had stacked books, and brought in pots of flowers and plants and herbs. A smile touched Selena's lips.

Tara was becoming quite the kitchen witch.

'We're all going to be very appreciative, I'd say,' Selena continued. 'What flavour are these?'

'Honey and walnut.' Tara grimaced then laughed. 'I'm trying to make them as healthy as possible.'

'And imbuing them with your love and caring. Which is as important as any other ingredient.'

Tara coloured slightly and glanced around at the books

she'd bought over the last month. There were several of them, and she'd pored over each one, drawn to the idea of making and serving magic through something so humble as tending her house and family.

And she did, she knew, consider everyone in the household her new family. The children especially, but Selena and Dandy too. She looked down at the counter, ran a fingertip through a small spill of flour. Even Damien felt like he was family.

Sometimes, she thought, the family you found and chose along the way, could be more supportive than the one you were born into. She still had her parents, but they lived in the North Island, and she saw them too rarely now.

Selena watched the thoughts flicker across Tara's face and smiled to herself. The young woman was finding her way, she thought. For a moment, she wanted to draw up a seat at the table and sit there with a piping hot cup of tea and just talk to Tara, ask her about how Clover was doing at the kindergarten. How Tara was finding all her books on witchcraft.

But she had to follow up the invitation of the small spirit owl who had landed on her shoulder.

There would be time for tea and chatting afterwards.

SELENA HAD TRIED TO FIND A SPOT IN THE BOTANIC GARDEN where she might sit undisturbed for an hour at a time to travel deeply into the Otherworld, but she had decided that there was really no such spot. It was a popular place, especially for the university students who were flooding back into the city in anticipation of the new semester. They ranged back and forth all around the large garden, and in flocks, like noisy geese.

There was the old cemetery, which spread along the flanks of an alarmingly steep hill, the nineteenth century graves facing feet first down the slope, as though placed that way to brace themselves, but although Selena liked the paths that wound around the quiet graves, she'd decided that using that place to do a spot of travelling might bring up more issues than she cared to deal with. The dead seemed quiet there, but she'd caught whispers, echoes. And although a cemetery really had no more cause to be haunted than any other place, still they often were.

The ghost tour operator, who trooped groups of wide-eyed people into the old cemetery at dusk, certainly spun a good story that it was so. Selena had stopped and listened to a snatch of his patter once, but it was the usual sort of thing – love stories gone wrong, early and tragic deaths. The human litany of sorrows.

And so, she climbed the stairs to the attic rooms. The larger of these she had taken for her own use, feeling like a pigeon nesting in the rafters.

But it was necessary, she knew, to make the best of what she had. And she had a room, and a spirit she'd taught to flex beyond the confines of body and room. That was plenty. She couldn't touch her feet to the earth, and she missed the caves of Wilde Grove, but this room was becoming a sanctuary, nonetheless.

The air was still, hot, but the room was big enough that it wasn't suffocating, and Selena switched on the fans she'd set up, the blades of which stirred the air to circulating. She went to her altar, already calming her breathing, doing it without thought, the result of fifty years of practice.

She touched the bowl of water, set carefully in the western position. Her fingertip wet, she marked her forehead with it.

'Spirits of the west,' she murmured. 'Spirits of water. The great salmon who returns home against the current each year, bless me with your instinct.'

The fans turned the still air in the room to a warm breeze against her back. Selena reached for the rock, the size of her palm, that she'd picked up in the Garden on one of her walks and brought home weighing her pocket down. It was volcanic rock, emptied from a mountain in a blaze of fire and ash ten million years ago.

'Spirits of the south,' she whispered. 'Spirits of earth, the rock under my feet, spirit of hare who burrows into the soil to birth her family, bless me with your earthy groundedness.'

Selena picked up a feather, also brought home from a recent walk and stirred it into the air, a slight smile touching her lips. 'Spirits of the east,' she said. 'Spirits of air, of the wind that rises with the dawn to trace secrets across the land, I ask you to whisper now to me.'

She stood still for a moment, feeling the breeze from the fans against her and closing her eyes, letting herself fall open like a flower in bloom. The breeze whispered, and she felt, briefly, for a moment, something threading through it, a cry, a call, but it was there and gone before she could tug it into sight. Selena opened her eyes, put the feather down, made her way around to the next point on her altar.

She lit the candle with a match that sparked and fizzed.

The flame took, leapt high, then sank down, fat and satisfied. Selena watched it, drew breath, spoke.

'Spirits of fire,' she said. 'Spirits of the north, I conjure you and bid your blessing upon me. Great snake who basks in the heat of the sun, lend me your wisdom.'

Selena paused, wondering for a moment if she'd got the elements of the directions right. Since changing them around for the southern hemisphere, she'd had to keep checking herself, to see that she was doing it correctly. It annoyed her, that her tongue seemed to stutter over them, but it was what it was. She sighed. It wasn't always easy to begin over.

Or begin at all, she thought.

But begin she must. Each day in this new land, this new house, with these new people. This was where she had been called to, and so the challenge would not be beyond her. One step at a time, she reminded herself, a smile on her lips again at the small, old piece of wisdom.

'Here I am,' she said into the warm air. 'My Lady, here I am, letting my purpose flow.' She took a long, slow breath, held it for a few beats of her heart, then let it softly out, following it with another, preparing herself. She picked up the string of seeds, conkers, and acorns she'd brought with her on the plane trip and slipped it over her head.

She picked up the two crystal balls, which had also come with her to this new land. They were heavy in her palms, one yellow citrine, one clear quartz. The sun and the moon.

Once, when she'd first begun her learning of the ways at Wilde Grove, she'd done her first travelling, and come to a maze, where a stone woman wept. There, in niches in the wall near her, had been a crystal sun and moon and she'd slipped them into her pocket, taking them on instinct.

Later, back in the waking world, she'd searched for their equivalent, and now they were part of her practice. She liked to hold one in each palm, the stones growing warm against her flesh. The sun in her right, the moon in her left.

Selena took the crystal balls and went to her chair. It was more comfortable than a cave floor, she thought wryly, settling herself in its padded depths and tipping it backwards so that she was almost lying down, her face towards the sunlight through the sky light, blinking in the brightness. She shook her head – that much light in her eyes would be distracting. She got up again and fetched a scarf, sat back down and adjusted it over her eyes so that the room was dim.

Here, there was no Morghan to drum or sing for her as she travelled. She let that thought waft about in her head for a moment then blew it away. She was where she was. Circumstances were what they were.

And there was the weight on her shoulder again. The small warm weight of a bird come to visit her in its spirit form. She could almost smell its feathers, see its wide round eyes.

She closed her own and the cloth over her face made the room dark. She listened to her breathing and slowed it down a fraction more. Her legs and arms became heavy, and she squeezed her muscles, then relaxed them.

With each breath, she let herself sink down further into the dimness, let herself relax so that her body became just something warm and heavy.

Then she wasn't in the armchair at all.

She wasn't anywhere she recognised at all, was she?

But she was, Selena realised a moment later.

She did recognise this place. It was one of the paths in the Botanic Garden.

This was not her usual way into the Otherworld.

She walked down it, her spirit body long and lean, stepping easily along the path, hands swinging.

Now, she could see the bird on her shoulder, its small claws digging into her flesh as it balanced itself there. She was an owl, Selena saw, a small, spotted owl, cream and brown, speckled, her eyes golden and warm.

'Hello little one,' Selena murmured. 'I'm pleased to meet you.'

The path under Selena's feet took her not into the Botanic Garden, but into the shadows and shades of the Wildwood, and Selena stopped walking, shaking her head in wonder. How things always surprised her, she thought. How things changed and adapted when circumstances did. Where before she'd followed the paths through Wilde Grove into the Wildwood, now she followed the path through the garden.

She hadn't known to expect that.

The forest of the Wildwood hadn't changed however, and a smile touched Selena's lips at the thought of Grandfather Oak somewhere in the thick of things, his huge branches hanging wide, his slow-flowing sap that vibrated with an eons-old song.

But it wasn't Grandfather Oak she'd come to see today. The small owl on her shoulder fluffed up her feathers and spread her wings in front of Selena's face, so that for a moment, she was blinded.

And then she was flying, and she laughed with the delight of it, looking out over her speckled wings, feeling the hollow lightness of her bones, and looking down at the treetops with eyes that saw the tiny movements of a mouse on the forest floor between the branches.

The forest was behind her then, and she looked down the flanks of great hills, where water pooled deep and green at the bottom. It was the harbour, she realised. The harbour in her new city, her new home.

But it was not the harbour she was getting used to, standing on the edge of the sports ground at the top of the hill up which the cemetery and Botanic Garden climbed, and where there was a great view of the harbour basin and the large ships that came slowly up the length of the harbour carrying their cargo.

This harbour was placid in the breeze and there were no ships slicing the surface. There were no buildings either, crowding towards the water.

There were only trees. A great carpeting of green and brown, bustling down to the water and back again up the hill.

Trees and a golden scimitar of beach, towards which Selena and the owl flew, feet outstretching to land.

3

THE SAND UNDER SELENA'S FEET WAS COOL, AS THOUGH IT had just rained, and she stood still, looking around, not sure what to expect. This was a part of Dunedin she had not explored.

She suspected it was a part not many did any longer.

But the little owl was still on her shoulder, smoothing her feathers and looking about as though pleased with herself.

'Where have you brought me, little one?' Selena asked, but even as the words left her mouth, she knew the answer.

She was here to meet the local Fae.

As if the thought had conjured them, a line of people emerged from the trees and made their way across the sand towards Selena. They were brown-skinned, and the woman in front had thick black hair that fell in a dark waterfall down her back.

Selena lowered herself to one knee, tucking her chin

down so that she could see only the sand and herself knelt in it. Her heart thumped against her ribs.

'So, this is who Ruru has brought to see us,' the woman's voice said, clear as a bell in the air.

'My Lady,' Selena said, still kneeling, not looking. 'I am honoured to be here.'

There was a pause, and then the voice again. 'You may stand.'

Selena did as she was told and got to her feet as gracefully as she could. She gazed at the woman standing several steps away, amazed and dazed suddenly to be there. She glanced at the array of Fae spread behind their Queen and her heart lifted in a sudden crest of joy.

'The wind whispered of your arrival,' the Queen said, tipping her head to one side. 'Until we were quite sure we needed to meet you.'

Selena bowed in acknowledgment. 'I thank you, my Lady Queen, for sending your owl for me. It is a great boon to make your acquaintance.'

'It is not often now that we meet those who can cross the borders.' The voice became amused. 'You caught my attention.'

'I am honoured.'

'You may introduce yourself.'

Selena straightened, and the small bird lifted from her shoulder and flew to settle upon the Queen's.

'I am Selena, Lady of the Forest,' Selena said. 'Formerly Lady of Wilde Grove.'

'Lady of the Forest,' the Queen repeated, her voice musing. 'All forests are one forest, and their wisdom is deep and wide. But you are far from home. What brings you here?'

The breeze fluttered the feathers woven into the Queen's cloak.

'I answered the call of the wind,' Selena replied.

The Queen's eyebrows rose.

Selena went on. 'The flow of my purpose took me from my homeland to yours, where a child needed me.'

'A child?'

'Yes. A child of my soul family, and of rare and strong talent.'

'Ah,' the Queen said. 'I have felt the ripples of the mind of the one of whom you speak. For certainly it is her.'

'That would be likely, I'm sure,' Selena answered.

They looked at each other, the Queen's gaze appraising, Selena keeping hers neutral, respectful. These Fae were extraordinary, she thought, letting the thought slip to the front of her mind. Regal and beautiful.

The Queen's gaze softened. 'You will come and eat with us,' she said.

Selena released a breath, bowed her head. 'I would be honoured to join you.'

At her answer, a great chattering broke out amongst the ranks of Fae behind their Queen, and they bustled away to prepare the feast, the atmosphere jubilant.

The Queen gestured for Selena to follow her back across the beach where a great fire had been lit now, and a pit uncovered on the other side of it, food being scooped up from the ground in leaf-wrapped bundles that made Selena's mouth water with the scent.

'My people came here alongside the first canoes,' the

Queen said, gesturing for Selena to take a seat beside her upon a carved log. 'We found a land to make our hearts sing, and we have walked here ever since.'

That was interesting, Selena thought. 'Were there any here before you?'

'Yes. Many trees and birds and creeping beasts graced this land. And others nearer to ourselves.'

Selena had heard of Fae travelling to new lands with the humans of their old homes. And had always suspected that there would be some already there in those new lands. For no land was truly new, was it? And no world empty of life.

'Things have changed however, since those days,' the Queen said, accepting a platter of food. 'We move in the shadows now, more separate than ever before.'

'Most humans deny your existence now,' Selena said with genuine regret, looking at the food given to her and savouring her first bite.

'Humans are fools more often than not.' The Queen blinked her dark lashes. 'They have let their spirits grow weak and flaccid.' She looked at Selena. 'Which brings us to you.'

'Me?'

'Your spirit is as strong as any I've ever laid my gaze upon.'

Selena swallowed her mouthful of sweet potato. 'I was trained from a young age for it to be so,' she said.

'Trained by whom?'

'I am next to last in a long line of priestesses whose task is to keep the old wisdom. The ancient way.'

'Next to last?' The question was fast, sharp.

'I left behind the one I had trained to take my place when the time came.'

'And the wind told you the time had come?' The Queen's gaze was astute. 'This was expected?'

'Not at all.'

The Queen laughed. 'You will be teaching the child the ways of seeing and walking?'

Selena looked down, thinking upon her answer. 'I am unsure,' she said.

'You are a fool too, then. For of course the child must be taught.' The Queen shook her head in disdain. 'More of you need to relearn the old ways. All of you need to relearn the old ways. To know and love the world again. How you could have forgotten it, I do not fathom.'

Silent, Selena considered the Fae's words. 'The child is young,' she said.

'The child is strong. But even she will lose what she has if it is not nurtured. Your world would have it that way.'

It was true, Selena knew. Clover's talent would be first muffled, then extinguished. 'Thank you,' she said. 'For helping me see clearly in this matter.'

The Queen tipped back her head and laughed again, her hair gleaming in a swatch of light. 'I will do so any time you need it.'

They ate then, a feeling rising inside Selena that had nothing to do with the succulent food, but everything to do with the company, the Fae people laughing and talking together, enjoying their feast on the shorefront. To be there with them made Selena's heart swell. She was in a new land, but she was not alone there. She could make the connections she needed.

With that thought came a new determination – it was past time that she explored and made the best of her new home. She could not leave, so she must somehow become part of it.

This was a challenge she had the skills to meet. And if she didn't have all the skills, she would develop them. For she must, she knew, be rooted where she was.

For that was the only way to living truly and deeply.

THE PHONE RANG AND TARA LOOKED UP FROM HER RECIPE book. It was full of recipes for creating meals to celebrate the wheel of the year, and she was filling a notebook with ideas from it. They'd just celebrated Lughnasadh – the first of the harvest festivals in the calendar that Selena followed, and although Tara was happy enough with what she'd pulled together for it, she wanted to be more prepared for next time.

Besides, she was having the time of her life. She felt like she was really living, wallowing gloriously in the world.

'I'll get it,' Dandy said, bustling into the room and snatching up the landline. 'Hello?'

Tara dipped her head back to the book, but her pencil stayed poised as she listened to Dandy speak to the person on the other end of the line.

Although, she wasn't doing much speaking. A lot more listening, and as she listened, she turned around to face Tara, who straightened and put the pencil down.

'We'll be right there,' Dandy said, and hung up.

'Which one is it?' Tara asked around the sudden lump in

her throat. The pencil rolled off the counter and clattered to the floor.

'Clover.'

Tara moved from behind the kitchen bench, tearing off her apron, and making for the sideboard where her keys sat in a blue bowl next to the phone. Her handbag was on a chair at the table, and she snatched it up, her face white, lips pressed together to stop them trembling.

'I'm coming with you,' Dandy said.

They made a beeline for the back door and threw it open, hurrying to the car.

Tara didn't ask what had happened until she had the car going, turning out of the driveway.

Dandy told her. 'She decided she wanted a nap apparently and lay down on some cushions and now they can't wake her up.'

Tara turned and stared at Dandy. 'They can't wake her up?' For a moment, her brain tripped over the words, and they made no sense. 'But it's not even lunch time.'

She'd thought a broken arm, perhaps. An accident on the playground. Maybe a broken leg or a concussion. She'd been prepared to go to the hospital.

'They can't wake her up?'

'Mind the road!'

Tara looked grimly back at the street, slowed for the intersection, put the indicator on. 'So, she's at the kindergarten still?'

'Yes.'

'Did they call an ambulance?'

Dandy didn't know the answer to this. The woman on the other end of the phone hadn't been all that clear. What

Dandy had heard more than anything else was the fright in the teacher's voice.

'I don't know,' she said.

The kindergarten was only a three-minute drive away. Tara walked there with Clover every morning, holding her small hand, singing along with her. Clover's favourite song was currently *Row Row Your Boat Gently Down The Stream* and the words tumbled around Tara's head suddenly. They'd sung it that morning, Clover wearing her sunflower dress and the yellow sunhat she barely went anywhere without.

Merrily merrily, life is but a dream.

Why couldn't she wake up? Why had she needed a nap in the first place?

Tara pulled into the parking space reserved for kindy drop offs and pick ups. She pulled the parking brake on and twisted the key roughly out of the ignition. Dandy was right behind her when she hurried to the kindergarten door.

'Where is she?' she cried to the first adult she saw. 'Is she all right? Why haven't you called an ambulance?'

There had been no sign of an ambulance outside the building. Surely you didn't take any chances with a child?

The teacher threw her hands up. 'Ms. Cross,' she said. 'She seems to be breathing just fine – and her colour's good. She just won't wake up.'

'Call an ambulance,' Dandy demanded, but Tara was shaking her head now.

'It'll be quicker if we take her there ourselves.' The hospital was three blocks away. Tara turned to the teacher again. 'Where is she?'

The woman didn't answer, simply turned and hurried

through into the main kindergarten room. Tara followed, Dandy on her heels.

'We're keeping the other children outside,' the teacher, whose name Tara couldn't for the life of her remember right then, said. 'We're trying not to frighten them unnecessarily.'

But Tara didn't care about the other children, her eyes were on the tight cluster of adults at the side of the room where all the cushions were kept. They were huddled over something and when Tara peered around them, she glimpsed a scrap of sunflower dress.

'Move,' she said roughly, reaching out to push the women aside. 'Move; let me see her!'

She fell to her knees, shaking her head, her hands going out to touch Clover, who lay on a big purple cushion, eyes closed, cheeks pink.

'What's wrong with her?' Tara wailed, and put her hands on her, touching her skin, feeling for a fever. She shook her gently, leant over her. 'Clover,' she said. 'Clover, sweetheart. It's Tara. Wake up now. Wake up now, okay?'

'Pick her up,' Dandy said, her voice brisk. 'We'll take her to the hospital.'

Tara sniffed, nodded, unaware that tears streamed down her cheeks. She cleared her throat, scooped her arms under Clover and picked the child up. Clover flopped loosely against her breast and Tara turned, ignored the pale faces staring at her, and lined up the path out of the room.

At the hospital, Tara carried her again, Dandy hurrying along with them, straight through the doors into the emergency department.

'Hurry,' Tara cried out. 'Help, our little girl won't wake up!'

Clover lay in her arms, looking for all the world like she was asleep.

A flutter of white coats surrounded them in moments, and Clover was taken from Tara's arms, placed quickly on a bed to be examined.

Tara wrung her hands, then reached for Dandy's hand. She clasped it tightly, stranded outside the room into which Clover had disappeared.

'Please Goddess,' she breathed. 'Let Clover be all right.'

4

It was not the little owl – Ruru, as she was told to call her – but Hind who waited to guide Selena back to the waking world. She stood in the shadows at the tree line as Selena took her leave, bowing a final time to the Queen.

'This way will lead me home?' Selena asked, seeing Hind there.

'It will,' the Queen agreed, then smiled slightly. 'All forests are one forest, remember.'

Hind led her deep into the darkness of the woods, her long legs stepping nimbly over the ferns that grew everywhere and the logs that had fallen to return slowly to the earth from which they came.

Gradually, Selena realised that the forest had changed. Instead of beech trees and others she didn't recognise, now there were oak and elder and ash, and she was within the Wildwood she knew from so many visits.

There was movement between the trees and Hind stopped, ears flicking, delicate nose twitching. Selena turned in the direction the spirit deer looked, and her eyes widened.

'What are you doing here?' she gasped.

'Lookin' for you.' Clover rushed forward and caught up Selena's skirt in a hand and grinned happily.

Selena shook her head. 'But how did you know where to find me?'

Really, the child was extraordinary.

Clover shook her head. 'Saw ya,' she said. 'In the deep an' wide.' She dropped her hand at Selena's perplexed frown. 'I wanted to have an adventure with you.'

Selena shook her head. 'Oh, my child,' she said and bent down to catch up the small girl in her arms. 'I don't know how you did this.'

Clover sat back in her arms with satisfaction. 'I ask the trees. They were tellin' me when I saw ya.'

'Goodness.' Selena stood in the forest, Clover in her arms, and didn't quite know what to do next. She'd never been in this situation before.

Clover snaked her arms around Selena's neck and rested her head against her shoulder. 'Can we go see the whales?'

Selena's eyes widened in the dimness. 'The whales?'

Against her shoulder, Clover nodded. 'I see 'em when I sleepin'.'

'The whales.' Selena was bamboozled. She glanced at Hind, who had turned to face them, her eyes dark brown and luminous. 'Do you know these whales?' she asked her spirit kin.

'They in the big pool,' Clover said.

Stilling, Selena looked down at the child in her arms. 'The World Pool?'

But Clover just shrugged. 'Dunno bout a worl' pool.' She wrinkled her nose. 'You shoul' ask the man.'

'The man?'

A nod.

'What man?' Selena asked carefully.

'In my sleepin,' Clover said, as though that answered the question. 'He showed me the whales.'

This, Selena thought, was fascinating. She nodded and set Clover back on her feet. 'Well,' she said. 'Let's go see the whales, and perhaps we will meet your man along the way.'

'You know the whales?'

'I know some whales,' Selena answered, stepping forward again, Hind trotting along the path in front of them.

Clover grinned and skipped, holding Selena's hand. This was a good day! She'd been playing at kindy when she saw Selena flying like a bird at the back of her mind and decided to go after her.

And look what had happened – she'd found her. Clover puffed her little chest out, proud of herself. This was more fun than she'd ever had before, even though she wouldn't say so to Rue, because she wouldn't want Rue to be sad that they hadn't had this much fun.

'This is the way!' Clover cried, delight making her shout. 'I seen this in my sleepin'.' She nodded and pulled Selena's hand, surging forward. 'The whales be down there.'

So, Selena thought, Clover had meant the World Pool. How...amazing that the child had found her way there.

Or had been brought there, she considered, thinking about the man Clover had mentioned.

Clover let go of Selena's hand and rushed to the edge of

the cliff where she dropped to her belly and peered over the edge. She turned her face back to Selena.

'Is a long way down,' she said.

Selena agreed. 'Don't go any closer to the edge.' What ramifications, she wondered, would an accident in the Otherworld have in the waking? This didn't seem a good time to test it out.

'I wanna swim with them,' Clover said, looking down over the rim of the cliff at the whales in the circular pool far below her. 'I swim with 'em before, las' time I come here.'

'With the man?'

Clover nodded, then grinned. 'He a wizard.'

'A wizard?'

Clover scrabbled around and sat up, her back to the drop behind her. 'Like in my fairy tale books.' She frowned. 'He looks a bit like Santa Claus 'cept he don' wear a red suit.'

Selena shook her head. The day was becoming more extraordinary at every turn.

Clover scrambled to her feet and took Selena's hand. 'Let's go swimmin'.'

They made their slow way down the hundred steps carved into the side of the cliff, Selena silent the whole way as she listened to Clover's chatter and turned over in her mind the implications of finding the child here.

The World Pool was a bright, pale blue, the pod of whales swimming around in its depths, milky blurs under the water. Clover stopped at the edge of it, on the narrow piece of ground beneath the cliff and frowned. She looked up at Selena.

'Did you talk to the lady?' she asked.

'The lady?'

Clover nodded. 'Someone wanted to talk to you.'

'Oh.' Selena considered the question. 'Yes,' she said at last. 'I did.'

Frowning, Clover nodded. 'She not a lady like you. What is she?'

Selena felt as though she was dreaming. Was there no limit to what the child could see?

'She's Fae,' she said.

'Fae?'

'A different type of people,' Selena said. 'One of the faerie folk.'

Clover's eyes widened. 'Fairies?'

'Yes,' Selena answered slowly, thinking of what sort of fairy stories Clover was likely to know. 'Sort of like that.'

Nodding solemnly, Clover turned back to the lake. 'Can we swim now?'

A DOCTOR SLIPPED OUT OF THE ROOM WHERE THEY HAD Clover, and Dandy reached out, grabbed his white coat.

'Is she all right?'

The man, who in Dandy's opinion looked barely old enough to shave, seemed for a moment like he was going to bolt rather than answer her.

'Has she woken up?' Tara asked.

He shook his head at that question. 'I'm going to get one of our senior paediatricians to see her,' he said. 'Someone will come and see you in a few minutes.'

'Can we go in and be with her?'

His head shook from side to side again. 'The room is

small,' he said. 'Best wait. One of the nurses will come be with you in a minute.'

He scurried off and Tara looked after him. 'Don't they usually just page doctors?' she asked.

'I don't know,' Dandy said. 'I wish we could be with her.'

Tara did too, and she turned anxiously back to stare at the window of the room where Clover was. It had a blind pulled over it, but she looked anyway, hoping someone would move it aside so she could see.

'We should call Selena,' Dandy said abruptly. 'She should know what's going on.'

Tara stared at her, then swallowed and nodded. 'I didn't think,' she said. 'She's at the house – we should have fetched her when the kindergarten rang.'

Dandy reached out and patted her with a trembling hand. 'I'll take care of it now. I'll try the house phone, then her mobile.' She dug around in her bag and pulled out her own mobile, flipped the lid on it, and scrolled through her short list of contacts before poking at their new home number.

The land line rang and rang with no answer.

Dandy grimaced, hit end, and looked for Selena's mobile number. She looked at Tara as the call went through, Tara staring back at her with a white face.

The phone buzzed in Dandy's hand as she waited for Selena to answer. But the call went through to voicemail and Dandy hung up on the mechanical voice that wanted to invite her to leave a message.

'I'll try again,' she said. 'Are you sure she was at home?'

Tara nodded. 'She came through the kitchen less than

an hour before you did.' She bit at her bottom lip. 'Before they called.'

Dandy hit call again and put the phone to her ear. 'Pick up,' she muttered. 'Pick up.'

She'd almost given up, was sure that the call was going to go to voice mail again when Selena spoke in her ear.

'Yes?'

'Selena?' Dandy frowned. 'Are you all right?'

There was a slight pause, then Selena's voice came back stronger. 'Yes, I'm fine. Dandy? Is something wrong?'

The words tumbled out of Dandy's mouth in a rush. 'It's Clover,' she said. 'We're at the hospital. She won't wake up.'

Tara's arm clamped on hers and Dandy looked up.

'I hear her,' Tara hissed. 'She's awake.' Her fingers let Dandy's arm go and pushed through the doorway of the room where Clover was.

Dandy blinked, spoke into the phone. 'She's just woken up. Just now. We don't know what's wrong with her.'

Selena spoke again and Dandy frowned. 'What?' she asked.

Dandy listened, not understanding, to Selena's instructions, then nodded and closed the phone, putting it back in her bag without noticing. She went into Clover's room.

'Is she okay?' she asked, skirting around the doctor who shone a penlight into Clover's eyes. Clover was perched in Tara's arms.

'Hi Dandy,' Clover said, pushing the light away. 'I feel dizzy.'

Dandy looked at Tara. 'Selena said to give her something to eat. Some chocolate.' She blinked. 'And a drink.'

'What?'

The doctor frowned at her, put his penlight away and caught Clover's little wrist in his fingers to feel her pulse. He shook his head. 'She seems fine, except for being mildly disoriented.'

'I don't have any chocolate,' Tara said helplessly.

Clover smiled at the doctor. 'I was swimmin',' she said.

His brow rose. 'Swimming?'

'With the whales. Me and S'lena.'

Dandy met Tara's gaze over Clover's head. They looked at each other silently for a long moment.

'I'll go to the hospital cafe and get some chocolate.'

'And a drink,' Tara said. She sat down on the bed and relief flooded through her with such force it took her breath away. She buried her face in Clover's hair just as the doctor went to feel under Clover's neck.

'She's all right now,' Tara said. 'Aren't you?' she asked Clover.

'I dizzy,' Clover said, and leaned against Tara. 'But S'lena and me had a 'venture.'

The doctor shook his head. 'She appears to be fine now, but I think we should run some tests, just to be on the safe side.' He nodded to the hovering nurse, who handed him a clipboard. 'Some blood tests, and maybe...' He hummed to himself.

Tara shook her head. 'She's okay now,' she said. 'We don't need any tests.'

'I think we ought to do them. It's not usual for a child to be so deeply asleep that we can't wake her up. It could be a symptom of a serious underlying problem.'

'Wha's he sayin', Tara?' Clover asked.

But Tara just shook her head. The doctor scribbled on

the paper on the clipboard and handed it to her. She looked at it.

'Blood tests,' he said. 'We'll begin there. Pop her across to the lab there, and get those done, and that should give us a good idea of what's going on.' He looked seriously at Tara over his glasses. 'If this happens again, don't hesitate – bring her straight in.'

Tara nodded just as seriously, while Clover yawned widely and burrowed in against her.

'He's letting you take her home?' Dandy asked a few minutes later, at the doors to the hospital.

'He wanted us to go and get blood tests done, and I thought for a minute he was going to insist that he admit her for observation or whatever.'

Dandy shook her head, handed Clover a piece of chocolate broken from a bar she'd bought at the hospital coffee shop.

Clover's eyes lit up and she ate the piece with gusto, letting the creamy sweetness coat her mouth. 'Yummy,' she said.

'Good girl,' Dandy told her, and passed her a juice box. 'Now something to drink.'

Clover sucked seriously on the straw, her blue eyes clearing even as she drank. After she'd downed half the small box she sighed.

'Much betta!'

Tara shook her head, but she kept her mouth closed all the way to the car, and all the way home.

She didn't really understand what had just happened.

And she certainly hadn't expected it.

5

RUE WALKED IN THE DOOR AND CAME TO AN ABRUPT HALT IN the kitchen.

'What's going on?' she asked, staring around at all the tense faces. Everyone was there. Selena, Dandy, Tara, and Damien, who was running his fingers through his hair so that it stood comically on end.

No one was laughing, though.

Tara was on the phone, hunched over it as though whatever the person on the other end of the line was saying, it was hitting Tara like it hurt.

Rue sidled further into the room, but no one was answering her question.

They were all listening to Tara, who shook her head. 'I can't persuade you not to do this?'

Rue's eyes widened and she dropped her backpack from her shoulders and stood holding it by the strap. She looked at Selena.

'What's going on?' she repeated.

But Selena only held up a hand for her to be quiet.

Tara was listening on the phone. 'Very well, then,' she said after a long moment. 'I'm sorry for the consternation caused. Thank you.' She replaced the receiver and straightened slowly.

'Is it Clover?' Rue said, and she dropped her bag. 'Where is she? Is she okay?'

This time Selena put her hand on Rue's arm. 'Clover is fine. She's upstairs having a nap.'

The relief made Rue's legs weak. She sank down onto a chair at the table and shook her head. 'What's happened, then?'

'That was the kindergarten,' Tara said. 'There was an incident.'

Rue rolled her eyes and half coughed with relief. 'There always is with Clover. Wow, is that all? I thought something real had happened.' She shook her head. 'They're kicking her out, aren't they?'

'Can they do that?' Damien asked, his voice rough. 'Can they tell you she's not welcome? Isn't that, I dunno, denying her legal education or something?'

'She's only three,' Dandy said. 'The legal need to go to school doesn't begin until a child is six, so yes, they can ask us not to bring her back, if that's what they want to do.'

'And that is what they want?' Selena asked. 'For her to not go back there?'

Tara leaned against the wall and squeezed her eyes shut. 'Marjorie – the senior teacher or whatever – said that today's...kerfuffle...gave them a very big fright.'

Rue narrowed her eyes. 'What kerfuffle?'

But Tara just shook her head briefly and continued. 'But

that isn't the reason she's suggesting that Clover might be better off at home.' Tara sighed.

'Let me guess – she's been saying things that freak them out,' Rue said.

'Yes.'

There was silence in the room, then Tara winced. 'She's been telling them things she shouldn't possibly know. Practically every day. They're really frightened by it, and Marjorie said none of them feel comfortable around her anymore, which means they can't do their best by her.'

'Then they are right to ask us not to bring her back,' Selena said.

'Well, I pretty much told you that would happen,' Rue said. She looked around the room. 'What kerfuffle, though? Did something else happen?'

Selena, sitting at the table beside her, laid a warm hand over Rue's. 'I went walking between the worlds today,' she said.

Rue stared at her. 'What does that mean?'

'It's an ancient practice that involves entering an altered state of consciousness and walking with the spirits.'

Rue heard that and had a lot of questions. She didn't know which to ask first. 'What spirits?'

Selena shook her head slightly. 'The spirits of the Otherworld, but I can explain that better another time. What happens, is that in this state, my spirit essentially leaves my body - my consciousness of myself isn't connected to my body anymore.'

Selena moved her hand away and leaned back in her chair. 'And Clover joined me.'

'Clover joined you?' Rue frowned, twisting around to stare at Selena. 'I don't get it.'

'She was at kindy,' Tara said. 'And went to sleep, according to the teachers. They rang me in a panic because she wouldn't wake up. We took her to the hospital.'

Rue's eyes widened. 'To the hospital?' She looked back at Selena. 'She what, left her body and went wherever you were in this other world?'

Selena nodded. 'In a nutshell, yes.'

Rue fell silent, her brows drawn together. Then she got up, picked up her schoolbag, and made for the door. 'I'm going to go see her.'

Everyone was quiet, watching her leave.

'So, what do we do now?' Tara asked.

'She needs socialisation,' Dandy added.

'She gets lots of that with us, though, doesn't she?' Damien said.

'We're adults,' Dandy replied. 'She needs to play with kids her own age.'

'Can't we ask her not to say stuff to the teachers?' Damien asked. He shrugged helplessly. 'And I don't know, not to pull a stunt like that again?' He gazed through the doorway into the hallway, wanting to go upstairs and give Clover a hug, relieved that she was all right.

'If we do that,' Selena said, remembering the Fae Queen's words, 'we risk stifling her gifts and then they will fade.'

'That might be a good idea,' Damien said. 'If it's going to get her kicked out of kindergarten all the time. What will happen when she goes to school?'

Selena shook her head. 'We can't risk her gifts. They are

too precious. Hopefully by the time she is old enough for school she might naturally have learnt some discretion.'

'I think we're going to have to teach her that,' Dandy said wryly. 'I agree that we don't want her to feel ashamed about what she can do and see, but teaching her to discern when it's appropriate to say something and when it's not, feels necessary.'

There were nods all around at that.

'I think I might have an answer,' Tara said slowly, straightening. She blinked. 'I think so anyway.'

She looked around the room at everyone, her chosen family, her new home. She glanced down at the books still open on the counter. Books on kitchen witchcraft.

'What about if I ran a playgroup here in the house?' Tara said. 'Then she could get the fun and games with other children that she needs, but I could help her learn how to manage her gifts around others.' She frowned. 'Or is that a really stupid idea?'

'What do you mean, a playgroup here in the house?' Selena asked.

'There's Barnardos,' Tara said and flushed at the fact that she'd looked this very thing up not all that long ago. Actually, she'd been searching parenting advice, and it had popped up, but she was glad to remember it now. 'There's a training course, and when you qualify, you can look after children in your own home for a number of hours a day.' She looked around. 'I think it might be a good compromise.'

'You're already doing so much though,' Dandy said, shaking her head. 'Training to be a childcare provider, and then looking after a bunch of kiddies several days a week – that's a big ask.'

'Dandy's right,' Selena said. 'You'll need to be sure.'

'At least the house is big enough,' Damien offered. 'If you really want to do it, that is.'

Selena shook her head. 'You need to be sure.'

'I think I am,' Tara said, pursing her lips, considering it. 'Yes, actually. I'd pretty much do anything for Rue and Clover, and if this is the best course for Clover until she goes to school, then that's what I'll do.' She felt a sudden relief. 'It's a no-brainer, the more I think about it.' She smiled, feeling like she'd just put down a heavy burden. 'I'll call Barnardos tomorrow and see when I can start the training.'

Selena considered Tara's proposal but could find no flaws in it. Clover would be able to have the social contact she needed, but in a controlled environment, cared for by someone who loved her deeply.

Because there was no questioning that Tara loved Clover and her sister.

Dandy was looking at her, however. 'What about the other thing that happened today?'

'The travelling, yes,' Selena said with a sigh. 'That was unexpected.'

'She only came out of it because I called you,' Dandy said. 'And drew you out of it.'

That was true. Selena tapped her fingers on the table.

'I've not run into a situation like this before,' she said.

RUE DROPPED HER BAG IN HER BEDROOM AND WALKED BACK along the hallway to Clover's room. She let herself in and stood for a moment on the other side of the door looking around. Clover was a little sausage roll under the blankets in her comfortable new bed, and in the other half of the room was a bookshelf full of new and old books, and a small child-sized table and chair piled with art supplies.

Rue spotted the shell she'd given Clover ages ago and smiled. It was still pride of place on the bookshelf.

She closed the door quietly and crept across the room, dropping softly onto the bed and curling up around her sister.

Clover snuffled a little and squinted her eyes open. 'Rue?'

'Yeah, it's just me, Clover Bee,' Rue said. 'Just checking on you.'

Clover nodded, her eyes gummed with sleep. 'I had a 'venture.'

'I heard. Tara took you to the hospital.'

'Dunno,' Clover said, then reached out and patted Rue's cheek. 'Me and S'lena went swimmin'.'

'Swimming?'

'With the whales. In the whirlpool.' That was what Selena had called it.

'What? The whirlpool? That sounds dangerous.'

Clover shook her head, waking up further. 'The whales are nice,' she said. 'They don' mind me swimmin' with them. They a whole fam'ly.'

'Where are these whales?' Rue asked, caught up in the story.

Clover frowned. 'Dunno. In the sleepin', I guess. In the deep an' wide.'

What had Selena said? Some sort of ancient practice of walking with spirits. Rue untangled one of Clover's curls.

'You have all the fun, kiddo,' she said.

Clover looked at her, blue eyes wide now. 'You can come too.'

'Don't know how.'

'You just go to sleep,' Clover said, her small face scrunched up with the effort to explain.

'I go to sleep every night and there aren't any whales.'

Clover shook her head. 'Not sleepin' like that. Its diff'rent.' But she didn't know how to tell Rue how it was different. 'You jus' gotta try,' she said in the end.

Rue sighed and rolled onto her back, looking up at the ceiling. Easy for Clover to say, she thought.

Clover sat up, peered down at her sister. 'S'lena show you how,' she said. 'Then we can do it together.'

But would Selena show Rue how to do it? Rue wasn't sure. She thought about the conversation they'd had before Midsummer. When Rue had asked her if maybe she could train to be a priestess.

Selena had shaken her head. Said that was a hard road to travel and she wasn't sure if it was Rue's path.

Why couldn't it be her path though? Rue stared at the ceiling, while Clover lay back down, her head resting on Rue's chest. Couldn't it be her path? She shook her head slightly. She knew, in her heart, that Selena had come all this way for Clover, but there wasn't just Clover, was there? There was her too. Sure, she didn't have all Clover's talents, but that didn't mean that whatever force had brought Selena all this way hadn't meant her to come for Rue's benefit as well.

Did it?

Rue thought about school. It wasn't as good as she'd expected it would be and she was having trouble settling in again. She felt jittery all the time there, as though she ought to be elsewhere, doing something else – even though she knew there wasn't anywhere or anything else she was supposed to be doing now. It was hard to relax, and almost impossible to concentrate.

'You okay, Rue?' Clover asked.

Rue nodded. 'Yeah,' she said. 'Just thinking about stuff.'

Clover snuggled closer. 'I miss you when you at school,' she confided.

Rue, her arm slung around Clover's shoulders, gave her a squeeze. 'I miss you too, Clover Bee.' She wrinkled her nose at the ceiling. 'Wish I didn't have to go.'

Clover wriggled upright and looked at Rue. 'Why you have to?' She shook her head, curls bobbing. 'You can stay with me an' Tara and S'lena an' Dandy.' She frowned. 'Damien goes to work.'

Why did she have to? Rue gazed at her sister's serious blue eyes. She'd thought she'd known why she had to go to school, apart from it being the law, of course. She'd thought she wanted to.

But it was turning out, in the couple weeks since school had started, that it wasn't that great. The stuff the other girls talked about made Rue want to roll her eyes.

Didn't they know how boring they were, and how tiny their problems and dramas were?

6

SELENA ROSE WHILE THE REST OF THE HOUSEHOLD WAS QUIET, enveloped still in sleep. Or so she thought.

'Morning,' Dandy said as Selena pushed open the kitchen door. 'I've just filled the pot, if you want a cuppa.'

'You're up early,' Selena said, surprised.

'Age,' Dandy said, shaking her head. 'Apparently it doesn't require as much sleep to run an eighty-something year old body.'

'But your room is comfortable?' Selena asked, looking longingly at Dandy's steaming cup. 'You're comfortable?'

Dandy nodded. 'My room is everything I need it to be, as is the whole house and the company in it.'

The answer made Selena smile. 'I'm very glad about that,' she said, and inched closer to the teapot. But she needed to go out and greet the day before she did anything else. So, she went to the door instead. 'I'll be back in a few minutes,' she said.

'Where's Rue?' Dandy asked. 'Doesn't she usually do this with you?'

'I'm up a bit earlier than usual,' Selena said. 'Trying to get back on track – I've let a lot of things slip since I've been here.'

Dandy's eyes widened. 'Really?'

Selena smiled. 'It's true.' She glanced out the window. 'It's time for me to settle in and get back to things. Really dig myself in to my new surroundings.'

'I can understand that,' Dandy said. 'There's only so long you can excuse yourself for a settling in period. After that you just need to do whatever it is that needs to be done.' She eyed the door into the rest of the house. 'Rue will be devastated if she doesn't get to greet the day with you, though.'

Selena stood still. 'She will?'

'Don't you think she will?'

'Yes.' Selena sighed. 'She will. She's been doing it with me every day. I was wrong to think it would be fine to do it differently, meaning she couldn't join me.' Abruptly, she got out a cup and poured herself some tea from the pot. She carried it over to the table where Dandy sat.

'It's been a long time since I had a young person following my teachings,' Selena said, sitting down and taking a sip of the tea.

'I thought you, you know, had to train someone?'

Selena nodded. 'Yes, to take over my position when I died – or as has happened, when I had to retire from it.' She smiled briefly. 'But Morghan is now in her thirties. I stopped actively teaching her years ago.'

'I think Rue wants to learn everything you know.'

But this made Selena shake her head. 'We're not in Wilde Grove,' she said. 'My job isn't the same.'

Dandy raised her eyebrows. 'Isn't it?'

'You think otherwise?'

'Weeeell,' Dandy said, pretending to think about it. She sipped at her tea then smiled widely. 'I do. I don't think your job with these children stops at saving them from neglect and hunger. Anyone could have done that – it was about to happen, right before you found them, with Heather taking them into foster care.' She put her cup down. 'So, considering that, your role – your calling – towards these girls must require more. Something that no one else could give them.'

But Selena was shaking her head. 'There is a soul family bond between them and I,' she said. 'It could be just that.'

Dandy looked shrewdly at Selena. 'You don't even believe that,' she said. 'And you're not going to convince me of it.'

Selena thought of the Fae Queen, and what she'd had to say. 'Of course the child must be taught,' she repeated.

But Dandy was shaking her head again. 'Not just Clover,' she said. 'Rue as well.'

'Rue has to go to school,' Selena said. 'And then to some sort of further education, and after that a job of some description.'

Dandy threw back her head and laughed. 'So will Clover – she'll have to do all the same things.'

Had Selena thought of that? She was shocked to realise that she hadn't, not really. Of course, there had been a lot of talk around Clover going to preschool, but had she thought, concretely considered, that after that came school, and university, and working?

She hadn't.

This wasn't Wilde Grove. There was nothing set up to support a fulltime priestess of the old ways.

Selena placed her hands on the table. Looked at them. At the ring on her hand that she'd put on when first taking her vows as priestess.

'I've known no other life than this,' she mused. 'Than that of a priestess of Wilde Grove.'

Dandy stayed quiet, listening, her hands relaxed around her mug of tea.

'My mother was a cousin of the Lady of the Grove before me – Anwyn.' Selena paused for another sip of tea. 'Anwyn took me in as a foster daughter, agreeing on it with my mother, so that my mother could continue her acting career, and Anwyn could train me to be a priestess.'

'Your mother was an actress?'

Selena nodded. 'Of some success, too.'

Dandy blinked at this.

'I'm not going to tell you her name,' Selena said, smiling at Dandy. She gathered her hands back into loose fists. 'I was a baby when fostered, so I've never known any other life. It was all I was brought up for.'

'Do you resent that?' Dandy asked.

Selena shook her head.

'But don't you wonder what your life might have been like, if your mother had brought you up? Who you might have been?'

Selena gave this some consideration. 'No,' she said at

last. 'I don't, because it was my path to follow Anwyn as Lady of the Grove.'

'But you weren't given any choice – you were just a baby. The path was mapped out for you.'

'Yes,' Selena conceded. 'It was – but under whose direction? Anwyn would not have taken me on if she didn't have a very good idea that it was my path to take in this life.'

Dandy shook her head. 'It all seems a little odd.'

Selena smiled. 'We each come into this life with a purpose.'

'Purpose is one of the things most of us struggle with,' Dandy said. 'We get up, go to work, have families, pay the bills – or try to.' She shrugged. 'And then we have to face death. How much purpose is there in all that? It's easy to see that your life had and has purpose, but the rest of us are mostly very ordinary.'

'The ordinary life can be a thing of beauty.'

Dandy thought on that one for a moment, and a memory came floating to the surface of her mind as though the conversation had tugged it up on a string. She was sitting in the slanting afternoon sun, long tanned legs stretched out while Teddy sat in his sandpit, which was an old dinghy that Frank had acquired from goodness knows where and set in the back garden, digging it into the soil and filling it with sand they acquired from half a dozen trips down to the beach. She remembered little Teddy singing to himself, and Frank, he was shirtless in the late afternoon, a hammer in his hand as he worked on turning the garden shed into a studio for her.

She shook herself from the memory but when she

spoke, her voice quavered slightly. 'You're right,' she said. 'An ordinary life can be extraordinarily beautiful.'

'What we need, however,' Selena said, 'is a way to combine the path I took, with the ordinary course of a life.'

'Well, that's like being a churchgoer, isn't it?' Dandy asked. 'I mean – not everyone wants to be the clergyperson up the front, leading the flock, but we can all fill the pews.' She flushed. 'If you see what I mean.'

'I do see,' Selena said, and smiled at Dandy. 'And I think you've answered a question I've been carrying around since I got here.'

'I have?' Dandy looked round-eyed at Selena. 'What did I say?'

Selena was nodding slowly. 'I'm without a Grove now,' she said. 'But the world still needs beacons, and a way to live the ancient way in the modern world. Where we go to school, have jobs, families, and so on.'

'That's Clover and Rue,' Dandy agreed, and then her face lit up. 'And not only them, but Tara too – have you seen the books she's been buried up to her nose in lately? All the green witchcraft and kitchen witchery and so on?'

'Yes,' Selena said. 'She's learning how to love the world, consciously, gracefully, with body and mind and spirit.'

'I saw Damien reading one of her books the other evening,' Dandy said, 'and he's been talking about his grandmother a lot, have you noticed? About the stories she used to tell him when he was a nipper. His heritage, and his spirituality.' Dandy laughed. 'Your influence is rubbing off on all of us. I don't know if you've noticed, but we're all keen to live the way you can teach us to. We've made a start, coming together in this house, but we can go further, all of us, I'm sure of it.'

There was the sound of someone running down the stairs, and Rue burst into the room, her hair wild and wiry around her shoulders.

'I haven't missed it, have I?' she asked, stopping when she saw Selena at the table with a cup of tea.

'No,' Dandy said. 'Selena and I were just jawing while we waited for you.'

Rue's face relaxed into a beaming smile. 'Are you coming out with us, Dandy?' she asked. 'To greet the day?'

Dandy opened her mouth to say she was too old to stand outside watching the sun rise, but she closed her lips on the words. It was late summer, for one thing, so it wasn't even cold out yet.

'Yes,' she said instead. 'I think I will.' She looked at Selena. 'If that suits?'

Selena nodded. 'I would be glad if you did,' she said.

Rue's face broke into a beaming smile and a sudden flush of wellbeing flooded through her. Selena had waited for her; Dandy was joining them. Clover was safe and well and all was okay in the important parts of her world.

The sun was stretching its light over the hills and into a blue sky. It would be another beautiful, clear day. Selena tipped her face towards the sun and let its warmth sink in.

Still strange, she thought, that it would be summer in February. It was like being in a new world altogether.

'Rising Sun,' she said, letting her body soak in its warmth. 'We welcome you to a new day. We welcome your living light, your strength, given to all of us creatures large and small for our wellbeing. Hail and welcome to a new day, Rising Sun.'

Rue closed her eyes and let the sun infuse her lids with a rosy glow. She repeated Selena's words fervently, letting the new day's heat radiate through her.

For a moment, Dandy felt awkward in her old skin. She didn't know how to stand, or where to look, and to begin with, Selena's words barely made sense to her. Then she took a breath, let it out, and relaxed.

I'm worried about seeming a fool, she thought to herself. No fool like an old fool.

She let herself feel thankful for the warmth of the blooming day. And as she let the heat sink into her, a feeling rose up in her to welcome it. Gratitude, she realised. Simple, loving, wholehearted gratitude. It suffused her like a balm.

'We stand in balance between sun, sea, and soil,' Selena said. 'We stand in balance and give thanks for the breath of our lungs, the ground under our feet, and the sun that heats our blood. Let us carry this balance through our day, to keep coming back to it.'

She opened her eyes and looked around. 'Greetings to you,' she called from somewhere deep inside herself. 'Greetings to you, spirits of this land. I am grateful to share these shores with you.'

'WHY I NOT GOIN' TO KINDY?' CLOVER ASKED, SPOONING UP the last mouthful of cereal and dropping her spoon to the table to lift the bowl to her lips, slurping the milk in the bottom.

Tara glanced at Selena, but it was Rue who came to the

rescue, answering the question as she hefted her backpack on and pressed a kiss to Clover's unbrushed hair.

'Because you freaked everyone out again, kiddo,' she said.

Tara grimaced. That hadn't been exactly the response she was hoping Rue would give.

But Clover just rolled her eyes. 'Can we go to the playgroun', then?' she asked.

Rue shook her head. 'I wish. I gotta go to school. Later alligator.'

'Bye crocodile,' Clover said and set her bowl down with a thump, scrambling down from the table to follow Rue to the door where she waved as Rue walked down the driveway.

'Can we go to the playgroun'?' she asked, coming back in and gazing at Tara and Damien.

'Don't look at me,' Damien said, standing up and stuffing his wallet into his pocket, checking he had his keys. 'I gotta go drive people around.'

'You can drive us to the playground,' Clover said. 'We're people.'

Damien laughed, picked her up and smacked a kiss on her cheek before setting her giggling on her feet again. 'You sure are,' he said. 'My favourite people, and I'm about as enthusiastic about going to work as Rue is about going to school.' He sighed. Lately, his job had not been giving him the satisfaction he was beginning to crave from life.

Perhaps it was time for a change.

Clover went over to Selena when Damien had let himself reluctantly out the door. She sidled up to lean

against Selena as she sat at the table. 'We go swimmin'
again?' she asked hopefully.

Selena smiled. 'Not today, I think,' she said.

Clover's face fell, then perked up again. 'Soon?'

'Soon.'

'Kay,' Clover said with a wise nodding of her head.
'Wha' bout the playgroun'?'

Selena laughed. She couldn't help herself. Clover was a
precocious and disarming child. 'Yes,' she said. 'When
you're clean and dressed, we'll go for a walk to the playground.' She glanced over at Tara. Dandy was in her little
suite of rooms, getting ready for her day at the shop giving
tarot readings.

'Will you come with us?' Selena asked.

'You bet I will,' Tara answered.

7

'HAVE WE GOT YOUR BOOK FOR THE LITTLE LIBRARY?' TARA asked after an hour of chasing Clover around the playground beside the rugby field at the top of the hill. From the playground they could see the house where the children had been living before Selena came along, and Tara didn't like the reminder. Next time, she decided, they'd go down the hill to the big playground in the Botanic Garden.

Clover fell to her knees and dug around under her pushchair before emerging triumphant with a book. She held it up for Tara to see.

'I like this one though,' she said. 'I wanna keep it.'

'If you keep it, then another little kid like you won't get to read it,' Tara said. 'And you want to choose a new one, don't you?'

The miniature library in the old phone box fascinated Clover, and she loved looking for a new book and leaving an old one. She frowned at the book she held then heaved a dramatic sigh.

'Kay,' she said, and went to clamber into the pushchair.

'Where is this library?' Selena asked.

'We discovered it by accident,' Tara answered, buckling Clover in then standing back up. 'I love walking around neighbourhoods – I like houses. All the ways that people make them homes interests me.' She pushed Clover out onto the footpath. 'Anyway, the little library is along the back road here. It's very quaint.'

Selena and Tara walked along in companionable silence, while Clover sat in her pushchair, book on her knees, singing to herself. It was a song she'd made up, about whales and wizards.

'Wanna book 'bout wizards, Tara,' she called out, then waved at a black dog looking over a fence at them as they passed.

'What's this thing about wizards all of a sudden, do you know?' Tara asked, her voice low on the sunny morning.

'In her travellings, Clover has met a wizard.'

Tara narrowed her eyes and looked at Selena. 'She's been travelling more than the once?'

'It seems so, yes.'

Tara shook her head in disbelief. 'She's something special, isn't she?'

It was true, Selena thought, and agreed.

'Who is the wizard, though?' Tara asked. She wasn't sure she liked the idea of Clover hanging out with strange men, wizards or not.

'I suspect,' Selena said carefully, 'that Clover's wizard is one of her kin. A spirit guide, if you like.'

Tara shook her head, not because she was refuting what Selena said, but because she could barely believe that she was having a conversation like this. She coughed a laugh. 'I never had conversations like this before I met you,' she told Selena, and shook her head.

'I never even thought about these things. That there even could be such things.'

'Didn't you?' Selena asked, tilting her head to look at Tara. 'Not even a nudging of them?'

Tara was about to answer no but went suddenly quiet. 'Well, maybe, come to think of it.'

'Yes?'

'I had this boyfriend once,' Tara said, rushing ahead. 'Ages ago, you know – but it was funny, I always knew if it was him on the phone before I answered it, and I knew if he was coming around too, before he'd turn up.'

Selena nodded. She wasn't surprised.

Tara sucked in a breath. 'It wasn't a great relationship, actually, but we ended up living together, and then I decided I had to leave.'

For a moment, her face got a faraway, pale look.

She snapped back to the present. 'I didn't tell him I was leaving. I just got up one day and when he'd gone to work, I started packing my things.'

Clover had stopped singing, had her book open on her lap and was looking at the pictures. Tara watched her for a moment, steadying herself in the present again.

'Anyway,' she finished. 'He left work and came home in the middle of me packing.' She blinked. 'Said he'd suddenly got this feeling that I was leaving, so he'd walked out of work to come stop me.'

Selena looked steadily at Tara. 'And did he?'

Tara nodded. 'I was so shocked, that I let him talk me out of going.' She sighed. 'So, I guess, when it comes down to it, I know there is more to everything than we're supposed to think.' Tara gripped the pushchair and found a smile. 'I did leave him in the end,' she said. 'And that was ages ago anyway.'

Selena nodded, reached out and touched Tara gently on the arm, then withdrew and lifted her head. 'What's that?' she asked, standing still.

Tara stopped walking and looked around. 'What's what?' she asked.

But Selena shook her head. 'I feel something.'

Something on the breeze.

She lifted her face, let the breeze whisper across her skin, looked around. 'That house,' she said.

Tara looked. 'What about it?'

But Selena was already moving, going to stand in front of the wall that marked the boundary of the old brick house. She frowned at the house, shook her head.

'What is it?' Tara said, pushing Clover over and looking at the house, perplexed. It was just another old bungalow. There were lots of them up and down the roads here. Tara thought the same architect must have designed them all, as they looked so similar.

'It's like the children's old house,' she said. Was that why it had caught Selena's attention? Tara couldn't see any other reason.

'Wha's goin' on?' Clover asked, who couldn't see over the brick wall. She looked at Selena. 'There's sumthin' wrong with the house?'

But Selena shook her head. 'I don't know,' she said, then looked at Tara. 'Can't you feel that?'

Tara's eyes widened. Feel what? She looked at the house again. The curtains were open in the bay window, but the room behind them was wreathed in shadow, and she couldn't see anything beyond the glass.

'I can't feel anything,' she said.

'Open your senses,' Selena said.

But Tara didn't know how to do that. She went to tell Selena that, then snapped her mouth shut.

Didn't she? Didn't she know how to do that, though?

Maybe unconsciously. But if there was a switch to flick, she didn't know where it was.

She looked at the house again, and took a breath, trying to open her senses, probing the...atmosphere.

'I don't know,' she said. 'Maybe I feel something.'

Selena shook her head. 'I've never felt anything like this, a house with this sort of energy.'

'Wanna see,' Clover said, wriggling around in her pushchair and dropping her book.

Selena gazed down at her for a moment, then reached down and unsnapped the buckles, lifting Clover out to hold her on her hip.

Clover wrinkled her nose, looking into the house and the deep and wide at the same time.

'What does it feel like?' Tara asked.

'Like the ringing of a bell,' Selena said. 'Like a great ringing and humming.'

Tara listened, cocking an ear towards the old 1930's bungalow. 'I don't know,' she said.

But Selena felt it. It was as though the house was vibrating, its spirit reaching out, calling to her.

It was extraordinary.

Clover shook her head. 'Don' like it,' she said.

'It's bad?' Tara asked. Clover reached out for her, and Tara took her.

'Hurts,' Clover said, turning her mind from the house. It was dark in there, and she didn't want to look at it anymore. It was like someone had fallen over in there a long time ago and was still crying.

Selena drew her gaze away and looked at Clover. 'Let's go, shall we?' She took hold of the pushchair and they walked away from the house.

They made it to the little library in the old phone box, and Clover forgot about the house as she looked at all the children's books on the lower shelf and decided which one she wanted to swap hers for.

They walked back a different way, taking the street over before heading down the hill home.

But Selena kept thinking about the house.

Natalie pressed herself against the wall, frowning at the two women staring into her house.

Who were they? What were they doing?

She shook her head and took a step back, making doubly sure she couldn't be seen. What sort of people stopped and stared at someone else's house? Even lifted their child to have a look?

She squeezed her eyes closed, trying to reason it out, but came up blank. Her breath quickened.

But when she opened her eyes, they were gone. Natalie sagged in relief, yet even as she did so, even as she muttered to herself that they were gone, that she was glad they were gone, somewhere deep inside her a small, lost voice piped up and wished them back.

Maybe they could help, the tiny voice whispered before Natalie squashed it back down to wherever it had come from.

No one could help her. Hadn't everything already proved that? Hadn't she established a long time ago that it wasn't safe out there in the world?

Nobody could help her, could they?

'Please help,' she whispered.

She waded through the dimness – the front room never did get any sun – back to the kitchen at the rear of the house and collapsed in relief down onto a chair at the Formica table, pressing the palm of a hand to her chest, counting the racing beats of her heart, willing it to slow down.

It had been a long time since she'd seen anyone staring over her fence. Sometimes the local children did it, and she knew they were whispering among themselves that her house was a witch's house – hadn't she done the same when she was a kid?

She nodded slightly, and her heartbeat slowed, the tightness in her chest eased. Walking to school when she was a kid, there was a house on the corner that was just an ordinary house but rundown, the grass around it long, and the windows of the house grimy with neglect.

Natalie looked up at her own windows. They were clean. At least on the inside.

A woman had lived in the witch's house when she was a

kid, and they'd all known she was a witch. She was ugly, for
starters, and sent them scattering whenever she poked her
head out of the house.

Natalie wrinkled her nose. Hadn't she had two daughters too? Perhaps. She thought so, and was sad for them, for
their mother too. Because of course she hadn't been a real
witch – there was no such thing – just a poor, unattractive
woman struggling to get along in the world.

The world was a terrible, hard place. Full of hidden
dangers.

Natalie pried herself out of the chair and looked
around the small kitchen. The table was squeezed into the
back of the room, in front of the wall of cupboards. There
wasn't much in the way of counter space, and one of the
oven elements had burnt out the week before. She was
trying to gather the courage to call in a repairman to
replace it.

But there were three more, so it didn't seem urgent.

What had she been going to do today? Natalie chewed
on her lip and tried to recall.

She'd been tidying up the living room, picking up the
cushions on the couch and giving them a swat to loosen the
dust before setting them back down when she'd caught a
glimpse of movement outside.

She'd stopped, frozen, one cushion in her hand, caught
like a deer in the headlights.

Then she'd dropped the cushion – it was probably still
there on the floor, she thought now – and crept to the side
of the room, flattening herself against the wall as though
that would make her thin and transparent.

She'd risked looking.

It had been a couple of women, staring over the fence at her house.

Her head had gone blank then, just snow playing on the screen of her mind, like the television when the channels switched off for the night.

She didn't know how long that had lasted, but when she'd come back to look again, the women were still there, this time one of them held a small child with soft, golden hair.

Natalie had blinked away tears. She'd looked like that child once. All round cheeks and bouncing hair.

That had been before. Before the protests. The bombing. The minute hand of the Doomsday clock moving closer to midnight.

Natalie shuddered. Before her parents had told her all about what an awful, unsafe world they'd brought her into.

How could she be happy when she lived in a world where people built bombs?

They'd thought she was crazy when she'd taken to hiding each time their talk turned to the bombs, to the nuclear testing. You can grow up and change things, they'd told her. But she couldn't – how could she change something that big? Her parents and brother kept trying to, and it made no difference that she could see.

Natalie closed her eyes. Tried to think what she had been planning to make that morning.

But she just saw the women looking over the fence at her. Why? Why had they stood there looking?

Natalie glanced down at herself, feeling like she'd forgotten to get dressed that morning. But she was wearing all her clothes. Shoes, jeans, jumper. Everything neat, tidy.

She bought them by mail order. They were delivered right to her door.

It was how she got everything.

A volunteer at the library brought her a pile of books and VHS tapes every week. Sometimes she picked books or movies that Natalie didn't like, but most of the time they were interesting. For a while, she'd even managed to talk to the woman – she was plump and older, like a benign auntie – on the doorstep, tucked safely into the shadow of the house, but recently she'd been pretending to be asleep or busy and unable to hear the woman's knock on the back door. The books and movies were always left in a paper bag on the step.

Ladysmith cake. That's what she'd been going to make. The recipe was in her old Edmond's cookbook, which was tattered, and stained with small smears of cake batter, but it was trusty nonetheless. She'd made all the recipes in it, and perfected them.

Natalie squeezed behind the table and opened the cupboard, getting the flour down.

The butter was already softening on the bench.

One and a half cups of flour. Natalie measured it out carefully into the big white ceramic bowl.

Baking calmed her. It pushed back the fear of everything that lurked outside the windows of her house. The people plotting war. The people building weapons.

In July 1985 they'd bombed the Rainbow Warrior.

Natalie shivered. Put the bag of flour down. Picked up the baking powder, measured out one teaspoon.

Her brother Tim had worked on the Greenpeace boat, going out to protest the nuclear testing at Muraroa.

He could have been killed. He hadn't been.

But it could have been him that died in the explosion. He'd been on the boat that night. Had jumped to safety.

She cut 175 grams of butter from the block and put it in her second bowl.

Went back to the cupboard. Got the sugar. Measured it carefully onto the butter. Three quarters of a cup.

And at school – she'd been nine, almost ten, the teacher making them practice a bomb drill.

Natalie creamed the butter and sugar together, head down, not looking out the windows.

They'd crouched under their desks, arms over their heads, waiting for the bomb to fall, knowing they were just pretending, but terrified anyway.

Although some of her classmates sniggered. Who would want to drop a nuclear bomb on New Zealand?

But Natalie waited for the whine as the bomb dropped from the plane. Then the rush of hot wind that would break all the windows and blast them, cowering under their desks, with broken glass.

She turned her back on the window, looked down at the bowl. What was next?

A new bowl. Three eggs. She broke the shells against the rim of the bowl, got a fork and broke the yolks. Mixed them together.

Tipped the flour into the creamed butter alternately with the eggs.

After the hot wind, she thought. What would there be then? She'd imagined it as whiteness that was so hot it incinerated her.

Crouching under the desk, arms wrapped around her

head. Incinerated. The glass in her hair would melt, and then she would. Until she was nothing but a shadow on the floor.

She divided the mixture into two bowls. Added two teaspoons of cinnamon into one portion, mixed it in, then spread that half into the bottom of the cake tin.

Her hand paused on the jar of raspberry jam, then lifted it up, unscrewed the lid. It was too bright to be the colour of blood.

The memory of waiting for the bomb to come had never left her. She'd been in town once, years later, in Penrose's department store – just before it closed, that had been – and she'd been looking for some new winter tights. Penrose's was the place to find all the little things you needed but generally didn't think of until the last minute. They sold black woollen tights, made of real wool. Which made the Dunedin winters just a little better.

Natalie spooned jam over the cinnamon layer, then carefully spread the second, plain half of the batter over it. That just left the sliced almonds, and those were in a glass jar in the cupboard. She sprinkled them on.

There'd been a loud bang out on the street, and a fire truck had screamed its siren as she'd been sifting through the bargain bin of tights and odd socks. Penrose's sold odd socks, and Natalie had never been able to figure out how they were able to fill a wooden trough with socks that were brand new but had no matching mate.

She'd screamed and dived to the floor, curling up in a ball, arms over her head, hearing the windows breaking at the front of the shop, the glass flying already, and waiting for it to hit her, waiting for the rush of burning air.

Natalie checked the oven. It was preheated to 180. She slid the cake in and turned the timer to forty minutes.

No one had helped her up. They'd just stood round staring at her as she cowered on the ground.

'Just a car backfiring, you silly cow,' a man said.

8

S<small>ELENA</small> <small>STOOD</small> <small>OUTSIDE</small> <small>THE</small> <small>HOUSE</small> <small>ON</small> <small>THE</small> <small>SLIVER</small> <small>OF</small> garden. How, she wondered, did she recreate her life here in this new land?

She had no stone circle. No woods through which to thread her way undisturbed. No stream to offer thanks to, and even though she'd met the local Fae, she was as yet unused to them – did they even venture into the city?

She didn't know, didn't think so, and looked around.

What did she have?

The house, tall and solid behind her. She felt it at her back and nodded. It was a good house and filled with good people as well.

Tara who pored over her new books on witchcraft, filling the kitchen with herbs and potted plants, turning it into an oasis of fragrant greenery. Selena smiled. There were simple household rituals and spells she ought to show Tara. Protections, cleansings, blessings.

Selena nodded. There was a way to become embedded

in her new home. By focusing on her home. Help Tara become immersed in the magic of hearth, home, and food. She could do that, could she not? It had been some years since she'd spent time in the kitchen of Hawthorn House, but there had been hours during her training when Anwyn had had her working alongside Mrs. Parker each and every day, learning the secret ways women had for hundreds of years blessed their home and family with simple, sacred magic. It had taught her many things, not least of which was how to participate fully in life.

Selena smiled at the memory. She'd not thought back then, when Anwyn had sent her to the kitchen, that she could learn anything from making pastry and peeling apples. But she'd learnt quietness and peace of mind, purpose and bliss.

Those were lessons she could pass on. To make the home, wherever it was, an oasis of calm and uplifting magic – a needed thing in a world that so often seemed off-kilter.

She glanced down at the garden, planted by Teresa and Rue over the summer, Clover helping, stabbing her toy gardening fork into the ground with glee, and now the herbs were well and truly up, the leaves of the mint and lemon balm green and luminous in the sun, while the lavender, liking their sandy sunny spot in a big planter by the house unknotted their tight purple flowers in front of the sun. It was a small but tender oasis, Selena decided, and she would tend it alongside Tara and the children. She did not have a forest anymore, it was true, but there were these plants, their small, luminous spirits singing joy into the day.

Could a Lady of the Forest become something else if she lost her forest? The thought wound its way unbidden into

Selena's mind and she shook her head. There was still the Wildwood – that would never be lost to her.

She turned where she stood and looked up the hill that curved away from the house. There was the big Botanic Garden, full of trees. And the Northern Cemetery, also full of trees. They did not have to grow in her garden, for her to incorporate them in her practice, did they?

Her mind spread outwards, and she closed her eyes, going back to an exercise she had forgotten she even knew, learnt way back in her teenage years, but when she looked at it, just as shiny and useful now as it had been then.

Selena let her imagination lift her into the spell of the world. Closing her eyes, she imagined a hot air balloon, its basket resting softly on the ground in front of her. It was waiting for her, bobbing gently in the warm air of the afternoon. No one was around to watch her clamber into the big basket, except perhaps the small fantail bird that fluttered and spun in delight, chirruping and chattering.

The balloon rose as soon as she stood in its basket, and she let it, going with it, her spirit rising above the land, the great balloon billowing over her. A rope dangled down from the basket into the garden, and Selena leaned to look, seeing that Clover's stone lion held the end of the thick tether in his strong jaws. She would not float off while he was there to hold her tight.

She laughed slightly. Was this imagination? Or the flight of spirit? She'd asked Anwyn that many, many moons ago, and Anwyn had refused a straight answer.

Did it matter, she'd asked instead?

What was real? What was unreal? Where did imagination and spirit intersect?

The balloon with Selena in its basket rose higher, until she looked down at the roof of the house, seeing its individual tiles, the sloping of the eaves this way and that way.

Then higher, and Selena turned her attention from the house to the city that spread out slowly at her feet. She gazed down at the houses in curving rows, following the roads weaving in and out of each other, and looked across the valley in which her part of the city lay nestled, at the slopes of the hills which rose rapidly on the other side, coated with trees and green, a red and orange roof here and there among them. She leaned over and peered down the thread of the main road, to the city proper, where the buildings were taller, although squat now as her balloon took her higher.

There was the Botanic Garden beneath her. The rugby fields. The cemetery. The great basin of the harbour. And sparkling in the distance, the ocean.

There was the world beneath her – her world. Her new world. The land dipped and rose and tucked itself around her; the ocean lapped at its shores.

The ocean spread out to the horizon, and then the horizon shifted, and Selena saw that there was more ocean beyond it, more land, lights, people, animals, trees, plants. The whole world lay spread out beneath her, singing in her vision and she knew she was part of it all, connected intimately to it, one of many, one of all.

She closed her eyes, feeling the threads that bound her to the world. Grateful for them.

The balloon drifted downwards again, lowering her calmly to the ground, but even as she clambered from the basket, she knew the land was still there, the ocean that stretched to the horizon and then further, and she felt it all tingling inside her.

'World to world to world,' she breathed. 'I stand in balance between you, earth, sky, water.'

For a moment she was unsteady on her feet, so strong had her vision been, and still was, held inside her, and then she stilled, paused, eyes closed again, looking for something that had caught her attention again.

A house.

The house she had seen earlier that day. It had almost seemed to call out to her, and it did so again. Selena shook her head.

What was it about that place? It looked an ordinary house. A little neglected, the grass a little long, the paint peeling around the windows, the garden overgrown.

And yet. And yet it called out to her, its energy ringing out on the breeze.

Selena went inside, sought out Tara who was at the kitchen table with Clover, both of them drawing, Clover with head bent, tip of her tongue poking out as she concentrated.

'Tara,' Selena said, going around the table to put her hand on Clover's smooth head.

Tara looked up.

'Is there any way to find out who lives in a particular house?'

Tara looked at her for a moment, then blinked. 'The house we saw this morning?'

Selena nodded.

'I drewed a house,' Clover said, putting down her

crayons and holding up her picture. She frowned, her tiny eyebrows knotting together. 'Is the hurtin' house.'

That caught Selena's attention and she looked at Clover's picture. It was a house with all the windows scribbled dark with black crayon.

Clover pulled a face and gave it to Selena. 'You can have it,' she said. 'I don' like it.'

'Do you see who lives in there?' Selena asked.

Tara opened her mouth to protest, but closed it again.

But Clover shook her head. 'She don' wanna be looked at.'

'She?' Tara asked.

But Clover just shrugged. 'I dunno.'

Selena dropped a kiss on Clover's head. 'You've been very helpful,' she said. 'And I'm going to keep your picture. Why don't you draw one of our house now?'

Clover considered that for a second then grinned and dived for her crayons. 'I goin' to draw all of us in our house,' she decided. 'You an' me an' Tara an' Rue an' Dandy and Damien.'

She bent over a clean piece of paper, a crayon gripped tight in her small hand.

9

RUE SAT LEANING BACK AGAINST THE WARM CONCRETE AT HER
back and held her lunch box loosely in her hands. Despite
the fact that Tara insisted on making lunch for her every
day, filling the plastic container with chicken filled rolls and
slices of carrot cake, Rue didn't feel like eating. She tapped
her fingers against the side of the lunch box. A quartet of
girls went giggling past, shining heads bent together over
some secret, something Rue wasn't part of and knew she
never would be.

Not her, on the outside of it all.

It wasn't because she was a goth. The uniform took most
of that away, except for her dark hair and the smudge of
dark eyeliner she put on each morning.

It wasn't even because the other kids were especially
snobbish. Some of them had made overtures, advances that
Rue could have taken as invitations into various friendships,
cliques.

Rue closed her eyes, letting the sun burn red against them. It was her, she knew. The way she was.

She didn't fit in.

One of the girls laughed. Made a comment about a cute boy in some band. The circle of girls contracted, shook with hooting laughter, expanded again. Rue had her eyes open again, watching them. One of the girls, tall, blonde, well-developed, glanced at her and Rue saw bafflement there in her eyes before she turned away.

Rue didn't care. The girls in the popular group were pampered, sleek and manicured.

None of them had broken into their neighbour's house to steal food.

None of them had lied and cheated and gotten up at two in the morning to change their bedsheets because their kid sister had had a nightmare and wet the bed.

She shook her head. She'd tried, but they lived in different worlds. Worlds that didn't appear to have any point of intersection.

Rue couldn't imagine laughing over some boy band. She closed her eyes again, drifted, the sun floating red and orange behind her lids.

Also, there was the other stuff. Selena's stuff. Rue's fingers twitched. Training to be a priestess.

No one here would understand anything about that.

Greetings to the Risen Sun, she thought, watching the rosiness of her eyelids. Bringer of light and strength.

A sudden idea flickered to life inside Rue. Selena preyed to a goddess she called Elen of the Ways. An ancient, antlered goddess. The thought of this goddess gave Rue a swimming sensation, as though she was about to faint.

She wondered if the school library would have any information on Elen. Or any of the old gods and goddesses. Opening her eyes, she sat up, reached for her bag and slipped her lunch box back in. It was worth looking. She wasn't doing anything out here except letting the sun give her a tan she didn't want.

The library was at the heart of the school and was pretty busy. There was a cluster of computers the kids could use during the lunch break, and always a milling crowd around them. Rue skirted them, formulating a plan to use one of the computers to do research if she couldn't find any books. She curled a lip. She'd have to find a way to come back during class time though, or after school, if she wanted to get to use one.

Tara had talked about getting a computer. It would be great to have one at home. Perhaps she could say she could use it for homework. It would even be true. Well, her English homework anyway. Whatever. It would be useful.

Rue glanced around at the shelves, wrinkling her nose at the Dewey decimal listings taped to the end of each, wondering where she ought to look. She wandered down to the 200s where the religious books were. But it was all Christian, and she kept going, scanning the shelves to stop at the section on mythology.

There were the Greek and Roman gods. She scanned past the two volumes, meaning to come back to them if there was nothing else. Next was a bigger section on Māori mythology. Finally, an encyclopaedia of world mythology, a book of Norse myths and legends, which she pulled from the shelf, because didn't Norse stuff happen close to Britain?

Then there was a lone book on Celtic myths, and she

nabbed that one too, flicking through it, stopping at a picture of a silver cauldron – that's what the caption called it – with a figure on it, antlers growing out of its head. A sudden rush of excitement coursed through Rue. This was it. This was one of Selena's ancient gods and goddesses.

'I think it's a crime they're called myths, don't you?'

Rue looked up to see a girl standing in front of her.

'What?'

The girl shook her head. 'I'm Ebony,' she said, and rolled her eyes. 'Blame my mother for the weird name.' But there was a gleam in her pale eyes that made Rue think Ebony didn't mind her name too much. 'I think she was just really into trees or something.'

'Hi,' Rue said diffidently.

'You're Tiffany,' Ebony said before Rue could offer her own name. 'I heard about you.'

Rue stiffened. 'What do you mean?'

Ebony shrugged. 'You robbed a bunch of houses to pay for food and stuff.'

'I did not!'

Another magnificent shrug. 'That's what I heard. For you and your sister, or something. And then you got put in care.' She frowned. 'Or was it Borstal?' Her face, broad and serene smoothed out. 'Either way, well done, is what I say.'

'None of that happened,' Rue said, humiliated at the thought that that was what was being said about her. 'Who's saying such rubbish?'

Ebony, who didn't resemble her name in any way, having very fair hair and eyes so light they were just a blush of blue, shrugged and changed the subject. 'So,' she said instead of answering Rue's question. 'Which goddess do you worship?'

Rue blinked at her in astonishment, unable to absorb properly what the other girl had said to her.

'What?'

'Which goddess do you worship?' Ebony repeated, then frowned. 'Or have I read you wrong?' she asked. 'I don't usually get it wrong.'

Rue swallowed dryly and her throat made a clicking noise. She hugged the books to her chest. 'Um. Elen of the Ways, I guess.'

Ebony's eyes widened. 'I haven't heard of her,' she said.

'I was looking for some more information about her,' Rue said, glancing down at the books, then back up at Ebony. 'What about you?'

Ebony pushed past and got one of the Greek mythology books from the shelf and flicked through the pages. She held it open for Rue. 'Her,' she said, beaming.

Rue looked at the page. 'Athena,' she read, then looked questioningly at Ebony.

Ebony turned the book around and looked at the page with satisfaction. 'She's a war goddess,' Ebony said.

'A war goddess?' Rue asked dubiously.

'Yeah, but she believed in going to war only when it was the last resort and there was no other way – like against Hitler or something. She would have gone for that.' Ebony shook her head. 'She's not like Ares.'

'Ares?' Rue looked down at the book in Ebony's hands, feeling off-kilter.

'Yeah. He's the god of war, you know?' Ebony grinned, showing a row of small, neat teeth. 'But he's always marching off to war, over the slightest little thing. Athena thought he was a jerk.'

Rue looked at her, bewildered.

'So,' Ebony went on. 'Who is this Elen of the Ways?' She blinked her faded blue eyes. 'What pantheon is she from?'

'Pantheon?'

'Yeah. Is she a Greek goddess like Athena? Or...' Ebony cast around for another example. 'Or a Norse goddess? I bet she's Norse, right? Like Freya? She's fierce.'

Rue shook her head. 'I think she's British.'

Ebony's fair eyebrows rose. 'British? I've never heard of her.' She wrinkled her nose. 'I don't know much about British goddesses. Who else is one?'

'Um.' Rue cast about in her mind. 'Brigid, I think.' She'd heard Selena mention a Brigid, she was sure of it.

'Cool,' Ebony said, sticking her book back on the shelf. 'I need to know more. Is there anything in your books?'

Rue looked down at the ones in her arms. 'I don't know,' she said. 'I was going to go have a look.' She hesitated a moment, then went on. 'Elen's an antlered goddess, and there's a picture in this one of a guy with antlers on his head.'

'Antlers?' Ebony asked. 'You mean like a deer or something? That's pretty cool.'

Rue nodded. 'I think she dates back to really ancient times.' Hadn't Selena said that she followed the ancient way?

Ebony sniffed. 'We should go look for books in the public library,' she said. 'They don't have much here.'

It was a minute before Rue answered. Could she be making a friend here, she wondered? Ebony seemed a bit kooky, maybe, but she was into goddesses and stuff too. Rue glanced around the library. There was still the milling, humming group of boys around the two computers where every now and then one hooted in excitement. The librarian was watching them, mouth downturned as though she wished she could expel them from her domain. Them and perhaps the computers too.

She looked over at Rue, as though she'd felt Rue's gaze on her, and her frown deepened.

'Don't worry about Mrs. Wallace,' Ebony said, following Rue's eyes. 'She would be happiest if no pesky kids were allowed into her library.' She gave her eyes a massive roll. 'Don't know if you've noticed this,' she said earnestly. 'But most teachers don't seem to like kids.'

Rue looked back at Ebony and made a decision. 'My name's really Rue,' she said. 'I don't go by Tiffany if I can help it.'

'Rue,' Ebony repeated, nodding solemnly as though she really got it. 'Hey, that's cool – now we're both named after plants.'

Rue smiled, tentatively at first, then more widely.

'You wanna get those books out so we can go find somewhere to sit to take a look through them?' Ebony asked.

Rue nodded, then stopped. 'You don't have friends waiting for you?'

'Ha!' Ebony shook her head and grinned. 'Do I look like I'm popular, in with the cool kids?'

Rue thought it polite not to answer that. Hopefully it was a whatchamacallit – rhetoric question. They were studying rhetoric questions in English right now, and their homework was to write a speech that made use of rhetoric. Rue wasn't looking forward to it.

Ebony slung an arm around Rue's shoulders, squeezed, then danced away. 'It's been just me, myself, and I, until you turned up, my new friend. This is my fifth month in this hellhole, and you're the first person who's even looked at the books in this aisle.' As though that was her criteria for friendship.

Rue was warming to Ebony. The girl was relentlessly, unashamedly, confidently herself.

'I didn't rob a whole street of houses,' Rue said in a low voice as they moved away to the desk where she could check out the books.

'Nah?'

Rue shook her head. 'No Borstal, either.'

That got a shrug in response. 'Thought that one was a little too good to be true.' Ebony slid Rue a sideways look. 'You got a sister though, right? That's what I heard. Something about just you and her on your own?'

Rue handed her books to Mrs. Wallace and waited for the librarian to issue them to her before answering. She thought of the months she and Clover had lived on their own. More than months, it had been years, really. When you got on down to it.

'Yeah,' she said when they stepped out into the sunshine. 'Her name's Clover. She's almost four.'

'Where's your mum?'

Rue could say it now without her voice cracking. 'She died when I was twelve.'

'Aw shit, that's rough,' Ebony said. 'Let's go sit out under the trees. I wanna show you something.'

Rue followed her across the playing field to a far row of trees by the school's back fence. Ebony ducked under the fringed canopy of a weeping willow.

'Wish my mum had called me Willow instead of Ebony,' she said, gesturing for Rue to follow her.

'Ebony's nice,' Rue said and stood up under the branches that shaded them like a green tent. 'Wow,' she said.

'I know – cool, huh?' Ebony stood with her hands on her hips, surveying the round, sheltered space with obvious satisfaction. 'I thought, first time I crept under here, that I was going to find this was like, a favourite spot with other kids, but no one comes here.' She wrinkled her nose. 'Can't sunbathe under here, I guess.'

Rue nodded. She'd long ago noticed that the older, cooler girls in the school like to stretch out in the sun, hitching up their uniform skirts so that their long legs were bare. Some of the more daring even hitched up their blouses too, tucking them under their bras and baring their midriffs.

Ebony moved around to the other side of the tree's trunk. 'This is really what I wanted to show you.'

Rue went to look. 'What is it?' she asked.

'It's a shrine,' Ebony said. 'So I can make offerings at lunchtime.' She sniffed, her shoulders rounding.

'Get Athena's help to make it through the school day.'

10

IT WAS SATURDAY MORNING AND DAMIEN BUMPED OPEN THE
kitchen door, which was the one they all seemed to use to
go in and out of the house, rather than the big front door,
which was sort of too formal and intimidating between its
twin pillars for everyday use.

'Heyho,' he called, setting down a bakery box on the
kitchen bench. 'Creamed doughnuts for everyone!'

Clover came running, Rue close on her heels.

'Doughnuts?' Clover asked, little face shining. 'The ones
with jam?'

'You got it,' Damien said, picking her up and tucking her
under his arm so that she giggled. He lifted her to the
cupboards. 'Get a plate already,' he told her.

'You wan' one?' Clover called to Rue.

But Rue shook her head, her mouth full already. She
swallowed. 'Unlike you,' she said. 'I can eat without
smearing everything in sight with food.'

Damien lowered Clover so she could put the plate

down. He popped her on the floor and loaded her up with a doughnut, winking at Tara when she came in to see what all the excitement was about.

'Doughnut?' Damien asked.

'They're almost as good as your baking, Tara,' Rue said.

Tara beamed, helped herself to one of the long, creamed buns and shook her head. 'I've got a long way to go yet when it comes to baking.' She looked ruefully down at the doughnut in her hand. 'And I'm going to be the size of a house, by the time I get good at it. The taste-testing is wreaking havoc on my waistline.'

'You look perfect to me,' Damien said, trying not to actually look as he said it. He carried Clover's plate to the table instead. 'There ya go,' he said, then looked around. 'Selena about?'

'Somewhere,' Tara answered.

'Someone asking for me?' Selena said, coming into the crowded kitchen with Dandy.

'That'd be me,' Damien said. 'I've just been to the customs warehouse.'

For a moment, Selena didn't know what he was talking about, then her face lit up. 'It's here?' she asked.

'Had to dismantle it to fit everything in the car, but yep, it's here all right.'

'What is it?' Rue asked, then put down her doughnut and looked at Selena. 'Is it your things? From Wilde Grove?'

They'd been sent by sea, on a container ship and Selena could barely believe they were finally here. 'Yes,' she said.

Rue stood up. 'I'll help bring them in.'

Clover stood on her chair, clutching her doughnut. 'Me too,' she said, her mouth full of cream.

Selena kissed her head, sat her back down. 'You can help me unpack them,' she said. 'When you've finished eating and have washed your hands.'

They carried the boxes all the way upstairs to the attic room Selena had chosen to be her workroom, Damien carrying the heaviest and Rue full of curiosity.

'Can we really help you unpack?' she asked, setting the last down on the floor.

Selena surveyed the eight cardboard boxes, hands on her hips. She nodded. Probably, she knew, she'd prefer to unpack the things from Hawthorn House herself, but if she let Rue and Clover help it would stop her from brooding and feeling teary with homesickness.

And she thought that was a very good thing.

She was no longer Selena, Lady of the Grove. That was Morghan's title now.

But, she told herself. She was still a Lady of the Forest, of the Wildwood, and that should be more than enough.

'What's in this one?' Rue said, getting to her knees on the floor beside a box that was long and narrow.

'Hmm,' Selena said. 'I'm pretty sure I know what that will be.'

Rue lifted shining eyes to her while Clover stood surveying the boxes with glee, rubbing her hands together.

'Have you got the box cutter Damien gave us?' Selena asked Rue.

Rue nodded, held it up, and Selena gave her the go-ahead to open the first box.

Rue chose the long narrow one, her curiosity burning. When she had the end open, she stood up and passed the box respectfully to Selena, then stood back with her hands tucked behind her back, waiting to see what treasure Selena would bring forth.

Because these were Selena's things from Wilde Grove. The name conjured images of exotic rituals and spells. Of men and women dancing in the moonlight around a stone circle.

She was holding her breath.

'I had to get special permission to bring these into the country,' Selena said, sliding a long, burnished piece of wood out of the box. Her hands touched the familiar smooth wood, and she felt a flooding feeling of relief, as though she had come home again.

Or perhaps home had come to her.

'Wha' is it?' Clover asked.

Selena stood the long carved and polished stick on its end, hand gripped around it in a position so familiar to her that she felt herself standing taller, automatically slipping into the state of prayer and power that she usually occupied when holding her staff.

'It's a staff,' she said.

'What's it for?' Rue asked.

That was a good question. How to explain? Selena pursed her lips. 'Well, a staff is used as a prop to focus your power,' she said, then paused, thinking that was an inadequate explanation.

'How does it do that?' Rue asked before she could carry on.

Selena gazed at her staff. 'This is made of oak,' she said. 'Gifted to me by Grandmother Oak who stands watch over the stone circle at Wilde Grove. Oak is all about strength and authority, so it felt right for my staff, which I use in community and ritual as a symbol of, firstly, my authority in the Grove as the priestess of the Goddess – she whose will I carry out – and secondly, when I plant the staff upon the ground, it becomes symbolically the central point of the Wheel, around which the worlds turn.'

'The wheel?'

Selena held back her sigh. It had been a long time since she had taught Morghan these things, and she hadn't been expecting to go back to the beginning of it all and teach it again. But Rue's face was rapt with attention, and even Clover was squatting silently on the carpet gazing at the staff, as though the child knew it was an object of authority and power.

'The Wheel is the pattern around which all worlds, all seasons, all lives, revolve. We help the Wheel – the natural and abundant order of things – turn with our singing.'

'Singing?'

'Our right thinking, our right actions, the strength and beauty of our spirits. That is our Singing.'

Rue sank back and nodded. She thought she understood and was pleased. It was pretty simple really. The world had order, a kind of proper flow to it, and this singing was just keeping things in this proper order.

She liked that. It was good to think there was actually order and a pattern to what usually looked like chaos to her.

Or had until Selena had come into her life.

'What's this say?' Clover asked, pointing a small finger at the symbols burnt into the wood in three long rows up its length.

Selena smiled, taking the staff from Rue and running

her fingers over the letters. 'It's a prayer,' she said. 'Written in Ogham.'

She anticipated Rue's next question and answered as Rue opened her mouth to ask it. 'Ogham as we know and use it today is the script of the trees,' she said, touching her fingers to the prayer again.

Clover leant closer to Rue. 'Tol' ya trees can talk.'

Rue shook her head. 'I never told you they couldn't.' She was intrigued by Selena's staff. 'Tell me more about the Ogham,' she said. The word felt awkward on her tongue.

Selena nodded. 'It's a written language found on standing stones and dating back to the 4th century, although suspected to be much older than that. What makes it so useful for me and others, is that each letter has a symbolic meaning. So, it can be read and used on several levels.' She looked at Rue. 'Have you heard of runes?'

Rue nodded eagerly. 'I got a book out of the library on Norse Gods, and it mentioned runes in that.' She thought back. 'Something about one of the gods hanging upside down from a tree for three days and then being given the runes?'

'That was Odin,' Selena said. 'And runes are similar to the Ogham. Both letters, sounds, and symbols. They can both be also used in divination.'

Rue nodded slowly. This was awesome, she thought, and immediately decided she wanted to learn more about both things.

'Wha's it say?' Clover asked. She was running her fingers over the strange strings of symbols.

Selena looked at her staff and debated whether she wanted to read the short prayer to them. But hadn't she known she'd need to when she invited their help in unpacking her things?

She moistened her lips. 'I made this,' she said, 'by my own hands, when I was formally initiated as the Lady of the Grove's successor.' She smiled slightly. 'This was my prayer I wrote for that occasion; my dedication to my path, so to speak.'

Rue took a breath, her head spinning with excitement. 'What does it say?' she asked in a low, reverent voice.

'Ogham are read from the bottom up,' Selena said, finding the beginning of the prayer.

'Here is the tree that grows strong in the Wildwood.
Here is the root that digs deep,
The branch that reaches high.
Here am I, in balance,
spoke of the great Wheel.
Here is my task to sing.'

Rue was silent, not sure if she was disappointed by the prayer or not. It seemed very plain, but she held the words in her mind a little longer, and they seemed to grow there, and blossom, bursting into life. It was simple, she decided, but it didn't need to be anything else. It was powerful.

She touched the staff again, tentatively this time. 'Can I make one of these too?' she asked.

'I think that sounds like a fine idea,' Selena answered, seeing the deep desire plain as day on Rue's face and remembering Dandy's words. She could not leave Rue out of her teachings, and no soul eager to learn should be denied. As Dandy had said, although not perhaps in so many words, it was the task these days to sing the ancient path while walking the modern road.

'Where do I find the wood?' Rue asked.

Selena nodded. 'We don't take it alive from the tree, unless the tree needs pruning. So, I think you'll be able to find something over the road in the Garden, if you go often enough and look. There's a lot of windfall there, in the forest parts.'

Rue beamed at the thought. 'What sort of wood, though? Does it matter - yours is oak for a reason, right?'

'Yes, but I suggest when you go walking there, that you learn the types of trees, and perhaps even the history and meaning of them, and hold in your heart the desire to make a staff and ask the trees that one of them offer a limb to you, if they would wish to.'

Rue blinked at the suggestion, then looked at Selena. 'That works?' she asked.

Selena laughed. 'It does.'

'I wanna staff,' Clover said.

'You're too small for one,' Rue told her. Then looked at Selena. 'Is there something else we could make her?'

Selena, who had been about to rebuke Rue for denying Clover so quickly, chastised herself instead. She should have known that Rue had more care and loyalty to her sister than that. So, she smiled instead and gestured to another box.

Rue got up and took the box cutter to the cardboard carton, eager to see what was in it. Pushing back the flaps was like revealing a treasure chest and her breath caught in her throat.

'Wow,' she breathed. 'How did you get all this stuff here? I thought you weren't allowed to bring things like this into the country.' They'd studied conservation once when she was at school, and part of it had been some talk by a customs officer who listed all the things that weren't allowed into the country.

You weren't supposed to bring wood of any sort in. Or feathers, or anything like that.

But Rue could already see, as well as the staff, a short length of wood, with beads and feathers attached to it.

'I got an exemption,' Selena explained. 'These are religious artifacts, tools.'

'Cool,' Rue breathed, and glanced at Selena. 'Can I lift them out?'

At Selena's nod, she dipped her hands into the box and brought out the short length of wood, holding it so Clover could stare wide-eyed at it.

It was a knotted knuckle of wood, that looked as though once it had had four branches growing from it, which had since fallen off, leaving dimples in which were lodged shining stones.

'Wow,' Rue breathed, turning it over in her hands. The wood was worn smooth, and one end fitted neatly in her palm as though made for it. 'What do you use this for?'

Selena smiled. 'I guess you could call that my wand,' she said.

Rue examined the leather strings that had been threaded through a hole drilled in the 'handle'. On the end of the long strings were beads and feathers. 'What sort of feathers are these?' she asked.

'Those are feathers from a crane,' Selena replied. 'A common crane. Specifically. They're being reintroduced to the UK after an absence of 400 years.'

Clover sat next to Rue and stroked the pearl grey feather with a delicate finger. 'Where you get it?' she asked.

'One of the conservation centres sent it to me when I asked them to,' Selena explained.

'Why a crane?' Rue wasn't sure what a crane looked like, even a common one, but she was definitely going to look it up when she met Ebony at the public library later.

Selena leaned back in her chair, enjoying the conversation. Rue and Clover were an attentive audience.

'Crane special,' Clover said.

'Yes,' Selena agreed. 'Crane walks with me as my spirit kin.'

A frown creased between Rue's eyebrows. Here was another thing she knew nothing about and yet felt a sort of desperation to learn. 'What's spirit kin?'

'We each have a team of spirit helpers, of kin, who walk with us throughout our lives, there to aid us and keep our company.'

'What's that got to do with a bird?' Rue asked, not understanding.

'Some of our kin are animals,' Selena said, a smile spreading across her face because she knew how unlikely that sounded to most people.

Rue didn't say anything for a long moment, looking down at the smooth wooden stick in her hand, and running the feather through her fingers as she thought. Finally, she looked up and met Selena's gaze.

'Do I have an animal kin?' she asked, tripping over the unfamiliar term.

'Yes,' Selena said.

'Everyone does.'

11

RUE WAS EARLY AND STOOD OUTSIDE THE LIBRARY SHIFTING from foot to foot, nervous that Ebony wouldn't show. She wasn't used to having friends, had got out of practice after looking after Clover had begun to take up so much of her time. Now, she felt awkward, not quite sure that Ebony had been serious when she'd suggested to go to the big library in town to continue their research.

She checked her watch again, saw that only three minutes had gone by, and shrugged. Even if Ebony didn't show, there was plenty that Rue wanted to do there. She scraped her shoes across the ground again, nervous and impatient to go inside and look on the shelves up on the second floor, see what the library had about goddesses and mythology.

And spirit kin.

Would she find anything about that?

Rue tugged her phone out of her backpack and flipped it open. No new messages. Ebony hadn't texted again.

Still, she'd been early, Rue reminded herself, and looked again at the time. And Ebony was only a few minutes late.

'Hey!' Ebony came bouncing up the stairs, fine fair hair flying, and raced up to Rue, grinning. She punched her lightly on the shoulder. 'You made it!'

Rue smiled back. 'Yeah,' she said. 'I thought I was going to be late – my kid sister wanted to come along.' She shrugged affectionately. 'Clover would make me take her to the library every day if she could.'

'This the sister you went to Borstal for?'

'I didn't go to Borstal!'

'Yeah, yeah,' Ebony said, still grinning. 'So you tell me.'

Rue rolled her eyes and laughed. Ebony was pretty funny.

Linking her arm through Rue's, Ebony steered them into the library. 'So,' she said, aiming them towards the stairs. 'Where do you live, then?'

'Up by the Botanic Gardens,' Rue answered.

But Ebony shook her head. 'Nah,' she said. 'That's not what I mean. Who do you live with? Not your mum or dad, right?'

Rue's steps slowed as she realised she hadn't had to answer this question yet. Ebony was the first person who had asked her. Well, Ebony was pretty much the first person who had talked to her properly.

Ebony tugged on her arm and dragged her up the stairs, then stopped dead and turned to look seriously at Rue.

'Listen,' she said. 'You don't have to talk about it, if you don't want to. That's cool by me, okay?'

Rue looked at her for a long moment, startled. Ebony

meant what she'd said – Rue could see it in her face. Finally, Rue shrugged.

'Nah,' she said. 'It's okay.' She remembered why they were at the library. 'It's pretty cool, actually.'

They started walking again, climbing the stairs.

'I live in a big house with my sister and four other people.'

'Jeez,' Ebony broke in. 'Must be a big house.'

'Yeah.' They reached the first floor.

'They your extended family or something?' Ebony asked.

But Rue shook her head. 'Well, Selena might be a sort of relative,' she said, not quite sure there was another way to explain her ties with Selena, or even if she should yet. 'Distant, you know?'

Ebony nodded solemnly as though she did know.

'Anyway,' Rue continued, looking around at the library shelves. 'Selena came over from England to find Clover and me when she heard that Mum had died.'

'But hadn't your mum died a long time ago?'

Rue shrugged. 'Selena didn't hear about it until last year.'

'What's she like?'

'Selena's amazing. She was going to take us back to England with her, but she couldn't take us out of the country for some legal reasons, so she's moved here to take care of us.'

Ebony was impressed. 'That's pretty amazing of her.'

Rue nodded, making her way through the maze of shelves until they came to the right one.

'Better selection than at school,' Rue said.

'Yeah. Like a million times.' Ebony squinted at the books in the mythology section. 'So,' she said. 'Who is your goddess again?'

'Elen.' Rue cleared her throat. 'Elen of the Ways.'

Ebony shook her head. 'Never heard of her – and you better believe me when I say I've been through all these books a bunch of times.' She cast a glance around. 'Maybe there's something about her online. We should put our names down to use the computer.' She turned and looked at Rue. 'How did you find out about her anyway?'

Rue tugged a book from the shelves on Celtic mythology and flipped through the pages. It was mostly stories, she saw. Interesting, but not exactly what she was looking for at the moment.

'Selena told me about her,' she said when she'd slid the book back onto the shelf and reached for another, opening it up and sliding a finger down the list of gods and goddesses. 'This one has them from all over,' she said, holding the book for Ebony to see.

Ebony leaned over the page. 'Hasn't got your Elen.'

'No,' Rue said, disappointed. She flipped through the pages.

'So, how does Selena know about her, then, when there's nothing in all these books?'

Rue paused, looked over at her new friend. Ebony would believe her, right?

'What?' Ebony said. 'Why are you looking at me like that?'

'We're friends, right?' Rue asked, then ducked her head. 'I mean, we only just met but...'

'You bet we're friends,' Ebony interrupted. She shook

her head vigorously. 'I've been waiting months for someone like you to turn up. I mean, someone who isn't completely boring.'

'Thanks,' Rue said.

'You're definitely not boring.' Ebony shrugged, diffident now. 'And you know, you believe this stuff too.' She gestured to the books.

'I want to be a priestess,' Rue blurted.

Ebony stared at her, then a slow smile bloomed across her face. 'Me too,' she said.

They looked at each other.

Finally, Ebony nodded. 'So, that's what we'll do then,' she said. 'That's who we'll be.'

Rue had a lump in her throat. She wet her dry lips with her tongue, then spoke. 'Selena was the priestess of a Grove, back in England,' she said.

Ebony's eyes widened slightly. 'What's a Grove?'

'It's like, a group of priestesses, who come together to, I don't know, learn the ways of the goddess or something.' She grimaced. 'Or at least, Selena said that's how it used to be. Now there's just her and Morghan.'

'Who's Morghan?'

'She's the new priestess. Selena trained her to take over. She said that's the way they've been doing it for hundreds of years – so they can keep the ancient ways alive.'

Ebony's eyes were as round as saucers now. She let out a low whistle. 'So, she can teach us, right?'

Rue's face fell. 'I don't know. I asked her to, but she said maybe not. That maybe it wasn't my path.'

'Bollocks!' Ebony shook her head. 'Of course she has to – why else would she be here?'

They stood close to the bookshelf, looking at each other.

'She's kind of teaching me already,' Rue said, and her voice was almost a low whisper. 'I mean. Without meaning to, right? She goes out every morning to greet the sun, and lets me come too.' Rue shrugged her narrow shoulders. 'We kind of pray together.' She blinked. 'And she let Clover and me unpack some of her stuff that finally arrived on the ship from her home and told us all about them.'

'What sort of stuff?'

'She has a staff and a wand – and I'm going to make one too. Selena told me I could, told me how to find the right pieces of wood for them.'

'I'm making one too,' Ebony said promptly. 'And you gotta remember the prayers, so you can teach them to me.'

'We do offerings too,' Rue said, excitement rising inside her until she felt she might almost start to float.

'Offerings? Like I've been doing?'

Rue nodded. 'We have a shrine to the goddess and the Fae outside, and there's a small jug to fill with milk or whatever, and you pour it onto the ground as an offering.'

Ebony's head was spinning, and she grasped Rue's arm. 'I gotta see all this,' she said, leaning closer as though sharing a secret. 'You gotta let me see it all.'

'Well, you can come around and see the shrine – it's in the garden. But I don't know if Selena will let you see her stuff.'

'That's okay. It's good enough.' Ebony stood back, her eyes shining.

'And we can go into the Botanic Garden to look for wood for a staff,' Rue said. 'Selena told me how to find it.'

They grinned at each other.

'When?' Rue asked. 'When do you want to do it?'

Ebony wrinkled her nose. 'I have to go visit my gran tomorrow. We go every second Sunday.' She heaved a sigh. 'What about after school one day?' She raised her eyebrows. 'Do you think I could stay over?'

'Oh.' The thought hadn't occurred to Rue. She'd never brought friends back to her house – when she'd had some, that was. She'd always been too busy looking after Clover, picking her up from day-care, taking her home and making dinner.

'Hey, it's okay if you say I can't,' Ebony said, her mouth turning downcast even as she spoke.

Rue shook her head. 'No, it's fine, honest. I've just never had a friend over before.'

'Will Selena mind?' Ebony asked, her face relaxing. 'What about the other people you live with? You haven't told me about them.'

'They're just people who helped Selena find Clover – that's my sister – and me.'

Ebony laughed. 'What, she just like, collected them along the way?'

Rue thought about it. 'Yeah, just like that, actually. There's Dandy – she used to be my neighbour back when Mum was still alive. And Damien, he drove Selena around everywhere when she flew over here, because she doesn't drive. And Tara, she ran the guest house where Selena stayed while she was looking for us.'

'And you all live together now?'

'Yep.'

'You know that's weird, right?'

Rue shrugged. 'We sorta turned into a family.'

Ebony thought about it for a moment. 'That's cool,' she nodded. Then her eyes lit up further. 'Right,' she said. 'You know what we need to do today?'

'What?'

'We need to write down some of this stuff in these books into a like, what are they called?'

Rue didn't have any idea.

'The books witches have – a Book of Shadows, that's it.'

'But we don't want to be witches,' Rue said. 'Do we?'

Ebony stopped, brow furrowing. 'I don't know,' she said slowly. 'Doing magic and spells and stuff would be pretty amazing.'

Rue thought about it. Then nodded. 'We kind of did a spell at the solstice. And Tara has a stack of books on witchcraft that she bought.' Maybe it did all go together.

'See!' Ebony crowed. 'What sort of spell?'

A librarian walked up to them, lips pinched together, and Rue saw with sudden dismay that it was the same one who had been so mean to Clover and her that day before Selena had come along.

Miss Meadows.

'I'll thank you to remember that this is a library,' Miss Meadows hissed at them in a low voice. 'An institution of learning,' she said, and looked them up and down in obvious distaste. 'I suggest you put that book back and move along,' she said, lip curling at Rue's black clothing.

'But we want to get this book out,' Ebony said.

'I don't think so,' Daisy Meadows said grimly. 'We won't have talk of spells and witchcraft in this library.'

Rue gaped at her. 'You can't decide who gets to look at which books!'

Daisy drew herself up to her full height. Which wasn't very tall, but sufficient to get the point across.

'I assure you, young lady, that I can have you thrown out of here in a flash.'

Ebony shook her head. 'This is a public library and we're the public.'

'You're a nuisance,' Daisy said and plucked the book from Rue's hands before Rue even had time to know it was happening. 'I'd like you to leave now.'

She narrowed her eyes at Rue. 'And don't think I've forgotten you,' she said, baring long yellowing teeth.

'Me?' Rue said. 'I didn't do anything wrong then, and I haven't done anything wrong now.'

'You are causing a disturbance in my library,' Daisy Meadows said. 'Do I need to get security to escort you out?'

'The library doesn't have security,' Ebony said, incredulous.

'Certainly, we do,' Daisy said, and sniffed. 'Out,' she told them.

Rue and Ebony exchanged glances.

'Fine,' Ebony grumbled. 'We'll go.'

Rue followed her out to the stairs.

'What a fascist,' Ebony said. 'Where'd they recruit her from?'

'She was a bitch to Clover and me once,' Rue said, clomping down the steps and refusing to glance behind her to see if the woman were standing there watching to make sure they left.

But she wouldn't put Miss Meadows past it.

'She used to work in the children's library. Clover hated her on sight.'

'I wouldn't put that woman within a mile of a small child,' Ebony said as they reached the ground floor. 'Well,' she said. 'What do we do now?'

Rue shrugged. 'I've got a little bit of money. 'You wanna go have a coffee?'

'Yeah. Sounds good.'

12

'CAN YOU BELIEVE WHAT JUST HAPPENED?' EBONY ASKED, shaking her head as they sat down with cups of coffee and a piece of cake each.

'Nope,' Rue said. 'Well, strike that – I can believe Meadows did that, I just can't believe she gets away with it.'

'We should march back in there and demand to see the boss, or head librarian or whatever. I bet Field Marshall Meadows would get fired.'

The girls sat a moment in silence, looking at their pieces of cake. They weren't going to go marching back into the library, they both knew that.

'Okay,' said Ebony at last. 'So, let's go shopping for a notebook to be our Book of Shadows. I want mine to be nice – like leather or something.'

Rue picked up her fork. 'What do you put into a Book of Shadows?'

The question had Ebony shrugging. 'Well, all the prayers and stuff you're learning, for starters. Then whatever spells we learn.' She sat up. 'And how to make a staff and wand and so on.'

'Why's it called a Book of Shadows?' Rue asked. 'I don't like that.'

Ebony sat for a moment. 'We can call it something else.'

Rue thought about it. 'What about Book of Ways?' She frowned, then nodded. 'I can't think of anything else at the moment, and I quite like that.'

'Hey Ebony.'

Ebony and Rue looked up at the greeting.

'Oh, hey Suze. What are you doing?' Ebony looked over at Rue. 'This is my cousin Suze,' she said.

'Hi,' Rue said. 'I'm Rue.'

Suze, a tall girl with the same colouring as her cousin, smiled at Rue shyly.

'We got kicked out of the library,' Ebony said. 'Wanna sit down with us?'

'Sure.' Suze looked at their plates. 'Is the cake good?' she asked.

Rue looked down at the banana cake on her plate. 'It looks good,' she said. She hadn't tasted it yet.

'I'll get some, just a mo,' Suze said and made for the counter.

'Does she go to our school too?' Rue asked.

'Nah,' Ebony said. 'She goes to St. Brigid's.'

Rue's eyes widened. 'The Catholic school?'

'Yeah. Her dad's Catholic. My auntie converted when they got married.'

Rue looked down at her plate. 'We never went to church when I was a kid. My mum wasn't religious.'

'Mine's not either,' Ebony said, then giggled. 'Mum's a

complete New-Age hippie.' She stabbed her fork into her cake. 'You know – crystals everywhere and mantras and meditation.' She shrugged, stuck the cake in her mouth and talked around it. 'She's a good egg, though. Lets me do my thing, right?'

Rue nodded and felt a pang of longing for her own mother. Then thought of Selena and felt better, ate some of her own cake.

'You guys heard about Sophie?' Suze asked, sliding into the third seat at their table.

'Sophie?' Ebony said around another mouthful.

Suze nodded. 'Sophie Raisin.' She giggled. 'I'm awful,' she said. 'I always laugh when I say her name.'

'Raisin?' Ebony shook her head. 'I'd change it if it was my name.'

Suze pointed her fork at her cousin. 'And you're happy being Ebony White, are you?'

Rue stared at Ebony. 'Your surname is White?'

'Yeah.' Ebony stuck her fork back into her carrot cake. 'And I'm changing it when I'm old enough to.' She paused. 'Or I might change Ebony – I haven't decided.' She tapped her fork on her plate, spreading crumbs everywhere. 'Maybe I'll take Athena as my name.'

'Can you do that?' Rue asked.

But Ebony just shrugged. 'Sure,' she said. 'Why not?' She stopped suddenly and looked at her cousin.

'What about Sophie Raisin?' she asked.

Rue, who had forgotten about what Suze had been going to tell them, followed Ebony's fork as it pointed at Suze.

'There's a ghost in their house.' Suze sniffed and ate a dainty bite of cake.

Ebony set her fork slowly down and sat back. 'Say that again?'

Suze shrugged. 'A ghost. That's what Robyn said, and she lives next door. Says there's banging and carrying on, and that Sophie said that her bedcovers keep getting ripped off her in the middle of the night.'

Ebony turned her head so slowly that it seemed to creak, and she looked at Rue across the table.

'A ghost,' she said.

'Yeah,' Suze spoke up again. 'One of those, waddayou-callits?' She frowned. 'Robyn called it something.'

'A poltergeist,' Ebony said gravely.

Suze nodded, ate some more cake. 'Thought you'd like that.' She looked over at Rue. 'You're not into all the same weird stuff that Ebony here is, are you?'

Rue hesitated.

'She is, thank you very much,' Ebony said.

Suze rolled her eyes, but she grinned at Rue in a friendly way. 'Don't let her drag you into anything,' she said.

Ebony shook her head. 'Tell me everything you know about the poltergeist,' she said.

'I already have.'

'No,' Ebony told her cousin. 'I mean every single little tidbit of information. All conversations word for word.' She'd finished her cake and held her cup of coffee now, peering at Suze over the rim, pale eyes sharp and focused.

'I'm not going to remember every word,' Suze said. 'No one can remember every word of a conversation.'

'You're going to try,' Ebony said.

Rue picked up her own cup of coffee, realising that her heart was thumping loudly under her clothes.

'Fine,' Suze said. 'It went like this: I saw Robyn at school during English, and she said to me have you heard about Sophie?' Suze gazed serenely at Ebony. 'Just like I said to you.'

Ebony rolled her eyes. 'Go on,' she said.

Suze did. 'I said no, why, what's Sophie done? And Robyn said she hasn't done anything except there's a ghost in her house, and I laughed and said there's no such thing as ghosts.'

Ebony snorted.

Rue took a sip of her coffee, still looking at Suze.

Suze poked her tongue out at Ebony then resumed her recital. 'That's not what Sophie says, Robyn said. Sophie says she keeps getting woken up by something moving around their house and then her door opens and she can hear footsteps and sometimes there's a creak in the bed when someone invisible sits down next to her, or her blankets get pulled off her.'

Suze fell silent and looked expectantly at Ebony. 'Well?'

Ebony was impressed, looked across the table at Rue. 'What do you think?'

Rue didn't know what to think.

Ebony looked back at Suze with her eyes narrowed. 'Is Sophie telling the truth?'

Suze shrugged. 'I don't believe in ghosts, and I said that to Robyn. I said I don't believe in ghosts and Sophie must be making it up, but Robyn shook her head and said Sophie swears it's true. But she's a bit of an attention-seeker.' Suze paused. 'Robyn, that is.'

Ebony pushed her cup away. 'Okay then,' she said.

'Okay what?' Suze asked.

Rue looked across the table at her new friend.

'We'll go see,' Ebony said, nodding, satisfied.

'Go see?' Rue asked.

'Do you believe in ghosts?' Ebony asked her.

'Um.' Rue looked at Ebony then Suze, then Ebony again. 'I've never thought about them,' she finished lamely.

'Well, have a think right now,' Ebony demanded. 'Do you believe in ghosts?'

Rue thought about the times Selena had mentioned spirits in her prayers. Animal spirits, helper spirits. Kin. Were they that different from human spirits? If one was possible, why couldn't the other be?'

'I guess so,' she said. Then shrugged. 'Yeah, I suppose so.'

Ebony nodded as though that question was all settled.

'Finish your cake,' she said to Suze.

'I've only just sat down,' Suze protested.

Ebony just stared at her until Suze heaved a sigh.

'Fine,' she said. 'Or you can go without me.'

'You're coming,' Ebony told her. 'You know Sophie.'

'Not real well.'

'Robyn knows Sophie,' Ebony said implacably. 'And you know Robyn. That's only one degree of separation. Plenty.'

Suze finished her cake.

'YOU KNOW BRIGID WAS ACTUALLY A GODDESS, RIGHT?' EBONY said as they got off the bus near Suze's school.

'So you've said about a million times,' Suze said, walking ahead down the street.

Ebony didn't let that stop her. 'Brigid was so popular that when the Christians came and tried to convert everyone, they couldn't stop people worshipping her, so they made her a saint instead.' She smiled smugly.

'Is that true?' Rue asked, hurrying to keep up.

'Of course,' Ebony said. 'If I wasn't dedicating myself to being a priestess of Athena, I'd be going with Brigid. She's cool.' Ebony blinked. 'If that fascist librarian had let us get some books out, you could read all about her.'

They followed Suze down the road and around the corner.

'What are we going to do?' Rue asked. 'Do you really think this house is going to be haunted?'

Ebony sniffed. 'Doors opening on their own in the middle of the night. Mysterious footsteps. An invisible entity sitting on the bed. Blankets being pulled off.' She gave Rue a pointed look.

'Yeah,' Rue said. 'I guess so.'

'What else would it be?'

'This Sophie girl could be lying?' Rue asked.

'A possibility, of course,' Ebony mused. 'Still. Bit of an adventure, don't you think?'

Rue nodded, but she suddenly wished that Selena was there to ask her advice. Then she straightened, because Selena wasn't there, and wasn't sure Rue should be a priestess. Well, perhaps looking into this ghost business would convince Selena that it was her path.

Rue was sure she'd make a good priestess.

She already knew most of the prayers Selena said off by heart.

'We didn't get the notebooks,' she said suddenly.

'Huh?' Ebony said. 'Oh, we'll get them when we go back into town.'

Rue nodded.

Up ahead, Suze suddenly stopped walking and looked across the road, lifting her hand to shade her eyes. Then she nodded over to Ebony and Rue.

'Sophie lives in that house up there.'

Rue followed Suze's gesture and frowned. 'Behind that fence?' she asked.

Suze nodded.

'But it's right on the edge of a cliff.' She shuddered, thinking she could forget about any ghost – just waiting for the whole house to slide off the cliff would keep her awake at night.

'How old is Sophie's house?' Ebony asked.

Suze shrugged. 'Dunno. Old?'

Ebony nodded wisely as though she'd expected just that answer.

'How do we get up there?' Rue asked.

'Road goes around and up,' Suze said, and sighed. 'Come on, then.'

They walked in silence up to the house then stopped and stood in a row, staring over the neat white picket fence at the weatherboard house.

'It's got to be over a hundred years old,' Ebony decided. 'Big villas like this were built when Dunedin was just getting going.'

Suze shrugged. 'What difference does it make?'

'It's haunted, isn't it?'

'Sure,' Suze replied. 'I mean, maybe. But even if it is – wouldn't we have heard something about it before this?' She paused. 'Robyn can't keep a secret to save her life.'

Ebony scowled at the logic, then shook it off. 'Maybe the ghost has just been at peace before this, and Sophie did something to upset it.'

Suze shook her head. 'What did Sophie do?'

'I don't know,' Ebony said, undeterred. 'Let's ask her. Go and knock on the door.'

Suze turned and looked at her cousin. 'Me?'

'You,' Ebony nodded. 'You know her, right?'

'Not very well. We're not real good friends, or anything.'

'Tell her we're here about the ghost.' Ebony was implacable. 'Tell her we can get rid of it.'

Rue looked at her in consternation, but Suze just laughed and went to the gate, opened it, then marched up to the front door.

'We can't get rid of a ghost,' Rue said.

'How do you know?' Ebony said. 'Have you ever seen a ghost before?'

Rue shook her head.

'Then how do you know what we can or can't do?'

13

Selena and Dandy walked out of the Botanic Garden at the top of the hill and looked both ways before they crossed the road. Just up the street there, opposite the tennis courts, was the house where Rue and Clover had been living when they'd finally found them. Both paused in front of its peeling gate and looked over the low concrete wall at the house.

It looked empty, and Selena wasn't too surprised. The place seemed ready to subside gently into the ground, the gutters hanging askew, pocked with holes and rust. Still, she smiled at the house and wished it well. It had, after all, for a time sheltered two people Selena cared dearly about.

Clover was down at the duck pond with Tara and Damien. Rue was out with a new friend. Going to the library in town, she'd said when she'd told them about it.

'I'm glad Rue's making friends,' Dandy commented, sighing at the house. 'It hasn't been easy, these last few weeks, trying to fit back into school when she'd been away so long doing an adult's job.'

Selena nodded. 'I'm very glad too. Every day I'm in awe of Rue, doing what she did. I want her to be able to relax into her life now.'

They nodded, both falling quiet, thinking about what a close thing it had been, keeping Rue and Clover out of foster care. Dandy touched Selena lightly on her arm.

'They're both going to be fine,' she said.

Selena nodded. 'Yes. I do agree.'

'It's just that parenting is hard,' Dandy said. 'Worrying over them.'

Selena smiled, drew breath, and turned to walk again. 'Rue and Clover are in the best of hands, with all of us looking out for them,' she said. Then looked ahead to the street she was heading for.

They stopped in front of the house, and Selena watched Dandy closely.

'Can you feel anything?' she asked.

Dandy pressed her lips together and tested the atmosphere. Then nodded slightly. 'I think I can,' she said. 'Sort of a shiver in the air.'

Selena turned her face towards the house, with its windows looking blankly out at the road. She could feel it strongly – a vibration that got under her skin and went all through her.

'I can't help but feel like it's calling to me,' she said, and a dizzy woozy feeling made her sway, her head suddenly fuzzy with the feeling she'd come to know was an affirmative to whatever she was asking or thinking. She nodded, waited for the sensation to subside.

'I think we should go knock on the door,' she said.

Dandy nodded, but slowly. 'What's our cover story?' she asked. 'We can't very well just rock up and say well hello there, we were passing and noticed your house has a very strange and potent energy to it.'

'We can't?' Selena said, turning to Dandy with brows raised. Then she relaxed and smiled. 'I know,' Selena said. 'Shame, isn't it?' She pursed her lips.

'We could pretend to be soliciting subscriptions for the bowling club,' Dandy said dubiously.

Selena shook her head. 'I don't think so.' She put her hands on the gate. 'Why don't we just go knock on the door and see what we come up with?'

Dandy opened her mouth to protest that she'd much rather be a little more prepared than that, but Selena was already pushing her way through the gate and up the driveway beside the house.

There was no car in the driveway and Dandy looked at the front windows, thinking how awfully dim it must be in the front room.

'I think we'll find the back door,' Selena said, gazing at the front entrance, which was festooned with spider webs. 'I don't think this one gets used very much.'

'I think you're right,' Dandy said in full agreement. 'And I don't like the size of those spiders.'

They made their way around to the back of the house.

'This isn't much better,' Dandy said. 'Although at least there aren't any spiders.' She looked back up at the windows. 'How sure are we that someone actually lives here though?' The curtains were open, but the windows were filthy on the outside. Dandy stood on her tippy toes, trying to see in. She thought she caught a flash of movement.

'Did you see someone in there?' she asked Selena.

Selena shook her head. She had her eyes shut, using other senses to feel out the house. The building's energy was just as strong, a sort of siren call. She stepped up to the back door and abruptly knocked.

They listened for someone coming to answer it.

There was no movement from inside.

'I was sure I saw someone inside,' Dandy said, perplexed. 'Perhaps they're disabled, can't get to the door.' She shook her head. 'But in that case, they wouldn't be alone, would they?'

'I don't know,' Selena said. 'I feel certain someone lives here, but unfortunately we can't make them come to the door to speak with us.'

'Knock once more anyway,' Dandy said.

Selena nodded, rapped her knuckles against the faded blue door. 'Hello?' she called. 'Is there anyone home?'

She flattened her palms against the door and leaned closer, listening, trying to feel her way into the space behind the walls. Then shook her head and looked at Dandy.

'I don't know,' she said. 'There's someone there, but that's all I can say.'

'Man or woman?'

Selena considered. 'Woman – but I'm mostly saying that because of Clover.'

'Right,' Dandy said, nodding. 'What did Clover call the house?'

'The hurting house. And she said the lady in it didn't want anyone to look at her.' Selena moved back to the path and stood with Dandy, both of them considering the house.

'Maybe she's a shut-in,' Dandy said. 'I had a friend when I was a child, whose mother never left the house.'

Selena nodded slowly. 'I wish we had something to leave for her. Some sort of gift.'

'That would probably just frighten the poor thing,' Dandy said on a sigh. 'We should leave.'

'Yes.' Selena followed Dandy reluctantly back down the path to the gate and closed it gently behind them. There was no way to make the woman in the house – if she was indeed there – answer the door and talk to them. No way to let her know they wanted to help, if possible.

Selena drew in a breath, sighed. 'Shall we walk back through the garden?'

'That would be lovely.'

They retraced their footsteps and entered the Botanic Garden, slipping into its fragrant shade.

'It is a strange thing,' Selena mused as they walked along the path under the trees, 'to come to a new country and spend so much time in a garden full of trees from all over the world.'

Dandy, who had never come often to the big public garden despite living in the city for all of her life, nodded. 'We're lucky though, to live right beside it. I've never enjoyed it so much.'

The path twisted down past a grassy area, on which several groups of young people lay sprawled in the sun, chatting and sharing picnic lunches.

'It's marvellous for all the students who live around here.'

Selena nodded, but her attention was caught by something else.

Someone else.

She nodded her head towards two young men skulking along the path that ran the other side of the lawn.

'Do you see those two?' she said, almost in a whisper.

'Oh,' Dandy said. 'Yes. I don't like the look of them.'

Selena shook her head. 'Nor do I. Their spirits are twisted.' She blinked. 'Particularly that of the man on the left. He feels...predatory.'

They stood still, watched a young woman from one of the groups stand up, brush off her jeans and say she had to run to the loo.

'I think we should follow her,' Selena said quietly.

The two men had lifted their head as though sniffing prey and were walking back down the way they'd come. Their path would intersect with the young woman's.

Dandy nodded, gripped Selena's arms, and gritted her teeth as they took the steep path that led upwards across the sloping lawn. 'We won't get in front of them,' she said. 'We're too far behind.'

'Behind is fine, as long as we're close enough for them to know we can see them,' Selena huffed.

Her legs worked as they climbed the path but most of her mind was elsewhere, encircling the young woman in a bubble of protection.

They reached the top of the path and turned hurriedly, saw they were still quite a way behind the two men, who were in turn shadowing the university student.

'The bathrooms are right by paths where not so many go,' Dandy said in between wheezing breaths.

'Excuse me!' Selena called out loudly. 'Excuse me!'

One of the men turned his head to look at her, then dismissed her and turned back.

'You two,' Selena called. 'Can you tell us the way to the aviaries, please?' She hurried forward, Dandy on her arm. 'We don't know which way to go.'

The man turned to look at them again. 'Follow the signs,' he growled.

'Oh!' Selena called. 'Follow you! Wonderful!'

She and Dandy watched the two men falter, realising that they couldn't keep shadowing the woman with whatever plan they'd had in mind. They stopped and both scowled at Selena and Dandy.

'Fuck off,' the one on the left said, and Selena looked at his face, into his eyes, and didn't like what she saw there at all.

'I'm sorry,' she said. 'We're both of us a little hard of hearing. Which way is it to the aviaries, then?'

'What, you blind as well?' It was the one on the right and Selena looked at him, feeling for the quality of his spirit. He wasn't as corrupted as his friend, but she still had to stop herself recoiling in distaste.

He would go along with whatever his friend came up with.

Dandy patted her arm. 'Oh look,' she said. 'There are the bathrooms. I need to go, don't you?'

The men glared at them, but Dandy put on her most cheerful, harmless-old-lady face and smiled blearily at them as she and Selena edged past them and scurried on to the bathroom block.

'We can't let her come out alone, you know,' she whispered when they were past. 'They'll wait for her to come out and then who knows what they've in mind.'

'Nothing good,' Selena said grimly, shaken at the unexpected turn of events. She flicked a glance behind her and saw the two still standing there, glowering. She pressed her free hand to her chest. 'Those two,' she said, then ran out of words and shook her head instead.

They bustled into the toilets, saw that one stall was still occupied and heaved a sigh of relief between them.

Dandy went over to the basins and washed her hands, dried them, then smiled at the young woman as she flushed and came out.

'Lovely day, isn't it?' she said, then stopped smiling. 'There are two men who tried to follow you here, dear, and we didn't like the looks of them.' Dandy glanced at Selena who nodded. 'So we followed you too, just in case.'

The woman straightened, her smile falling away. 'Followed me here?'

'I'm afraid so,' Selena said. 'They had a very predatory look about them.'

'And this bathroom block is just a little way from the forest walk,' Dandy added.

'Are they still there?' the woman asked. She went to the door and peered out, then turned back to the two women. 'There are two men just down the path I came along.' She blinked. 'Are those them? Are they waiting for me to come back?'

Dandy took a quick peek.

'Yes. Those are the two. I'd call the police on them, except lurking isn't a crime. They gave us the willies, though, and got very angry when they realised we were right behind them.'

The woman narrowed her eyes. 'Thank you,' she said. 'I had no idea they were following me.' She blew out a breath. 'It's not safe anywhere anymore, is it?' She glanced outside, then back at Selena and Dandy. 'I'm Melanie, by the way. Will you walk back with me? They're probably hoping you'll go a different way.'

'We will definitely walk back with you,' Selena said.

'And maybe we'll have a word with some of the gardeners here, let them know a couple of creeps are stalking women,' Dandy added. 'They can keep an eye out.'

They left the bathroom together, in a safe little knot.

14

SUZE TOOK A BREATH AND LIFTED THE KNOCKER ON THE FRONT door. There was no point not doing it – if she didn't knock on the door, then Ebony would. Either way, Sophie was having visitors.

Suze stood back and hoped no one was home.

But the door opened, and Sophie stood there, surprise on her face. 'Suze,' she said. 'What are you doing here?'

Ebony ran lightly up the path. 'Hi Sophie,' she said.

Sophie's eyes grew confused. 'Who are you?'

'She's my cousin,' Suze said, with what sounded a lot like regret.

Ebony gave her a little poke. 'Suze told us you're having trouble with a ghost,' she said, then smiled widely. 'We've come to help you with it.'

Sophie paled and she looked at Suze. 'Who told you that?' she asked.

'Robyn told her,' Ebony said.

Rue crept up to stand behind them.

Sophie blinked at them then shook her head. 'It's not true,' she said, mortified.

'Your mum and dad here, Sophie?'

Sophie frowned at Ebony. 'What? Why?'

Ebony softened her voice. 'Listen, we know it's true – Robyn said to Suze here that you told her all about it. And we know neither you nor Robyn are liars.' She jerked her head to indicate Robyn's house next door.

Sophie swung her head around to look, even though it wasn't visible on the other side of the wooded garden.

So did Rue.

'You don't know me at all,' Sophie said. 'And Robyn had no right to repeat anything I told her.'

But Ebony waved the comment away. 'You know what it's like,' she said. 'No one keeps their mouth shut about anything.' She jerked her thumb at Rue. 'There's gossip going round at our school about this one that's much worse.'

Rue gaped at Ebony, then looked over at Sophie who was now staring curiously at her. She sighed, then shrugged. 'Yeah,' she said. 'And there's some truth to some of it too.'

Ebony ploughed on. 'Listen,' she said. 'We're not here to judge you, or to laugh at you, or anything like that. I believe you. We believe you. And we want to help.' She gazed at Sophie, urging her to let them in, talk to them. This was too exciting an opportunity to pass up. A ghost! Ebony had always wanted to see a ghost.

Sophie blinked at her, perplexity on her face, a small frown between her eyes. They didn't think she was making things up? Everyone thought she was making it all up. Robyn hadn't believed her; she was sure of it. Doubly sure of it now that she knew Robyn had gone running off to spread word around.

Ebony was still talking, her voice low, confidential, confident. 'Listen, we can help. Let us in, tell us about it. You'll feel better.'

For a long moment, Sophie stared at them dubiously, then without a word, she stood back and held the door open.

Ebony bolted inside, grinning, all but rubbing her hands together. 'I'm Ebony,' she said and then waved a hand at Rue. 'This is Rue – her foster mother is a priestess of Elen of the Ways, so she knows a bit about ghosts and stuff.'

'I do?' Rue asked.

But Ebony just shrugged. 'And what we don't know, we'll just learn as we go along. Are your mum and dad home, Sophie?'

Sophie shook her head. 'Jeremy and Reece have a karate tournament today. They won't be home until later.' She flicked a glance at Rue. 'Jeremy and Reece are my brothers. Who is Elen of the Ways?'

'Um,' Rue said. 'She's an ancient British goddess.'

Sophie's eyes widened. 'We're Catholic,' she said.

Ebony broke in. 'We can still help you,' she said emphatically.

'My parents don't believe me,' Sophie said. 'They think I'm just making things up.' She looked abashed for a moment. 'I had an imaginary friend when I was little, and now they don't believe this is anything but my imagination again.' She looked down at the floor. 'Or they say that Jeremy and Reece are playing tricks on me.'

'What do your brothers say when they tell you that?' Suze asked, interested despite herself.

Sophie gave a tight shrug. 'They howl and whine that they're not doing anything, so Mum and Dad just shake their heads and look at me then and ask if I'm not too old to still be making up things like this.' There were bright spots of colour on her cheeks now. 'I've stopped telling them anything, since they don't believe me.'

They were still standing by the front door, and Ebony turned now and closed it, looking about the hallway. It was a really nice place, light and bright for an old house. She couldn't say it looked like the typical setting for a haunting. Shouldn't it be old and dusty? There was a thick runner of carpet on the polished floorboards and Ebony clomped her shoe against it then nodded wisely. 'Good floor for hearing footsteps,' she said, then peered into the front room on her right. 'This your room?'

Sophie shook her head. 'That's my parent's. Mine is that one.' She pointed to the one opposite, then chewed on her lip. 'I'm in the kitchen though. You want something to drink? I have a bottle of coke.'

Ebony was peering into Sophie's bedroom, taking a quick inventory of its contents. The bed was neatly made. There was an old wardrobe on one wall, the door closed, the key in its old-fashioned lock. 'This where all the action happens?' she asked.

Rue glanced in the room.

Sophie winced, her face still white. She licked her lips.

'I'd like a coke,' Rue said, then smiled diffidently. 'If that's okay?'

Sophie looked relieved. 'Sure,' she said. 'This way.'

Rue cast Ebony a pointed glance as they followed Sophie down the central hallway, through the living room and to the kitchen at the back of the house. 'She's scared,' she whispered.

'That's because she has a ghost haunting her,' Ebony whispered back.

'Maybe, but don't rush her, okay? And I don't think she wants to go into her room.'

Ebony sighed, then nodded and Rue was satisfied for the moment.

'She can tell us all about it from the safety of the kitchen,' Ebony said.

They filed into the kitchen, which also looked like it had been renovated recently. It was a big, open plan room for cooking and dining. Sophie went to the fridge, pulled out a big plastic bottle of Coke and got glasses down from the cupboard.

'You wanna watch a movie or something?' she asked, pouring the drinks and handing them around. 'We went to Video Ezy last night, got a stack of them out.'

'Yeah?' Suze said. She loved movies. 'What did you get? Did you get the new Pride and Prejudice?' She sighed dreamily. 'I've seen that twice already. Matthew MacFadyen has such beautiful eyes.'

Ebony rolled her own eyes. 'We're here to talk about ghosts,' she said. 'So unless you've got The Amityville Horror in there, I don't want to hear about it.'

Sophie looked horrified. 'The Amityville Horror?

'Or Fog,' Ebony added. 'Or War of the Worlds.'

Rue hadn't seen of any of them. She knew pretty much

all the words to Matilda, but she didn't think that would impress Ebony.

'My parents wouldn't let me get any horror movies out,' Sophie said, shuddering. She turned to Suze. 'I love Pride and Prejudice too. I've got my own copy of it – I got it for my birthday.'

'Good grief,' Ebony said. 'Tell us about the ghost, then we'll leave you two to have a Jane Austin party, all right?'

Sophie sat abruptly down at the table, clasping her glass of Coca Cola.

Rue lowered herself to a chair beside her and looked carefully at Sophie. 'It's really bothering you, isn't it? Something is.'

Sophie gave her a grateful look, then nodded. 'I keep noticing these strange smells, you know?'

'Nope,' Ebony said, but her voice was gentler. 'Why don't you tell us?' She sat down as well, and a moment later, so did Suze.

Sophie stared at the bubbles rising to the surface of her drink, her mouth turned down at the edges. 'It started a month or two ago, right after we moved in.' She looked around. 'I was really excited about moving here – the people renovated it before they sold it to us, and we'd never lived in such a nice house, right?'

Everyone nodded and Rue looked around again. 'It's really nice,' she said. 'I like the colours.'

The walls were a soft, buttery yellow. Clover, Rue thought, would be right at home here.

'Tell us about these smells,' Ebony demanded.

Sophie gazed at her for a moment. 'It's just the flowers in

the garden,' she said. 'There are some roses. They smell really nice.'

'That's not what you told Robyn,' Suze said unexpectedly.

'She wasn't supposed to tell anyone what I said.' Sophie shook her head. 'She promised.'

Ebony broke in before things could be derailed. 'She was frightened for you.'

Suze nodded, although privately, she thought that gave Robyn too much credit. Robyn had been practically salivating to tell her all about the ghost at Sophie's new house.

'So,' Ebony asked. 'Do you really think you're smelling the flowers in the garden?'

Sophie lowered her gaze, shook her head, then sighed. 'It's weird. Every now and then, I'll be in my room, or the hallway, and I can smell perfume, or at least that's what it seems like. A great cloud of perfume.'

'Do you know what kind it is?' Rue asked, leaning forward, letting herself get fascinated.

Sophie looked at her, then back at her drink. 'No,' she said. 'It's really old-fashioned, which is why I thought it had the be from the garden when it first happened. I went outside and sniffed all the flowers, but nothing smelled like it.' She paused, tapped her fingers against her glass. 'And when it happens, it really is like a cloud of it. You can walk through it, then turn around and walk back through it again.' She looked confused for a moment. 'I mean, like it's not everywhere, right? It's just in one place.'

Everyone nodded, getting what she meant.

'I kept believing that it was just wafting in from the garden anyway, because what else could it be?' Sophie looked at the other three girls in turn, then shrugged. 'I mean, there's nothing else it could be.' She grimaced, continued.

'But then it happened at the petrol station.'

'At the petrol station?' Rue asked.

'Yeah. Mum had gotten out to put petrol in the car, right? And suddenly the whole inside of the car smelled like this floral perfume.' Sophie shook her head. 'It was so strange. And Jeremy and Reece were in the back seat and when I asked them if they could smell it, they just laughed and asked if I'd farted.' She wrinkled her nose.

'They couldn't smell it?' Ebony asked.

Sophie shook her head miserably. 'Nope. Only I could – so I must just be imagining things, right?'

Rue looked at Sophie and didn't think she was making it up, not from the expression on her face.

'What else has been happening?' she asked gently, with a glance at Ebony and Suze.

Ebony bared her teeth in a humourless smile. 'Robyn said your bedcovers were getting yanked off, and that someone keeps climbing into bed with you.'

Sophie's eyes widened. 'That's not true!'

'She might have exaggerated it,' Suze said, her voice apologetic. 'She was pretty excited.'

'Great, Sophie muttered and sat up straighter. 'I should never have said anything to her at all. I can't believe she's running around telling everyone and making stuff up too.'

'But what else is happening?' Ebony asked, impatient with the recriminations.

'Well, no one is yanking my blankets off my bed,' Sophie said, then her eyebrows rose, and she stared into her glass again. 'But sometimes I feel like someone has sat down on the bed with me.' Her face crumpled. 'And I catch a glimpse of her sometimes.'

'Her?' Rue interrupted.

'Yeah.' Sophie met their eyes. 'In the mirror of the wardrobe, mostly.'

'What does she look like?' Ebony said, unable to believe her luck. A real live ghost! Or rather, a real dead ghost. She frowned a moment. How did you describe that? But it didn't matter, and she looked expectantly at Sophie again.

But Sophie was shaking her head. 'I don't know,' she said. 'It's more like just catching a movement, than really seeing anyone. I mean, I can't make her out, I just...' She fell silent, frowning, trying to think how to describe what she meant, what she saw without really seeing. 'I dunno,' she said at last, giving up. 'It's just this flicker, right? And I know she's there.'

'If it's just a flicker, how do you know the ghost is a woman?' Ebony asked.

Rue looked at Sophie with interest. She half wished she had Clover with her. It would be super interesting, she thought, to see what Clover had to say about it. Maybe she should bring Clover around sometime.

But what if the ghost or spirit or whatever was scary? She couldn't do that to Clover.

And Sophie did look pretty freaked out about it.

Maybe she should invite Sophie back to her place. Clover knew things about people she met on the street; she'd be able to tell if something was going on. Rue frowned to herself, wishing she had even a fraction of Clover's gifts.

Goddess Elen, she thought, let me see and know things

too. Please? She swallowed, her skin prickling with the strangeness of having just said the small prayer.

'Because of the perfume, I guess,' Sophie said, then jumped up.

'What?' Ebony asked, standing up too, looking back down the hallway in the direction of Sophie's gaze. 'What is it?'

Sophie stared down the hallway. The front door had frosted glass in it, and she thought she'd seen something cross in front of it, a flicker.

'Sophie?' Ebony demanded. 'Do you see something?'

Sophie shook her head, then sank back in her seat. 'I thought I saw something – her, I suppose.'

She hugged her arms around herself.

'I'm just really jumpy.' She squeezed her eyes shut. 'You try living with a ghost.'

15

THE SUN WAS SETTING, AND NATALIE WAS GLAD. ANOTHER DAY almost done, she thought, standing in the living room looking between the curtains out to the street. How many more did she have left, she wondered?

There were three hundred and sixty-five days in a year. She was only thirty-five.

A lot of days, then.

A lot of days to spend cooped up in this house.

She couldn't spend them all in there, baking in the morning, napping in the afternoon, tossing around under the sheets, gripped by nightmares every day.

She'd slept that afternoon, and the dream that always came did again. She was a child again, hiding under her school desk. The linoleum was cold under her knees, and her left foot was cramping. But she didn't dare move, not an inch, not a muscle. Her head was tucked down over her knees, her hands clamped over her head in the position the teacher had taught. She could smell the sour stench of her own sweat. It was fear that made it smell like that, and she was terrified.

She squeezed her eyes shut tight, waiting for the blast to come, the shattering window, and the terror grew and grew in her chest until she could hear her heart knocking against her ribs.

There was a low, whimpering sound, and Natalie scanned the lawn outside the window before realising the noise was coming from her own throat. She pressed a hand to her chest, and listened to it again, feeling the vibration inside herself.

She should go outside, she thought abruptly, dropping her hand.

She should go outside and walk around her own house, and she'd see that nothing bad would happen.

Closing her eyes, she gripped the curtain in one hand, concentrating on sucking air into her lungs.

Go outside?

Where had that thought come from?

She hadn't been out of the house in so long.

She wondered what the air smelt like. Would it smell like trees and flowers?

A voice inside her warned her against it, against the sure panic that would come.

Natalie shook her head and turned from the window, walking through the house on legs she could barely feel. She was heading for the kitchen.

For the back door.

She was going to do this?

She was going to do this.

'Enough is enough,' she croaked. 'I want out. I want this to end.' She pressed her head against the door. 'Oh god,' she moaned. 'Someone help me.'

Her hand was cold on the doorknob, her fingers stiff. She could barely feel the metal beneath them.

The trees would smell good, she told herself.

Nothing would happen if she went outside for a minute.

Just a minute. Into her own front yard.

Her lips were dry. Mouth too. Her head ached, a thin steel thread of pain through her brain. She lifted her hand from the doorknob and touched her head. Pressed the pads of her fingers to the thread of pain.

Then made herself put her hand back on the round doorknob.

All she had to do was twist it. Pull.

It wasn't a grenade pin. It wouldn't blow up. Nothing would explode.

It was a door. Just a door. On one side of it was her kitchen, where she'd had casserole for dinner. She could still smell the lentils she'd simmered all day in the slow cooker.

On the other side of the door were two steps going down to the path. Natalie blinked, making herself imagine it. The path turned and followed the house around the corner, beside the driveway. She didn't have a car.

The grass would be long, she thought. No one had come to mow it recently. The last time it had been mown, the noise of the mower had frightened her, and she'd had to lie down on her bed with her pillow over her ears.

Maybe there were flowers still in the garden, she thought, breathing heavily. The air would be silky warm.

The door was open. When had she turned the knob? When had she pulled the door open? She had no memory of doing either.

But the door was open, her hand still on the knob, the metal now warm beneath her touch.

The room was spinning, and she didn't know if she was still in her body because she couldn't feel it. Her legs were moving though, stumbling outside down those two steps, her fingers letting go of the doorknob and flailing at the air.

Which was warm and silky.

Natalie was distantly aware of it against her cheeks. Of a breeze that lifted her hair and cooled her hot neck. She looked down, but the path was so far beneath her that she tipped her chin back up, black specks floating in her eyes, and she swam down the path, around the corner of the house, taking great gulping breaths of air, hearing her breath rasping in and out but not feeling it filling her lungs.

Something rough was under her fingers and she scraped them along the sudden surface, then realised somewhere high up inside her head that it was the outside of her house and she flung out her other arm for it, groping for it, collapsing against the wall, pressing a cheek against the bricks that were still warm from the sinking western sun.

Her eyes closed, Natalie opened her mouth, gulping at the air like a fish pulled from the water.

She was outside. Her heart pounded.

She was outside. She scraped a knuckle against the brick.

Outside.

Natalie forced her eyes open, forced her lungs to let the air into them.

The black dots swirled in her vision. She blinked.

Staggered upright. Turned, pressed her back against the house.

What was she doing? Why was she outside?

What had possessed her to do this?

For a moment, the black dots swirled away, and her vision cleared. Her heart thumped in her ears, but she could see.

There was the sky above her, spreading with a velvet darkness. There was the first star!

There'd been a rhyme, she thought. There'd been a rhyme.

Star light, star bright, first star I see tonight.

'Give me the wish I wish tonight,' she croaked from a throat drier than a desert.

What was her wish? She pushed herself further upright, the old brickwork rough against her back, scraping her skin where her shirt rode up.

She wanted to smell the trees, the flowers. Wasn't that it?

'Should have opened a window,' she croaked again, then there was another sound, terrible, rasping, and she realised she was laughing.

Natalie snapped her mouth shut, her tooth catching her lip. The taste of copper filled her mouth.

Then, her legs were moving again, jerking along under her as though they belonged to a puppet, as though she was a puppet, a marionette, someone above her pulling the strings, sending her clawing along the side of the house, towards the front.

Towards the front!

Go back inside, a voice in her head told her. You keep trying this and it never works.

Maybe this time, she argued.

Maybe this time it would work.

She just wanted to smell the trees. See the sinking sun. The flowers closing up for the night, their petals curling in to cover their small faces.

She wasn't far from the Botanic Garden. Perhaps she would hear the last goodnight calls of a tui.

She was swimming again, only dimly aware of her legs jerking along under her while from the waist up she was swimming, her body swaying, the world blurring in front of her.

But then she was at the corner of the house and there was the front yard, and on the other side of it, the fence between her and the world.

Once, not that long ago, not so long ago, she'd been able to come out here, into the yard, and stand on the grass, feeling it tickling the soles of her feet, smelling the clean astringency of the eucalyptus trees that grew by the children's playground down the road. She'd been able to come out and, if she kept her head bent and didn't look too far, she'd been able to cut roses from the climbing bush in front of the bay window, taking the fragrant flowers back inside with her. A little piece of beauty she'd been able to save from the world.

And then one day, one summer just like this one, she'd gone out, the shears gripped in her right hand, and it had been in the yard waiting for her, the dread. It washed over her like a wave, tumbling her around in it until she didn't know which way was up, which way was down, couldn't see for the heavy drift of it, couldn't do anything but scuttle back down the driveway on her hands and knees, dirt on her face, her hair hanging loose and damp with her suddenly sour sweat, while the mailman had called after her, his words lost in the roar of terror that filled her head with blinding whiteness.

She thought she'd screamed at the mailman to leave her alone. She'd dropped the pruning shears under the rosebush.

They were probably still there.

There was no room to go further now, if she wanted to hang onto the house. The snarled and twisted branches of the rosebush pushed her away.

Staggering, Natalie took three steps into the middle of the small pocket of ground that was her front yard. She groped at the air, dimly surprised she was still alive. She could hear the thumping of her heart, a gong beat that pushed every other sound from her.

If she wanted to hear the tui, she'd have to calm down.

If she wanted to smell the trees, she'd have to breathe.

Natalie forced air into her lungs, made herself breathe through her nose, made herself stand there, swaying slightly.

And there was the scent of the trees. The eucalyptus trees just down the road, their oil heated from the day's hot sun. She let her eyes close and breathed.

For the first time in seven months, she stood outside on her too-long lawn and breathed.

Something cracked nearby and her heart took up its hammering again.

What was that?

She opened her eyes, looked wildly about.

There. Another crack. A footstep on a twig.

And there, by the fence, right by her, only a few metres away – what was that shadow?

It moved, detached itself from the darkness and the light from the streetlamp shone on it, turning it from shadow to a man.

A man. Staring at her, a wide, leering smile on his face.

She gaped at it, panting, breath coming quick and fast – too quick and fast, like a rabbit's.

He didn't speak, and she stood frozen in his grin.

She wanted him to speak. To say something.

Beautiful evening, isn't it?

Something normal.

And then walk on.

But he said nothing, did nothing, just grinned at her, eyes dark over the whiteness of his teeth.

Run, she heard herself scream inside her head. She thought it was inside her head. But she couldn't run. She tried, spilling over her own legs, legs she couldn't feel and couldn't get to move.

She hit the ground and lay there for a moment, and a heavy weight fell on her, pinning her down, hands grasping her wrists, holding her there, hot breath in her ear, a rasping, insinuating voice.

Wanna dance? it said. Wanna dance?

The words shocked Natalie, made her head jerk, and then she realised there was no heavy weight on her back, no hot breath in her ear that stunk of onions and cigarettes. Her hands were free.

She'd imagined it all. She'd imagined it.

She scrabbled for a moment in the grass and the dirt and then she was on her feet, arms outstretched for the house, her own sobs in her ears, but she was moving. She was moving. The house was under her hands once more and she knew it would lead her to the door again, it had to, and she was ripping her palms on rose thorns, her hair tangled in the straggling bush, her voice spilling from her throat in a low terrified whine.

She tore herself free of the rose bush, feet tripping over each other, and found the corner of the house.

Almost safe.

Natalie flung her head around. Perhaps she had imagined the man altogether. Perhaps he wasn't there, had never been there.

Or perhaps he was gone, just an ordinary man walking home after work, shaking his head at the crazy woman who lived at number three.

He was there. Still looking at her. Still the grin on his face.

And someone was with him now. Another man. Another dark, grinning face.

Natalie whimpered, felt something hot and wet gush against her legs.

Then she was spinning, scrabbling, clawing her way around the house, rushing in a tidal wave back to the door, scraping her nails against the wood, scrabbling for the doorknob, falling into the house, shoving the door closed, fingers slipping against the key, but it was okay, she'd turned it, locked it.

Her limbs went loose, and she sank to the floor, washed

up back into the safety of her house, sobbing, wet, her mind just the slip slide of terror and relief.

Then she lifted her head, thought tunnelling back into her mind.

Were the windows closed?

Was the door locked?

The windows were always closed.

She'd locked the back door.

The front door hadn't been opened in years.

But still, Natalie got up off the floor and made herself look. First the back door. The one she'd just crashed through.

Locked.

The front door. Locked.

She whimpered.

The kitchen windows. All of them shut, secured. Bathroom. Laundry. Dining room. Spare room. Bedroom. All of them shut, secured.

That left the living room windows.

They faced the street and she faced them. Standing in the living room, the crotch of her jeans cold and sticking to her thighs. She didn't notice. Her hands bled where the thorns had torn them.

There was a bruise of soil on her cheek.

She had to check the living room windows were closed.

They were. She knew they were, but she had to check. Just in case.

But what if they were still out there, the men? They would see her.

The curtains were thick, a heavy, dusty, lined brocade.

She twitched one away two centimetres from the wall, put an eye to the gap.

The windows were closed.

The men were gone.

Natalie sank to the floor, the inside of her head white with relief.

16

EARLY ON MONDAY MORNING, NATALIE MADE HERSELF GET
out of bed. She'd gone to bed on Saturday night and stayed
there all Sunday, only getting up to go to the toilet, then
flushing and turning right back around and going back to
bed, sliding under the covers and turning her face to the
wall.

She padded into the bathroom, did her business, then
walked into the kitchen. She felt hollow, slight, a slender
stick of willow that wouldn't stand up against any breeze.
Inside her head, it was almost silent.

She stared around the room for a moment as though she
didn't recognise any of it, then blinked, and opened the
cupboards behind the table. She pulled out the bag of flour.
Reached in for the baking powder, cocoa, slab of chocolate.
Her movements were automatic, floaty, and she kept her
eyes on the bags and boxes of ingredients, not wanting to
look at the windows behind her, afraid of what she'd see out
there.

Someone watching her. Grinning, wild-eyed and evil.

The weight of the windows at her back was too much and she turned around, the baking powder in one hand. She looked down at the small cardboard box, read the words on it.

Edmonds Prize Baking Powder. Established 1879.

She carried it carefully past the table to the kitchen sink, put it down on the aluminium bench and finally, slowly, lifted her eyes.

Outside the wind was up, and the trees at the back fence bent and swayed in the gusts, their splayed twiggy fingers waving their leaves at her.

She caught her top lip between her teeth and bit down on it. Not hard enough to break the skin, but hard enough to hurt. But she barely noticed.

There were so many places out there for someone to hide. Trees along the fence line. And the small old single garage to the left between the house and the fence. Someone could crouch behind that, and she'd never see them.

Natalie paled at the thought and leaned over the counter to squint out the window. Was someone there? Had she caught the briefest of movements? Her fingers whitened against the cold metal of the counter, and she stood back, spun on her heal and dashed to the back door to look at the lock.

Was it locked? She put her fingers to the doorknob, then moved them to touch the key in the lock. It was just a skeleton key, the lock old, out of date.

Why hadn't she had it replaced with a nice, shiny deadbolt?

Then another thought occurred to her. A question.

Had she locked the door when she'd come back inside on Saturday? She'd been in the grip of a panic attack – she could easily have not remembered to lock the door.

She thought she had, but the terrible idea occurred to her – could she trust her memory?

Her fingers went back to the doorknob. To see if the door was locked, she had to twist it, try to open it.

Natalie heard a panting noise, realised it came from her, the breath rasping quickly in and out of her open mouth, too quickly. She was going to hyperventilate if she wasn't careful.

Her fingers closed around the knob, and she twisted it. The door didn't budge.

She sagged against it, pressing her forehead against the door as relief flooded over her. A sob heaved itself out of her chest, rising like a great wet bubble, and then there were tears streaking down her cheeks.

It was locked, she thought. It had been locked the whole time. She was safe.

She was safe.

Defiantly, she wiped the tears from her face, sniffed, and walked back to the kitchen.

She was safe and there was no one outside.

The trees bent under the breath of the wind. The garage was the same as it always was. Folding dirty white door closed, the glass squares in it so grimy she couldn't have seen through them had she stood pressed up against them.

Nothing moved behind the structure. There was no one lurking there.

She was safe.

Her breath was slowing, catching every little bit in her throat, but it was slowing. Natalie put her hand to her cheeks, and they were wet again. She reached for the tea towel and wiped them dry, then looked at the baking powder. Edmonds Prize Baking Powder.

Since 1879. Her mother had used it, the few times she'd tried baking something for them.

Natalie sniffed. Not there, she told herself inside her mind. Don't go there.

She was shaking her head.

'Don't go back there,' she croaked, and the sound of her voice made her jump. 'Don't go anywhere back there.'

Her throat was dry, and she picked up the baking powder, then put it down again and went to fetch the flour, the other ingredients.

There wasn't anywhere in the past that was safe to land, she thought. All of it was painful. Humiliating. Why did it have to be so bad? And sticky. It wanted to hold her fast like a fly helpless in a web.

Chocolate cake, she thought. Chocolate mud cake.

She'd never had that when she was a kid. Her parents had been too busy for baking. They'd bought her birthday cakes.

She got out a single bowl. Her biggest. She held the bowl in her hands for a moment, feeling the weight of it. It had been in the kitchen, tucked far in the back cupboard when her parents had moved in with her brother and her. A crockery bowl. Probably fifty years old, at least.

She liked that about it. The bowl's history became hers. It had been a grandmother's and she and the grandmother had creamed butter and sugar in it, baked cakes and pies and puddings in it.

That was better. Natalie drew in a deep breath. Went to the oven and turned it to 150C to preheat. Nodded to herself. Heard the grandmother's voice tell her the secret to a dense and fudgy chocolate cake is to bake it low and slow.

'Low and slow,' she repeated.

She'd bake the cake for an hour and a half. It would fill the whole house with the smell of chocolate.

She got a pot out of the cupboard, and she was humming to herself now as she melted the butter and chocolate, stomach cramping with the rich scent, but she bent over the pot and stirred it with a wooden spoon – also the grandmother's, she was sure. When the chocolate and butter was melted and mixed, she turned off the heat and glanced up at the window.

In a moment, the illusion was shattered, the grandmother gone, the wooden spoon just one she'd bought from a mail order catalogue.

Something had moved outside. She was sure of it. She'd caught it just out of the corner of her eye.

Someone was there.

Outside.

Watching her.

A leering grin on his face.

Natalie, holding the spoon dripping with butter and chocolate, opened her mouth and screamed.

. . .

Selena was getting into a routine now, and she cast a sidelong look at the others outside with her, stretching their hands to the rising sun, and smiled.

Who would have believed it, she thought?

They were all there. Rue, her face earnest, still creased with sleep. Tara beside her, taking deep breaths, eyes closed, face tilted towards the sun. Damien as well, a small shine of self-consciousness still on his face, but what did that matter? He was there with them, greeting the sun, greeting the day, being part of the world.

And Dandy. Selena turned her head and looked to her other side where the older woman stood, still surprisingly spry, blessed with good health. Dandy, Selena realised, had become a friend, and wasn't that a wonder? Someone to fill the space where Teresa had used to walk.

'Greetings to you, Rising Sun,' Selena said. 'We begin our day in gratitude for your strength and your light, without which, none of us would be.' She lifted her face to the sky. 'We walk in balance between you, Sky, Earth, Sea.' She thought of the coastline just a few miles away, of the tide that swept in and swept out in the rhythm of this world, as though the ocean breathed in and out and in and out.

'Our hearts are open,' she continued. 'Our hearts open, our hands ready, for we walk in this world in balance with it, in reciprocity to it, in gratitude, and kindness.'

She closed her eyes, spoke to the others, guided them.

'We let our spirits relax and flow and flex,' she said. 'Our spirits spread out around us, touching the world, tasting it, and we are part of it all. Part of the woods, part of the houses.'

She breathed deeply of the morning. 'We are kin to

those driving their cars to work, making breakfast, beginning the day. We are them and they are us. We are the trees,
the sky, the sea, the great hum of life.'

Selena was part of it all. A small, grateful speck in it.

'May we follow the path today with grace and strength,
may we walk with our kin, in the flow of our purposes,' she
finished, and lowered her arms to her middle. 'We bring
ourselves back to our centre. We do this whenever we are
frazzled, or uncertain, or overwhelmed. We live from our
hearts.'

One more deep breath, held, then exhaled.

The small circle came to life around her, and everyone
shook their limbs to loosen them, their eyes glowing.

'I'll get Clover out of bed,' Tara said, hurrying inside, her
face alight with enthusiasm for the new day.

'And I'll get to work, I guess,' Damien said. With not
quite so much vigour. But then he grinned, his face beaming. 'Terrific way to start the day,' he said. 'Makes me feel
good.'

Dandy hugged him then hung off his arm, smiling.
'You're a treasure,' she said. 'Who are you driving about
today?'

'Couple property developers, or something, I think,'
Damien answered, then frowned and shook his head. 'I
know I need a job and all, but I'm about fed up with this
one.'

'Is that so?' Dandy asked. 'What would you prefer
to do?'

Damien shook his head. He'd been asking himself that
exact question for the last couple months. Since they'd all
moved into the house. His life felt different.

'I don't know,' he said. 'Just something...more, you know?'

Dandy nodded. She thought she might, at that.

'Start paying attention to your dreams,' Selena said.

'My dreams?'

'Yes.' Selena smiled at him. 'They're the most direct link you have to your heart and soul. They're a conversation that you're constantly having with yourself – and if you want to know which direction to turn in, the answer is probably coming through in your dreams already.'

Damien turned and watched the sun rise higher over the hills. It was going to be a grey, windy day.

'My dreams, huh?'

Selena nodded. 'Start writing down what you remember.'

Damien looked at her. 'You do this?'

'I do,' Selena smiled. 'I have since I was a child.'

'And it really helps?'

'Yes. Dreams seem cryptic, because they speak a language of images and associations, but once you begin to understand, it's like opening the guidebook to your soul.' She paused, tipped her head to the side, thinking. 'In fact, perhaps we could get into a new habit of sharing our dreams together over breakfast.'

Damien grinned suddenly. 'That sounds like a great idea,' he said. 'I could do with some signposts along the way.'

He followed Dandy and Selena inside.

'Goodness Tara,' Selena said, seeing that there was another fresh loaf of bread sitting steaming on the bench. 'What time do you get up to make bread for the morning?'

Tara, Clover on her hip rubbing at her eyes, smiled. 'It's my pleasure,' she said. 'And I've always been an early riser.'

'It's my pleasure,' Damien corrected her, picking up the bread knife. 'You've spoiled me for any other bread but yours, now.' He sliced into it, cutting enough for them all.

The aroma of fresh-baked bread was heavenly. Damien cut the crust into four small squares and gave one to Clover. Rue was already rummaging in the fridge for the milk.

'For the house,' Clover said, nodding. She put the crust to her nose. 'Sniffs good!'

Tara laughed and set her down. 'I'll put the tea on,' she said.

Rue had poured a dollop of milk into the small jug, as she'd been doing every morning for a while now. 'Ready, Clover Bee?' she asked.

'Yup.'

The two of them went out into the entranceway and in procession to the shrine they'd made back at the solstice for the house spirit.

'Hello bootiful lady,' Clover said, gazing up at the statue Rue had chosen to personify the spirit of the house. 'I got your off'ring.' She glanced at Rue, who nodded back at her, then turned to the table on which the statue stood, and reverently placed the square of fresh bread in the small bowl at the statue's feet. 'Thank you for bein' our house,' she said. 'We love you.'

She stood to the side, making room for Rue, who came forward and poured the milk into another small bowl.

'We make this offering in gratitude and honour to you,' Rue said, having learnt the words from Selena. 'We are safe within your walls. You are the heart of our home, and we are blessed by you.'

Rue stood up and looked at the statue. She'd been making the offerings every morning with Clover for weeks now and there was a small, niggling dissatisfaction at the back of her mind.

'Clover,' she said, pitching her voice low, so no one in the kitchen would hear her.

'Yeah?' Clover turned to look at her.

'Can you feel the spirit of the house?' she asked.

Clover's brow knotted in a delicate frown. 'Course,' she said.

Rue looked at the empty jug in her hand. 'What does it feel like?'

But Clover just shrugged and pointed to the statue. 'Like her,' she said.

'Like a statue?'

'Like a person,' Clover said, then grinned. 'A happy person. She likes us. An' the bread and milk.' The frown came back. 'No one talked to her for a long time. So she went to sleep. But she's waken now.'

Rue nodded. 'Okay.' She sighed. 'Let's go have breakfast.'

Clover skipped off to the kitchen but Rue lingered a minute longer, thinking about how Clover and Selena could see or sense spirits. How even Sophie could see a ghost.

'I wish I could see you,' she whispered to the statue.

17

NATALIE SHOOK HER HEAD, THE SCREAM DYING AWAY INSIDE IT.
No, she thought. It wasn't real.

Melted chocolate and butter ran down the spoon onto her hand.

She'd scared herself, that was all. There was no one there.

She had an overactive imagination. That was all.

Just an overactive imagination.

She was inside. Where it was safe. In her kitchen – her favourite room in the house.

Everything was all right.

Natalie nodded slowly, lowered the spoon, licked the drips on her hand.

The chocolate was rich, warm on her tongue. She swallowed it. Closed her eyes.

Where was she? What was next?

Sugar. It was time to mix in one cup of caster sugar and one of brown sugar and a tablespoon of instant coffee.

She measured them out and tipped them into the bowl. Stirred in the melted 250 grams of butter and 200 grams of chocolate.

There was nothing outside the window. The two men had given her a fright the other night, but they weren't there now.

Nothing was out there except for the world she hated. Was afraid of. The world where she wasn't safe. Where no one was really safe.

But in here, in the warmth of her kitchen, here she was just fine.

Everything was okay. Natalie nodded. She wasn't stupid. She knew she hadn't seen anything. The men hadn't been there.

To prove it, she looked out of the kitchen window.

The trees were there. The long grass. The garage, nothing behind it.

See? Nothing there.

Time for the eggs. They were ready, room temperature – she didn't keep them in the fridge. She cracked the first one over the bowl and broke the yolk with her spoon, stirred it in. Then did the same for the next two. Then the milk, pouring it in a slow stream while she mixed with the spoon in her other hand. One and a half cups of milk.

One tablespoon of vanilla essence.

Then the flour. One and a half cups of flour. Half a cup of cocoa powder. One teaspoon of salt.

Finally, the baking powder. Natalie picked up the box and measured out a level tablespoon of the white powder. Tipped it in her bowl and mixed.

She was humming again. The inside of her head white with silence.

The kitchen already smelt of chocolate.

T ARA HAD A B ARNARDOS WORKSHOP TO GO TO, PART OF HER plan to look after children a few hours a week. So that Clover could have some friends, and not, as Rue so succinctly put it, freak teachers out with her weirdness.

'Are you sure you're going to be all right?' she fretted, looking from Selena to Clover, knowing she was being silly, but the question had popped out anyway.

'Of course we will be,' Selena said. 'We'll go for a nice walk, I think.'

'An' feed the ducks?' Clover asked, bouncing in her chair at the thought of it.

'And feed the ducks,' Selena agreed.

Among other things.

Tara nodded, cheeks red with embarrassment. She grinned. 'I'm like an overprotective mother hen,' she said and laughed. 'Who would have fathomed it?' Shaking her head, she picked up her handbag and notebook, kissed Clover on the top of her curly head, and made for the door.

'We goin' to the forest?' Clover said, turning seriously to Selena.

'Yes, I think so,' Selena said, amazed once again at how easily the child picked up information.

Clover nodded. 'I wanna swim with the whales again.'

'We'll just see what happens, shall we?' Selena answered, smiling.

'Kay.' Clover climbed down from the table and went

over to take Selena's hand. 'Where we doin' it?'

Selena took Clover upstairs to the room under the eaves. Clover ran over to the staff and squatted down to trace a finger along the burnt letters of the Ogham on it. 'Rue wants one,' she said.

Selena lit a candle and nodded. 'We'll go collect some wood for one on the weekend, perhaps.'

'Can I have one?' Clover asked.

Selena turned around and smiled at her. 'Why not?' she said. 'I don't think there's any reason for you not to have one – you'll need help to make it, of course.' Her lips twitched with a smile.

'You can help me,' Clover said, nodding emphatically.

'Yes,' Selena told her. 'I expect I can, at that.'

Clover nodded. Moved on to the table Selena had set up in the room she considered her private working space. 'What's these?'

She was poking her small fingers at a group of three dice, esoteric symbols burnt into each side.

Selena came over and looked at them with her. 'I made those,' she said. 'Many moons ago, when I was learning about magical symbolism.'

Clover frowned. 'What's that?' She tried looking for the answer in Selena's mind and squinted. 'Like a drawing?' she asked.

'A drawing, yes,' Selena said, marvelling. 'A little drawing of something much bigger.'

Clover shook her head, not sure she understood. 'I like 'em,' she said anyway, turning one of the dice over in her hands, looking at the pictures. 'This one stands like we do when we sayin' nigh-nights to the sun,' she said.

Selena looked down at the symbol Clover was showing her and nodded. An upright line with arms out each side reaching toward the sky. 'It does – and that's almost what it means too. When we stand in balance between earth and sky.'

Clover nodded, put the dice back, picked up the second. 'This one got a circle,' she said. Rue had taught her the names of shapes when she was two.

'That's right. A circle to mean everything. The wheel of life.'

Clover's tiny finger traced the outline of it. Selena lit the second candle on her altar. Reached into a wooden box and brought out one of the small herb bundles Teresa had made for her before returning to Wellsford. She brought it to her nose and sniffed gently. Thyme. A good opener of the senses, she thought. Protective and connected to the intuition.

It would do well.

Clover was looking at her.

'What we goin' to do?' she asked.

'We're going to clear the space in the room first,' Selena said.

'Move the cushions?'

Selena smiled and shook her head. Morghan hadn't been this young when she'd begun teaching her. A preschooler was quite a different proposition.

'We're going to make a magical space,' she said. 'And invite our kin to be with us.'

'Who's my kin?' Clover asked, plumping herself down on one of Selena's floor cushions.

'I'm hoping we will find that out,' Selena answered.

Clover thought about that for a moment. 'Wha' is kin?'

'Our kin are those spirits who walk with us through our life, there to guide us.' Selena pursed her lips, trying to think how to explain it simply enough for a three-year-old to understand. She didn't know if she could, even one as advanced as Clover.

'Can we see 'em?' Clover asked.

'When we are...in the deep and wide,' Selena answered. 'And we can feel them with us even when we're not in the deep and wide, if we practice.'

Clover nodded solemnly. 'Kay,' she said. 'Who's your kin?'

'Crane, a big white bird, walks with me,' Selena said. 'And Hind – she's a small deer.'

'I saw her!' Clover said and got up, coming over to where Selena was now sitting at the wide table. 'I saw her – she was with you when we went to the whirlpool.'

'The World Pool,' Selena said and nodded. 'Yes, she was.'

Clover nodded too. 'Who else?'

'Well,' Selena said. 'There is the Fae Queen. She helps guide me in my life.' Selena blinked and fell silent. Would she still be answerable to the Queen? It was a tie all Ladies of Wilde Grove had, but she was no longer Lady of the Grove.

Perhaps things would be different now.

Selena didn't know.

She cleared her throat. 'And there's the Goddess,' she said. 'The Lady of the Ways.'

Clover's eyes were round. 'We gonna see her?'

Possibly, Selena thought. That wouldn't change, would it?

'Perhaps,' she said. 'When I first began travelling to the deep and wide, I was taught the ways of it by another as well as Crane and Hind.' Selena's lips curved in a smile. 'Her name was Isleen.'

'Isleen,' Clover repeated. 'Was she nice?'

'Very,' Selena said, smiling widely now.

'Who my kin gonna be?'

Selena had anticipated being asked this. She leaned forward and stroked Clover's hair. 'I don't know,' she said. 'I thought perhaps we could go to the Otherworld today and find out. Perhaps meet your wizard.'

Clover's forehead creased. 'The Otherworld?'

'The deep and wide.'

Clover nodded. 'Kay,' she said. 'Sounds fun.'

For a moment she sounded so grown up that Selena had to shake her head. 'Clover,' she said. 'You are extraordinary.'

Clover looked at her then nodded and swung against Selena's legs. 'So's Rue,' she said.

'Rue?' Selena was surprised.

'She's sad,' Clover said, frowning.

'She's sad? Why is Rue sad?'

'She wanna see the spirit of the house,' Clover said, then looked up at Selena, her face hopeful. 'You can teach her to see her, right?'

'Hmm. I didn't know Rue was sad about that.' Rue had been managing well to keep up with the morning and evening prayers even since school had started. There'd been no inkling in her that Selena had been able to tell, that she wanted more skills than she was already gaining.

Clover put her hand on Selena's knee and gazed up at her, so serious, so trusting that Selena nodded. 'Of course,' she said. 'I can teach her to see the spirit of the house.'

Clover nodded too and clapped her hands together. 'Good,' she said. 'Now, let's do it.'

Selena laughed, unfolded herself from the chair. 'First, we make the space nice, okay?'

'The space?'

'The room.' Selena held the end of the herb bundle to a candle flame until it caught, then let it burn a moment before waving the flame out, letting the herbs smoke instead. She reached one hand out, and Clover took it.

They walked to the corner of the room.

'Spirits of the South,' Selena said. 'May you bless and protect us in our travelling.' She glanced down at Clover, then moved them to the next compass point and held up the smoking bundle of thyme.

'Spirits of the west,' she said. 'May you bless and protect us in our travelling.'

Clover, holding her by the hand, nodded. 'Bless us in our travelling,' she repeated.

Selena smiled at the words coming from the mouth of one so young.

'Spirits of the north,' she continued. 'Bless and protect us in our travelling.

'Spirits of the east. Bless and protect us in our travelling.'

She led them to the centre of her room.

'We are spokes on the great wheel,' she said, drawing in a deep, slow breath. 'We sing the world to weaving. We weave the world with our singing.'

The smoke curled lazily to the roof.

'As above, so it is below,' Selena said, her eyes closed, the forest of the Wildwood gathering around her.

'As within, so it is without.'

She paused, feeling the trees filling the room around the two of them, then stepped lightly to the table and put the herbs into her ceramic pot, and turned to Clover, who she saw was half through the veil already.

'There are trees,' Clover whispered as Selena led her to one of the cushions and laid her down upon it before taking a seat on the one beside it.

'An' I see your deer,' Clover whispered.

Selena closed her eyes and slipped into the Wildwood beside Clover.

The air was cool under the shade of the trees and Selena stood there a moment, letting herself breathe in and out, sinking deeper into the trance state that let her walk here in this other world.

'Look,' Clover said, reaching for her hand. 'There's your deer.'

'So it is,' Selena replied, nodding her head at Hind. 'We are well met,' she said to the deer, who regarded her with eyes deep and knowing.

'I want an aminal,' Clover said.

'You must ask for yours to come to you, then,' Selena said.

Clover turned wide eyes to her. 'Just gotta ask?'

And Selena nodded.

Clover giggled, then called out. 'Where's my aminal?'

A breeze rustled through the Wildwood, picking up Clover's curls and tickling her neck. She glanced up at Selena then turned back to look around.

'Where are you?' she cried. 'Please let me see you!'

Selena stood still, waiting to see what would happen. She had no idea. She'd never come to the Wildwood with one so young. Not like this.

Something rustled and there was a fluttering of dark wings. Clover tipped her shining face to the trees and looked, a wide smile spreading over her face. 'Look S'lena! A bird! Is that it? Do I have a bird?'

Selena looked, and the bird, its feathers black suede, beak yellow, hopped down from the branch upon which it stood, and came to rest on the leaf-littered path in front of them. It was Selena's turn to smile.

Blackbird, she thought. How apt.

'Hello birdie,' Clover said. 'Are you my frien'?'

The bird hopped closer and cocked its head, looking directly at Clover.

'He's a blackbird,' Selena said softly to Clover. Blackbird was a guide familiar with the paths of the Otherworld, to the secrets of the soul, and Selena felt a swelling in her breast at the sight of him. This child was blessed indeed, she thought.

'Blackbird,' Clover said carefully. Then pointed to herself. 'I'm Clover.'

The bird bobbed his head, then turned and hopped along the path before stopping and looking back over his wing at them.

'We gotta follow him!' Clover said and grabbed Selena's hand again.

They followed the bird, deeper along the paths of the Wildwood, until Selena knew they had moved truly into the Otherworld.

'Where we goin', Blackbird?' Clover called, but the bird continued on, leading them along a path that wound around a hill. Clover squealed.

'I bin here,' she said.

'Here?' Selena asked, looking around. She had not.

But Clover was nodding and now she let go of Selena's hand and pointed to the hillside, where there was the entrance to a tunnel.

And standing in the hillside was a wizard.

Clover's wizard, Selena thought. Just as she'd hoped.

'Clover,' she said. 'Wait for me.'

But Clover had darted forward, Blackbird taking to the air in a flapping of black wings around her head, and in a moment had disappeared into the darkness behind the wizard.

Selena approached more warily. Bowed her head in greeting, trying to not crane her neck to see behind the venerable figure at where Clover might have disappeared to.

'I am Selena,' she said. 'Lady of the Forest.'

The wizard nodded over his white beard. 'I know who you are, Lady Selena,' he said, and his voice was low like a night breeze amongst ancient trees.

Selena waited, expecting the man to introduce himself, but he said nothing more, merely stood looking pleasantly at her.

She licked her lips, suddenly apprehensive. 'I wish to follow Clover,' she said. 'Please stand aside. She is too young to be without me.'

The wizard regarded her without a change in expression. 'She is safe,' he said.

'I would be with her,' Selena insisted.

Now, he shook his head as though with regret. 'You may not follow her.'

'I may not?' Selena stared at him. 'Why not?'

'Your charge is to take care of and teach her in your world, but here, she is ours.'

'I do take care of her and teach her,' Selena said, barely able to believe what she was hearing. 'Do you not know who I am?' she asked, shaking her head, standing straighter, gathering her true power around her. 'I am the Lady of the Forest,' she said, and now her voice was the rustling of slender branches. 'I am a Lady of the Goddess of the Ancient Way. I sing the worlds together.'

The wizard bowed his head slightly. 'Yes,' he said. 'We chose a protector well for the child in this lifetime.' He smiled slightly and turned away with a flourish of his long robes, and then he was gone into the darkness of the tunnel.

Selena stood still where she was, shocked at the turn of events. For a moment she just looked into the passageway into the hill, then she gathered herself, took a breath and prepared to step into the tunnel. She would follow and she would find Clover.

How dare they keep the child from her.

Clover appeared in the darkness of the tunnel and came rushing out.

'S'lina!' she said and grinned up at her. 'I saw all the wizards!'

Selena looked down at the child, then into the tunnel and nodded.

More than one wizard? What did all of this mean?

She'd never come across such a thing before.

18

'Rue!'

She turned at the hissed voice and saw Ebony threading her way through the lunchtime rush and waved.

Ebony grabbed her by the elbow and steered her away from the crowds, not letting go until they reached the playing field.

Rue rubbed at her elbow. 'What's going on?' she asked. Ebony's eyes blazed, and she was bouncing on her toes.

Ebony practically squealed in glee. 'What's going on?' she asked and shook her head, her grin wide across her face. 'Let me tell you what's going on!'

'Okaay,' Rue answered. 'Why don't you tell me what's going on, then?' Despite her drawled reply, Ebony's excitement was contagious, and Rue felt her skin prickling with anticipation. She hugged herself.

Ebony threaded her arm through Rue's and leant forward in a conspiratorial whisper. 'We're going for a spot of ghost hunting this afternoon.'

Rue stood straighter in surprise. 'We're what?'

'You heard.' Ebony did a little dance on the grass. 'Ghost hunting.'

'I heard,' Rue said. 'I just don't understand.'

Ebony looked at her and giggled. 'Let me explain then, my new friend.' They ducked under the fringe of the willow, and she threw down her backpack and knelt on the grass beside it, undoing the zip. 'In here,' she said, 'we have the technology to determine if indeed our other friend Sophie is being haunted by a spirit of the dead.'

'Technology?' Interested despite herself, Rue got down on the ground beside Ebony.

'Ta da!'

Rue looked at the gadget in Ebony's hand and frowned. 'A TV remote?' she asked.

Her response made Ebony cackle. 'Nope,' she said. 'It's an EMF meter.'

'A who what where?'

'An EMF meter,' Ebony said more patiently. 'It's a gizmo designed to measure electromagnetic fluctuations in the atmosphere.'

'And that has what to do with ghosts?'

'Well.' Ebony turned the device around in her hand and gazed happily at its small display. 'People who know about this sort of thing...'

'How do you know about this sort of thing?' Rue interrupted.

'I read a lot,' Ebony said. 'Online. There are some major online ghost hunting communities, you know.' She blinked in the sunlight. 'I'll send you some links.'

'I don't have a computer,' Rue said.

'Huh.' Ebony wrinkled her nose. 'That's a shame. Anyway.' She held up the meter. 'It's long been established that when a spirit is around, there's a noticeable increase in electromagnetic energy.' She nodded at Rue. 'And we know when that happens, because we have this.'

Rue looked at it and felt a stirring of her own excitement. Clover and Selena could see or sense spirits or whatever, but perhaps, she thought, there was a way for her to do so too. Differently, but still. There were, she decided, possibilities.

'Cool,' she said.

'And that's not all!' Ebony grinned, gave the EMF meter to Rue to hold, and dived back into her bag.

'What is it?' Rue asked.

'This is a video camera,' Ebony said, unzipping the back case and displaying the camera in all its glory. 'We'll set it up to record in Sophie's bedroom and see what it captures.' She pulled out another camera. 'This one's just a Polaroid camera, but we'll use it to photograph everything. Who knows?' Ebony grinned again. 'Maybe we'll capture the ghost on film, or some orbs or something.'

Rue was impressed. 'What are orbs?'

'They're like, glowing lights that move around on their own, like they have consciousness.' Ebony nodded knowingly. 'You can more easily see them on film than with the naked eye. They're weird like that.'

They sounded weird, Rue thought. 'Where did you get all this stuff?' she asked.

Ebony packed the two cameras carefully back into her bag and reached for the EMF meter. 'I saved up my money for this little baby,' she said. 'And the cameras have been lying around home for yonks. I just borrowed them.' She winked at Rue. 'So,' she said. 'How about it? We go around to Sophie's after school?'

'Does Sophie say we can?'

'Sure. She said we could come back, right? And her parents don't get home until almost six.' Ebony admired her EMF meter. She'd bought it online and it had arrived in the post really quickly. She tucked it away in her bag and looked at Rue.

'You in?' she asked.

Rue hesitated only a moment before nodding.

'I'm in,' she said.

THEY COLLECTED SUZE FROM HER HOUSE AND WALKED THE short distance up the hill to where Sophie's house clung to the edge of the cliff over the harbour.

Sophie hesitated before letting them in. 'I didn't think you'd be back so soon,' she said.

'Not a minute to lose,' Ebony said.

'What?' Sophie stared at her.

'Have you heard or seen anything else?' Ebony asked. Then added, 'or smelt?'

Sophie shook her head, although that wasn't quite true, was it? She sucked in her bottom lip, looked down the hallway to the kitchen, where her two brothers were raiding the fridge.

'Look,' she said, making a decision. 'Come into my room. My brothers are home.'

They crowded into the front room that was Sophie's and Rue looked around in appreciation.

'This is a really nice bedroom,' she said.

Sophie nodded. Then told the other girls the truth. 'I haven't smelt the perfume since I saw you last, but I keep feeling like she's around.'

'She being the ghost?' Ebony asked. She had put her backpack on Sophie's bed and was unloading it in a brisk, business-like manner.

'Yeah,' Sophie said, then reddened. 'If it is a ghost, that is.'

'Why wouldn't it be?' Suze asked, sitting herself down on the stool in front of the dressing table.

'Good question,' Ebony said. She looked at Sophie with raised eyebrows. 'You were pretty sure the other day.'

Sophie stood near the door and twisted her fingers together. 'Well,' she said. 'I don't know. It's just a bit scary, that's all.'

'It hasn't done anything to hurt you, has it?' Rue asked. 'Since we were last here?'

Sophie worried at a hangnail. 'No,' she said. 'But it's spooky.' She glanced around the room. 'I mean – did she die here? A ghost has to be someone who died, right? Maybe in my room?' She grimaced.

'I guess so,' Rue said.

'What else could it be but the ghost of a dead person?' Suze asked. 'I mean – what else is there? Are there other types of spirits?'

'There are demons,' Ebony said.

Everyone stared at her. Sophie shook her head, aghast. 'It's not a demon.' Her throat worked as she swallowed.

'You seem pretty sure,' Ebony said, taking the video camera out of its case and looking for a place to set it.

'God, it can't be a demon,' Sophie said and cast around for a reason. 'Demons don't wear perfume, right?' She screwed up her face. 'The thought of a demon in my room is worse than the idea that a woman died here.'

'And it's a woman because of the perfume,' Rue said, then shrugged. 'That makes sense, right?'

Sophie shook her head, still jittery over the suggestion of a demon. 'Look,' she said. 'Maybe this isn't such a great idea.'

'We should use an Ouija board,' Suze said at the same time.

Everyone paused in the room, then Ebony set the video camera on the wooden headboard above the bed and pushed record. It had a full battery charge, and while she'd rather have it run when they weren't all there, she had to take it back home with her when they left, so it was a case of anything being better than nothing.

She picked up the Polaroid. 'That's an awesome idea,' she said.

'An Ouija board?' Rue said.

'Yeah.' Suze jumped up. 'We can make one.' She looked at Sophie. 'Do you have a piece of paper and a pen?'

Sophie shook her head. 'I don't know,' she said. 'I don't know if it's a good idea.'

'Sure it is,' Suze said, excited about the idea. She wasn't really certain she believed in Sophie's ghost.

'What if it is a demon?' Rue asked. She wasn't sure about the Ouija board idea either.

Ebony shook her head. 'I know I suggested that,' she said. 'But Sophie is right – demons don't wear perfume, do they?' She looked at her cousin. 'How do we make an Ouija board?' Her eyes widened. 'We could set the EMF meter right by the board and see what it shows.'

'What's an EMF meter?' Sophie asked. Her hands were knotted together.

'It's a device that shows if there are any ghosts in the room,' Ebony said.

There was a banging against the door behind her, and Sophie jumped, yelping. One of her brothers hooted with laughter.

'BOO!' he yelled. Then his footsteps thudded off at a run back down the hallway.

Sophie swallowed, then nodded. 'Okay,' she said. 'Let's do it. Maybe we can ask it to go away.'

Suze was digging in Ebony's bag and pulled out a pad of paper, tore a page off. 'We'll write the alphabet on this,' she said. 'Put the letters around in a circle.' She pursed her lips, looked at Sophie. 'Do you have a glass or something? Made of crystal, preferably.'

'Have you done this before?' Rue asked. It certainly sounded as though Suze knew what she was doing.

But Suze shook her head. 'No,' she said. 'But I read a book a while ago where they made an Ouija board.'

'What happened in the book?' Sophie asked.

Ebony looked over, interested too. Maybe it was a book she could read. There was often stuff you could learn, even if it was fiction.

'Well,' Suze said, getting Ebony's pencil case out and snagging a pen to write the letters. 'It was a bit different in the book because they weren't trying to talk to a ghost.' She paused, frowned. 'Well, they kinda were, as well.'

Ebony snapped a photograph of her. 'Just tell us,' she

said. The camera hummed and delivered a photo into Ebony's hand. She waved it in the air.

Suze sniffed. 'Okay, so it was a sort of time travel book, right? And the people in the present used an Ouija board to try to contact their friend who had gone into the past.'

'Did that work?' Rue asked, wondering if it possibly could.

'Yeah, it did, in the book,' Suze said. 'Because there was still a bond between them, right, and because of time stuff. Like when they were talking to her from the present, she was dead by then, or something.' Suze shook her head. 'It was a good book, but time travel is hard.'

Ebony looked over at Sophie. 'Got any friends who hopped back in time recently?' she asked.

Sophie shook her head.

'Then I think it's still probably a ghost.'

'Or a spirit,' Rue said. 'Although what's the difference?' She answered the question herself. 'I know what the difference is – a ghost is the spirit of someone who was once alive, right? A person? But a spirit could be that too, or it could be a spirit of something that was never a person or alive like we think of it.' She was thinking of the spirit of their house, the statue she poured an offering to every morning. 'Maybe it's just the spirit of this house,' she said.

'What?' Ebony scoffed. 'Houses don't have spirits.'

Sophie looked worried.

Rue looked over at Ebony. 'Selena says houses have spirits,' she said firmly. 'She says everything has spirit.'

Ebony opened her mouth to retort, then closed it again. She frowned instead. 'Really?'

'That's what she says, although it's probably more complicated than it sounds.'

Suze had finished writing the alphabet down and was slowly tearing the paper into small squares, one letter to a square. 'Who's Selena?' she asked.

'My um, guardian,' Rue said. 'My sister and I live with her.'

'She's the priestess,' Ebony said, then swivelled around and took a picture of Rue. 'When do we get to meet her, by the way?'

The camera spat out another picture and Ebony laid it on the bed next to the one she'd taken of Suze. She aimed the camera at Sophie next and pressed the button.

'Meet her?' Rue asked.

'Yeah. You know – we go to your house, after school or on the weekend, I'd be happy with either – and you take us up to her, and you say, Selena these are my new friends Ebony, Suze, and Sophie, and then you turn to us and you say, guys, this is Selena.' Ebony took the photograph and laid it beside the others, then turned the camera around, held it out at arm's length, and snapped a shot of herself. 'And we all say pleased to meet you.' She looked archly at Rue, eyes dancing. 'It's pretty easy, really. Happens all the time.'

'Oh,' Rue said. 'Um. Right.' She'd told Ebony, hadn't she, that she could come over? 'You all would want to?'

'Sure,' Ebony said, putting her photo on the bed without looking at it. 'Why not? I'm free this Saturday.' She looked at the others. 'What about you lot?'

Suze glanced up. 'Sure,' she said. 'I've never met a priestess before. Got to be more interesting than Father

Arnold at St. Joseph's.' She looked at Sophie and giggled. 'Right?'

'What does a priestess do?' Sophie asked.

'Um,' Rue said again.

'She worships the goddess, of course,' Ebony said.

'But what does that do?'

Ebony looked at Rue, brows raised.

'Um.' Rue was blank for a moment, not knowing how to answer the question. She hadn't been expecting it. 'Well, I guess, she came all the way over here from England because she dreamed of us and talked to the spirit of my mother,' Rue blurted. Then felt her cheeks heat when everyone gaped at her.

'Whoa,' Ebony said. 'Back up just a minute, will you? You never told me this juicy story.'

Rue wrapped her arms around herself. She was sitting on the window seat. 'It's kind of hard to believe,' she muttered.

'But I am a believer,' Ebony said. 'Tell it from the beginning.'

Sophie was staring at her with wide eyes and Rue flushed. 'It's just like I said. The wind told her she had to look for us.'

'You didn't say that,' Ebony broke in. 'Not about the wind.'

'How does wind tell someone something?' Suze asked. She'd stopped tearing the squares of paper to look at Rue, fascinated. Maybe there was something to all Ebony's carry-on after all.

'I don't really know,' Rue said over the lump in her throat. She shrugged. 'She says we each have an affinity to one or more of the elements – those are earth, air, fire, and water, I think – and hers is air.'

'But the wind can't talk,' Sophie said.

Rue shrugged. 'Maybe it can,' she said. 'Maybe we just don't know it can and so don't listen.' She nodded. That was it. 'Selena knows how to listen. And the wind told her that we needed her, and she dreamed of our mother, and met her in the Otherworld.'

'What's the Otherworld?' Suze asked.

'It's like this um...' Rue tried to find a way to explain. 'It's like this part of the world that we can't see except when dreaming or in some sort of trance, but it's right there next to ours.' She blinked and sat straighter, triumphant. 'It's a world of spirit.'

Everyone was quiet for a moment, impressed.

'She came all the way from England?' Sophie asked.

Rue nodded. 'Found Clover, she's my sister, and me, just when we needed her.'

More silence, as everyone digested this.

'Right,' Ebony said finally. 'We are coming over on Saturday and you are definitely going to introduce us.' She looked around at the room. 'Right?'

'I'm in,' Suze said.

Sophie looked at Rue, then nodded.

'Me too,' she said.

19

'Sophie, go and get a glass,' Suze said, then paused. 'And a coffee table or something? Something we can sit around?' Her lap was full of small white squares of paper, a letter written on each.

Sophie nodded, let herself out of the room.

'Make it a crystal glass!' Suze yelled after her.

There was another great banging on the door and Suze shook her head. 'Brothers,' she said. 'Annoying little gits.'

'I consider myself fortunate not to have any,' Ebony said, who was an only child. She glanced at Rue. 'You've only got a sister, right?'

Rue nodded. 'She's almost four.'

'Bet she's annoying too,' Suze said, plucking up the letters.

'No,' Rue answered. 'We're really close. She's cool.'

Ebony nodded. 'You were looking after her by yourself, right? Before Selena found you?'

'What do you mean?' Suze looked startled.

'My dad works out of town,' Rue said, looking down at her fingers. 'I had to take care of Clover.'

'Her mum died,' Ebony said, and for once, her tone was gentle, kind.

'That's rough,' Suze said. 'I'm sorry.'

'Thanks, Rue replied. 'Everything's okay now.' She couldn't help but smile. 'We live with some really nice people now.'

'I thought it was this Selena you live with?'

'And a couple others.' Rue was interrupted from replying when the door opened and Sophie shuffled in with a small round table.

'This okay?' she asked, putting it down in the centre of the floor.

'Perfect!' Suze said and began arranging the letters around the edge of the table. 'What about a glass?'

'We don't have any crystal glasses, but I think this sugar bowl is crystal,' Sophie answered, putting the small ornate bowl down in the middle of the letters. 'It was my grandmother's.'

'Ooh, it will do really well,' Suze said, and finished arranging the letters in the alphabet around the table. 'Right, are we going to do this?'

'Wait – I'll get the EMF meter,' Ebony said, snatching it off the bed and bringing it over. She knelt on the floor and the other girls joined her.

'What do we do?' Sophie asked, a thread of nervousness in her voice.

'We ask for the spirits to talk to us,' Suze answered matter-of-factly.

Rue looked at her. From their conversation about horror

movies, she never would have thought Suze knew how to do this. 'You've done this before? I thought you just read about it?'

'I read about making your own board,' Suze said. 'My cousins – my other cousins, on my dad's side – we played with the Ouija board the Christmas before last.'

'Did anything happen?' Ebony asked, kneeling down on the rug to look at the table.

Suze laughed. 'My aunty went off her nut when she found us. Said it was a sin against God, or something.' She shook her head. 'But other than that, nah, not really. Bit of mumbo jumbo about boyfriends – but that was what Lorna and Chrissy were asking, whether their crushes knew they existed.'

'If nothing happened,' Sophie said, 'why do you think it will be different this time?'

'Because your house is haunted,' Suze said. 'Apparently.'

Sophie knelt down at the table too, but she was chewing on her lip again.

'I think we need to be specific about who we want to talk to,' Rue said.

Ebony nodded straight away. 'I agree, and Rue knows what she's talking about. Selena talks to spirits all the time, right?'

'Actually, yeah,' Rue said. 'She kind of does.'

'What, ghosts?' Sophie's eyes were wide.

But Rue frowned. 'Not ghosts,' she said. 'I haven't ever heard her talking to dead people – but she could, I'm sure, if one was around.'

'One's around here,' Ebony said with conviction. 'So why don't you begin for us, Rue?'

Rue flushed. She'd never done this before. Why have her do it? 'Wouldn't Suze be better?'

'Nope,' Ebony said before Suze could say anything. 'You know more.'

Did she though? Rue felt out of her depth for a moment, but then she straightened. She thought of Clover. Didn't she come from a family, and live in a family, where weird stuff was their bread and butter? She thought of Tara's witchcraft books, Selena's wand and staff. She could do this.

If she wanted to be a priestess, then she'd better start acting like one.

Suze turned the sugar bowl over and nodded. 'We have to all put our fingertips on it, like this,' she said, resting two fingers lightly on the upturned bowl.

Everyone else did the same. Rue shivered.

'This feels weird,' she whispered.

The others nodded. 'Go ahead,' Ebony nudged her. 'Start us off.'

Rue's mouth was suddenly dry. How should she start them off? What should she do? She tried to imagine what Selena would say, but she couldn't imagine Selena sitting around a homemade Ouija board trying to talk to spirits in the first place.

Rue sucked in a breath. Selena had the luxury of doing things differently. Rue did not. She cleared her throat.

'We come here in peace,' she said, remembering the words Selena had said back during the solstice.

'We come here in peace,' she repeated. 'We hold only peace in our hearts.' She glanced around at the others, and Ebony was looking at her, impressed, and Rue felt a rising elation.

Perhaps she could do this sort of thing after all. Perhaps she really had been a priestess once, and now was back on that path. Maybe it really was her path in this life too.

She wanted to tell Selena.

But first, they had to make a good go of this. Rue imagined getting Sophie's spirit to speak, and telling Selena about it, what she'd done.

She cleared her throat. 'We want to speak only to those who wish us no harm.'

There. That ruled out any demon.

Ebony grinned at her, and she let herself smile back.

This was cool.

'We want to speak to the spirit who has been appearing to Sophie,' Rue continued, her voice growing stronger, more sure. 'We want to talk to the spirit who brings with her a cloud of perfume. Talk to us. Tell us who you are. What you want. If there's anything we can do for you.'

She sat back slightly, and Suze spoke up.

'Are you there?' she asked.

The crystal bowl jerked under their fingers, slid an inch across the table, halted.

'It can sometimes take them a while to get the hang of it,' Suze said.

Rue thought that could go for her as well. She drew in a breath, held it like Selena had taught her, then let it out slowly, relaxing with it.

The small, upturned bowl moved again, slid hesitantly to the word *YES*.

They looked at each other, eyes wide.

'Do you have a name?' Sophie asked

The bowl moved backwards slightly, then appeared to

hesitate. After a moment, it moved again, circling around the letters as though searching out the right one.

'You're pushing it,' Ebony said.

'Am not,' Suze retorted. 'You are if anyone is.'

'I don't think any of us are,' Rue said in amazement. It was such a strange sensation, the bowl moving on its own under her fingers.

'If it spells out Captain Howdy,' Ebony said, 'we are packing up and getting out of here.'

'Who's Captain Howdy?' Sophie asked.

'The demon in The Exorcist.'

Sophie shook her head. 'Rue said no one wishing us harm could come through.'

They were silent after that as the bowl completed its second perambulation around the board.

'Look at the EMF meter,' Ebony whispered.

The needle was swinging to and fro in the display.

The sugar bowl homed in on a letter.

'H,' Suze said. 'Someone should write this down.'

But they all had their fingers on the bowl.

'O,' Ebony said. 'M.'

The bowl jerked again, made another round of the letters, then homed in on *E*.

'Home,' Sophie said, then shook her head. I don't get it.'

'Is this your home?' Suze asked.

The sugar bowl slid straight to *YES*.

Everyone sat stock still, eyes wide, looking at each other.

Sophie spoke around a lump in her throat. 'Can you guys smell that?' she asked.

Rue lifted her head, sniffed the air. She was about to shake her head, answer no, but then she did. She smelt it.

'It's perfume,' she said, and shook her head in wonder. 'It really is.'

'Why are you here?' Suze asked, determined to get the question in while they had the spirit on the line. So to speak.

The bowl moved under their fingers.

'H,' Ebony said. 'Are you going to spell *home* again?'

The bowl slid to YES.

She nodded. 'Okay, so this was your home,' she said.

'And still is,' Suze said with a delicate shudder. She could still smell the slight fragrance of flowers. 'I can't believe this is real.'

'It's real, all right.' Ebony looked at the EMF meter, still showing activity, and tried to think what to ask next. She mentally went through everything she knew about ghosts. 'Did the house renovations disturb you?'

'What?' Suze said. 'Like she was sleeping, or something?'

The bowl was reversing, then slid towards YES again.

Ebony shrugged. 'I read somewhere that a lot of spirits get more active after a place has been renovated.'

'They completely redid this house before we bought it,' Sophie said. She looked at the board. 'Can we help you?'

'With what?' Suze asked her.

Sophie shrugged. 'Shouldn't she, like, cross over, or something? She's dead. She shouldn't be stuck here.' Sophie shivered. She didn't want to end up stuck in the house where she'd lived, when she died.

It seemed awfully sad.

The bowl was moving again, made a circle around the letters, then stuttered to a halt once more. The girls waited, fingers lightly on the crystal sugar bowl, but it didn't budge.

'Guess not, then,' Ebony said.

'Or she doesn't know how she can be helped,' Rue said, already planning to ask Selena what ought to be done in this situation.

'Wait! It's moving again.' Suze nodded. 'Much stronger too.'

It was stronger. The bowl made another circuit of the home-made board.

It moved from one letter to another.

'What?' Ebony said. 'MCDXXVII. That doesn't spell anything.'

'Yes it does!' Suze crowed, taking her hand off the crystal bowl and jumping up. She grabbed the pen and pad of paper and came back to the table with it, writing the strange jumble of letters down. 'We studied this in school ages ago.' She looked over at Sophie. 'Remember?'

Sophie shook her head.

'It's Roman numerals,' Suze said. 'It's a date.'

The sugar bowl, under everyone's fingers except Suze's, slid to *YES*.

'Oh my god,' Ebony breathed. 'This is so cool.'

'1427,' Suze said, putting the paper down and placing her fingers back lightly on the bowl with the others. 'Is that right?'

The sugar bowl backed up a little then moved again towards *YES*.

'That's when you were alive?' Ebony asked.

The bowl moved again, round the alphabet of letters. *D, I, E, D.*

'Died? That's when you died?' Rue glanced at Sophie again, who sat transfixed.

YES.

Rue sat back. She had a funny feeling. 'This house wasn't around in 1427.'

Everyone looked at her.

'You're right,' Ebony said, and looked down at the bowl. She licked her lips. 'Are you the same ghost we were talking to before?'

The bowl zipped over to *NO.*

'This is getting freaky,' Sophie said. 'What's going on?'

'But you are a ghost, then?' Ebony asked.

The bowl didn't budge.

'It doesn't want to answer,' Rue said in amazement.

'What do we ask it then?' Ebony said.

No one knew.

Ebony nodded. 'I have a question. What country did you live in?'

The bowl hesitated. Picked its way around the board. Spelled out *FRANCE.*

Then it kept going.

MCCLXXXIX

Suze worked it out with a shake of her head. '1289.'

MDCCLV

'1755.'

CDXXI

'421.' Suze shook her head. 'That was a long time ago.'

LVIII

'That's a weird one,' Rue said.

'It's 58,' Suze answered, then addressed the board. 'Is that a year too?'

YES.

'Wow.' Ebony gave a low whistle.

The bowl was moving again.

MMCC

'That one's easy,' Suze said. '2200.'

'It's going forward in time again,' Rue said.

The bowl moved to *NO*.

'No?' Ebony asked. 'I don't get it.'

Suze shook her head. 'BC,' she said.

'What?'

'BC. Before Christ.' Suze stared at them all, then looked at the board. 'Is that right?'

YES.

'Who were you then?' Ebony asked.

RUE.

'Whoa, hold on,' Ebony said, looking at Rue with wide eyes. 'Your name was Rue in the year 2200 BC?' She shook her head. 'I don't think so.' Ebony glanced around at the others. 'Do you reckon Rue was a name back then?'

The bowl moved again under the light touch of their fingertips.

IAMRUE.

In silent agreement, everyone took their hands away.

'What do you think it means, Rue?' Sophie asked.

Rue shook her head. She felt faint. 'I don't know.'

'Wait,' Ebony broke in. 'I have another question. Put your hands back.'

Rue did, but her head was swimming. Whatever she'd expected, it wasn't this.

'You say you're Rue,' Ebony said, frowning, trying to find the right way to say what she wanted to ask. 'Are you, um, a past life?'

Of course, Rue thought. Then shook her head, not in disbelief, but awe.

YES.

'Why are you here?' Rue blurted.

Everyone looked at her, then down at the board.

The bowl moved swiftly, around and around the circle of letters. Once, twice, three times.

Then it came to a stop.

'What?' Ebony cried. 'Is that it?'

Rue shook her head. 'Do you feel like it's just gone? That whoever it was, they're just gone?' she asked.

They all stared at the silent bowl, then one by one took their hands away.

'What was that about?' Ebony asked. She shook her head.

'Wow.'

20

'I GOT A BLACKBIRD,' CLOVER SAID THAT NIGHT, SITTING UP ON Rue's bed while Rue was at her desk, bent over some notebook. She'd been bursting to tell Rue all day, but Rue got home late and then it had been dinnertime and then Damien had read to her three whole books, and it had been bath time. It was bedtime now, but she wanted to tell Rue first.

'What?'

'A blackbird,' Clover repeated. 'He got an orange beak.' She pointed to her eyes. 'And orange around here.'

Rue turned finally and frowned at her. 'What are you talking about?' she asked.

Clover sighed. 'I'm talkin' bout my bird,' she said.

'What bird?'

'My bird. I got a blackbird I said.'

Rue looked at her. 'What? You mean a drawing of a bird?' Clover was always drawing and colouring now. It was practically her favourite thing to do.

'No,' Clover said. 'S'lina an' me went to the far 'n wide and I got a bird.'

Rue put her pen down. She'd been working on her Book of Ways. She liked that name better than Book of Shadows. She was writing down everything that had happened that afternoon at Sophie's place.

She still wasn't sure what it all meant.

'You went to the Otherworld again?' she asked, comprehension dawning at last. 'Where the whales are?'

'We didn't see the whales,' Clover said. 'I got a blackbird.'

'Why?' Rue asked.

Clover rolled her eyes and flung herself back on the bed. 'I tol' S'lena you sad,' she said.

Rue felt the blood drain from her face. 'I'm not sad,' she said.

Clover sat up again, looked at her sister. 'Yes, you are.'

Rue shook her head. 'No, I'm not.' She paused. 'What did Selena say?'

'She said she'd teach you to see the spirit of the house.'

Staring at Clover, Rue felt a tickling of excitement. 'Really?' she said. 'Selena really said she would?'

Rue hadn't decided whether she was going to tell Selena about what had happened that afternoon. She wanted to, but every time she thought of it, she kept hearing Selena saying that it probably wasn't her path to train as a priestess.

But this changed things. Rue pressed her hand against her stomach, feeling excitement building there.

'Course,' Clover said. 'Wonder what you get?' She wrinkled her nose in contemplation, then rolled over and frowned at Rue, narrowing her eyes.

'What?' Rue asked.

'Shh,' Clover said. 'I tryin' to see.'

'See what?'

'Who you got?'

'Who I got what?'

Clover just shook her head and let part of her sink down into the deep and wide. It was probably more of a spreading out in spirit than a sinking down, but Clover didn't have the words for it. She just knew that if she relaxed and looked, she could see things that were there and not there at the same time.

She sat up suddenly and squealed. 'I saw it, Rue! I saw it!'

Rue shifted, unable to help scanning the room around her. 'What?' she asked and shook her head. 'I don't really know what you're doing, Clover.'

Clover shook her head. 'I seein' your bird,' she said slowly and patiently. 'Your bird frien' in the far 'n wide.'

'What?'

Clover gave up and slid from the bed. 'We go get S'lena to 'splain.' She made for the door, looked back at her sister. 'Come on.'

'Okay.' Rue got up, not exactly knowing what was going on, but there was that excitement in her still. Clover was going on about something – and it seemed she was seeing something.

Rue just didn't know what.

On impulse, Rue swept up her notebook and brought it along with her.

'S'lena!' Clover scampered down the stairs and stuck her head in the living room, then bounced in when she saw that

Selena and Dandy were both in there. 'S'lena, I saw Rue's bird frien'!'

Selena looked up from Teresa's book on trees and raised her eyebrows, glancing at Rue slipping through the doorway behind her exuberant sister.

'You did?' she asked. 'How did you see that?'

Clover climbed up onto Selena's lap, setting the book on her own and looked seriously at Selena. 'I looked hard in the far 'n wide,' she said. 'Lookin' lookin' lookin' for it.'

A smile touched Selena's lips. 'And you saw it?'

Rue perched on the couch and looked at Dandy and Clover and Selena. 'What is she talking about?'

Clover groaned. 'Your bird frien'!'

Selena touched her arm gently. 'Rue might not know about spirit friends,' she said gently.

'Rue doesn't,' Rue said.

Clover shook her head and looked at Selena. 'You tell her,' she said.

Selena laughed, then did so. 'Clover is talking about our spirit kin,' she said. 'She and I travelled to the Otherworld – which is part of what Clover calls the far 'n wide, I think – and while we were there, she commented on my animal kin.'

Rue blinked, trying to follow, feeling a tiny bite of envy. She'd never envied Clover's gifts until now. Taking a deep breath, she tried to tamp the small impulse away before it could grow.

And reminded herself about what had happened that afternoon.

IAMRUE.

'Your animal kin?' she asked.

Selena nodded. 'Each of us has kin who walk with us through our lives, there for support and wisdom along the way. We tend to forget our purpose when we are born into flesh, but they do not, and they are there to remind us.'

Rue glanced at Dandy, to see if she knew about this.

'I've always called them spirit guides,' Dandy said.

Rue shook her head briefly. She felt like her brain was going to explode.

'How do we know who our spirit kin are?' she asked. Then looked at Clover. 'She can see them?'

'Clover can see spirit,' Selena explained gently, seeing the emotions flitting across Rue's face and remembering what Clover had said about Rue being sad she couldn't see the spirit of the house.

Goddess guide me, she thought now, before continuing. And Dandy had been right, she thought too. She did need to teach both girls to be priestesses.

Even if they didn't have a Wilde Grove to grow up in.

'Which is a gift Clover was born with, but one the rest of us can cultivate.'

'We can?' Rue said.

'We can,' Selena agreed. 'There are a few tricks to it, but anyone can do it.'

'Rue's bird frien' is big,' Clover murmured. She was getting sleepy. It was past her bedtime now. 'Has 'normous wings.'

'What's it called?' Rue said, leaning forward. Big? Enormous wings?

But Clover shook her head, eyelids drooping. 'Don' 'member.' She forced her eyes back open. 'Is a picture of it in Damien's book.'

Rue straightened. 'I'll get it,' she said, and only minutes later she was back with the big book of New Zealand birds.

'Where is it?' she asked.

Clover slipped from Selena's lap, yawned, and knelt down on the floor with the book. She turned the pages, looking for it.

'There,' she said, and looked at the big word at the top of the page. She could read some words, but this one was too hard.

'Albatross,' Rue said, then leaned back shaking her head. 'But they're amazing birds. They can fly for ages without landing.'

'Your albitruss is big,' Clover said, spreading her arms like wings.

Rue nodded, leaning over the book. 'With strong wings, the albatross can fly the oceans for years at a time without needing to land.' She sat back. 'I always thought that was amazing, when I was younger. I've always loved albatrosses.'

'Your long affinity with them makes sense,' Selena said.

Rue thought about it. 'What does it mean to have one as your kin, though?' she asked. 'You said they are guides. How do they do that?'

'Such good questions,' Selena said. 'When it comes to animals and birds as spirit kin, then we need to learn the animal's attributes to know some of the wisdom they carry for us. There are messages in their strengths and weaknesses for us.'

'Do you have a bird?' Rue asked.

Selena nodded. 'Crane is my kin,' she said.

'And what does Crane teach you?' Rue tugged a cushion off the couch and settled more comfortably on the floor with it, then glanced at Clover and snagged the throw rug and put it over her. Clover was almost asleep, stretched out on the rug beside the open book.

'Crane,' Selena said, glancing over at Dandy to see her grinning and nodding, 'is a bird with much to teach in regards to patience and focus, as it stands for hours looking into the water waiting for fish.'

Rue nodded to show she was following. Clover gave a little snore.

'Crane also stands on the edge of water and land and so is a liminal creature,' Selena said, feeling a slight sense of deja vu, remembering having much the same conversation with Morghan. Many years before.

'What's liminal?' Rue asked.

'A liminal place is anywhere that's a border. A beach, for example – because it's where sea and sand mingle. A river bank.' She searched her mind for other examples. 'A mountain top – between earth and sky. A tunnel.' She stopped speaking for a moment, distracted by thoughts of Clover's wizards. She still didn't know what to make of them and their refusal to let her in.

But she would try again, she thought. Next time she travelled to the Otherworld.

'A tunnel?' Rue prompted, and Dandy had laid down her knitting needles, enjoying the impromptu lesson. She wasn't too old yet to learn more and deeper ways of the world.

'Right,' Selena said, coming back to the room. 'A tunnel is the liminal space between inner and outer.'

'So it works all sorts of ways?' Rue asked, thinking she

needed to make notes. She had her Book of Ways with her, but she wanted that to be tidy and organised.

She'd just have to remember it for later.

'It does. And being a liminal creature – and all birds are to an extent because they bridge earth and sky – Crane is also a guide to the Underworld.' She blinked. 'The Underworld specifically because Crane is a water bird, rather than a high-flyer.'

Rue was lost. 'I'm not following,' she said. 'What's the Underworld? I thought you always called it the Otherworld.'

Selena laughed. 'You're completely right,' she said. 'And the trouble is here that to explain one thing, I have to explain ten others.'

'We've got an hour or two,' Dandy said, then had a thought. 'Perhaps we should invite Tara and Damien in to hear all this too.'

'Then it really would be like teaching school,' Selena said, not sure if she was ready for that. She looked at Dandy, saw the older woman's arched brow, and grimaced, then laughed. 'I thought my teaching days were over.'

'I think they might be just beginning,' Rue said, shaking her head, unaware how grown up she sounded all of a sudden. 'There's so much to learn. So much I want to know.' She paused. 'Need to know. I need to know it.'

Selena stared at her for a long moment. Then nodded. 'Yes,' she said quietly. 'I see that you do.' She remembered the vision the Fae Queen had shown her and Morghan before she'd left Wilde Grove. 'You're to be a beacon,' she said. 'We're all to be beacons. I see that now.'

'What do you mean?' Rue asked, feeling a shiver even though the room was perfectly warm.

'I had a vision once,' Selena said. 'Of a world over which darkness and confusion crawled, threatening to overtake it.' She paused, closed her eyes, seeing it again. 'But there were lights holding out against the darkness. Beacons of light.'

Rue's mouth was suddenly dry. 'Beacons of light,' she repeated.

And Selena nodded.

21

'What are you doing today?' Dandy asked as she and Selena watched their housemates scatter. Damien was off to work, Rue, clutching a nicely bound notebook, walked to school, and Tara and Clover were busy getting ready for a parent and child playgroup Tara had found to take Clover to in the meantime while she was getting her home-based childcare qualifications.

'You were very good last night, by the way,' Dandy added, pouring them both a second cup of tea.

Selena shook her head. 'It felt very strange.'

'Not strange at all,' Dandy said. 'I went to a spiritual development circle for years when I was younger. Last night was just like that except better.'

'Better?'

Dandy eyed up Tara's fresh loaf of bread and debated whether to take a second piece. It was still warm from the oven and so good with the plum jam they'd bought from the farmer's market. She gave in and put another slice on her plate.

'Much better,' she said. 'You've a gift for teaching, and a wide range of skills.' She looked over at Selena. 'And good on you for stopping and bringing Tara and Damien in on it. You're talking about stuff everyone should know.' Dandy spooned a healthy dollop of jam onto the bread.

'Maybe it's what I'm supposed to be doing,' Selena mused.

'Lighting beacons,' Dandy agreed. 'I'd say so.'

They were silent for a minute. 'So,' Dandy reminded Selena. 'Plans?'

'I've been reading the book on native trees that Teresa got me while she was here,' Selena said. 'I thought I might make myself a new set of Ogham, using native trees. I'm rather interested to see how that would work.' She stared unfocused over the rim of her cup. 'It's become tradition now to align the Ogham with specific trees, but I think it might go well with some of the native trees here, and then I'd have a sort of blending of things that echoes the fact that I'm in a new country.' She tapped her fingers against the cup. 'Or I wouldn't mind looking into what forms of divination are traditional here, if any are.'

Dandy looked at her. 'I haven't the faintest idea what you're talking about,' she said. 'What are these Ogham things?'

Selena laughed. 'Sorry,' she said.

'Don't be,' Dandy told her. 'Just explain.'

'Just briefly, then,' Selena said. 'The Ogham is a very old – some say ancient – script, similar to runes, if you've heard of those. I use it, as many do now, for divination. But I'm interested in getting to know the trees of my new home, and I thought making a new set of Ogham would be a good way.' She pursed her lips. 'Unless there's already such a thing, perhaps in Māori lore and understanding?'

'I wouldn't know, unfortunately,' Dandy said, shaking her head and wiping a spot of jam from her lip. 'Maybe Damien would – or could find out from his gran. She sounds like the one to ask.'

Selena nodded. 'I should very much like to meet her before too long.' She sighed. 'I would also like to go back to the Otherworld and see what this business is with Clover's wizard.'

She'd told Dandy about it the day before.

Dandy nodded. 'What about the house up the road. Any more thoughts on that?'

'I've had thoughts, but no enlightenment,' Selena said, knowing straight away which house Dandy referred to. 'How about you?'

'Nope. I've never really heard of anything like it,' Dandy said. 'I mean, I've been into the odd house with a bit of an off atmosphere, as though something a little unsavoury had happened in it at one time or another, but I've not seen more than that, and – for me, at least, because I'm not very sensitive to atmosphere – it's been pretty rare.'

Selena shook her head. 'I don't know that you ought to put it like that.'

Baffled, Dandy looked at her across the table. 'Put it like what?'

'Words are important,' Selena said. She took a sip of the tea. 'More important than most people realise.'

'What did I say wrong?' Dandy asked dubiously.

Selena smiled. 'See,' she said. 'The trick is to remember to give room for things. Even in the way we speak, because words are a sort of spell.'

Dandy only looked more baffled and ran her words back in her mind, then shook her head.

'You said you're not very sensitive to atmosphere,' Selena explained. 'But saying such a thing is a declaration to the world, to spirit, and it doesn't leave any room for change or improvement.'

Dandy nodded, lip pursed. Huh, she thought. She learnt something new every day. Even at her age.

'So, what should I have said, then?'

'That's easy,' Selena told her. 'Something along the lines of – I have yet to cultivate a sensitivity to atmosphere.' Her eyebrows rose. 'Do you see the difference?'

Dandy thought about it and decided she did see the difference. 'I see what you mean about leaving space for things,' she said. 'If I'd said it your way, it opens up space for that to be different going forward.'

'And different now,' Selena added.

Dandy shook her head. 'You should write a book.'

Selena laughed. 'I warmed to teaching last night, actually. It's been so long since I went through all this with Morghan, and now that I'm getting over my resistance to it, I think I'm enjoying it.'

'Maybe not a book, then,' Dandy said. 'But a spiritual development circle. Just like the one I used to go to through with the Spiritualist Church.' She tipped her head to the side. 'Or not just like that. Your version of it.'

'I think I did that last night.'

It was true. Rue had even taken notes, running up to her room for paper and writing earnestly before tucking it in the back of her notebook.

'The shop I do readings at – they'd fall over themselves to have you do something like this.' Dandy grinned. 'And remember what it's called?'

Selena nodded. 'Beacon.'

'See?' Dandy reached for the last bite of her bread. 'Meant to be.'

Selena considered this. More than mere serendipity, this did feel meaningful, and hadn't she been brought up since a child to see the meaning in the strands of the web?

'Perhaps,' she said. 'I will think upon it.'

Dandy held her bread up and nodded. 'You do that,' she said.

SELENA MADE HER WAY UPSTAIRS TO HER ROOM UNDER THE eaves. She would go travelling again, she decided, while Clover was out busy having fun. She'd already told the child not to follow her into the Otherworld, if she was out of the house. Inside, with Selena, was the only place and time Clover should venture there.

Clover had nodded, looking only a little vexed. And then Tara had called her to get ready, and the girl skipped off happily.

Selena thought she was getting used to travelling now from inside the house. Back at Wilde Grove, of course, there'd been the woods to walk though while stepping into the Otherworld, and for more concentrated, ritual travelling, there had been the caves. She'd seldom travelled lying on the floor or leaning back in an armchair. It felt all a bit decadent, really, but since it didn't make any difference that Selena could tell, it certainly was easier on bones that were getting that much older now.

She sat at her altar for a few minutes, pouring a new offering to the Antlered Goddess, and running her prayer beads through her fingers, feeling the stone and crystal beads warm under her hands.

'Here is the path I seek,' she murmured, eyes closed, her spirit unfurling around her, seeking connection with the invisible web of the worlds.

'It is your path I seek, Elen, Lady of the Ways. It is your flame I tend, Brigid of the Hearth. I walk the path with my heart and head on fire, bright with the beauty of the soul.'

She paused, listened to her breathing for a minute, feeling her chest rise and fall slowly, feeling her senses expand so that, even with her eyes closed, she could see, could feel the worlds touching inside her. She was a spoke upon the great wheel, and the axis too, holding the worlds within her. They spun around her, flowing from the cauldron below her ribcage. The centre from which she would step forward.

'I am the spoke on the wheel,' she said quietly, her voice calm and clear in the hush of her room. 'I am the spinner and singer of worlds. I am one bright soul amongst many, and I would sing us into harmony. World to world to world.'

Without breaking the spell that felt to have fallen over her, Selena rose from her seat in front of the table that held her altar and lit the bundle of herbs, letting the smoke waft from it. Her spirit was alive, flowing around her, and she swayed slightly where she stood, on the cusps of worlds.

'Spirits of the south,' she said, walking to the south side of the room and letting the smoke billow. 'Bless and protect me in my travelling.' She paused before moving on, in the flow, in the great stream of the world. 'Beloved Stag of the Wildwood, greet and lead me in my travelling.'

Selena moved to the next point, holding the smoking herbs.

'Spirits of the west,' she said. 'May you hold space for me this day.' Again, she paused before going on, and a vision rose in her mind. 'Let me drink from the cauldron of inspiration. Cerridwen, I call upon you for blessing in my travelling this day.'

She moved around the room, barely seeing it, her spirit bright and flowing, her head swaying with that particular dizziness that came with the trance state that she would soon step fully into.

'Spirits of the north,' she said, and her words whispered around the room as though carried on a breeze. 'Spirit of the Phoenix, who lives, is consumed by fire, and lives again, let your wisdom gained from all your new beginnings lead me in my travelling.'

Selena breathed in, deeply, and the scent of the herbs filled her. She offered her exhale back as her own blessing.

'Spirits of the east,' she finished, moving to the part of the room that faced the rising sun. 'Spirit of the eagle who once flew over this land, eyes bright, eyes sharp, seeing and knowing, guide me in your love for this land.'

The eagle native to her new country was now extinct,

but she knew that somewhere, its spirit flew on, and she closed her eyes, a smile touching her lips, feather-light.

Selena brought the smoking herb bundle back to her altar and set it down safely to smoulder. She lit the candles that stood either side of the statue of the antlered goddess.

'Bless me in my travelling, my Lady,' she murmured. 'Guide me in my seeking.'

Now, she was ready, and she sat down, letting her body rest comfortably, even as she left it to stand in the Wildwood.

Her lips curved in a smile as she remembered Clover looking around wide-eyed and wondering.

'There's your deer,' she'd said, and Hind was here now as well. Ears flicking as she gazed at Selena, seeing if she was ready.

'I'm ready,' Selena told her. And followed the deer along the paths of the Otherworld, moving deeper into the heart of it.

Hind stopped in front of the same cliff and tunnel entrance that Selena recognised from her last travelling. This was Clover's tunnel. The child hadn't told Selena what she'd done when she'd disappeared into it, only that she'd talked to 'the wizards.'

This time, Clover was happily with Tara at the play-group, and that was fine by Selena.

She could still go into the tunnel and look for her, because the Otherworld was a place where you could meet in spirit, and right now, that was exactly what Selena intended to do. She was going to seek that part of Clover that walked these ways.

For it seemed to her that there was always a part that walked the paths and tunnels of the Otherworld.

Selena slipped into the dimness of the tunnel and stepped forward into the hill. This was the correct tunnel, and ahead of her, she saw a door.

Clover's Otherworld soul aspect was behind that door, Selena was certain of it. Her hands tingled with nerves when she reached to push it open.

The door opened silently, and Selena stepped forward, looking at the group of wizards in astonishment. They were clustered together in a loose circle, and she couldn't see what they were doing, what they were busy with.

And she couldn't see Clover anywhere.

She knew she wouldn't see Clover here this time as the small child she knew. Whenever she met the spirit of someone in this world, they were different than the face she knew. They were in their spirit form, which in the Otherworld sometimes looked much different.

One of the wizards – and they were, to Selena's eyes, exactly as one would expect a wizard, whether in movie or storybook, to be – looked up and saw her. She saw the shock on his face when he realised her intrusion.

Then she was blasted backwards, her whole body flying, arms and legs splayed, outstretched.

She landed, shocked, on her backside, in the path outside the tunnel.

Hind wandered over, bent her head down, and sniffed at her.

Selena sat in the dirt, her mind a blank, and then she shook herself, scrambled to her feet and looked furiously at the tunnel.

Who did they think they were? How dare they expel her like that! She had as much right as any to see Clover. More – she was Clover's guardian.

Selena dusted the dirt from her backside, fuming.

Hind twitched her ears again, wrinkling her delicate nose.

'I know,' Selena said, 'but still, how dare they!'

The outrage rose again, and for a moment, Selena stood poised on the threshold of the tunnel, ready to storm back up to the door and demand to be let back in, to see what their business was.

'But it's not my business, is it?' she said finally. Her rump throbbed, as did her dignity. Never had she been so unceremoniously thrown out of anywhere!

'Come on,' Selena said to Hind. 'Let's get out of here.' Whatever the wizards were up to, they weren't going to invite her to be a part of it.

Her job – she remembered the wizard's words from the previous visit – was to take care of and teach Clover in the waking world.

Here, she is ours, he had said.

Selena walked away, shaking her head. What an extraordinary situation, she thought, and then straightened. She'd best do her part of the job well, then, since there was so much more to the child than she'd ever contemplated.

Finally, a smile hitched itself onto her face. Not one wizard as Clover's guide and kin, but a whole bunch of the fellows. The smile widened and she shook her head at it all.

It was not necessary, she decided, to know everything. What was important was to follow the path you were on, to do what was required of you at each step of the way. And currently, what was required of her was not to understand everything, but to tend instead to Clover's wellbeing, to bend herself to that task.

'I follow the path of my purpose,' she murmured.

22

HIND MOVED DOGGEDLY ALONG THE PATHS OF THE Wildwood, and Selena followed her, head down, thinking, considering, until she realised that something had changed in the quality of the light, and that without noticing, the track had taken them out of the forest and onto the beginning of another, particular path.

This was where Selena usually entered the Wildwood. Not always, but mostly, when she went into trance to travel to the Otherworld, she stepped onto this path and into the Wildwood of the Underworld.

But the path did not go in just one direction, into the woods. Hind left the trees behind and walked on, and Selena lifted her head, alert as she followed her.

They were making for the bridge to the Middleworld.

This world was the reflection in spirit of her own waking world.

The old stone bridge curved gracefully from one world to the next and Selena crossed it, looking around, wondering where Hind was taking her, and for what purpose.

There would be a purpose, of that she was sure.

They came off the bridge to a road that Selena recognised. It looked different, seeing it in this manner, but she knew it all the same, and walked beside Hind now, not needing to be shown the way.

They stopped in front of the brick wall, and Selena gazed over it at the house. She shook her head – she could feel the call of it as strong as before. It was like listening to the wind howling around the corners and under the eaves.

'Why is it like this?' Selena asked Hind, but her spirit kin merely looked at her, and Selena shook her head. 'I know,' she said.

'That's my task to find out.'

Selena put her hand to the brick wall that was the fence and thought for a moment that she could feel it vibrating under her hand, as though the very fabric of the house was humming at her. She shook her head slightly and went to the gate, unlatched it, and pushed it open.

It opened silently.

A stillness had fallen over the house, as though it now held its breath. Selena looked at the windows, the curtains tightly drawn closed behind them.

Who lived here?

Selena thought she was about to find out.

The back door opened under her hand as though it had been left unlocked for her. She stepped in, pausing on the threshold to listen, but heard nothing. She entered the house and Hind followed her. The door closed with a soft snick.

Selena hesitated, then walked into the kitchen, but it was empty, spotlessly clean. She stepped through into the next room, but it too was empty.

As was the living room, and each of the other rooms whose doors hung open.

Which left only what Selena surmised was a bedroom. The door was closed, and she put her fingertips to the wood, as though she would be able to feel through its surface to who lay behind it.

The door pushed open at her light touch, and she looked into the dimness.

It was empty too.

Selena glanced back at Hind. 'There's no one here,' she said, whispering, unsure why she was keeping her voice down. Perhaps because the house was so still.

But Hind ignored her, looking around the room with her soft brown eyes.

Selena followed her gaze, saw nothing, turned to leave, to go through the other rooms again because perhaps she'd missed something, then hesitated.

Then realised there was a tent made from blankets tucked beside the wardrobe and the wall. Selena looked at it in silence.

She moved softly forward and got down onto her knees.

'Hello?' she said in front of the fold of blanket that hung down over something, a chair, perhaps.

Tentatively, Selena pushed the blanket aside, and peered into the dimness behind it.

Something was there. Selena crouched down further, hunched over her knees.

Someone was there.

'Hello,' she whispered softly to the figure crouched down on the floor of the wardrobe. 'I almost didn't see you there.' She smiled gently. 'You have a very wonderful tent. Did you make it?'

The small girl blinked at her but didn't budge from her nest in the shadows.

Selena sat down, crossing her legs under her. She wiggled a little until she was comfortable, ready to spend however long it took down on the floor, talking to the little one in the tent.

She looked around. 'What a good spot you have here,' she said, making her voice warm and calm. 'I almost didn't see you at all, but my friend thought you might be in here.'

The child's eyes widened, and she looked past Selena's shoulder.

Selena leaned slightly to the side so the girl could see the spirit deer behind her.

The girl looked startled at the sight of the deer and glanced confusedly at Selena.

'She's pretty, isn't she?' Selena said. 'And a very good friend of mine.' She smiled. 'Do you have any friends?'

The girl stared at Selena, then nodded her head.

She held up a teddy bear, its fur soft and worn from hugs.

'My goodness,' Selena said. 'He's a beauty, isn't he?'

The child's expressive eyes blinked at her, then she shifted slightly, and Selena watched her digging in the shadows for something.

She brought out a teapot, and set it on a small ledge, added two teacups. Smiled shyly at Selena.

'Oh,' Selena said. 'How wonderful,' she smiled. 'Is this where the two of you have tea parties?'

The small girl stared at her, then nodded. 'We like it here,' she said, her voice almost too soft to hear.

'It is a wonderful tent you've made for yourself – did you make it?'

The little girl looked up at the blankets draped over two chairs and nodded.

'It's our best place,' she said.

'Your best place?'

The girl nodded, hugged her teddy to her thin chest. 'We can play in here and imagine all sorts of nice things.'

Selena nodded. 'What about outside? Do you play out there?' She drew in a long, quiet breath.

The child shook her head. 'I don't like it out there. Mummy and Daddy talk about scary things.'

'I see,' Selena said, glad for once it was talking the parents were doing that was scary, not more.

'I'm Selena,' she said. 'And I'm very pleased to meet you.'

The little girl gazed at her, a new expression dawning in her eyes. She clutched her teddy in front of her.

'Where did you come from?' she asked, her voice little more than a whisper. 'Are you magic?'

Selena smiled. 'Yes,' she said. 'I suppose I am a little bit magic, to come and find you here.' She shifted slightly again so that Hind could rest her velvety head on Selena's shoulder and gaze at the girl. 'Hind brought me here. I followed her and she brought me to you.'

The child's eyes were wide, round, entranced. She scooted forward, until she was almost at the entrance to the little tent.

'Can I pat her?' she asked.

Selena nodded and moved back. She didn't think Hind would mind. In fact, Hind was already shifting so that she could lower her head further.

The little girl reached up and touched her fingers to Hind's nose. She slipped out of the tent onto her knees and patted the soft fur between Hind's ears.

'I like her,' she whispered.

Selena nodded. 'She likes you too. She doesn't let everyone pat her.'

Those wide eyes turned to Selena again. 'Who doesn't she let?'

'Hmm.' Selena thought about it, watching the child. She couldn't be more than seven or eight. Just a little older than Clover. 'She doesn't like people who scare little children,' she said. 'Has someone scared you?'

The child withdrew her hands, held onto the stuffed bear again and looked at Selena, forehead wrinkling. 'Mummy and Daddy keep talking about bombs,' she whispered.

'Bombs?' Selena said in surprise, but the child nodded.

'They say we could all die.'

The girl's beautiful eyes welled with sudden tears, and she crouched down in the entrance way to her tent, shaking her head. 'I don't wanna die,' she said.

Selena reached out and stroked the girl's hair. 'Hush,' she said. 'It's all right. It's all right to be afraid of something like that. It's very scary to hear your parents say those things.'

'We have to practice hiding from the nuclear bombs,' the little girl said, her face half buried in her teddy's fur. 'I made my tent cos it's the only safe place.' She sat up a little and looked at her bear. 'Me an' Bear stay in here all the time because we don't have to worry when we're in here.'

She looked up at Selena with wide, soft eyes.

'Where do you live? Are you a friend of Mummy and Daddy's?'

Selena shook her head. 'No,' she said. 'I'm a friend of yours, when you're grown up.'

It would soon, Selena thought, be the truth.

'When I'm grown up?' The girl looked confusedly at her, then nodded. 'Am I dead when I'm grown up?'

Selena looked at her in consternation.

'No,' she said. 'You're not. You're perfectly alive.'

The girl was silent for a long moment, then nodded at Selena.

I knew you were magic,' she said, and looked around, a frown on her face. 'I don't think you'll fit in my blanket tent. I don't want to come any further out. I'm afraid. I'm going to live in it always, and be safe – that's how I'm not dead when I'm grown up, isn't it?'

Selena looked at her, compassion filling her chest and making a lump in her throat. 'It's very scary living in a world where people talk about bombs, isn't it?'

She tried to think how to reassure the child, but realised she wasn't quite sure what to say. The threat of nuclear bombs had subsided to a certain extent, but what of everything else? She thought of the crawling darkness the Queen had shown her.

There was nothing certain about the world, or its future.

'By the time you grow up,' she said, finding a place to

begin, without lying, 'you won't have to worry so much about bombs.'

The girl stared at her horrified. 'They all go off?' she said. 'But you said I wasn't dead!'

'No!' Selena hadn't been clear. 'No,' she said again, shaking her head softly. 'There are agreements not to use them.'

It wasn't a subject she knew much about. When had the agreements been made? Then she realised that didn't matter. They were there and this traumatised child needed to know that.

'Nobody's gonna blow me up?' the little girl said.

Selena shook her head. 'No,' she said.

The girl thought about that then had another question. 'Mummy and Daddy worry about it.'

'Yes,' Selena agreed. 'It's a frightening thing to think of.'

The child nodded. 'My name is Natalie,' she whispered, then looked over Selena's shoulder at Hind. 'Will you come and visit me again?'

Oh yes.

Selena nodded and stroked Natalie's hair. 'Yes,' she said. 'I'd like that.'

'Soon?'

'Definitely,' Selena answered, knowing she was going to make that happen, because it was going to hurt her heart to have to leave the small child hiding in her blanket tent, where she'd been all these long years.

Satisfied, Natalie nodded. 'I'm tired,' she said, and she looked it, dark rings under her eyes. And with that, she tucked herself back into her nest, her teddy in a tight hug, and closed her eyes.

Selena looked at her there in the shadows of the tent, then slowly, quietly got up. She nodded at Hind, looked around the bedroom, at the small bed tucked into one corner, the shelf full of books, a row of stuffed bears.

And ordinary child's room, to look at, she thought. But the world was full of things for a child to be afraid of, particularly if their parents let themselves be scared too.

The question was then, how do we not let the frightening things in the world overwhelm us?

Selena moved through the doorway, Hind following her. In the eighties, when this child had been part of the world, there had been a great deal of fear over the nuclear issue.

That issue had been replaced with others. Always there were other things to make us feel unsteady and uncertain. Sometimes it was things like illness and poverty.

Sometimes it was other things also. It was 2006 now, and there had been devastating hurricanes, riots, wars, bird flu fears. And there was always a list like this.

She had to help Natalie. Hind stepped up to walk beside her and looked at her as Selena thought this.

Selena knew the spirit animal agreed with her.

Selena came downstairs on legs that were a little unsteady. She didn't know how long she'd been in her attic room travelling the byways of the Otherworld – it always seemed longer than it was – but she stumbled on the steps, righted herself, then blew into the kitchen.

Dandy wasn't there. She paused and listened to the house, checking to see if anyone were home with her.

Dandy?

Her face suffused with the odd heat she'd long ago recognised as an affirmative answer to whatever question she was asking.

Dandy was still home. That was good. Selena had already come to value the woman's level-headed wisdom.

She slipped out of the kitchen and went to the room Dandy used as her private sitting room and knocked on the door.

'Dandy?' she called.

'Come in, please.'

Selena opened the door and stepped into Dandy's preserve. 'Thank you,' she said.

'Of course,' Dandy answered, then frowned at Selena's expression. 'What's going on?'

Selena drew in a long breath and sat down on one of the chairs. 'I've just done a journey to the Otherworld,' she said.

Dandy nodded, holding her deck of cards in her hand. She'd just laid out a spread and a presentiment came over her. The card's message would coincide with Selena's.

There was the Ace of Hearts, but it was reversed. Trouble in the home. And the Queen of Hearts, which indicated a woman, lighter hair and eyes. Not Tara in this case, Dandy was sure of it.

With the next two cards, Dandy heart sank. She touched her fingers to them, cleared her throat. 'The Eight of Clubs,' she said. 'And Three of Spades. Confusion. Tears.' She looked over at Selena.

And Selena nodded.

'This is about whoever lives in that house, isn't it?' Dandy asked.

Another nod. 'Natalie,' Selena said. 'Her name's Natalie.'

Dandy's eyes widened. 'How did you find out her name?'

'I met her,' Selena said flatly. 'In my travelling. Hind, my spirit kin, took me to the Middleworld, the spirit equivalent of our own, and to the house.'

Dandy nodded, fascinated despite the sense of urgency that was growing inside her.

Selena blew out a breath. 'And I found a small child hiding in a tent she'd built from blankets.'

'Wait. A small child?' Dandy's gaze went back to her cards. There was no indication of a child there. A grown woman, yes, but no child.

Selena nodded. 'The child is a soul shard, splintered off during a time of great stress in the woman's life, and still caught in it.' She sighed, ran her hand over the arm of the chair. 'I've seen a lot of this in my travels around the Otherworld. It happens so easily, to almost all of us. Where there is trauma, there is splintering of the soul aspect.'

Dandy thought about this for only a moment before nodding. There was a logic and resonance about it that seemed right.

'This child was one of these...splinters?' she asked. 'From whoever lives in the house now?'

'I believe so, yes,' Selena said, then shifted slightly in her seat. 'In fact, I am sure of it.'

'So, we need to do something.' There wasn't any question in Dandy's voice. It was a statement, plain and simple.

'Yes.'

They were in agreement, and Dandy wanted to jump up right then and there and go do whatever it was needed doing. But she stayed sitting on the sofa, the coffee table spread with cards in front of her. She looked over at Selena.

'I don't know,' Selena confessed to Dandy's unspoken question. 'I don't know what we do.'

'We have to make her answer the door, and then we have to get inside, get her to trust us, whoever she is.'

Selena nodded.

Dandy grimaced. 'It's asking a lot, isn't it?'

Selena stood up. 'Yes, but we're going to try.'

'Now?'

'I think so.'

23

THE DAY WAS OVERCAST, AND DANDY CAST HER FACE TO THE sky. 'Autumn's coming,' she said. 'I can feel it.'

Selena squinted, confused for a moment. It was February. She shook her head. 'I have so much trouble with this back to front thing with the seasons. What is winter like here?'

'Cold, damp, and windy,' Dandy answered, turning to follow the path through the gardens up the hill. 'I hope we manage to heat the house nicely through it.'

Selena grimaced. She didn't like being cold. 'I'm sure we will,' she said, then turned her mind back to their day's mission.

How were they going to get themselves introduced to the person in the house?

Natalie. Selena was almost one hundred percent sure they were going to see a woman named Natalie.

They walked the rest of the way in silence and drew up in front of the now-familiar low brick wall.

'We should have come up with a plan,' Dandy muttered, pushing the gate open.

'We tried,' Selena said.

A sigh from Dandy. 'Nothing sounded reasonable,' she said.

They went around to the back door again. The front looked as though it were never used.

'I'll knock,' Dandy said, and did just that, standing back and listening for movement inside the house.

'How do we get her to answer?' Dandy said after two minutes of silence. She knocked again.

Inside the house, Natalie froze where she stood in the kitchen. Was she expecting any parcels?

She couldn't remember, wasn't sure what day it was. She glanced at the calendar on the kitchen wall – a cheery, plump Victorian child smiled back at her from the picture on it, a little black and white puppy in her arms – and realised it was a weekday. She'd lost track.

Slowly, she inched forward to the window, but yesterday – she was sure of that, if not the date – she had gone looking through the old boxes of her mother's sewing things, neatly packed into the spare room, and found a length of lace fabric to make a curtain for the kitchen window.

Natalie had covered it up so she wouldn't see the trees moving, the shadows stepping out from behind the garage.

She couldn't see anyone on the other side, and she didn't dare twitch the curtain out of the way to look. Natalie glanced at the back door, but the glass in it was frosted and all she could see was a shadow of a person, perhaps two.

The men from the other night? She blinked at the thought and froze again, still cradling a bag of rolled oats with one arm.

Her breath came in short, hitching gulps.

'OH HELLO, ARE YOU FRIENDS OF NATALIE'S?'

The courier smiled cheerily at Selena and Dandy, a package in her arms. 'She needs more friends, this one, does Natalie.' She swung the box down onto the step, gave a quick knock at the door.

'Natalie, love, it's Nikki. You've got a package!' She grinned at the other women, then went back down the drive, whistling merrily.

Selena put a hand to her chest, took a step backwards, and thanked the Goddess.

Inside the house, Natalie heard the knock again, then suddenly Nikki was yelling out to her, and she bent over, putting her hands on her knees, dropping her head down and taking slow relieved breaths of air. She went to open the door.

Two women stood there, and she froze on the doorstep.

There was also a box. Natalie's gaze slid down to it, then away, back to the women. The box was too big to just bend down and grab. It would take more than a moment to pick up.

Her mouth was dry. 'Who are you?' she asked, and it seemed to her that the words rasped against the inside of her throat as she spoke. She shook her head.

'I don't talk to solicitors,' she said, wanting to back into the house and close the door, but needing the box. She couldn't leave it out there. What if they took it? She couldn't afford to lose whatever was in it.

'My name is Selena, and this is Dandy,' Selena said, letting herself relax, letting her spirit flow outwards from her, and taking a small step forward so she could soothe the frightened woman on the doorstep.

Natalie shook her head.

'I don't want whatever you're trying to sell,' Natalie said, and it hurt to speak. 'Please go away.'

Dandy was trying to think of something rational to say. She glanced at Selena, who was probably attempting to work out the same thing.

'We're here today because...' Selena faltered. What could she say?

'Because we thought you could use some friends.'

Natalie stared blankly back at her.

'We noticed, you see,' Dandy said. 'That you don't get out much and thought you might like some company.' She smiled. 'A little visiting. A little chatting over a cup of tea. Does wonders, that does.'

Natalie looked at them like they were crazy. 'Are you Mormons?' She croaked. 'I don't believe in God.'

Selena shook her head, her gentle smile on her face. 'We're not Mormons,' she said. 'We're your neighbours.' She gestured vaguely away from the house, knowing she was stretching the truth, but willing to try it anyway.

'I've never seen you before,' Natalie said, then stopped still, her heart beating quickly beneath her sweatshirt.

Except what she'd said wasn't true, was it? She had seen them before.

'You were staring at my house. Standing on the footpath staring at my house.' She had a sudden image of the two men leering at her from the shadows and blanched. 'I have to go back inside now,' she said, trying not to look at the women or the garage behind them, or the trees and the shadows that moved behind them. 'I want you to go away now.'

Selena took another tiny step closer. 'We were looking at your house the other day,' she said. 'Wondering if we ought to introduce ourselves.' She stretched out her spirit, exuding calmness and reassurance.

Dandy held out the biscuit tin she'd stashed in her bag. 'We brought you some muffins. As a gift.' She hoped Tara wouldn't miss them before she could explain their disappearance.

Natalie's eyes widened and she shuffled a step backwards, shaking her head. 'No,' she said. 'Please go away. Leave me alone.'

The last was an anguished cry and Natalie would have slammed the door closed already if it wasn't for the box on the doorstep.

Selena bent down and picked it up, held it out to her. 'Here,' she said. 'Take this, Natalie. We'll be on our way. Thank you for talking to us.'

Natalie snatched the box from her, backed up and closed the door before running back to the kitchen, setting the box on the table and collapsing with relief into a chair.

She held her head for a while, thinking in a minute she'd get up and make a nice cup of tea. A nice cup of tea did wonders.

Where did she get that thought from?

She shook her head. She didn't know those women. They were strangers. She'd never spoken to them before in her life.

'Well,' Dandy said, closing the gate behind them. 'I don't think we can call that a roaring success.'

'No,' Selena sighed. 'She's too frightened to even let us talk to her.'

'Such a shame,' Dandy mused as they turned back down the hill towards their home. 'It's no life for a pretty thing like her being stuck inside the house.' She shook her head. 'It's no life for anyone.' A glance at Selena. 'What makes people so afraid, do you think?'

'It's easy to become afraid,' Selena answered.

'You don't seem to have much trouble with fear,' Dandy said, then thought further on it. 'Or me. I've never had much, and I lost my Frank and did without him all those years during the war and so on, and things were plenty hard during all those times, but I kept on. I always had the feeling that things would be all right.' She put the biscuit tin back in her bag. 'Why do some of us manage, and others don't?'

Selena thought of the small child hiding in her makeshift tent, with only a well-worn stuffed bear for company.

'A lot of it has to do with resiliency. Which is something we learn – or not – as we grow up, and a lot of things contribute to that.' Selena pursed her lips, thinking. 'I don't think our culture has done much for us, really.'

'What do you mean?'

'We no longer grow up knowing we have a soul's purpose – or even, much of the time, that we have a soul – and so we flounder in the great river of our lives.'

'You believe we all have a purpose?' Dandy asked.

'I do.' Selena smiled at her. 'It isn't always necessarily grand. We don't all come here with the need to do big things by our culture's standards. But we do all come here, every time, seeking the joy and privilege of being flesh and blood.'

'Not a lot of joy in it for many, however,' Dandy said.

'No,' Selena agreed on a sigh. 'We've lost the knack of joy and contentment.'

They walked along in silence for a time, until Dandy voiced the question they were both asking themselves.

'So, how do we help her?' Dandy shook her head. 'Is it really any of our business?'

'Yes,' Selena said softly. 'It's our business.' She sighed. 'But as to how we're going to get her to let us help, that I do not know.'

'We can't force ourselves on her again,' Dandy said. 'I wouldn't even feel good about going back to her door.' She shook her head to emphasise her words.

'I agree,' Selena said. 'Which means, we do it the other way.'

Dandy paused, looked at Selena with confusion. Selena stopped walking too, and stood gazing at the rhododendron trees, their curling, curved trunks and branches shading either side of the path. The silver in her dark hair gleamed in the glimpses of sunlight.

Selena turned to Dandy and smiled. She stretched out her arms in a gesture of openness.

'We allow things to flow into their right place,' she said. 'And we align them to do so, and we ask the Goddess and Natalie's own kin to aid us.' She turned back to the path. 'And so, it will happen.'

'It will happen?'

'The opportunity to speak properly with Natalie, and to help her in whatever way she needs, will come.'

'Simple as that?'

'All things, when they come down to it, are simple,' Selena said, then smiled radiantly at Dandy. 'Simple does not mean easy, however.' She shook her head slightly. 'When we are in the flow of our purpose, things open up to us, we are led along the path that is right for us. But there is nothing to say that this path does not go through some thorny places, however.'

Dandy nodded, digesting this. She thought of all the hard times she'd had in her life, all the times she'd got through by hanging onto her faith that she was strong enough to deal with it, and that if she could just hang on long enough, she would get through and things would turn out fine.

'Not everyone manages to hang on through those thorny places,' she said out loud, thinking of the woman they'd just glimpsed, prisoner in her own house, held there by her fear.

'No,' Selena said with genuine sorrow. 'Which is why we must build such strong foundations, must learn to flex our spirits, and to learn the larger picture of the world.'

'Which is?' Dandy asked, curious to hear what Selena would say.

Selena smiled at her. 'One which you and I know and live with every day – that we are not alone, that this life is but one small part we play, that there is more to everything, and that at heart, the world is beautiful. We can be beautiful.'

Dandy nodded. She thought that about summed it all up.

24

Rue hung around the back door looking slightly sick. Damien raised his eyebrows at her.

'I'm sure it's going to be fine,' he said.

Rue shook her head. 'I've never felt so nervous in my life.'

Damien laughed. 'You're having your friends come over,' he said. 'What's to be nervous about?' He leaned against the doorway. Outside, the sun was shining, although a cool wind rustled around the house like it had important business to get on with. Clover was in the garden, humming to herself and playing with the set of model animals she'd begged to have. Damien grinned, watching her as she lined them up, nodding and singing, a big adventure going on in her mind.

He looked back over at Clover's sister. 'Rue,' he said, softening his voice. 'What's really bothering you about your friends coming to visit? How can I help?'

Rue shook her head, stuffed her hands deep in the

pocket of the full black skirt she'd recently made, and peered out from under the brim of her black sun hat.

'I've never had friends over,' she said, her voice low, fretting.

'Then I'm glad you can now,' Damien told her.

But Rue just nodded.

'There's something else, isn't there?' Damien prompted.

Rue turned around and looked at Damien, indecision looming large on her face. 'I told them about Selena,' she said at last. 'And now I keep thinking I should have asked Selena if I could before I um, did.' She looked down at her feet, scuffed a boot across the path.

Damien wanted to reach out and hug her. Instead, he smiled. 'Rue,' he said. 'Selena isn't going to mind you talking about her to your friends.'

Rue shook her head. 'She's so different. How can you be sure?'

'Well, for starters, Selena is completely comfortable with who and what she is, and never makes any effort to hide it from anyone.'

Damien remembered Selena telling him and Tara how she'd come to be looking for the children she'd sought. I dreamed it, she'd said. I spoke to the spirit of their mother.

No, Selena didn't mind being herself.

Rue still looked a little sick.

'And also, this is important, so listen to me,' Damien said, straightening.

Rue looked at him from under her hat, dark eyes showing a glimmer of hope.

Damien continued. 'These are your friends. It's okay to talk about our lives with our friends. It's part of what makes a friendship a good thing – we share stuff, and feel accepted, right? Selena and the rest of us will be totally okay for you to be able to talk about us with your friends. I can say that knowing it is the complete truth, hand on my heart.'

He actually put his hand on his heart and grinned at Rue. 'All right, then?'

Rue nodded. 'Yeah,' she said. 'I suppose so.' Her shoulders tightened in a shrug. 'I guess I'm just not used to having friends – or a family.'

Now Damien did hug the girl, stepping forward and wrapping his arms around her. 'I'm so proud of you,' he said, then stood back. 'And I love the new clothes.'

Rue relaxed, did a little twirl and grinned self-consciously. 'It's pretty neat, I think.' She shook her head. 'I can't thank Tara enough for the sewing machine.'

'I reckon she knows how much of a hit it is with you,' Damien said. 'You deserve it, and you've a real talent for designing and making clothes. We all love seeing you use it.'

Rue shoved her hands back in the skirt's big pockets, but now she was glowing from pleasure.

'I think they're here.' Damien nodded to the gaggle of teenaged girls coming up the driveway, their hair shining in the sun, their faces bright, turned towards the house.

Rue flashed a smile at him then turned, met them halfway.

'You never mentioned living in a mansion, Rue my friend,' Ebony said, flinging an arm over Rue's shoulder and gazing up at the house, shaking her head.

'I'm pretty sure I said it was big.'

'There's big, and there's mansion.' Ebony gave a low

whistle. 'I think we need to get you a dictionary, so you know the difference.'

Suze, face tipped upwards to gaze at the house, nodded, mouth open. 'For once, I agree with Ebony,' she said. 'This place is big. And old.'

'Really old,' Sophie added.

But Rue shook her head. 'It's not that old. Before Selena came here, she lived in a house built in the seventeenth century.' She grinned at her friends, glad to see them. 'That's old. And it was built on the foundations of a house that was burnt down.'

'Seventeenth century?' Sophie was wide-eyed, gazing at Rue.

'Was burnt down?' Ebony asked, looking pointedly at Rue. 'Not just ordinary everyday burnt down?'

Rue laughed. 'In the early sixteen hundreds, the then Lady of the Grove, which is the line of priestesses from which Selena is descended, was hanged as a witch, and her house – Hawthorn House – was set fire to and burnt to the ground.'

The other girls stared at Rue.

'I am so glad I met you,' Ebony said at last. 'Between you and Sophie here with her ghost, I am living the life I dreamed of my whole...life.'

'Yeah,' Suze said, nudging Ebony in the ribs with her elbow. 'All fifteen years of it, most of which you spent crawling around in nappies.'

Ebony pushed out her lip in a mock pout then burst out laughing. 'All the same,' she said. 'I am living the dream.' She grinned at Rue and took her by the arm. 'Lead the way, my friend. Introduce us to everyone in your mansion.'

Rue nodded, and they headed for the garden. Clover looked up at them, then stood up with a plastic bird in her hand.

'These your frien's, Rue?' she asked.

'Yeah,' Rue answered, feeling her cheeks colour slightly with a sudden burst of pleasure. These were her friends. An unlikely bunch, perhaps, but she wasn't sure she'd ever find better.

'Hiya little one,' Ebony said, then dropped Rue's arm and stepped forward, holding her palm up. 'Gimme a high five already.'

Clover giggled, transferred her bird carefully to her other hand and slapped her palm against Ebony's. Then she squinted at Ebony and Rue recognised the look on her face.

'Oh, no you don't, Clover Bee,' she said, and pushed Suze forward. 'This is Suze. Say hello to her.'

But Ebony bent down so that she was at Clover's level. 'Oh no don't what, Clover?' she asked.

Clover blinked at her, reached out and touched Ebony's blonde hair. 'You got pretty hair,' she said.

Rue relaxed a fraction.

'Thanks, little Bee,' Ebony said. 'You're not so shabby yourself.'

Clover giggled, then looked down at the bird in her hand and held it up. 'I got a bird,' she said.

'So you have. A blackbird.'

'Yeah,' Clover agreed. 'He's my frien','

'Good friend to have.'

Rue realised her hand was still clamped on Suze's arm and she dropped it.

Clover squatted down and looked at her collection of

animals. Tara had bought them for her from the bookshop and they were solid and well made. She picked one out and held it up for Ebony to see.

'Here,' she said. 'This is your frien'.'

Rue, who had expected Clover to open her mouth and say something freaky, hadn't expected this, of all things. A great curiosity welled up in her.

'What do you mean?' she asked.

Clover looked at her. 'This her frien',' she said. Then pursed her lips. 'Her spirit kin,' she said carefully, remembering what Selena had called Blackbird and Hind.

'Whoa,' Ebony said and looked at Rue, eyes wide and gleaming. 'We're not even in the house yet, and the fun has begun.' She turned back to Clover and shook her head. 'Spirit kin?' she asked, and took the model elephant, turning it over in her hands as though she'd been given a treasure. She looked up at Rue.

'What's spirit kin?' she asked.

Rue remembered what Selena had said just the other night. She licked her lips. 'They're guides who walk with us through our lives. Some are always with us, others come and go for specific purposes.'

Ebony's eyes widened. She looked back at Clover. 'And you see an elephant walking with me?'

Clover nodded, matter of fact. 'El'phant always with you,' she said.

Ebony rocked back on her heels, stunned. Finally, she handed the plastic elephant back to Clover. 'Thanks,' she said.

'You welcome,' Clover replied, a sunny smile returning to her face. She put the elephant down with the other birds and creatures, then turned to look at Rue.

And saw Sophie. Clover's mouth dropped open, and she gaped at the teenager.

Rue saw her and glanced at Sophie. 'Clover?' she asked.

But Clover just frowned, looking at something none of the rest of them could see, and then she was bolting for the house.

'S'lena!' she yelled.

'What is that about?' Ebony said.

Suze shook her head, looked at Sophie. 'She saw something when she looked at you.' She turned and blinked over at Rue. 'You never said your sister was psychic.'

But Rue was looking at the house, wondering. 'Yeah,' she said absently. 'Totally, absolutely psychic.' She gestured at the door. 'Come on, let's see what's going on.'

Sophie didn't move. 'What did she see?' she asked.

Rue glanced back at her and shook her head.

'Ghost dust,' Ebony said. 'You've got it all over you.'

Sophie stared at Ebony. 'That's not really...a thing, is it?'

'Of course not,' Suze said, coming and putting her arm around Sophie, then looking at Rue. 'Is it?'

Rue didn't have a clue. She went inside. 'Clover?' she shouted, then saw Damien coming out of the big walk-in pantry. 'Hi,' she said. 'Did you see Clover come tearing through here?'

'I heard her calling for Selena,' Damien said, then looked at Rue's guests. 'Gidday,' he said. 'I'm Damien. I live here with Rue and Clover.'

'Shit,' Rue said. 'Sorry, I didn't mean to be rude. Damien – this is Ebony, Suze, and Sophie.'

'This is a cool house,' Suze said.

'And you've only just seen the kitchen,' Damien grinned. 'Can I get any of you anything?'

'Can I have a glass of water, please?' Sophie asked. She felt like the day was running ahead of her.

Or running over her.

Damien got her a glass without a word, a small frown creasing his forehead. Then, he couldn't help it. 'Are you feeling all right?' he asked.

Sophie nodded. 'I just need some water,' she said.

'Sophie is being haunted,' Ebony said, and she peered out of the kitchen at the big entranceway. There was a fancy staircase there and she thought Clover must have gone running up it. 'I think Clover might have seen by what.'

Damien had to run these words back though his head before he could make them sound like anything sensible.

'What the heck the who now? Haunted?' He looked over at Sophie. 'Sit down at the table. You look like you're about to fall down.'

Sophie sank down into a seat and opened her mouth to say something, but took a sip of the water instead, because she didn't know what to say.

She wanted to snap at Ebony that she shouldn't have said anything, but the truth was, she was too tired. And wouldn't it be a relief if someone other than the four of them knew and believed her?

No one at home believed her. Her mother just rolled her eyes and told her to quit bothering her.

Clover came running back into the room, then skidded to a stop, suddenly shy, looking from under her curls at Sophie.

'I got S'lena,' she said.

'Yeah,' Rue asked her. 'But why?'

But Clover, uncharacteristically for her, just shook her head. She had no idea how to describe what she was seeing when she looked at Rue's friend.

She looked at Selena when she walked into the kitchen. 'Wha' is she?' she asked.

Ebony gazed at Selena and listened to her heart beating loudly under her shirt. For once, she couldn't decide on a single thing to say.

This was Selena, she thought. The woman who had spoken to spirits and listened to the wind and travelled all the way around the world to find two children because of it.

Ebony's mouth was dry.

Here was a real priestess and she was standing there in the same room as her.

Selena smiled at the cluster of girls. 'Hello,' she said. 'I'm Selena. Rue might have mentioned me?'

Ebony nodded wordlessly. Had she ever, she thought. Selena was old, Ebony thought, but she was beautiful. It was like she glowed, and Ebony took an unconscious step closer. Selena was wearing a long, dark blue dress, similar to the things that Ebony's mother wore, but she looked like...like a priestess, Ebony thought. Selena's thick hair was caught in a knot at the back of her head, held there by something that flashed silver, something Celtic in design, and Ebony wished she could look at it more closely, because it seemed to have a long necked and legged bird in it.

'I've told them a bit about you,' Rue admitted. Then shook her head. She wasn't going to get embarrassed about that again, not right now, at least. 'What did Clover see?' she asked instead.

Selena looked at Clover, who stood tucked beside Rue, staring at the girl seated at the table, a glass of water in front of her.

She didn't answer Rue's question directly but held up a hand and looked at the girl at the table.

'What's your name?' she asked, moving over to sit down. She looked at the group of teenagers, stopping at Rue's reddening cheeks.

'Why don't you all sit down?' she said. 'And tell me what's going on?'

25

For half a minute, everyone was talking at once, until Selena held up her hands again. Silence fell around the table.

'One at a time, please,' she said. Then shook her head a little. 'From the beginning.'

Rue looked down at her hands. They were trembling slightly. She should have told Selena all about it, she thought.

Why hadn't she?

'Rue?' Selena asked.

Damien, looking at the four girls sitting around the table with heads down and cheeks red, took Clover by the hand.

'Let's go play with your animals outside, shall we?'

'Wanna stay,' Clover said.

'Yeah, me too,' Damien answered. 'But I reckon we should leave them to it.'

Clover nodded reluctantly, glanced over her shoulder at

the girl Rue had called Sophie, then trailed outside with Damien.

'Well?' Selena prompted. 'I know something's going on.'

'What did Clover see?' Rue asked. 'When she looked at Sophie?' She paused. 'What do you see?'

'Ghost dust, I told ya,' Ebony said, but she said it low, almost under her breath.

Selena gazed over at the girl called Sophie and smiled comfortingly. 'It's all right,' she said. 'Both Clover and I are particularly sensitive to things of spirit.' She paused a moment. 'And you have...' She glanced at Ebony, her lips quirking. 'Ghost dust on you.'

'See,' Ebony said, lifting her head in amazement. 'I said so, didn't I?'

'It's not really a thing, is it?' Rue asked. 'Ghost dust?'

'Well,' Selena said. 'It's not really dust, no. Just...an echo, perhaps.'

The girls looked at her in awe. Until Selena gazed pointedly back at them.

They told her about Sophie's ghost.

Sophie took something out of her bag and put it on the table. She slid it over to Selena with a dry mouth.

'Ebony was snapping pictures,' she said.

'And taking video,' Ebony interrupted, then shook her head. 'But there was nothing on that.' She craned to see the Polaroid. 'I'd forgotten about those,' she said.

'They were on my bed, after you were all gone.'

Selena looked down at the photo. It was of Sophie, but there was something partially obscuring her. A white mist in front of her.

'My room really is haunted, isn't it?' Sophie asked.

Selena nodded. 'I think we can safely say that, yes.'

'Rue told you what else happened, right?' Ebony said. 'With the Ouija board?'

Selena lifted her gaze to meet Rue's. 'She hasn't told me any of this,' she said mildly.

'It was really weird,' Ebony said, throwing an astonished looked at Rue.

Selena nodded at Rue. 'Perhaps you would like to fill me in now?'

Her cheeks burning a dark red, Rue nodded. She wasn't quite sure why she hadn't told Selena any of this. She'd meant to. Hadn't she?

'Um, first we were talking to Sophie's ghost,' Rue said.

'But it wasn't very good at communicating,' Suze broke in. She cleared her throat. 'It was my idea, by the way, to make an Ouija board and use it – I don't want Rue to get in trouble for it when it was all my idea.'

Selena shook her head. 'Rue isn't in trouble.'

Suze was nonplussed for a moment. 'Oh,' she said. 'Okay then, that's good.' She looked wide-eyed at Rue.

Ebony waded back into the conversation. 'Rue said a prayer to start us off, so that no one bad or who meant us harm would come through. So, we were being careful.'

Selena nodded.

Rue was staring at the table.

'Anyway,' Ebony said, with another glance at Rue. 'First, like Suze said, Sophie's ghost came through.'

'It's not my ghost,' Sophie said. 'I just have to live there, is all.'

'Yeah.' Ebony shook her head. 'Anyway, it – she – came

through and just spelt out *home* a couple times, and then we all smelt perfume.'

'That's how I mostly know she's around,' Suze said. 'I smell this really flowery, old-fashioned perfume. At first, I thought it was just the roses and stuff in the garden.' She shook her head. 'But it's not. It's the ghost.'

Selena nodded. 'What happened next?' she asked patiently.

'Well, that's when it got a bit strange,' Suze said, when it was clear that Rue wasn't going to pick up the story. 'Suddenly the crystal bowl we were using as a you know –' She tried to think of the word.

'Planchette,' Rue said in a low voice. She'd looked it up.

'Yeah, that thing. Anyway, it started moving much faster, and then it spelt out these letters that I figured out were actually dates, in roman numerals.'

'Dates?' Selena asked.

Dandy had come into the room, stopped in surprise at the sight of Selena and the girls around the table, and hesitated. Selena waved her over.

'They've been using a spirit board,' Selena said.

Dandy's eyebrows rose almost to her hairline. She sat down. 'I have to hear this, then,' she said.

Selena nodded, looked back at Suze, and nodded for her to continue.

Suze cleared her throat. 'Right,' she said. 'Well, it gave us one date after another, and we were all sure we were talking to someone else now, not Sophie's ghost.'

'It's not my ghost,' Sophie repeated.

Selena looked at Dandy. 'There's a spirit that's been making her presence known in Sophie's house.'

'Ah,' Dandy said. 'I see.'

Rue lifted her head and looked at Selena. 'When we asked who this new spirit was, it spelt out *I am Rue*.' She knotted her fingers together.

There was silence for a long moment, and everyone looked at Selena, to see what she would say about that.

But it was Rue who broke the silence. 'I've been dreaming about her,' she said.

'Who?' Ebony asked. 'You never told me this?'

Rue hunched her shoulders a little. 'I thought they were just dreams, until right now, actually.'

'What do you mean?' Selena asked.

'There's this woman in my dreams,' Rue said, twisting her fingers around, a frown between her eyes. She shook her head. 'I don't know. I just got the strong feeling, when Suze was talking about it, that the spirit talking through the Ouija board is the same one I've been dreaming of.'

'Who is she in your dreams?'

Rue looked across the table and winced. 'I don't know. She's maybe from a long time ago, and she's wearing this blue dress. Except it's not really a blue dress, it's more like a long piece of fabric, held up at the shoulders with some sort of pins or broaches.' She tugged her hands apart and indicated her shoulders. 'I could draw it, I guess.'

Selena was nodding. 'What is she doing, when she appears in your dreams?'

Rue wrinkled her nose. 'I'm not sure. She's doing things I don't know what they are.' She looked down at the table, then met Selena's eyes. 'Sometimes I'm looking at her, and sometimes I'm like, inside her. I am her.' She blinked, almost winced. 'And I think we're doing magic.'

The words seemed to hang over the table for a long moment.

'The second spirit said they were Rue's past life, or lives, I guess,' Suze said, her voice slightly squeaky.

But Ebony was looking excited. 'That's right! And now you're dreaming of her – that's amazing.'

'It is amazing,' Selena agreed. 'I hope you're writing these dreams down?'

Rue flushed, then nodded. 'You told Damien he should write down his dreams, and he said I should do the same.'

'That's a very good idea. An aspect of yourself is obviously wanting to make contact with you.'

Dandy looked with interest at Selena. 'That can happen?'

'It happens all the time,' Selena said. 'But since contact, not just with our past lives, so to speak, but with all manner of ancestors, happens most often during our dreams, most of us miss it.'

Again, there was silence around the table, then Ebony shifted in her chair.

'I'm going to start writing down my dreams,' she said.

'I don't remember any of mine,' Suze said. 'Or not many, just the weird ones, right?'

'How do we know what they mean, though?' Sophie asked. She shook her head. 'Mine are always about going to school, and not being able to find my classroom or stuff like that.' She trailed off, her cheeks turning pink.

Dandy began laughing. She looked at Selena. 'You've got your work cut out for you now,' she said. 'Development circles, and now a dream group.'

Selena wasn't sure that was funny at all. What was she

getting herself in for? Back in Wilde Grove, it had been simple – teach Morghan.

Here it seemed more of a case of – teach everyone.

'Well,' she said. 'We'll work something out.' Then she took a breath. 'So,' she said. 'Rue. Do write down those dreams and pay attention to them. I've a feeling they're important for you to look at.'

She looked around at the other girls, nodded. 'What are we going to do about Sophie's ghost?'

Sophie sighed. 'It's not my ghost.'

Selena smiled. 'No, my dear. You're right.'

'I've got some ghost hunting equipment,' Ebony said, practically chortling.

Selena's eyes widened. 'What is ghost hunting equipment?'

'Sounds dangerous,' Dandy added.

Ebony shook her head. 'It's not dangerous - it's just a couple cameras, and an EMF meter, which measure the electromagnetic waves, which are usually stronger when there's a spirit present. Its needle went way up when Soph... I mean the ghost was communicating.' She glanced across at Sophie and grinned.

Selena blinked at her. 'What do you need that for?'

Ebony was aghast. 'To determine whether there's a spirit there? To prove you know, life after death and all that.'

'I don't think we have to prove that,' Selena answered. She glanced at Dandy. 'What I think we need to do, is help the poor soul stuck wandering in Sophie's house.'

Ebony fell into awed appreciation. 'Can we help?' she asked. 'You're going to cross her over, right? Can we help?'

'Please?' Suze added, thinking this was all much more

exciting than she'd ever anticipated one of Ebony's enthusi-asms being. 'I suggested that we needed to help her cross over,' she added.

'I did too,' Sophie said. 'I said it was sad that she's just stuck there in the house she used to live in.' She looked at Selena. 'The house was all done up before my parents bought it a few months ago. We think that's what disturbed the ghost.'

'Yeah,' Ebony added. 'It's well known that home renova-tions and what-not disturb spirits and make them bump around. They don't like you changing the way they had their house.'

Selena nodded. 'I'm sure that's right,' she said. 'I do think we need to do something about her.' She smiled at Sophie. 'You're right too – it is sad that she is still in the house where she lived, instead of moving on to the next world as she should.'

'So, what are we going to do, then?' Rue asked.

Dandy looked over at Selena, a smile on her lips.

'Yes,' she said. 'What are we going to do?'

26

'WHAT ARE YOU GIRLS PLANNING FOR THE REST OF YOUR DAY?'
Damien asked, sitting at the picnic table in the tiny garden
as the girls milled around, their faces dazed and excited.

Selena was going to talk to Sophie's mother – Sophie
didn't have high hopes of that going well, but Selena had
insisted – and sometime the next weekend, would go over to
the house, and see what could be done.

'Oh,' Rue blinked in the sunlight and tried to remember
their original plan. 'Um, we were going to go to the Botanic
Garden to look for sticks suitable for making staves.' She
coloured slightly and glanced for confirmation from the
others.

'I for one,' Ebony said. 'Am still keen on that.'

There was general nodding. Rue looked at Sophie.

'Do you want to?' she asked.

Sophie nodded. 'Yeah,' she said. 'I'd like that.' She felt
rather bedazzled, as though she'd just stepped out of a dim

room inside her head, into the sunlight. She couldn't believe that Rue's foster mother had not only believed them about the ghost but was actually going to do something about it.

Selena, Sophie decided, was brilliant.

'Me come too,' Clover said, gathering up her model animals and dumping them in Damien's lap. She looked expectantly at Rue. 'I get my shoes?'

Rue was about to shake her head, tell Clover she had to stay at home with Damien and the others, but she stopped herself and looked at her friends instead.

'Do you guys mind if she comes with us? We hardly ever get to do anything together anymore.'

'I be very good,' Clover said seriously, her little chin tipped up. 'I wanna staff too.'

Ebony jumped forward, picked Clover up and swung her around until she squealed, then set her on her hip and looked at the others.

'I say we take the kid,' she said.

Rue relaxed and grinned. 'You hear that, Clover?' she said. 'You're part of the gang.'

'Grove,' Ebony corrected her.

Selena, come out to stand in the doorway, spoke up. 'What did you say?'

Ebony looked slightly abashed. She set Clover back on the ground and coloured a little. 'Um,' she said. 'Rue said gang, and I said grove.' She winced. 'You know – like a grove of priestesses.'

Ebony straightened, and some of her natural bravado came back. After all, this woman was a priestess herself, so she knew all about it, and she believed them about Sophie's spirit, so Ebony knew Selena was just as cool as Rue had made her out to be.

And today was such a brilliant day. She'd been told by the little kid, Clover, that she had an elephant as a spirit animal.

Which was very awesome.

'All of us want to be priestesses,' she said. 'I have dedicated myself to Athena, and Rue here to your Elen of The Ways.' She nodded.

'I see,' Selena said, with a glance at Damien, who had his eyebrows lifted, a wide grin on his face. She looked back at the girl Ebony, with her very fair hair. She looked a little like Clarice, she thought, and felt the familiar pang of desire for Wilde Grove; felt it and let it go.

She was here.

With, apparently, her own little grove of apprentice priestesses. She shook her head, a small smile lifting the corners of her mouth.

Life was an odd thing.

'Best you all go looking for fallen wood for your staves, then,' she said. 'And when you've found them, I'll show you how to finish and consecrate them.'

The girls, all four of them, stared at her with round eyes, and Selena smiled, then turned back into the house, the group erupting into excited babbling behind her.

THEY WALKED ACROSS THE ROAD AND SLIPPED ONTO THE PATH that wound through the century old rhododendron dell, where the trees grew taller than usual in their own little ecosystem, and gracefully twisted around each other and over the pathways in a dance.

'I can't believe Selena is going to talk to your parents about the ghost – spirit, I mean,' Ebony said to Sophie. She'd decided to call it, and all others she came across, spirits. It seemed cooler.

Clover, hanging onto Rue's hand, twisted around to look at Sophie with wide eyes.

'Can you really see something, Clover?' Sophie asked.

Clover blinked, then nodded, but she was frowning. She didn't know how to describe things like this. Not out loud in words. 'Is like you gotta smell,' she said.

Ebony laughed. 'A smell?'

Rue looked at her sister. 'You mean, being around a spirit leaves a sort of smell?'

But Clover shook her head. 'Not a real smell,' she said.

'Residue,' Ebony pronounced. 'Like ghost dust, right?'

Clover looked at her and giggled. 'Ghost dust,' she said, and giggled some more.

Sophie ducked under a branch, then untangled it from her hair. She had thin, fine hair, and grimaced as it snagged. 'Selena could see it too,' she said, free again. 'I think so, anyway.' She nodded. She didn't mind having ghost dust all over her, she guessed, if people like Selena could see it and wanted to do stuff about it.

Rue nodded. 'I wish I could see spirits.'

'Me too.' Ebony brushed her fingers through a leafy branch, then swung round to walk backwards a few steps, facing her friends. 'Do you think she'll let us go with her? When she goes to help the spirit cross over, I mean?'

'She said she'd think about it,' Suze answered. She glanced at Sophie. 'You'll be there; it's your house.'

'I won't be there if Selena says I can't be,' Sophie answered.

'Well, I hope she lets us all be there,' Ebony said. 'I think I've found what I want to do with my life.'

'What's that?' Rue asked. 'You mean ghost hunting?'

But Ebony shook her head. 'No,' she said, then corrected herself. 'Well, not really. I mean, I want to go find them still, go into haunted houses and so on, but I want to talk to the spirits, help them cross over and whatever, you know?'

Rue nodded. 'Do you think we could learn to do that?' she asked.

Ebony stuck an elbow in Rue's side. 'I bet you could – you're already dreaming of doing magic.'

Rue shook her head. 'I don't know what those dreams are about.'

'I bet you were a priestess in your past life, and now you're trying to remember it all so you can be one again.' Ebony nodded emphatically. 'We can do it together,' she said.

'Do what?' Suze asked.

'Help spirits,' Ebony said, and stopped walking to face the others. 'Like, find out who murdered them, then when the killers are brought to justice, we can help the spirits cross over.'

Suze's eyes were like saucers. 'What?' she spluttered. 'Where'd the murder bit come from?'

Ebony just shrugged. 'Or it might not be that dramatic. But still – you get the idea, right?'

They did. They all got the idea.

A thought occurred to Rue. 'Do you think Selena could always see spirits? Some people can, can't they? Like they're born that way, or something.' Rue paused, looking down at Clover. 'Or do you think she learnt to?'

'Probably learnt to,' Ebony said. 'As part of her training. After all – you're not born a priestess, are you?'

'I guess not,' Rue said.

'But you can definitely have died as one,' Ebony chortled. 'Hurry up and dream some more, Rue. We want to know every one of those lives.' She shook her head, thinking what an amazing idea that was. 'I want to get in contact with my past lives,' she said suddenly. 'I wonder who I was?'

'Not the Queen of England, and not Cleopatra, either,' Suze said, giggling. 'So don't get any ideas!'

'You don't know this,' Ebony said. 'I could have been either, or even both.' She shook her head, lips quirking. 'But probably I was some poor sassy Irish lass who perished during the great potato famine.'

'We probably all were,' Rue said, but she was almost trembling with excitement. She was definitely going to write down all her dreams. She glanced down at Clover, who was standing beside her on the path, her little face serious as she tried to follow the conversation.

'Come on,' she said. 'Let's keep going. It's cooler out of the sun.'

They turned their feet to the path again, up into the garden proper. At the next intersection of paths, Rue stopped and looked around.

'Where do you think we should look first?' she asked.

'For branches, I mean? There ought to be a few around – we had some windy days during the week.'

'I don't suppose there are any olive trees in here?' Ebony said hopefully. 'Olive trees are associated with Athena, so that's what I'd like best.'

Rue nodded, her mind turning to what tree might be coupled with Elen. She didn't know if Elen was really her goddess. It wasn't like she'd had a sign or anything, but she didn't even know if it worked that way. But Elen was who Selena followed, and who the Wilde Grove had always followed, so Rue thought it would be good enough for her too.

'I want one made of pōhutukawa,' Suze said. 'I don't know if we'd find a branch long enough to make a staff, though.'

'Pōhutukawa?' Ebony asked. 'Why on earth that?'

But Suze just shrugged. 'I love pōhutukawa trees,' she said. 'When we went on holiday to Auckland one year, there were heaps of them all along the beaches. And I just really like them.'

'There's one up the top of the hill,' Rue said. 'Its flowers aren't red though. They're pink, I think.' She paused. 'Or yellow. It's really special, anyway.'

'Good,' Suze said. 'That's what I want, then.' She turned to Sophie. 'What about you?'

Sophie nibbled at her lip, thinking about it. 'Um. I don't know much about trees,' she said. 'Maybe I'll just look for one while we walk?'

That seemed a good enough plan.

'I think I want oak,' Rue decided. 'There's an oak grove not far from here. In fact it's just past the Mediterranean part of the garden. Which is where I'd guess we'd find an olive tree if there is one.'

She looked down at Clover. 'You want an oak staff too?'

Clover didn't know, but she'd have whatever Rue had. She looked up at her big sister with a shining face and nodded. Then blinked. 'I want a long stick like my wizards.'

'Wizards?' Several of them spoke at once.

Clover shrugged. 'They look after me in the far 'n wide,' she said.

Ebony shook her head slowly. 'I am so glad I met you, Clover. You are one cool kid.' She looked around at the group. 'Hell, I'm glad I met all of you!' She slapped Rue on the shoulder. 'Lead on, Rue of the Oaks.'

Rue laughed, but the impromptu name rather pleased her, and she took the path to their left, leading them across the sloping hill. Her steps were light, and she felt strangely exhilarated.

She was glad they'd all met, as well.

'You know your way around here really well,' Suze said.

'Clover and I lived just up the hill from here,' Rue said. 'And we used to come here a lot, didn't we, Clover Bee?'

Clover nodded. 'There's ducks,' she said. 'And swings. Rue pushed me real high on the swings.'

'Well,' Ebony said, doing a leaping little dance on the path. 'When we've found what we're after, let's go see these ducks, ask how you doin' ducks!'

Clover giggled. Ebony was funny.

'All right,' Rue said. 'This is my favourite part of the Mediterranean garden.' She led them down a short path to a stone-paved terrace, with a square pool and fountain in the middle of it. There was a low columned stone fence at the front overlooking the lower levels of the garden, right down to the road at the bottom.

'Wow,' Ebony breathed. 'How come I didn't know about this place?' She spun slowly around and shook her head. 'I've lived in this city my whole life and never been here. I am going to have to have serious words with my mother. She has been depriving me of culturally and educationally appropriate expeditions.'

Clover tugged away from Rue's hand and ran over to the shallow pool, dropping to her knees and dangling her hands over into the water.

'It is pretty neat here,' Rue agreed.

'Neat? It's more than that,' Ebony said, clasping her hands to her chest and spinning around again in another slow circle, shaking her head as she took it all in. 'I love this place. I have found my spiritual home. I'm going to come here every week and make offerings to Athena. Like it's her home away from home.'

'Can you do that?' Sophie asked.

Suze shook her head. 'Ebony does whatever she wants.' She punched her cousin lightly on the arm. 'Isn't that right?'

'Ebony does the Goddess's bidding,' Ebony said. 'And the Goddess wants offerings given here on a weekly basis.' Ebony grinned, then shook her head. 'Seriously though. This is an amazing place, and I'm totally going to do it.' She looked away from the terrace and at the trees. 'Any of these an olive tree, do you think?'

'No idea what an olive tree looks like,' Suze answered.

'Me neither,' Sophie said.

Rue, sitting on the wide rim of the pool now, next to Clover who was splashing in the water, looked around thoughtfully. 'I don't think so,' she said. 'Now that we're here, I think it's mostly shrubs and stuff in the Mediterranean garden. And this terrace, of course.'

'Which is worth the visit on its own,' Ebony said. 'So, let's keep going then, and see what we see.' She nodded happily.

'This is going to be the best day ever!'

27

THERE WERE FIVE OR SIX GORGEOUS BIG OAK TREES STANDING on the hillside, spreading their branches out to touch the sunshine. Rue stopped on the path, then grinned at Clover and skipped around onto the grass under the trees.

The acorns were just starting to fall, and Clover dropped to her knees and scooped up one in each hand.

'What are these?' she asked.

'Acorns,' Suze answered, squatting down with her and picking one up and showing Clover. 'Look, it's wearing a little hat.' She dug in her backpack and found a felt tip pen, drew a face on the acorn and gave it to Clover, who held it up with glee.

'Look Rue,' she called. 'The 'corn gotta face an' he's wearin' a hat!' She put the acorn carefully down and took off her own little backpack and began filling it with acorns. 'Goin' to make a fam'ly of 'corns,' she said.

The other girls roamed around, peering at the ground, looking for sticks that might make a nice, solid staff. They didn't really know what either staves or wands were used for, but the thought that Selena would teach them was exciting. Rue picked up a good sturdy branch that came up just above her waist when she turned it end up on the ground. She tested it to make sure it wasn't rotting, but it was solid, and nicely knobbed part way down in a way that made a natural place for her to rest her hand.

She was delighted with it.

Ebony, who had ranged farther away, came back brandishing a slim length of wood. She was grinning broadly in triumph.

'Well,' she said, re-joining the group. 'I've found my staff.'

'I've found mine too,' Rue said, holding up her length of oak. She frowned at Ebony's.

'What tree is that from?' she asked.

Ebony laughed, tapping her fingers on the stick. 'Something called a quaking aspen. Which totally tickles my fancy.'

Rue nodded. 'I like it,' she said. It was completely different to her piece of oak, but that was all right. She turned to Sophie. 'What about you? Have you found anything?'

Sophie shook her head. 'I'll look for something as we go,' she said. Then grinned. 'A nice big stick like yours.'

Ebony laughed. 'You sound as though you're planning to clobber someone with it once you find it.'

Sophie bared her teeth in a grin, and laughed, shaking her head.

She shrugged, looked over at Suze, who was still on the

ground with Clover. 'We should go find your pōhutukawa tree,' she said.

'And your clobber stick,' Ebony said.

Sophie looked over at Clover. 'We have to fit in a visit to the ducks too, remember.'

'And I'm getting hungry,' Suze said. 'There's a fish and chip shop down there, isn't there? I wouldn't mind that for lunch.'

Rue looked at Clover. 'Ready to go?'

'With about half a tonne of acorns,' Suze laughed.

Rue's eyes widened. 'Wait,' she said. 'We need to thank the trees.'

'Thank the trees?' Suze asked.

'What's this about thanking the trees?' Ebony asked.

'It's something that Selena said,' Rue explained. 'She said that it's important to ask the trees if you can take anything of theirs – although since we're just picking up fallen stuff, we're probably okay not having done that, but we have to thank them afterwards.'

Sophie frowned. 'But they're trees, they're not people.'

Clover got to her feet and went over to the oak tree. She put her arms around it. 'Trees are people,' she said. Then planted a smacking kiss against the trunk. 'Thank you for the 'corns, tree.'

'Selena says all things on this earth have spirit,' Rue said quietly. 'And trees are living beings.' She went over and stood next to Clover, took a breath, and spoke, her cheeks burning at the fact that she was speaking out loud in front of her friends.

But it was important.

'Dear Oak Tree,' she said, casting around for what might

be the proper words. 'Thank you for the branch you let fall to the ground and which I've found. I'm going to use it for a staff, the strength and wisdom of yourself a big part of it. I feel very lucky to have it.'

She glanced at the others, defensive and slightly defiant, but Ebony was grinning.

'We have to go over to my quaking aspen,' she said. 'I need to thank it for its most excellent branch.'

Rue nodded, and they made their way farther around the hillside to where a pair of aspens flanked an off-shooting path.

Clover gazed up at their small green leaves that fluttered in the breeze and pointed at them. 'They dancin',' she said in wonder, then ran up to the trunk of the tree on the left side, and pressed her palms against it. 'Does quakin' mean dancin'?'

Ebony leaned her head back and admired the trees. She nodded. 'You know what, Clover? I reckon it does.' She gave a little shimmy of her own, then laughed as Clover copied her.

'We dancin' like the trees!' Clover crowed and did the wriggling movement again.

Ebony, holding the long branch, stepped up to the other of the aspens and placed a hand on it, ducking her chin solemnly.

'Graceful, dancing aspen,' she said. 'I have a branch from you, which will make a beautiful staff. Thank you for dropping it where I could find it. It's going to be gorgeous and magical just like you.' She looked slyly at Rue for a moment. 'And may I someday make myself quake in awe at the magic we do together.'

Rue grinned.

'Rue?' Clover came sliding over to her, slipping a small hand into hers.

Rue looked down at her. Clover's face was pale, strained. 'What is it?' she asked, shocked by the sudden change.

'I don't like them,' Clover said in a whisper.

Rue looked around. 'Who?'

'Nor do I, little Bee,' Ebony said, joining them in a small cluster and no longer joking around. She gestured to Suze and Sophie, who stepped into the group, and they all watched the two men.

'They look like creeps,' Sophie whispered.

'They bad men,' Clover said.

The two men came slinking down the hill, boots crunching on the gravel path. They saw the girls staring at them and held their gaze as they went past on the main path.

Rue realised she was holding her breath, and that Clover was squeezing her hand tightly. If Clover had been bigger, it would have hurt.

Clover was staring at them as though they were the big bad wolf, heading off to grandma's house.

She was glad they were going a different way, that they wouldn't have to brush past them to get by.

But even the sight of their backs gave her the creeps.

One of them stopped walking, and Rue heard Suze gasp. He turned, looked back at them, lifted his hands into claws.

'Boo!' he shouted, then leered at them, licked his lips, and turned to catch up with his friend.

'What a jerk,' Ebony muttered. 'Creeps like that should stay out of the park.'

Rue shook her head. 'They looked so ordinary,' she said. 'Why were we so afraid of them?'

Clover looked up at her. 'They bad men,' she said.

'That's why,' Ebony said. 'And that's good enough for me – besides, couldn't you feel it? There was something wrong with them.' She shuddered visibly.

They stood clustered together a minute longer, glad the men had taken the path out of their sight.

Rue shook herself. 'I gotta go to the loo,' she said. 'What about you, Clover? Do you have to go too?'

Clover shook her head. 'Nope,' she said.

'Okay.' Rue looked at the others. 'You want to take Clover with you, and I'll meet you at the pōhutukawa tree?'

'We don't know where it is,' Suze said.

'That's easy,' Rue said, and pointed. 'Follow this path, then when you get to a sort of intersection, go straight up to the edge of the path, then turn right. The tree is at the end of that path, where it meets one of the driveways into the carpark.'

'I know the way,' Clover said. 'I show ya.'

'Done deal, Clover Bee,' Ebony said. 'We'll meet you there.'

'Cool.' Rue turned and took the path straight up the hill. She'd nip to the toilet, then meet the others. If they were lucky, the pōhutukawa would have lost a couple branches in the wind.

Rue reached the bathrooms, leaned her staff against the wall and did her business humming a tune under her breath.

She felt good. She thought that Selena would probably

still have a word with her about not mentioning the Ouija board session, but that was all right.

Rue didn't know why she hadn't told her.

Selena had looked at them so kindly, and listened to them so seriously, and that made Rue's heart sing. That and the fact that she was having dreams that might really mean something. She almost couldn't wait to go to sleep that night, to see what happened.

Perhaps there was a way to contact the spirit during the day too. Her past self. What did it want?

Rue smiled, delighted with the day so far. She laughed as she flushed the toilet. She was still shaking her head in wonder when she stepped out into the sunshine a moment later, one hand wrapped around her new staff.

The two guys were loitering outside the loos. One of them blocked the path back to her friends.

The other stood casually on the grass, looking around at the lawn and trees behind him.

Rue looked too. The hairs at the back of her neck stood on end as she hesitated in the doorway to the concrete bathroom block.

What were they doing there? Had they stopped around the corner down the hill to listen to her conversation with her friends?

They must have. Rue was suddenly very glad that Clover hadn't needed to come with her. Whatever was about to happen, Clover was well out of it.

Her skin prickled and she realised her heart was beating fast under her thin tee shirt.

She wanted to retreat back into the toilets, pull the door closed behind her, lock it.

But the locks on the doors were flimsy. They wouldn't hold anyone out. Not if someone wanted to break in.

And these guys did want to. Rue saw that in a second. Saw what was going to happen. She'd go back into the bathroom to hide and one of these guys would come in behind her, pushing the door open, his hand already unbuckling his belt while his mate kept watch.

Even having her staff wouldn't help. It wasn't a clobber stick, even if she needed it to be.

Rue's knees felt close to buckling.

'My friends will be along any minute,' she said, voice thin, uncertain.

She watched the men check around them again, seeing if the way was clear.

And before she knew it, she was running, straight up the drive beside them, sneakers thudding, hair streaming behind her, hand still clamped around her stick. Her breath rasped in her throat.

And then she was at the road, not knowing which direction to go. The road was narrow, there was no place to hide. She lived on this road, but too far away to run to.

Rue flew across the street and dashed onto the track on the opposite side, leading into the bush.

The path was under her feet, and she followed it, but they were running after her, and she realised her mistake.

They'd wanted her to come here.

Here where it was private.

Her side burned, and there were dark flecks in her vision. She couldn't keep going. She was going to faint.

But she didn't faint. Instead, there was a sudden calmness inside her, and she was pushed aside by this stillness, an abrupt, clear focus.

It wasn't Rue who stopped running then, but another part of her, someone she'd been so long ago, lifetime upon lifetimes ago, and this different Rue, one who had once been called Bryn, turned instead to face the way she'd come, and for a moment, she stood still upon the path, her hands making a complicated gesture that Rue, watching from the background far away, didn't recognise, and her mouth uttered sounds Rue didn't know the meaning of.

The air swelled around her, a great pressure, and Bryn pushed it away from her, back towards the men only meters away, their grins wild in the dimness of the bush.

Then they were stumbling, tripping, one smacking his head into a suddenly looming tree, the other falling over him.

Bryn didn't stop to watch. She knew what these men were after, and they weren't going to get it.

Not while she could do something.

She veered off the path, skipping between the trees seeking somewhere to crouch down, to conceal herself.

There was nowhere to hide. The copse of trees was narrow, with nowhere to stay out of sight, nowhere to be hidden.

Bryn straightened, looked briefly around her, and picked up a slim stick the length of her leg. She hefted it for a moment, weighing its strength, then, fist tight around it, she stalked through the trees back to the path.

The path was bordered by stones the size to cup in a hand, and she knocked one out into the path with her foot.

She could hear the men - one of them, at least - stumbling along the path towards her.

Then, she could see him.

He stopped and stared at her, a graze high on his cheek, and he swiped blood from it with the back of a hand, his smile spreading across his face in a wide leer.

Bryn leaned Rue's oaken staff against the nearest tree, not taking her eyes from the man several meters away. The corners of her lips curled up in a small smile of her own, and she grasped her new, shorter, light-weight stick in one hand and with the other, dipped into Rue's pocket.

She brought out a pocket knife, flipped the blade expertly open, never taking her gaze from the man's.

Her smile widened slightly.

She took the knife and put it to the end of the stick, slicing a sliver of wood from it.

Fashioning a sharp point.

The man stared at her, blinked, hesitated.

Bryn let herself smile wider. She knew he wasn't seeing a scared fifteen-year-old. He wasn't even seeing Rue anymore.

He was seeing Bryn, expert huntress, and priestess of the ancient goddess.

She who brings strength and joy and the power to confront everything.

When he turned tail and ran, Bryn laughed.

CLOVER, WHO HAD BEEN DOING FORWARD ROLLS ON THE LAWN by the pōhutukawa tree, stopped suddenly and burst into tears. Suze, startled, knelt down beside her.

'What's the matter?' she asked.

'Rue,' Clover said. 'Got a bad thinkin'.'

'Thinking?' Ebony asked, frowning from where she'd been lounging on the grass.

'I think she means feeling,' Sophie said, and looked around. They'd been waiting by the pōhutukawa tree for a while, but there was still no sign of Rue. 'How long has she been gone?'

Ebony shook her head. She bent and picked up Clover, who sobbed into her shoulder, fright shaking her small body.

'Where are the toilets?' Ebony asked. 'Let's go look for her.' She glanced at the others, a dark thought intruding on the bright day. 'You don't think those men...?'

She was met by shocked looks. Suze put her hand over her mouth, spoke around it.

'Let's go find her,' she said.

They turned, then Ebony shook her head. 'I don't know where the toilets are,' she said. 'I've never been up here before.'

Clover lifted her head. 'That way,' she said, then buried her face in Ebony's neck again.

They went that way.

'Rue!' Suze was running ahead. 'Rue!'

They got to the carpark, where two cars were closed up and locked. A bird from the aviary screamed out, and Ebony jumped.

Suze and Sophie dashed into the women's toilets, then came out a moment later shaking their heads.

'Rue!' Ebony screamed out, then handed Clover over to

Suze and put her hands around her mouth to yell again. 'Rue!'

'Where is she?' Suze said frantically.

'She might have gone back down the hill to where we were,' Sophie said, pointing at the path. 'That way.'

'We should split up, look for her,' Ebony said, then she shook her head. 'No way we should do that - not with those creeps prowling around the place.' She paused. 'She said she'd meet us at the pōhutukawa tree.' She looked at the others. She had a bad feeling about this too.

Clover, her face streaked with tears, lifted an arm - pointed. 'There she is.'

Everyone turned around, knees weak with instant relief, and ran up to Rue, who walked down to meet them.

'What happened?' Ebony cried, flinging her arms around Rue. 'Jeez, we were so frightened.'

Clover clamped onto Rue's leg and sobbed, this time with relief.

Rue untangled herself from Ebony, gave her the staff she was still carrying, and a shorter, sharp stick. She heaved Clover into her arms.

'I'm okay,' she said, but her voice shook.

'What happened?' Suze asked. 'We were so scared when we couldn't find you. We thought those guys had got you.'

Rue shook her head, face white, lips set. 'They tried to.'

'What?'

'They chased me,' Rue said, face pale in the shadows from the great pine trees beside them. 'I thought they were going to get me in the toilets, but I ran instead, right through the middle of them.' She closed her eyes for a moment, beginning finally to shake. 'Which was what they wanted me to do - because the only place there was to run to was into the bush across the road.' She kissed Clover's head. 'Where it's you know, private.' She looked around, shadows accumulating under her eyes.

'But I ran anyway,' she said. 'Faster than I've ever run and then - I wasn't running anymore.'

Everyone stared at her.

Rue shook her head. 'It wasn't me anymore. It was her - the spirit from the board, from my dreams, she was the one running.' Rue hugged Clover harder and looked over her head at the others. 'I was kind of just hovering inside my head while she was doing it all.'

She blinked. 'She did this. Standing on the path waiting for them.' She nodded at the end of the second stick, now a spear. Then dipped a hand into the pocket of her skirt. 'With this.'

Rue put Clover down and looked at the pocket knife in her palm. 'It was my father's.' She looked up. 'I put it in my pocket this morning, thinking it might be useful for cutting wood or something.'

Rue looked at the roughly sharpened end on the stick then back at the others.

'Whoa,' Suze said. 'Just who were you in your past life?'

'I don't know,' Rue said and stared at them, eyes wide and dark.

28

'I don't understand,' Rue said. 'Lots of women get murdered or raped and no past-life spirit comes in to save them.' She leaned forward where she was perched on the edge of the couch and shook her head.

Clover was upstairs in bed, but Rue didn't want to go to her room just yet. It had been a hell of a day and she needed to unwind.

She needed to understand. Looking over at Selena, she shook her head. 'So why did it happen?'

Selena got up, went over to sit down beside Rue, taking her hands in her own and rubbing them gently to warm them.

'I don't know,' she said.

Rue shook her head. 'Is this why she came through on the Ouija board the other day, and why I've been dreaming of her? To save me from this?'

Selena frowned slightly, thinking about it. 'My sense of it is no,' she said.

'No?' Damien looked at them from the other couch. 'So, what, it was a happy piece of luck she was there with Rue?'

'It was definitely a happy piece of something,' Dandy said. She gathered one of the throw rugs up and patted it over her knees. The evenings were growing shorter and colder.

Selena looked at Rue, thinking. 'There are plenty of accounts of people in dire circumstances who tell of being suddenly either overcome by a different personality or accompanied by another, until they are safe again.'

'Third man syndrome,' Damien said, nodding. He'd been doing some reading and research of his own. 'Climbers and hikers tell of getting in deep trouble and another person, a spirit, comes to lead them to safety.' He pursed his lips. 'Sometimes even carrying them, but usually just there, like in your peripheral vision, urging you on in the blizzard or whatever, in the right direction.' He paused. 'It's a pretty well-documented phenomenon.'

Selena shook her head. 'But that doesn't ring true here for me,' she said. 'At least not in its entirety.'

'What do you mean?' Rue asked. She looked down at her hands, which Selena was still holding. 'Do you think she's here for another reason?'

'Here?' Tara said. 'Do you mean still here?'

Rue shrugged.

'You said you'd dreamed of her,' Selena said.

Rue pressed her lips together and frowned. 'I have been,' she said. 'Or at least, I think it's her. Mostly, the dreams are about one woman. Sometimes I'm watching her, and sometimes I am her.' Rue shook her head.

'And the spirit coming through your Ouija board said it was you,' Dandy reminded her.

'What?' Tara asked. 'What's this?' She'd been out most of the day.

'Rue and her friends played with an Ouija board,' Dandy said succinctly. 'One spirit came through, said she was Rue, and gave a bunch of dates.'

Tara's eyes widened.

'She's a priestess,' Rue said quietly, and looked at Selena. 'In my dreams, she's a priestess. That's what she's doing. Like in your Wilde Grove, like how you said it was there in the beginning.'

She stopped talking, not wanting to say out loud what she was thinking, that if past lives were a real thing, she might once have been a priestess in Selena's own Wilde Grove. Wasn't that possible?

Selena was nodding. 'I believe you,' she said. 'We've glimpsed that about you before, haven't we?'

Rue looked at their hands again and nodded. 'But what's it mean?' she asked. 'What do we do about it?'

Selena paused only a moment before answering. 'You keep dreaming, and writing them down, and see what she's trying to tell you. You listen for her, ask her what she wants from you.'

Rue looked at her, wide-eyed. 'And then what?' she asked.

'Then we do what she wants, I expect,' Selena said with a smile.

They were silent for a while, all of them.

'I want to see my spirit kin, too' Rue said suddenly. She

looked at Selena. 'Clover can see them. You can see them.' She shook her head, and when she spoke again her voice was small, wistful.

'Do you think I'll be able to one day too? Properly, I mean. The way you and Clover can?'

'Yes,' Selena said, then smiled. 'At least the way I am able to.'

Rue gaped at her. 'Really?'

'You can learn to,' Selena said. 'Yes, it comes naturally to Clover, but I had to learn it.' She shook her head.

'It's a faculty we all used to have, millennia ago, because we used it. The ability to be close to spirit in a way we've since forgotten.'

Rue's mouth was suddenly dry. She took her hands back and rubbed her palms on her skirt. 'We can learn to?' she asked.

'We can remember what we've forgotten,' Selena said. She looked over at Dandy. 'Don't you think so?'

'Well.' Dandy thought about it, then nodded. 'There's a saying in tarot circles, that anyone can learn to read the cards. Anyone can develop their psychic abilities.' She nodded. 'So, then, yes, I'd say so, for sure.'

'I want to,' Rue said, very certain of it. She looked earnestly at Selena. 'I want to be a priestess – like maybe I used to be in a past life – and I want to learn to be as close to the spirit world as you are.'

Selena looked back at her silently.

'You have to teach me how,' Rue said. 'Me and Clover.'

'Me too,' Damien added.

Rue nodded. 'All of us.' She straightened in her seat.

'This is important,' she said. 'I need to understand this.' She frowned, sucking on her lower lip for a moment. 'Look,' she said. 'The world's a mess and it has been for a long time. Is this the answer? Your ancient ways?'

She shook her head. 'Isn't that why there's been a Wilde Grove all these hundreds of years? Why it's been kept alive?' Rue wished they could go live in Wilde Grove.

'You're not allowed to take us to Wilde Grove,' she said. 'So can't we make our own here?' She closed her eyes, subsided.

'I need to know this stuff,' she whispered.

Selena laid a hand on Rue's knees. 'I do the Goddess's bidding,' she said.

'The Goddess brought you here,' Rue answered, suddenly tired, miserable. Her eyes were heavy, and she thought she might cry. What a day it had been.

'She did,' Selena agreed, casting a glance around at everyone else in the room. 'She brought me here to you. You are all already learning my ways.'

'That's not enough,' Rue burst out, and now there were hot tears behind her lids. She blinked her eyes. 'You have to teach us like you mean it. What else are you here for?' She shook her head and a tear dripped down her cheek. 'We could have just gone into foster care. It probably would have been okay.' She didn't believe that. Not with Clover the way she was, but the words were out now.

'I want to learn to see the way that you and Clover do,' she said, winding down, swiping the tear from her cheek. 'I want to understand it all. Now that I know it's there.' She was quiet a moment, then spoke again. 'I mean – I want to be a fashion designer, but there's no way I can just go live a normal life now, not when I know there's so much more to the world. How do I go and be normal now? It was bad enough just living with Clover and seeing what she could do.'

Rue looked momentarily abashed at her outburst, but then she clenched her fists and carried on.

'But now I know that this sort of stuff – Clover's world – is really all around us, and any of us, so you say, can touch it, feel it, see it.' She took a deep breath. 'I can't go back to not knowing, not when this is better. When we'd all be better off living like this.' She glanced around the room, then thought of another point.

'I mean, today, I talked to a tree, thanking it for giving me one of its branches, and I meant it. Wouldn't the world be a better place if we knew trees were, like...' She blinked. 'What's the word?'

'Sentient?' Damien said. 'A living, knowing creature.' He was remembering his grandmother's stories.

Selena nodded, and Rue did too.

'Yeah,' Rue said. 'People wouldn't be in such a hurry to burn down the Amazon rainforest if they knew they were murdering beings who have as much right to be on earth as we do.'

She shook her head, sank back against the cushions, spoke more quietly. 'I have to research how fabric is made for my class at school, and you know what I've learnt so far?'

Everyone looked at her.

'I've learnt that the whole industry is built on what's basically slave labour, and that it's a huge pollutant as well.

Not to mention that fast fashion is just unsustainable.' She blew out a breath. 'I can't become a fashion designer in that sort of world. I just can't. So, I need to know more, to build my life on something different.'

'There's a lot that needs to be done differently,' Damien said. It was his turn to shake his head. 'Back to the old ways, or at least integrate them with new ways.' He frowned. 'I don't know,' he said. 'But we have to start living in harmony again. With everything.'

'I don't know how to do it differently,' Rue said, but she was thinking furiously.

'I do,' Selena answered. 'I know how to do it all differently.'

Everyone looked at her.

She smiled. 'You begin by building a foundation. A strong spirit in a world built on reciprocity and balance.' She closed her eyes.

'We go back to the original reason humanity was born.'

Damien's eyes widened. 'What was that?' he asked.

The small smile was still on Selena's lips.

'For the sheer joy of the experience,' she said. 'To walk in flesh and blood in a world full of wonders.'

The room fell to silence, as they contemplated this. It was Rue who broke the spell.

'It's not too late?' she asked. 'To do things so differently?'

Selena shook her head. 'We can't control the whole world,' she said. 'We can't change everything and everyone, but we can walk the path ourselves.'

'If we did that,' Dandy said, grinning, 'we'd shine like your beacons, Selena.'

Selena nodded.

'Sounds good to me,' Damien said.

'Me too,' Tara said.

'And to me,' Rue added.

Dandy picked up her teacup, held it up.

'Here's to shining.'

29

NATALIE CURLED HER LEGS UNDER HER AND SAT BACK ON THE couch clutching her cup of hot chocolate. She'd made it, warming the milk in a saucepan over the stove, hoping it would settle her nerves so she could go to bed.

It was after midnight. She ought to be asleep.

Lately though, since the day she'd gone outside, she'd been having problems sleeping.

Sleeping meant closing her eyes and relaxing. It meant letting go of consciousness, being okay with not hearing whatever might be going on outside, whoever might be walking past the house, looking over the fence at it.

She sipped her hot chocolate, eyes darting around the room, taking inventory.

There was the couch, an armchair by the window, where she'd used to sit reading, the light coming in to light the pages.

There was the television, with the video player under

the table. The screen was blank now, and she could see her reflection, pale and slightly distorted, in the glass.

There was a voice outside, shouting, and Natalie startled, spilling a drop of chocolate on her hand. She grasped the mug tighter, the heat burning into her fingers, reddening the skin.

A burst of laughter, a shout in reply. Natalie relaxed an inch. Just people on their way home, or somewhere. Students, probably.

Everything was all right. She should put a movie on to watch, if she wasn't going to go to bed.

She couldn't go to bed. Natalie shook her head. Going to bed would mean closing her eyes, going to sleep.

How could she listen out for danger, if she was asleep? What if those men came back, and this time they opened the gate and crept down the path, found their way into the house, into her bedroom?

Natalie put the mug of hot chocolate down on the coffee table. It wasn't going to help. Or not yet, anyway. She needed to go check the back garden again. Check that the back door was locked.

She winced at that. Checking that one was locked meant turning the doorknob or the key, and what if it opened? What if it wasn't locked and she opened the door?

It was locked. Natalie took a breath and told herself it was. She'd checked it before she made the chocolate that was supposed to calm her down. She'd checked it again while she was warming the milk, dashing to the door, putting her hand to the cold metal of the knob, and twisting it, holding her breath, letting it out in a huff of relief when the door didn't move.

She told herself she didn't need to check it again.

Her mug steamed in the dimness. The light wasn't on, but perhaps she should turn it on.

If it was on, wouldn't someone think she was up?

Maybe she should turn the television and the light on, so someone would hesitate, thinking maybe she had visitors.

She could put a record on. Turn it up loud, with the television on, a movie playing.

That way, maybe someone would think she was having a party.

Natalie sat in the dark room and groped for her mug again, picked it up and pressed her palms against its hot side.

If she turned all those things on, she wouldn't be able to hear someone outside.

She wouldn't be able to hear the gate squeal when someone pushed it open.

Or the crunch of their footsteps up the driveway.

She got up from the couch and tiptoed through the house to the kitchen, stood looking out the window, holding the curtain open just a fraction.

Scanning the back garden for movement, heart thudding inside her ribcage.

Was that someone there, behind the garage again? Natalie held her breath, eyes looking looking looking.

No one. No one was there.

But the door. Was that still locked? She hadn't accidentally unlocked it last time she checked it, had she?

She put her mug down on the bench and pressed her burning palms to the cold surface.

'Calm down,' she muttered. 'You're going crazy.'

That made her laugh.

A movement outside caught her attention, and she froze, only her eyes moving, as she stared at the tree beside the garage.

Was someone there?

The hairs on the back of her neck prickled.

Someone was watching her.

Natalie choked on a sob.

Someone had been watching her for days.

She was sure of it. You could feel when someone was watching you, she knew. Everyone said so. She'd accidentally watched a show on the television, where someone somewhere was being stalked. They knew they were being watched, they'd said, even when they couldn't see where the person was.

You knew. You knew when someone was spying on you, Natalie thought. She dropped the curtain and backed away from the window, heart in her throat, trying convulsively to swallow it back down, then ran through the house back to the living room.

She'd turn the television on, she thought. Put on a movie. She'd put a record on her old player, throw all the lights on.

Make it look like a party.

Her hand froze in the air, fingers outstretched in the act of reaching for the television's on switch. She sank slowly to the floor.

If she turned the television on, and the record player, and all the lights, then no one would be able to hear her scream.

She whimpered, crawling over to the wall beside the television and huddling there, her hair falling over her face.

Selena turned over in her bed. She was dreaming. Dreaming and seeing and knowing, and the dream made her cry out in her sleep, a cry of alarm.

It was dark in her dream, and cool; she was outside.

But the house next to her wasn't her own, wasn't the house she lived in with Rue and Clover and the others.

Selena shook her head in her dream.

It was the house up the road, the one that kept calling out to her.

Someone else was in the darkness with her and she stilled, listening to the wind, and the person's quiet, stealthy steps.

She followed them – him – down the driveway and watched him slip into the shadows in the back garden. He'd been here before, she thought. He knew his way around.

And there was something familiar about him. Selena moved closer, invisible, just a dreamer in a dream, and waited for the skid of moonlight to fall across his features.

Yes, she thought. I know you. I've seen you. She and Dandy.

And so had Rue and her girlfriends.

Selena turned and looked at the house, following the man's gaze. She looked at the kitchen windows, the darkness thick behind the glass.

All the lights were off. Asleep. The house and its occupant were asleep.

The wind gusted, swooping down like an owl to brush its feathered touch across Selena's cheeks.

The house wasn't asleep. It had called her here.

Selena glanced at the man. He leaned slightly forward, gaze fixed on the house. She could feel the tension in his body.

He wouldn't watch for long.

He was primed to move. Selena reached out and touched his mind with hers, and saw he'd already decided which window he'd jimmy to get in.

He knew the woman was alone in there. Knew she was always alone in there, never went outside. Selena felt his hunger and his glee.

And she woke up, eyes wide in the darkness of her bedroom.

She got out of bed, switching on the bedside lamp and picking up her clothes, pulling them roughly on, dropping her nightdress to the floor.

In the dim hallway, she hurried to Damien's room, knocked quickly on the door then flung it open.

'Damien,' she hissed. 'Damien, wake up.'

He woke up instantly, blinking at the figure in his doorway. 'Selena?'

'Get out of bed and dressed,' she said. 'We've got to go.'

He threw the covers back and reached for his jeans on the floor beside the bed where he'd thrown them.

'What is it?' he asked. 'Is it Clover or Rue?'

'Neither,' Selena said, her voice steady now, and grim. 'Meet me downstairs.'

She turned and moved again, pausing in the hallway to decide. Tara or Dandy?

Someone had to stay, with the children in the house.

She ran down the stairs again and through to Dandy's room, sorry she had to do this. But Dandy would be a calming, stable presence, and Selena knew this would be invaluable.

Once the danger had been dealt with. If she was right about it.

She knew she was right about it.

'Selena?' Dandy's voice was clogged with sleep as she groped out a hand and switched on the bedside light. 'What's going on?'

'She needs us,' Selena said. 'The woman in the house. She needs us right now.'

Dandy sat up, gaping at Selena.

'Please,' Selena said. 'There's no time to explain, I just want you to come with me.'

Dandy closed her mouth, nodded, and got out of bed. Selena went back out to the kitchen.

'What's going on?' Tara asked. Her eyes were wide, hair mussed from sleeping.

'We've got a situation,' Selena said. 'Please can you stay here with the children?'

Tara nodded. 'Of course,' she said. 'But what's going on?'

'The woman up the road in the house we keep wondering over needs us,' Selena said, relieved to see Damien coming into the room, fully dressed, heavy boots on his feet, and car keys in his hand.

'The woman?' Tara tried to understand. 'But how do you know?'

Selena shook her head. 'There isn't time, I'm afraid. I just know. I dreamed it.'

Dandy appeared, pulling on a warm jacket. 'I'm ready,' she said.

Tara looked at her, wide-eyed but believing. How could she not? She nodded. 'Shall I call the police?'

'What's going on?' Damien asked.

'There's a man outside the house of a woman we know – been trying to know,' Selena said quickly. 'He's planning to break in through the laundry window.' She pursed her lips. 'I think he's one of the men who tried to attack Rue.'

Damien looked at Tara. 'Call the police. Have them meet us there.' He turned to Selena. 'Do you know the address?'

Dandy spoke up. 'It's number 3 Border Street.'

Damien nodded, opened the door. 'Let's go,' he said, face set, grim.

THE CAR CLIMBED THE SILENT HILL, ITS HEADLIGHTS SLICING across the trees. Selena sat in the passenger's seat, one hand on the dashboard as she leaned forward against her seatbelt, gaze focused on the road that wound up past the Botanic Garden on one side, and the tract of forest where Rue had hidden earlier that day.

Or rather, Selena thought. The day before. It was after midnight.

'Are we too late?' Dandy asked tensely from the back seat. 'Is he already in the house?'

Selena shook her head. 'I don't know. I'd have to focus and reach out to know.'

'We're going to be there any moment, anyway,' Damien said. His hands were strong on the steering wheel.

There was a wail of a police siren from the other side of the gardens.

'Maybe they'll beat us there,' Dandy said.

'They must have had someone close,' Damien said, and then he was at the top of the hill, ready to turn into the warren of roads, past where Clover and Rue had used to live.

The police car, siren howling, lights strobing the night, beat them to the turn. Damien made it right behind them.

Then pulled up on their bumper at the house. Damien was out of the car in a flash, striding across to the officer.

'Back away, sir,' the officer said, reaching for the gate.

'We're the ones who called you.'

The second officer looked at Damien. 'The callout is for a suspected intruder.'

Damien nodded. 'He was spotted lurking outside, and it's the same guy who attacked a friend of ours in the gardens yesterday afternoon.' He looked down the pathway where the first officer had disappeared out of sight. 'Look, we're wasting time.'

'I'm going to ask you to stay where you are,' Sandy Rice, the police officer said. She held up a warning hand, and Damien nodded, although he was bouncing on the toes of his boots, ready to bolt down the driveway at the first yell.

Selena and Dandy came and stood beside him.

'What do you think?' Dandy asked.

'If he wasn't inside already, the sirens would have had him getting the hell out of there.' Damien shook his head.

They could see the light from the officers' torches, and their loud rapping on the door. A light went on in the house.

Selena pushed through the gate, and after a pause, Damien and Dandy followed.

The back door was open a fraction and Selena caught a glimpse of a pale, frightened face, before it opened wider, and the first officer slipped through.

'It doesn't look like he got in,' he was saying, but let's search to make sure.'

'He didn't get in?' Selena asked, pressing a hand to her chest, feeling relief swell there.

Sandy Rice looked at her. 'There are jimmy marks on the laundry window, but it's still secure.' She moved away from the step and began sweeping her torch around the garden, searching for signs the man had been there.

Damien joined her without a word.

Selena glanced at Dandy, then slipped into the house, Dandy on her heels.

There was a woman standing shivering in her kitchen, and Selena went straight over to her, speaking softly.

'My name's Selena,' she said. 'We met the other day, on your doorstep, do you remember?'

Natalie looked at them with hollow, shadowed eyes, then nodded. Her teeth were chattering.

'You're in shock, poor thing,' Dandy said, and looked around for something she could put around the woman's shoulders. There was nothing in the kitchen, and she didn't want to interrupt the man doing the search, so she took off her jacket and tucked it over her shoulders.

Natalie looked at her dumbly. 'I couldn't sleep,' she said, her body shaking. 'I could feel him watching me.'

The police officer came back into the kitchen, eyebrows

going up at the sight of the three women. He looked at Natalie.

'There's no sign of him,' he said. 'But I've called for more officers to search the neighbourhood for him.' He shook his head briefly. 'Someone definitely was trying to break in. I'd say you were lucky that he was seen.'

Natalie squeezed her eyes shut and suddenly her breath was coming hard and fast.

'Whoa,' Richard Ames said. 'Are you all right?' He looked at the two women flanking her. 'Does she need an ambulance?'

Natalie jerked upright in horror, shaking her head.

'She's in shock,' Dandy said. 'We're going to take her to sit down, give her a minute to calm herself.'

Richard nodded. 'I'll need to ask a few questions shortly. I'll be back, right?'

But the women were already going through into the living room, and he shook his head, and stepped out to help his partner and brief the others when they arrived.

30

Natalie's breath whooped in and out, and Dandy sat her down on the couch, arm around her shoulders.

'It's all right,' she soothed. 'Everything is going to be all right now. I want you to take some nice slow breaths from your belly now, okay?'

Natalie fastened her gaze on the older woman and tried to do as she said, but she was light-headed now, dizzy.

'She's going to faint if we don't get her breathing slower,' Dandy said.

Selena lowered herself to the floor in front of Natalie and took her hands in hers.

'Hello Natalie,' she said, looking into Natalie's eyes and letting her spirit swirl around her, and around Natalie as well, seeping into Natalie's aura, calming her.

'That's it,' Selena said, concentrating on relaxing herself into Natalie's space. 'That's it. That's so much better. Nice slow breaths now.' She swayed a little where she knelt, feeling fuzzy and diffuse, not quite inside her body.

But Natalie's breathing was slowing, and her cold fingers clasped hold of Selena's.

'That's better,' Selena crooned. 'Everything is going to be so much better now.'

Natalie licked her lips, blinked.

'Who are you?' she asked in a whisper. 'Where did you come from?'

Selena smiled gently as Dandy took the jacket from around Natalie's shoulders and wrapped a rug around her instead, tucking it snugly against her.

'We live nearby,' she said. 'Practically neighbours.'

Natalie felt a dull flush heat her cheeks. They knew, then, she thought. They knew how strange she was, how useless.

'Did you call the police?' she asked. Then closed her eyes. 'I was so scared. I couldn't find anywhere to hide.'

Dandy glanced at the door, but the house was quiet. Everyone was outside. The lights of the police car coloured the curtains in rhythmic pulses.

'Yes,' Selena said. 'We called the police.'

Natalie twisted her hands around Selena's. Her breathing was back to normal now, and somehow, she felt warm and almost calm. 'There was someone outside. I could sense him watching me, and then I heard him at the window.'

She wanted to lift her gaze from that of the woman in front of hers, but it felt safer not to. The woman holding her hands was making her feel better.

Selena nodded. 'Yes. But the police got here in time and scared him away.'

Natalie jerked back but kept hold of Selena's hands. 'He'll get away?'

'They'll find him, I'm sure. They'll look until they find him.'

'I could feel him out there,' Natalie repeated. 'I thought I was being silly though.' A tear leaked down her cheek. 'Always imagining the worst.'

Selena shook her head. 'No,' she said. 'You were right. You weren't imagining it.' She was coming fully back to her body now, and her neck was stiffening from looking up at Natalie. Gently, she got to her feet and sat down beside her instead.

Natalie clung to her hands. Looked at Selena with anguish. 'Do you know about me?' she asked.

'Know what about you?'

Natalie looked down at their hands. 'I don't leave the house,' she whispered.

'Ah, that,' Selena said, casting a glance over Natalie's head at Dandy. 'Yes. We guessed.'

Natalie nodded, suddenly more tired than she ever remembered being.

Sandy Rice came into the living room and gave Natalie a kindly smile. 'We've got officers searching the neighbour-hood now,' she said, sitting down on the edge of an armchair. 'Can I ask you a few questions?'

Natalie looked alarmed.

Sandy looked at Selena and Dandy. 'Your friend outside said you made the call to the police?'

Dandy cleared her throat. 'Our other friend did, while we came straight here.'

Sandy frowned. There was something odd about all this, she thought. 'You came here in a car.'

It wasn't a question. She'd seen them.

There was silence in the room. Natalie untangled one hand and used it to tug the blanket tighter around herself.

'Where do you live?' Sandy asked. 'Do you all live together?'

Dandy nodded. 'We live down on Lovelock road.'

'But that's some distance from here,' Sandy said. She'd taken out a notebook and pen, and wrote down the name of the street, then frowned at it before looking back at the older women. 'Were you at home when you became aware of what was happening here?' She shook her head. 'No,' she said. 'That's impossible.'

'We were at home,' Selena said, her voice calm and clear.

'Then how did you know?'

Dandy looked over at Selena. Exactly how were they going to answer this one?

'I dreamed it,' Selena said. 'I was aware of this house, and Natalie, and when this man was threatening her, I knew.'

Sandy stared at her, sitting very still and trying to make what had been said make sense. She blinked finally.

'I'm sorry,' she said. 'I don't understand. You dreamed someone was breaking in here?'

Natalie was looking at Selena. So, for that matter was Dandy.

'I did, yes,' Selena said.

'And does this sort of thing happen regularly to you?' Sandy asked dubiously.

'Reasonably regularly, yes,' Selena agreed.

Sandy's eyes closed. She shook her head. 'I'm sorry,' she repeated. 'You're going to have to explain this to me.'

'She's psychic,' Dandy broke in. 'It's a real thing.'

Sandy's gaze transferred to Dandy. 'Psychic?'

'Yeah,' Dandy said. 'Haven't you watched the new Sensing Murder show on TV?' She shook her head. 'It's like that.'

'I don't believe in ghosts,' Sandy said.

'That's fine,' Dandy retorted. 'Considering the man who we disturbed breaking in here is flesh and blood.'

Sandy held her hands up. 'Let's take a breath here, ladies,' she said. 'And start over.' She held her pen over the pad of paper on her knee.

Then set it back down and looked at them in dismay. 'You say you dreamed this man was going to break in here?'

'Yes,' Selena said. 'We've already had two run-ins with him, and he's on my radar, so to speak.'

This wasn't all the truth, because it didn't take into account Natalie, but Selena thought it was probably the best starting point if she wanted the poor policewoman to have a hope of understanding her.

Sandy perked up. 'Two run-ins?'

'Yes,' Selena said, and squeezed Natalie's hand. She could feel the uncertainty and fear rising in the woman on the couch next to her.

'We saw him and another man creeping around the Botanic Garden a couple weeks ago,' Dandy said. 'They were looking at the young women there in a way that didn't seem right.'

Sandy nodded. 'And did you do anything about this?' she asked.

'We spoke to a couple of the gardeners there, told them to look out for these guys.' Dandy shook her head. 'We would have come to you, but it's not a crime to be slimy now, is it?'

Sandy's lip quirked. Despite the weirdness of it all, she found herself warming to the feisty old woman.

'No,' she said. 'It's not a crime to be slimy.'

Dandy sniffed.

'And the second time?'

It was Selena who answered. 'My teenaged foster daughter was accosted by two men yesterday in the Gardens. These men acted threateningly towards her and chased her into the bush.'

Sandy's eyes widened. 'I heard about that!' She shook her head. 'We were briefed about it at the beginning of my shift.' Now she was frowning. 'You're saying it is the same man – or one of them anyway?'

'Yes.' Dandy and Selena answered together.

'But how do you know this?' Sandy demanded.

That was actually, Dandy thought, a good question. She looked over at Selena.

'It is the same man, isn't it?'

Selena nodded. 'I'm sure of it.'

'I saw him,' Natalie said, then winced when everyone looked at her.

Sandy leaned forward. This was more like it. An eyewitness sighting.

'When did you see him, Natalie?' she asked.

Natalie shuddered, shook her head. 'I don't know what

day it was.' She squeezed her eyes shut, hunched in on herself, then looked at the police officer, focusing on the notepad on Sandy's knee.

'The days blur together,' she said.

'Tell me what you do remember.'

Natalie nodded. Wondered if she was dreaming.

'I...I went outside,' she said. 'It was early evening, and I...I had a panic attack.' She ducked her head. 'I'm agoraphobic.'

Selena patted her hand.

'When I looked up, there was a man watching me on the other side of the fence, just standing there watching me.' Natalie took a deep breath. 'He was watching me have a panic attack and he was smiling. Grinning. Then another guy came up behind him and they both stood there.'

She stopped abruptly.

'What happened next?' Sandy said.

But Natalie shook her head. 'I ran inside.' She rammed the heel of her free hand into her eye and rubbed, holding the tears back.

'Ever since then I've felt like someone has been watching me,' Natalie said, and stared at the floor, shivering again.

'Someone has been, I'm afraid,' Sandy said. 'We've found clear evidence that at least one man has been repeatedly hiding behind your garage, and in the bushes, likely watching you inside the house.'

There was silence for a long moment. Natalie grasped Selena's hand and looked up at her.

'You saved me,' she said. 'You stopped him.'

'In the act of breaking in,' Sandy said. 'Right in the act.' She blew out a breath. 'How did you know?'

'I dreamed it,' Selena said again. 'I dreamed I was right behind this man, right outside this house, and I could feel what he was thinking, and he was getting ready to break in.' She nodded. 'He'd been watching the place on and off for a while.'

Sandy stared at her. Then down at her notebook. So far, she'd barely written anything down.

'That's not possible,' she said, her voice weak.

'Yet that's what happened.' Selena told her. 'I woke up, got Damien and Dandy, and our other friend Tara called you while we drove up here.'

'And got here in the nick of time,' Dandy added.

There was a squawk from the walkie talkie on Sandy's shoulder and she got up with some relief. 'Excuse me,' she said. 'I'll go see what is happening.'

Everyone watched her leave the room, then Natalie turned to Selena.

'Did you really dream it?' she asked.

'Yes.'

'You're psychic?' Natalie looked at Dandy. 'I don't know your name.'

'It's Dandy.'

Natalie looked confused.

'I mean, my name is Dandy.' Dandy smiled.

'Oh.' Natalie looked back at Selena. 'You're psychic like Dandy said?'

'Something like that, yes,' Selena said, deciding that was the quickest, easiest answer.

'But why me?' Natalie asked. 'Why did you come around the other day? Did you know something then?'

'Yes,' Selena said. 'But we didn't know what it was, only that you need help.'

Natalie frowned, sank back into the cushions.

'I sent you away,' she said in a small voice. She couldn't think why now. There was something so comforting about Selena. About both of them.

But especially Selena. Part of her felt like they'd already met.

'It's okay,' Selena said. 'We were just strangers turning up on your doorstep.'

Damien came striding into the room. 'They've caught him,' he announced.

Dandy jumped up, looking at him in delight. 'They've caught him?'

'Yeah. A guy a few streets away called the police because some dude was in his garden when they got up for a drink of water.' He nodded. 'And of course, it was our guy.'

'What a relief!' Dandy all but clapped her hands.

'And they're bound to get his mate as well,' Damien said, dropping to the chair that the police officer had vacated. 'Guys like that won't think twice about dobbing the other one in.'

'We hope,' Selena said.

Damien looked at Natalie with open curiosity. 'Hi,' he said. 'We haven't met. I'm Damien.'

Natalie blinked at him, gave him a tentative smile. 'I'm Natalie,' she said.

'So glad we got the bastard before he could get in here,' Damien said, then yawned. 'Most excitement I've had in the middle of the night for a while, that's for sure. Just glad it ended well.'

Sandy came back in a moment later. 'We caught him,' she said, jubilant. 'You're safe now.' She nodded, looked at all of them. 'We'll need you all to come into the station tomorrow to give a statement.'

Natalie stared at her in horror. 'I can't,' she said. And shook her head.

'Right,' Sandy said. 'Sorry. Listen then, I'll get someone to come around to get it from you, is that all right?'

Natalie wasn't sure it was all right at all, but it was better than having to go to the police station. The thought of navigating her way there, and all the things that could – would – go wrong made her feel faint. She nodded weakly.

'Right then, that's all good. We'll be off, but someone will back tomorrow to take some more photos of the damage to the window, and the footprints and so on outside. So, ah, don't go disturbing anything.' She coloured slightly, realising that this was one witness who wouldn't even be going out to look at the evidence.

31

THE POLICE FINISHED UP AND LEFT, THEIR PARTING WORDS reminding everyone to come and make their statements the next day. Natalie listened to them with her head down, cringing.

'I thought I was making it up,' she whispered, when the house had fallen silent, and the shadows she'd seen in the yard flickered across her memories. 'I thought I was imagining things.' She squeezed her eyes shut. 'I'm always imagining things.'

'But you weren't making it up,' Dandy said, and she was looking over Natalie's back at Selena, eyebrows raised. What next, she was asking. What do we do with her?

'You just didn't trust what you were seeing, that's all,' Dandy said. 'It's a mistake that's pretty easy to make.'

'I could have died,' Natalie said. She was leaning forward over her knees, hands clasped tightly together. 'You saved me.'

Damien came into the room, the question of whether

they were ready to go home dying unspoken. He looked at Selena too.

'Natalie,' Selena said. 'I think we need to take you home with us for the night.'

Dandy nodded. That was a good idea. The girl couldn't stay here, not like this, not after what had happened.

But Natalie had lifted her head and was looking at Selena with a mixture of horror and desperation. She shook her head.

'I couldn't,' she said.

But Selena just smiled at her. 'I think you can,' she said. 'I think you need to.'

The whites of Natalie's eyes showed as she shook her head, her breath coming quickly again.

Selena took her hands. 'Hush now,' she said softly, letting her warmth spread back over the woman. 'Everything is going to be all right. We want to help you. We want to take you somewhere where you won't be alone, and where you'll be safe. Just for a while, until this man's friend is found, and the police have it all wrapped up.'

That wasn't the whole reason, of course, but it was a compelling one. Natalie needed help, significant help, and Selena knew there was no way she could just walk away from this fact.

'Let's go and pack a small bag for you, shall we?'

Natalie stared at her. 'Go with you?' she said in a small, uncertain voice.

Selena smiled again and spoke to the little child she'd coaxed once already out of the blanket fort where she'd been hiding.

'Yes,' she said. 'Come and stay with us for a while. Would you like that?'

Natalie, dazed by the events of the whole night, found herself nodding. She didn't want to be on her own again, she realised, and she didn't want to let this woman, who somehow made her feel so safe, walk away without her.

'I trust you,' she whispered, and it was said wonderingly, with awe. 'I don't know why.'

Selena squeezed Natalie's hands. 'You can trust me,' she said. 'It's all right. Now, let's go pack a bag, okay?'

'I haven't been anywhere for a long time,' Natalie said, gaze fixed on Selena's.

'Just a quick trip down the hill. We have a house with plenty of space for you to stay a little while.'

Natalie looked around at Dandy, and at Damien, who was sitting on the edge of the armchair looking at her.

'Do you all live there?' she asked.

'Yes,' Dandy answered. 'Us and a couple others.'

'Others?' Natalie shied away.

'Tara and Rue and Clover,' Damien said. 'You'll love them.'

'They won't mind?' Natalie tried to reason through what was going on – she was going outside? But inside her head it was as though a lot of glass had been broken, and she squeezed her eyes shut. She felt shattered by everything that had just happened.

'Come now,' Selena said, standing up and pulling Natalie with her. 'Let's get your things together, shall we?'

Natalie followed her from the room without another word, hunched over, Selena's arm across her shoulder.

Selena asked which room was hers and Natalie pointed towards a door. They went in.

Natalie stood shivering in the middle of the room. She looked vaguely around, then shook her head. 'I don't think I can,' she said.

'Of course you can,' Selena said. 'You've forgotten how strong you are.' She came and stood in front of Natalie. 'You're very empathic, and you have a marvellous imagination, and I can see your spirit, Natalie, and it's beautiful.'

Natalie blinked at her, tears welling behind her eyelids. 'I'm a mess,' she whispered. 'Everything scares me. The world scares me.'

'The world is both terrible and beautiful,' Selena said. 'Learning to live in it is hard. But it can be done, and it can be done well, with practice, and knowledge, and help.'

Natalie stared at her. 'Who are you?' she asked slowly.

'Someone who's going to help you,' Selena said just as softly. She put her hands on Natalie's shoulder, then kissed her forehead softly, knowing she was reassuring the child in the tent of blankets as well as the grown woman.

For a moment, Natalie sagged at the knees so that Selena had to catch her, and the face that gazed up at her had a childish look of hope on it.

'You came back,' Natalie whispered

Selena smiled down at the child looking at her. 'Yes,' she said. 'And I'm going to take you home with me for a little while. Is that all right?'

Natalie gazed at her with wide eyes, then nodded.

'Good,' Selena said. 'Let's get your things together, then.'

The child inside Natalie blinked, then withdrew, and it was the adult Natalie in Selena's arms again.

'We're really going?' she asked.

'Yes,' Selena said, and set Natalie back on her feet.

Natalie found herself helping, getting things out of her drawers and putting them into a bag Selena had uncovered in one of the cupboards. She moved as if in a dream, part of her whispering harshly inside her head, asking her what did she think she was doing?

But the voice went unanswered, Natalie following along behind Selena, fetching toothbrush and hairbrush, fresh underwear, packing her clothes for all the world as though this was something she was going to do.

Leave the house. Go with these people.

She followed Selena back out into the living room and Dandy stood up, smiling with delight.

'We're ready, then, are we?'

Selena nodded.

And Natalie nodded too.

Damien took the bag from Selena, got out his car keys.

'Where are your house keys, dear?' Dandy asked, and for a moment, Natalie couldn't think of the answer.

'In the kitchen,' she said finally. 'In the drawer.' She never really had to use them. There was a key in the back door, and she never used the front.

They went through to the kitchen together, and Natalie watched, feeling her breath grow shorter, as Dandy sifted through the drawers, pulled out her house keys.

'I want my cookbooks,' Natalie said. 'Please. I need them.'

'Of course,' Selena said, and touched Natalie on the cheek. 'You get them, and we will take them with us.'

The touch was warm against her skin, and Natalie

pressed her hand against the spot. She nodded, drawing in a slower breath, and went to the shelf where her books were.

She looked at them, unable to decide which to take.

'Which is your favourite?' Dandy asked.

'This one,' Natalie said, tugging it down and tucking it under her arm. 'We should take my cake too.' She blinked. 'I made a cake.'

'Nice,' Damien said. 'What sort of cake?'

Natalie stared at him, then blinked. 'Marble cake,' she said. 'I was experimenting with new flavours.'

Damien raised his eyebrows and nodded. 'It sounds delicious,' he said. 'Where is it?'

Natalie pointed to a cake tin on the shelf. It was pink, with white polka dots.

Damien drew it down. 'Definitely taking this,' he said. 'Are we ready to go?'

Natalie didn't think so, but her feet walked her to the door, and her hand grasped Selena's when she reached out for it.

She gasped when the cold air hit her face and shied away.

Selena tightened her grip on Natalie's hand and spoke to the small child and the grown woman.

'It's going to be all right,' she said.

'Can I close my eyes?' the child asked, stepping out of her hiding place.

'Yes,' Selena answered. 'I'll lead you.'

Natalie squeezed her eyes shut, concentrated on Selena's fingers around her own, and shuffled forward.

The day was lightening. They'd been up long enough

for the sun to rise. Selena felt its first touch on her face and closed her own eyes for a moment.

'Blessed sun,' she murmured. 'Blessed day. We step forth confidently into your arms.'

'What was that?' Natalie whispered. 'What did you say?'

'A little prayer,' Selena answered, leading Natalie down the path beside the driveway while Dandy locked the door behind them.

'What was it?' Natalie asked again. 'I want to say it too.' She paused and her throat worked. 'I'm afraid.'

'I'm with you,' Selena said. 'The prayer goes like this: Blessed day.'

Natalie, eyes still closed, took another few steps. 'Blessed day,' she whispered.

'Blessed sun,' Selena said. 'Do you feel it on your face?'

Natalie tipped her head up. Held Selena's hand tighter, gripped Selena's arm with her other hand. 'Blessed sun,' she repeated.

'Good girl,' Selena said. 'You're doing brilliantly. The last line is: we step forth confidently into your arms.'

Natalie panted for a moment, then spoke. 'We step forth,' she said. And took another step. She opened her eyes slightly, saw the light, and the sky, and the path, and grew dizzy, held tighter to Selena and squeezed her eyes closed again.

Better not to look.

'What was the rest?' she asked. Were they there yet?

Selena walked her through the gate onto the footpath. Damien had the car door open, ready.

'We step forth confidently into your arms.'

'Whose arms?'

'The day's,' Selena replied.

'We step forth confidently into the day's arms.' Natalie was crying as she said it.

Selena slid them both into the car, and Natalie buried her head in Selena's shoulder.

'I can't look,' she said.

'That's all right,' Selena said.

'I don't feel very confident,' Natalie whispered.

'And yet, here you are doing it,' Selena answered. 'Stepping forth into the day. How wonderful that is. How extraordinarily courageous.'

'I don't feel like I'm courageous.' Natalie heard the car doors close and the engine start. She bit her lips and held her breath.

'Courage always smells of fear,' Selena said. 'You're doing brilliantly.'

Natalie whimpered as the vehicle pulled away from the kerb and she wanted to cry out. She wanted to scream at them to take her back home.

But she didn't. Instead, she took great shuddery breaths all the way down the hill.

NATALIE CLUNG TO SELENA AS THEY BUNDLED INSIDE, through the back door into the kitchen. Tara, kneading bread with furious concentration, looked up, her eyes widening at the sight of Natalie.

'This is Natalie,' Dandy said. 'She's going to stay a few days with us.'

Tara nodded, smiled with relief. 'I am so glad you're all

okay – I heard the sirens.' She dropped the dough into a bowl to rise.

Selena eased Natalie into a chair at the table, where she sat blinking, looking around gingerly, head tucked down into her shoulders.

'A pot of tea is called for, I think.' Selena said, taking the seat next to Natalie and touching her hand.

'I'll get it,' Damien said. 'And a pot of coffee, for myself and anyone else who needs more of a kick.'

'Me, please,' Rue said, trailing into the room with Clover right behind her rubbing her eyes. They stopped short when she saw Natalie.

'It's the sad lady,' Clover said, and stared at her curiously before going around the table to where Natalie sat and climbing up on the chair on the other side.

She planted her small hands on the table and leaned around to look closely at Natalie.

'Clover,' Rue said. 'Give her some space.'

But Clover shook her head, and continued staring. She frowned at what she could see in the deep and wide, then looked over at Selena.

'She goin' to stay with us?' Clover asked.

Selena nodded, while Natalie looked at Clover through the curtain of her hair.

'Good,' Clover said, and sat down, suddenly smiling. 'I have a coffee too,' she said.

Then, everyone but Natalie was laughing, the tension of the night seeping away leaving limbs and minds tired but clearer.

Natalie managed a smile, and some impulse had her

reaching over to touch one of Clover's small hands. 'What's your name?' she asked, her voice low, tentative.

'I'm Clover Bee,' Clover said. 'I'm gonna be four soon.' She nodded, proud of the fact, then pointed at Rue. 'She's my sister. Her name is Rue.' She went around the room. 'And that's Damien, and Tara, and Dandy, and S'lena. They all my frien's.'

Natalie looked cautiously around the room, conscious that she was somewhere different than her own house for the first time in years. The thought, once it snagged on her mind, had her breath quickening, but Selena took her hand again, and a wave of calm washed over her. She breathed it in as though it was air and she needed it to survive.

'Do you all live here?' she asked. Her mouth was dry, voice raspy, but she felt a small tick of joy at being able to ask, at being able to sit at this strange table with these strange people, and ask.

And no one laughed at her, or her question. No one was looking at her as though she was stupid, as though she was embarrassing herself and them.

'We do,' Tara said, helping Damien behind the kitchen counter. 'We all met last year and how we came together was a sort of magic.' She laughed, but she meant what she'd just said. It really did feel like it was magic that had brought them together.

'S'lena found us,' Clover said. She was resting her head on one hand, elbow on the table, and examining Natalie again. 'Now she found you.'

Dandy hooted with laughter, coming to sit beside Rue at the big table. 'We're all Selena's strays.'

Selena shook her head. 'That's not the case at all.' She

smiled, a beautiful smile on her tired face. 'You're all my shining lights.'

No one said anything for a long moment after that, and Damien and Tara brought the coffee and tea to the table, then stood there, Damien's arm slung around Tara, his other hand on Rue's shoulder. They were their own little community, he thought. An odd, brilliant sort of family.

Suddenly, he was filled with the desperate desire to go home again, back to his whānau, his family – and take these people with him, introduce them all to each other. He took a breath, held it, let it out slowly. He'd do it, he decided. Next school holidays.

At the table, Natalie swallowed, looked around in the sudden silence and felt the warmth of it. Felt drawn into the harmony of the moment, and with a burst of bravery, reached for her teacup.

Then noise and bustle swelled into the early morning kitchen, and Damien said something about pancakes and then there were eggs being broken into bowls and flour tipped in, a pan heating on the stove, and Natalie sipped her tea, barely looking over the rim of her cup but listening to the sounds, the comforting, familiar sounds of batter being mixed and plates clattering.

She didn't know what to think about it all, so she just sipped and listened.

And for a nice long while, the kitchen and the people in it were all that existed.

32

Natalie didn't think she'd be able to sleep, when Selena led her to a bedroom, set her bag down, smiled, and left her to rest.

For a while, adrift in the centre of the room, she didn't think she'd be able to do anything but stand there, frozen.

Not my room, the voice in her head said. Not my room, not my house.

She waited for the panic attack to come, braced herself for it, putting her hand across her mouth so that no one would hear her when she started crying.

And panic did prickle at her, but somehow, she got her eyes closed and forced herself to breath slowly and deeply.

Then she went and sat on the bed, put her bag on her lap, then on the floor, found her nightshirt and changed into it. The sun was rising and reached through the window to turn her skin to a burnished bronze.

She drew the nightshirt over her head, gulping in the sight of the sun, watching as it turned the backs of her eyelids to copper. She got into the bed bathed in the light, and lay there inside it, closing her eyes and sliding finally, thankfully, into sleep.

She dreamed of the small girl. Clover.

Clover came into her room, something in her hands, and went over to the rug on the floor and crouched there, playing.

Natalie knelt down with her, a little girl herself once more, and they played together, the sun shining on them, turning Clover's hair to a bright halo, and between them, a sweet brown teddy bear came to life and played too.

In her dream, Natalie smiled, felt the bear's soft fur, and let herself relax, playing with her new friends as the morning light grew stronger.

RUE MET EBONY ON THE FOOTPATH OUTSIDE OF THE SCHOOL, grabbed her by the elbow and nudged her away from the school gates.

'We're not going in,' she said.

'What?'

Rue shook her head. 'I texted the others on my way, and we're going to meet Sophie and Suze.' Rue cast a glance around to make sure no one was paying them any attention. 'Pretend we gotta go to the shop on the corner,' she said.

She was already walking Ebony in that direction.

'We're skipping classes?' Ebony asked, as they got to the corner and kept going.

'That's exactly what we're doing,' Rue said, her voice determined. She tugged Ebony across the road just in time to jump aboard the bus pulling up and paid the fare for both of them before hustling Ebony to a seat.

'I am most in favour of this plan,' Ebony said. 'But what has brought it on?' She narrowed her eyes at Rue. 'And how on this great green earth did you get Suze to agree to skipping a day's school?'

'A morning's school,' Rue said. 'We can go back for the afternoon classes.' She glanced at the old woman in the seat opposite them who was gazing narrowly at their school uniforms.

'We're meeting at the library,' Rue said.

'The library?'

Rue nodded, shrugged. 'I wanted to go there anyway – we never did get out the books we wanted last time.'

Ebony leaned back in her seat. 'Field Marshall Meadows.'

'Yeah, well, she isn't stopping us this time.'

Ebony looked approvingly over at Rue. 'What else?' she asked.

Rue raised an eyebrow. 'What else?'

'You said *anyway*. You wanted to go there *anyway*.'

'Right.' Rue nodded, looked over at the woman in the seat opposite. 'Some things are more important that science class and a free period.'

The woman looked away. Rue thought she was probably still listening though, and she discovered she didn't care.

Important things were happening.

'The police caught the guy last night,' she said.

Ebony stared silently at her for a moment, mouth hanging open.

'What?'

Rue nodded. 'One of the creeps who tried to attack me yesterday.'

The old woman stiffened in her seat, but Rue ignored her, looking at Ebony. A curious elation bubbled up inside her. She'd always known the world was different than everyone thought – thanks to Clover and her spectacular gifts – but now Rue felt like she was swimming in it, actually a part of all that difference.

It excited her. Life seemed, since meeting Selena, and even Sophie, Ebony, and Suze, deeper now. Deeper and wider.

Just like Clover said.

They got off the bus in the city and walked up to the library.

Ebony listened in astonishment to Rue's story. 'And now this woman is staying at your place?'

'Yep.' Rue lifted her shoulders in a shrug. 'Don't know how long for, though. A few days, apparently.'

'I should develop an issue,' Ebony said. 'And get myself taken in as well.'

Rue laughed. 'You can visit whenever you like, is that good enough?'

Ebony grinned and looked pleased. 'Rue,' she said. 'The day I met you should be made into a public holiday.'

Suze and Sophie were waiting in the courtyard outside the library, self-conscious in their uniforms and trying to hide it.

'About time,' Suze said. 'We've been waiting ages, hoping we don't meet anyone we know to ask us why we're bunking off school.'

'Don't worry,' Ebony said airily. 'You can tell all at confession on Sunday.'

Suze gave her a flat look, then turned to Rue. 'Are you all right?'

Rue nodded. 'Thanks for doing this,' she said, colouring slightly. 'Meeting me, I mean.'

'I was glad to,' Sophie said. 'After what happened yesterday.' She grimaced. 'I'm still a bit freaked out about it all, to be honest.'

'They caught him,' Ebony said. 'One of them.'

'What?'

Suze and Sophie looked from Ebony to Rue, who nodded.

'He tried to attack another woman in her house last night, but the police caught him – in the nick of time.'

Suze's eyes were round as saucers. 'Was she all right? The woman?'

'Here's where the story really gets juicy,' Ebony said, a smug smile on her face. 'You won't believe it when you hear it.'

Except they did.

Rue told them everything that had happened while she lay asleep in her bed the night before – as told to her by Tara that morning, out of hearing of the new woman, Natalie.

'What do you think?' she asked them at last.

Suze shook her head. 'That's unreal,' she said. 'And Selena dreamed it was happening?'

'She dreamed she was standing right next to the guy, outside the house, and she could hear what he was thinking.'

'Wow.' Sophie was shaking her head. 'That's incredible.'

'I want to be Selena when I grow up,' Ebony announced.

Rue nodded. 'Me too.'

'She needs to open a school for priestesses,' Ebony said.

That made Rue laugh. 'I'll tell her – but I think she already is. She said she's going to teach me. Finally.'

'What about the rest of us?' Ebony asked.

'We still have to learn how to magic up our staves and stuff,' Sophie said. 'And get rid of the ghost in my house. Not that I've told my parents anything about making a staff.' She shook her head. 'I don't think they'd understand.'

Rue looked at her, then Suze. 'Same for you?' she asked.

Suze nodded, then shrugged. 'If they can believe in a virgin birth, then I can have a magic stick.'

Rue nodded. 'She was planning to do the staff thing with us next weekend – and go to your house sometime, Sophie, to help the spirit cross over if she can.' Rue paused. 'But I don't know if she will now. She might be busy with Natalie for a little while.'

'Has this poor Natalie person really not left her house for years?' Suze asked.

'I don't know if it's been years,' Rue said with a shrug. 'But it's been a long time.'

'I feel sorry for her,' Sophie said. 'That's really rough.'

They were silent for a long minute, then Rue nodded.

'I want to get some books out of the library,' she said. 'Selena can't teach us every day or anything, so I want to read as much as I can and learn as much as I can around what she can do.' She closed her mouth, thinking about her dreams, the woman in the blue dress, the way she'd taken over when the two men had been after her.

The priestess.

'I wish we could live somewhere like Wilde Grove used to be,' she said.

'Yeah,' Ebony agreed. 'That would be much more fun than Mr Evans and trigonometry.'

'Or Madame Jeoffrey and French,' Sophie said.

'I thought you liked French?' Suze asked her.

'I do,' Sophie sighed. 'But it's not very useful, is it?'

'Unless you go to France,' Ebony said.

'Unless I want to teach high school French,' Sophie said. 'And no way do I want to do that.'

Rue looked curiously at her, at all her new friends. They still stood outside the library, the morning sun lighting them. 'What do you all want to do when you leave school?' she asked. It was only a couple years away.

'I want to be a ghost hunter,' Ebony promptly said. 'Just like I told you the other day. Except instead of just proving they exist, I want to help them.'

Suze looked at her with a straight face. 'What subjects do you need for that?' she asked.

'Dunno,' Ebony said and heaved a sigh. 'I'd probably be better off dividing my time between in there...' She stuck her thumb out at the library door. 'And out in the field. I'm taking geography though, in case it's useful in some way. And history, because well, history is about dead people and ghosts are dead people, right?'

'I guess so,' Suze said. She laughed. 'I want to be a doctor,' she said to Rue. 'Lots of years of study in front of me, then.'

Rue nodded, looked at Sophie. 'What about you? If you don't want to be a teacher, what do you want to do?'

'I want to travel,' Sophie said shyly. 'All over the world. That's why I'm taking French. I'd take more languages if our school taught them. I don't know how to make money while I'm doing it, though.'

They fell silent, thinking about that.

'Let's go get some books out,' Rue said at last. 'We've all got things we want to do, but I think this is important no matter what.'

The girls nodded.

'It's about living, right?' Rue said. She'd taken a few steps towards the library doors, but now she stopped, turned back to look at her friends.

'No matter what we do after we finish school, it's about how we want to live. And I want to live like this, no matter what. No matter what I do. I want to live from my heart in this much bigger world, where there's still magic.'

33

NATALIE OPENED THE BEDROOM DOOR AN INCH AND BLINKED through the narrow gap into the hallway, trying to find the courage to step out into the strange house.

She'd woken only minutes before, sitting up in her bed, wide awake suddenly with the sensation that just before she'd sat up, something had moved on the bed, fallen to the floor.

A bear, she thought, the detail seeping through from her dream. It had been a bear, someone's teddy bear. Had someone opened her door while she was sleeping and brought in a bear? She'd looked around, but there was nothing on the floor except for her clothes, in a heap where she'd left them.

It had been just a dream, then.

And now she needed the toilet. Where was the bathroom? How was she supposed to go out there and find it?

Someone was sitting by the door, and Natalie opened it wider in surprise.

Clover stared at her, mouth blossoming into a joyous smile. 'You waken!'

'Hello,' Natalie said. 'What are you doing?'

Clover, surprised by the question, looked down at the small chair she'd dragged from her room to put by the door so she could sit and wait.

'I waitin' for you,' she said. Then held up one of her model animals. 'This one for you,' she said. 'We was playin' with it.'

Natalie stared at the small, realistic model bear, and licked her dry lips. 'We were playing with it?'

'Yep,' Clover said. 'Little you an' me.' She held the animal out until Natalie reached tentatively out and took it from her. 'You keep it,' Clover said. 'To 'mind you.'

'Mind me?'

'Yeah. He's your frien'.'

The door wide open now, Natalie straightened, turning over the figure in her hands. 'I dreamed it,' she said.

'Yep,' Clover said, standing looking delightedly at her. 'Me too, 'cept I wasn't sleepin'. Was fun playin' with you.'

Natalie squeezed the plastic bear in her hand and the world swayed slightly around her.

Clover shook her head. 'Is alright,' she said. And held out her hand. 'I show you where the bathroom is. You can have a shower, if you like.'

Clover's hand was warm and small, and Natalie, who didn't remember putting out her own hand to hold it, was glad for it. The child was odd, she thought.

But lovely. She looked at the little girl, and something welled up inside her. She didn't recognise the emotion at first, then, startled, realised it was happiness.

Something inside her was happy. Some piece of herself, long forgotten, was happy.

'I can stay here while you have a shower, if ya like,' Clover said. 'I can get my chair.'

'Don't you have other things to do?' Natalie asked at the bathroom door.

Clover shook her head. 'I can wait for ya.'

Natalie slipped into the bathroom, used the toilet, then looked at the shower. Looked all around the bathroom, in fact.

This was a new place, she said to herself. She was in a different house. She'd never been here before. Natalie shook her head. She wanted to close her eyes. It was too strange, being in this room, in this house. Her hands tightened into fists, her breath hitching.

Something dug into the tender flesh of her palm, and she straightened out her fingers and looked at the plastic bear.

It made her feel better. She opened the shower door and put it on the soap dish, looked at it dazedly for a long moment, then turned the water on.

Afterwards, Clover walked back to her room with her, dragging her small chair. Natalie tried to concentrate on what the child was saying, but Clover's voice came as though from a long way away.

'You get dressed, okay?' Clover said. 'I wait, and then we can have lunch.' She patted her tummy. 'Tara makes us lunch. Is so good.'

Natalie paused on the threshold, gripping her dressing gown closed in one hand, and the bear in the other.

'I don't know,' she said. The idea of going downstairs

made her feel faint. She'd got through breakfast with everyone – but now she wasn't sure.

'I wait,' Clover said, and planted her chair in front of the door and sat down, folding her arms over her chest.

Natalie stared at the child wide-eyed for a moment, then turned and stumbled into her room.

The room was good. It made her feel better, being in there, with the door closed. She changed into fresh clothes, looking at the rug at the end of the bed, and remembering her dream.

Her dream of playing with Clover and a small bear cub, its fur so soft and thick. She'd put the model bear down on the bed and now, dressed, she shook her head slowly.

Clover had spoken as though she knew she'd been part of the dream.

Natalie's head buzzed. She sat on the bed, staring at the bear, then looked up as there was a knock on the door.

'She gettin' dressed,' Clover told Tara. 'She takin' a long time. Is lunchtime.'

Tara smiled at the child. Clover had insisted on playing outside Natalie's door. She'd barely budged from the spot.

The door opened a smidge and Tara transferred her attention from Clover to Natalie.

'Hello,' she said softly. 'I thought I'd just come and see if you wanted something to eat. Would you like to come downstairs and eat in the kitchen with Clover and me?'

Natalie took a shaky breath but opened the door wider. 'Where is Selena?' she whispered.

'Selena and Dandy are out for a bit, and Damien is at work. It's just us three.'

Tara waited, hoping that Natalie would agree to come

down. Selena had warned her that Natalie would perhaps not want to, but that Tara might try gently to encourage her.

Natalie looked at Clover, who was smiling at her, small face bright. She nodded.

'Thank you,' she said.

'Lovely!' Tara was pleased, and she stepped back so Natalie could walk with her.

Clover skipped ahead.

'Selena tells me you enjoy baking?' Tara walked slowly, matching Natalie's speed, seeing how the woman seemed to shy away from everything. It must be all very strange for her, she thought.

Natalie nodded. Grasped the thought of her mixing bowls and measuring cups and held it to her. 'Baking calms me.'

'I'm trying to learn,' Tara said. 'What do you like making?'

Natalie's mouth was dry. The staircase was wide, lots of steps. Had it had so many when she'd gone up it?

'I like making cakes,' she said. Then grasped another thought. 'I brought my favourite recipe book.'

She looked down at her hands. She was holding the bear again.

'You did?' Tara sounded delighted. 'That's wonderful.' She paused. 'Could we make something from it this afternoon? I need the practice.'

Startled, Natalie forgot herself and looked at Tara.

'You want to bake with me?'

Tara nodded. 'I'd love to,' she said.

'Okay,' Natalie agreed, then nodded. Baking. That was something she could do. Already, she imagined the calmness of measuring flour and creaming butter and sugar. She followed Tara through to the large room that was the kitchen.

'What shall we make?' she asked.

'I've a lot of apples,' Tara said, pulling a chair out from the table so that Clover could climb onto it. 'We could make something with those, perhaps. Do you have any recipes?'

Natalie almost laughed at the question. She nodded instead, sitting where Tara indicated and keeping her head down, only risking looking up and around in little visual gulps.

She'd been in the kitchen before, Selena's hand on her arm, and it felt at least a little familiar.

At least a little safe.

'Yes,' she said at last, as Tara laid out fresh bread and salads.

Clover reached for a slice of cheese, then sat back nibbling on it, watching Natalie with satisfaction.

The bear was on the table beside Natalie's plate.

'I have two recipes I like to make with apples,' Natalie said, risking a glance at Tara. 'One is a chocolate apple cake, and the other is spicy with a crunchy topping.' She looked momentarily perplexed. 'Wait,' she said. 'The chocolate cake uses courgettes, not apples.'

'What are 'gettes?' Clover asked, looking dubious.

'They're a sort of vegetable,' Tara answered. 'We have some growing in the garden – the zucchini.'

Clover looked even more startled. 'You don' put vege'bles in cakes.'

Natalie giggled, then clapped a hand over her mouth,

eyes round at the sound that had come from her own self. When had she last laughed?

'I think sometimes you do,' Tara told Clover seriously. Then she looked over at Natalie. 'How about we try your crunchy one first, though?'

Clover nodded. 'Crunchy good.'

Natalie nodded, reached for a slice of bread and some lettuce. 'It takes 125grams of butter for the cake, two teaspoons of mixed spice, half a teaspoon of ground cloves, one cup of brown sugar, one egg, 2 apples – we grate those, with their skins on – and 1 and a half cups of flour.' She blinked, laid some sliced tomato on her bread. 'We can use either plain or wholemeal. I like wholemeal because it seems to go with the texture of the cake well.' She paused, hand in mid-air, holding another slice of bread for the top of her sandwich. 'Oh. And a teaspoon of baking soda. Soda, not powder. That's for the cake. Then there's extra for the topping, which is the crunchy bit.'

She looked at Tara, and blushed. 'I'm sorry,' she said. 'I didn't mean to go on like that.'

Tara shook her head, a wide smile on her face. 'That was amazing,' she said. 'You know the recipe off by heart.' She took a deep breath. 'I'd like to be able to do that one day.'

But Natalie shook her head. 'Baking keeps me calm, but I think I get a bit obsessive about it.' She clenched her hands. Looked at the model bear, then over the table at Tara's hands. They were deftly building a sandwich for Clover.

'I get scared a lot,' Natalie said. 'Panic attacks.'

She closed her mouth then, not sure why she'd said what she had.

But Tara just nodded, pressed down the bread lid of Clover's sandwich, then cut it deftly in half. 'Selena said this is the first time you've been away from home for a while.'

Natalie looked at her sandwich, neatly made now on her plate. She nodded.

Tara glanced at her. Reached impetuously across the table and touched her hand to Natalie's. 'It's going to be okay,' she said. 'You're doing great.'

Natalie's cheeks burned with embarrassment. 'I shouldn't be like this,' she muttered. 'I should be stronger. Able to cope.' She shrugged her shoulders, then reached out and touched the bear.

'That's your frien',' Clover said.

Natalie shook her head. Looked at Tara. 'What does she mean by that? She keeps saying it.'

'Ah,' Tara said, tousling Clover's curls. 'There's a question.'

'I dreamed Clover and I were playing on the rug in the sunshine with a little bear cub. I think it was a teddy bear, but it seemed so real.' Natalie blinked. 'I don't really know what's going on,' she said.

'I know exactly how you feel,' Tara said. She opened her mouth to say more, then thought twice. What should she say? How should she try to explain things? Natalie was sitting in her chair like a frightened child.

'We was playin',' Clover said, swallowing her mouthful of sandwich and nodding vigorously. 'We was playin' with your bear.' She nodded towards the figurine. 'He your frien'.'

Natalie shook her head. 'It was a dream. You can't play in my dream.'

Clover giggled, turned to Tara. 'Can an' did,' she said. 'You 'splain.'

Tara shook her head, looked at Natalie and blew out a puff of air. 'Selena's the one who will really explain things to you,' she said. 'But our little Clover here – well, she has some very particular gifts. If she says she was playing with you in your dream, she probably was.' Tara pressed her lips together and hoped that Natalie wasn't about to stand up and demand to be taken straight home.

Natalie stared at her. She shook her head. There was the sound of static in her head, as though her brain had tuned itself between stations. She swallowed, wanted to go home, thought about that for a moment, shied away from the thought of being alone there.

'Perhaps we could make that cake now,' she said limply.

Tara nodded in relief. 'Definitely,' she said. 'Cake making sounds just the way to spend the afternoon.'

'Are you sure this is the way to do it?' Dandy said.

Selena laughed and nodded. 'Natalie is going to need a lot of help. Let her spend a little time with Tara and Clover – Tara is a very grounding person to be around – so that she can settle in to being somewhere new for a while, without the pressure of all of us fluttering around.'

Dandy eyed Selena. She shook her head. 'Fluttering?' Another shake of the head. 'I just can't imagine you fluttering, Selena.'

Selena looked at her, a smile quirking her lips. 'I don't flutter?'

'Nope.' Dandy gave it some thought as they walked

along the path through the garden and up the hill. She was getting so much fitter with all this walking around tree-hugging. 'Glide, perhaps.' She nodded. 'Yes, that's the closest I can come, perhaps. Glide. You glide along, Selena, as though you know exactly where you're going and what you're doing.'

'Hmm.' Selena considered that. 'I don't always know what I'm doing, or where I'm going,' she said. 'But I do know my purpose, and that keeps me...' She tried to think of the right word.

'Serene,' Dandy offered. 'Unperturbed. Confident, in a glowing sort of way, not an arsehole sort of way.'

Selena's brows rose. She smiled. 'My practice grounds me on my path,' she said. 'I don't always know what is around the corner, but yes, I have the confidence, of the glowing sort, I do hope, that I can weather any storm and find true north.'

'That's a valuable thing, these days,' Dandy said.

'It's a valuable thing in any time or place.'

They reached the top of the hill and crossed out of the Botanic Garden into the patch of woods that lay between the garden and the cemetery.

'What do you make of Rue's spirit, then?' Dandy asked suddenly, looking around them. They were walking through the same area Rue had hidden in. And sharpened a stick to make a pretty handy spear while she did.

'I am not sure,' Selena said, frowning softly over the question.

'You said it was a past life. Or that's what Rue seems to think, anyway.'

Selena nodded. 'And so it seems most likely.'

'But?' Dandy asked. 'I sense a but in there. You don't think she turned up just to keep Rue safe yesterday?'

'I think it was mostly just good fortune that she was there to help Rue.'

Dandy digested that nugget for a moment. 'You mean, there's another reason?'

'Something else is going on there, I'm sure of it,' Selena said. 'But what that something is, I don't know, as yet.' She smiled at Dandy. 'It's around a corner in front of us,' she said.

Dandy nodded. 'Better keep walking the path, then.' She paused, had another thought. 'You're going to teach them?'

They left the shade of the trees and slipped into the cemetery to follow the path through the old gravestones. Selena was heading for a particular tree. Dandy was with her to make sure they weren't disturbed when they got there.

'Yes,' Selena answered. She drew in a deep breath, scented with the roses that grew unkempt but beautiful around many of the old plots. 'We should have anticipated, I think, that Rue would be talented, or have a deep purpose, since she came into this life in such close proximity to Clover.' She smiled. 'Yes, I am going to teach her. And her friends. Beginning with making their staves, since they'll find that fun.' She thought for a moment. 'And I'll teach them the foundation of grounding and centring, which is how we all begin to safely work with spirit.' She shook her head. 'It's not enough to just greet the day with me, and perform those small rituals that Rue is already doing.'

Dandy raised her gaze to meet Selena's. 'It's not?'

'No, because it's not all I'm doing during it. I'm not just

greeting the sun and dedicating my service to the day; I'm aligning my spirit. Grounding myself. Becoming clear and centred.'

'Sounds like what I do to prepare for a reading,' Dandy said.

'We all need to do it, every day. All outer work is really inner work.' Selena said, then smiled as they reached the tree she had been seeking. 'Ah,' she said. 'Here we are.' She looked at the huge sequoia. 'How did this tree get to be here?' she asked Dandy, shaking her head. 'It's as far from its natural home as I am.'

Dandy tipped her head back and looked at the sweeping, spreading branches of the giant redwood.

She shook her head. 'I've no idea,' she said. 'But they certainly grow well enough here.'

They admired the tree in all its perfectly formed splendour for a moment, then Selena smiled at Dandy.

'This is going to look a little strange,' she said. 'And it's in a public place, which I'm not used to.'

'What exactly are you going to do?' Dandy asked.

'Every Lady of the Grove...' Selena stopped talking and frowned a moment. 'I suppose I'm still one.'

'You're definitely still one.'

She nodded. 'Every Lady of the Grove has an affinity to trees, simply because of the fact that we practice alongside them. If we lived and practiced in a different type of landscape, then it would be otherwise.'

Dandy nodded. 'Lady of the Cactus, perhaps.' She laughed.

'You may snigger,' Selena said, smiling widely, 'but that

is perfectly possible. All creatures have things to teach, cacti included.'

'I don't doubt it,' Dandy replied, but she was still grinning. 'So, what are you going to do with the tree?'

Selena gazed upwards into the high branches again and patted the sturdy trunk. 'I've come to know this tree,' she said. 'On my travels around the area.'

She'd thought that she would go to one of the oaks in the Botanic Garden, but this tree was better situated, and she resonated with it. They were both strangers in this land, and the tree stood sentinel over the graveyard, which was another sort of place altogether, the realm of the dead, and she could easily imagine the tree growing in the Otherworld as it did here.

'I'm going to ask it to help...top up my energy levels. To give me a little of its tree magic.'

Dandy nodded slowly, giving the tree another assessing glance. 'Well,' she said. 'You couldn't have picked a finer, stronger specimen.'

'Hopefully, it will agree to do so.'

This surprised Dandy. 'They don't always?'

'Good heavens, no,' Selena said and patted the tree again. 'Trees have personalities almost as varied as we do. Some are more vigorous, some more dreamy. I need a vigorous tree to do what I'm about to – and this one has a great deal of wisdom as well.' She smiled. 'Perhaps it will share some of that with me also.'

Dandy nodded slowly, her mind buzzing. This was a thing that people did? That could be done? She'd heard of tree hugging before, but this was taking it to a whole new level.

It was very interesting, she thought.

'I'll head off any nosy passers-by,' she said. 'So that you'll be as little disturbed as possible.'

'I'd be grateful,' Selena said. She was already turned to the tree, breathing slowly, letting herself relax and expand.

34

THE SEQUOIA'S BARK WAS ROUGH UNDER SELENA'S HANDS AS she placed both against it and leaned in close. Her eyelids slid down, and she breathed in the clean, healing scent of the tree, letting herself sink deeper into its song with each breath out.

For the tree sang softly to itself, as it stood, guardian of the dead, in the old cemetery.

Its voice was low and deep, here in its dreaming, and Selena bowed deeply to it, greeting it, listening to its song.

She asked for her favour and the tree rumbled in pleasure at her request.

Certainly, it would fill her with its song, it told her. And began to hum, its sap rising as it sang, its energy rising from its roots, up toward its branches, and then down again, in its great looping life force.

Selena pressed palm and forehead against it, felt the energy pass into her, fill her, felt the buzzing humming life of it, and joined her own dreaming voice to that of the tree.

They sang together for a long time. How long, Selena didn't know. It could have been the time it took for a seed to fall to the ground, or for the time it took for a sapling to reach full height. For a season, or for a moment.

'Do you know what I plan?' she murmured to it in the midst of their singing.

I do, the tree hummed back at her. And it sang its energy through her once more, for she had a great task and required the strength of a thick trunk, and the conviction and instinct of a tree who knew when to spring forth, and when to sleep and dream.

Dandy nodded at a dogwalker and her spaniel, and stood with her hands in her pockets, blocking Selena from interruption. The dogwalker gave them a curious glance and hurried on her way, the spaniel wagging his tail at her side.

Selena surfaced, kept her head pressed against the tree a moment longer, thanking it, giving it her blessing, then she stood back and sighed.

'All good?' Dandy asked.

Selena closed her eyes and breathed in. She felt the wind in her hair and felt strong and tall and full of the song of the seasons.

'Yes,' she said, opening her eyes. 'Very much better.'

Dandy looked curiously at her. 'You don't look as tired either,' she said. 'Perhaps I should give that a go, considering how little sleep we had last night.'

'Perhaps you should,' Selena said, stepping to the side and gesturing at the tree.

Dandy was about to shake her head. After all, she'd been joking. She hadn't meant it seriously.

'What do you do?' she asked.

'Be quiet until you can hear the song of the tree,' Selena answered. She touched her chest. 'Slow your breathing, feel for the tree, for its energy, its voice, its song.' She took another step from the tree and nodded. 'Then ask what you need of it and listen to its answer.'

Dandy hesitated, thinking how silly she'd feel doing all that. But Selena really did look less tired. Her face had regained its quiet serenity.

'Maybe I will,' she said softly, and approached the tree, glancing around to see if the dogwalker was gone, if they were alone.

She placed her hands on the tree as she'd seen Selena do. Palms flat to it, then leaned in so that her cheek brushed against the reddish-brown bark.

'Hello tree,' she whispered, feeling foolish. She shut her eyes, remembering what Selena had said.

Breathe slowly, feel for the tree, listen for its voice.

She tried to breathe more slowly. Sucking in the scent of the tree, feeling its knotted bark against her skin. She held her breath a moment, let it out. Listened for the tree's singing.

Couldn't hear anything.

Dandy felt vaguely silly.

There was a touch on her shoulder, and Selena's voice.

'Hush,' Selena said. 'You're making too much noise inside your head. Just breathe.'

Dandy breathed, and felt herself sink suddenly, and jerked her feet, steadied herself.

'That's it,' Selena said. 'Let yourself sink down into awareness of the tree and nothing else. Let it sing to you.'

Dandy swallowed, slowed her breathing again, and let herself flow down into the darkness behind her eyes. Except it wasn't all darkness there. There was warmth, and something low and sweet there with her.

Something with a heartbeat that was deep and wide and vibrated through the world.

Was this what Selena had meant, this heartbeat?

Perhaps, Dandy thought, listening to it. Perhaps this was a sort of a song, for the heartbeat seemed to her to hold everything in the world within it. Its whole history, the history of the tree and its forest and all forests, for trees, she discovered, had long memories, and grew in many worlds.

She listened to the heartbeat until her own seemed to beat in time with it, and then she didn't know how long she stood there, part of the heartbeat of the worlds.

Dandy blinked in the light when she drew away from the tree and looked stupidly around. Selena was standing next to her, one hand still on her shoulder, a smile on her face.

Dandy shook her head. 'Did you hear that?' she asked.

'Hear what?'

Another shake of the head. 'I heard the tree's heart beating.' She squeezed her eyes shut. 'But trees don't have heartbeats.'

'Trees are one of the heartbeats of the worlds,' Selena said. 'They are the history keepers, the guardians of liminal space.'

'Liminal space?'

'The edges between here and there, this and that. Above and below. Inside and out.'

Dandy shook her head. 'What did you do to me?'

Selena raised her eyebrows.

'When you put your hand on me,' Dandy said. 'I wasn't having any luck before that.'

'I just helped you hear,' Selena said. 'Helped you go that bit deeper.'

'How?' Dandy gazed around, looking at the paths, and the gravestones, and feeling as though behind everything, there lurked something else now. Something more. Another world.

Worlds.

'How can you do that?' she asked. 'Make me go deeper just by touching me?'

'I am used to walking the worlds,' Selena said. 'I hold them within me all the time. Which,' she smiled, 'has taken many years of practice to perfect.'

Dandy shook her head slowly. 'Learn something new every day,' she said, then looked at Selena. 'Is it time to go?'

Selena nodded. Natalie waited for them back at the house.

'S'LENA'S COMIN',' CLOVER ANNOUNCED, SLIDING OFF HER chair at the table and running to grapple with the door to the garden. She swung around on the doorknob, barely able to turn it, and let go when it swivelled around under her hands.

'S'lena!' Clover crowed. 'We made cake!'

'That sounds yum,' Selena said.

Dandy shook her head. 'Wait a minute, munchkin,' she said, narrowing her eyes. 'What sort of cake?'

Clover grinned and did a little hopping dance. 'Crunchy

cake! Nat'lie knew the recipe off by her heart.'

'Did she now?' Selena asked. 'That's very clever.'

'An' it tastes real good,' Clover said. 'We saved you some.'

They went into the kitchen, a small procession led by a dancing child. Dandy sniffed the air appreciatively.

'That smells marvellous,' she declared.

'It certainly does, doesn't it?' Tara replied, from where she was sitting at the table, her books spread in front of her, including her own large notebook where she was writing in the attributes associated with various herbs and flavourings.

'Did you know,' she said, 'that every flower or plant or herb contains its own particular magick?'

'Hmm,' Dandy said, sitting herself down at the table and reaching to feel if the teapot was still warm. 'I like the idea of that.'

Tara nodded. 'Tea's hot,' she said. 'I just made it.'

'Where's Natalie?' Selena asked, pausing to pour herself a cup of tea too. She tapped Dandy on the arm. 'You should have a piece of that cake,' she said. 'It will ground you after your small adventure.'

'Your 'venture?' Clover asked.

'Yes,' Dandy said. 'I had a go at being a tree for a while.'

Clover narrowed her eyes. 'A tree?'

'You betcha,' Dandy said, eyes twinkling.

Tara looked at Selena. 'Natalie is in her room, resting.'

'How did she do this morning?'

Tara nodded. 'Really well, I thought. Very skittish, but once we got to baking, she calmed down and seemed to relax. She's a whizz in the kitchen. The police coming and taking her statement was a bit of a shock, but she coped well, I thought.'

332

'I gave her my bear,' Clover said, bouncing on her chair. 'She got a bear, you see.'

Selena did see, and she smoothed her hand over Clover's curls. 'That was very kind of you.'

'I take it the bear is one of Natalie's spirit kin?' Tara asked, hearing the words coming out of her mouth with a certain disbelief. She'd never known she would one day be speaking of spirit animals and so on with such casual acceptance.

Life had certainly deepened and widened and grown more beautiful, more meaningful.

'Yup,' Clover said, and nodded under Selena's hand. She twisted around to look at Selena. 'I played with little Nat'lie in her dream. We played with the baby bear.'

Selena gazed down at Clover, thinking for the hundredth time how broad the child's gifts were. Everything she did was possible for others to do as well, Selena knew this, but Clover was able to perform without training, without years of practice. She wondered how this had come to be, what lives this soul had lived, because it was obvious that a great many skills had been learnt over time by it.

'You played with little Natalie?' she asked finally.

Clover nodded, feeling pleased with herself. 'I like her,' she said, then frowned. 'She lives in the blanky tent, though.' She gazed up at Selena. 'Is it comfy 'nuff in the blanky tent?'

'I think we'll have to find somewhere better for little Natalie than that,' Selena said.

Tara shook her head at the same time that Clover was nodding at Selena's answer.

'Whoa there,' Tara said. 'You've gone right on by me –

what do you mean Natalie lives in the blanky tent?' There was consternation on her face.

Selena took a sip of her tea. She decided that discussing Natalie within this circle of those dedicated to helping her was not only acceptable, but probably required.

'Natalie had something of a traumatic childhood, I think,' Selena said softly, holding her teacup in one hand and stroking Clover's curls with the other. 'Part of her retreated then, to the safest place she could find, and is there still.'

Tara looked confused. 'A blanket tent?'

Selena nodded. 'She made it in a corner in her bedroom and retreated to it.'

Tara was appalled. 'But,' she said, then shook her head. 'That's terrible.' She gazed at Selena. 'That really happens?'

'All the time,' Selena said. 'Once, in our long-ago societies, it would have been dealt with as a matter of course. But as we became more civilised...' Selena raised her eyebrows. 'We stopped that sort of thing, and as a result, there are a lot of us walking around who are not whole.'

Tara looked around the room, dismayed, then shook her head. 'Can you help her?' she asked Selena.

'Yes,' Selena answered. 'I believe so. I am certainly going to try, although reintegrating her lost child is only part of what she requires. Important, but only one aspect of it all.'

Tara swallowed. 'I want to help too,' she said. 'Tell me what I can do to help.'

Selena smiled. 'You can teach her to be grounded and strong upon the earth she stands on.'

Tara blinked. 'I know how to do that?'

Selena indicated Tara's books. 'You are learning it.' She

pointed at the drift of books on the table, and nodded. 'I can tell from the way you are in the kitchen, that the lessons of these books are sinking in – that when you are cooking and baking for us all, the kitchen becomes your sacred space.'

Tara bent her head, thought about that, then nodded. 'Yes,' she said. 'I feel really grounded and present now, whenever I'm working on something in the kitchen. Really calm, and it's like I see and do everything from a different perspective.' She shook her head. 'I don't really understand it yet, but it's really powerful.'

'You're working from your body and your heart, Tara,' Selena answered with a smile. 'Whenever we are up in our heads, listening to all the chatter that goes on in there, we tighten up, our hearts clench like a fist, and everything is more difficult. But when we relax into whatever we're doing, and be mindful about it, calm and sweet, then our heart relaxes, blooms like a rose, and the moment is spacious enough to live a whole life in, and do a great deal of magic.'

Tara nodded, her face relaxing into an expression of joy.

'This is where you start,' Selena said, putting her hands on Tara's shoulders and beaming at her. 'This is where each of us starts. We cannot straddle the worlds if we are not strong in our own centre.' She looked at the others in the room. 'And that is where real magic is done – from the strong, centred heart. That is how we find our soul purpose, the flow of our lives.'

'We're all going to learn this,' Selena said.

Clover looked up at her. 'Even me?'

'Even you,' Selena said.

'Everyone.'

35

SELENA STOPPED QUICKLY IN HER ROOM, THEN WENT ALONG the hallway and knocked quietly on Natalie's door.

'May I come in?' she asked.

There was a reply almost too soft for Selena to make out, but she opened the door, stepped into the room, and closed the door behind her. She brought with her into the room the trees of the Wildwood, folding them around into a burrow, a cocoon of warmth and safety. She did it almost without thinking.

'How are you, Natalie?' she asked.

Natalie sat on the bed, back against the headboard, knees tucked up to her ribcage. She shook her head.

'I think I ought to go home now,' she said. Her brown eyes closed for a moment, then blinked open, wide and skittish. 'You've been terribly kind,' she said. 'Helping me yesterday, and bringing me here, but I think I'm better off going home now.'

Natalie flicked her gaze away from Selena and looked at

the painting beside the door instead. It was of a cottage in the woods somewhere.

Selena followed her gaze. 'I like that picture,' she said conversationally, easily, sitting down on the end of the bed. 'I look at it and think what a lovely calm place to live.'

Natalie shook her head. 'It's Grandmother's cottage in the woods,' she said.

'Grandmother's?'

Natalie swallowed, tightened her arms around her knees. 'Yes,' she said. 'The Big Bad Wolf is on its way to it. He's in the shadows in the woods somewhere.'

She turned her eyes from the picture, but they landed on Selena, so she dropped them and stared at the bedcover instead.

'I really do think it's time I went back home,' she said.

'Natalie,' Selena said, and shifted slightly on the bed, wondering which was the best approach to take. 'Do you like living the way you do? Not leaving the house?'

Natalie stared at her in surprise. Then shook her head disbelievingly. 'Like it?' she asked. 'What's there to like about it?' She blew out a breath and looked away, stared at the floor. 'I hate it.'

'Then you want to change it?'

Natalie shook her head. 'I can't change it,' she said.

'You'd want to, if you thought you could?'

'Of course.' Natalie replied, dropping her head to her knees so that her words were muffled. 'But it's too late.' She paused, and a question rose to the surface from deep inside her. 'Isn't it too late?'

'I don't think so,' Selena said quietly, feeling a soft breeze stirring inside her. 'I don't think it's too late.'

Natalie held herself still at the answer. 'I saw someone for a long time. A psychologist. It helped, and the medication helped.' She paused.

'Until none of it did.'

'I can help,' Selena said. 'I can help you help yourself. So that you can go back to the psychologist and the medication if you need. But you must want to help yourself.'

Natalie lifted her head, looked at her, not saying anything for the longest time.

'How?' she said at last, the word almost a sigh. She went to say something more, something about no one being able to help, and then she remembered how warm Selena's hands had been the night before. How when Selena had touched her, everything had felt a bit better.

A little safer.

'How?' she asked again, whispering. She closed her eyes. 'Please help me.'

Selena didn't answer straight away. She was looking at the corner of the room, at the shadows there.

She was looking because she could feel the child stepping out, sidling up to her, taking her hand. Staring around at the room, at the trees Selena had brought in with her, at their solid trunks, their bright leaves woven together to create a room.

Little Natalie's hand was tiny in hers.

Selena looked over at Natalie sitting hunched on the bed.

'I've got a little girl here with me, Natalie,' Selena said slowly. 'She wants me to help her, and you.'

Natalie looked up, confused. 'You mean Clover?'

Had Clover come in? Natalie hadn't seen her.

Selena shook her head. 'No, it's not Clover. It's you, when you were young.'

'I don't understand.' Natalie pressed her back against the headboard, suddenly frightened. 'What do you mean?' she whispered.

'You're about eight, I think,' Selena said. 'Around that age. Why does she live in a tent made of blankets, Natalie?'

Natalie stared at Selena in shock. 'I don't know what you're talking about.' Her voice was hoarse.

'What happened when you were eight or nine?'

'Nothing,' Natalie whispered. 'Nothing happened. She swallowed. 'My brother didn't get bombed until I was ten.'

'Bombed?' Selena's eyes widened.

'The Rainbow Warrior bombing,' Natalie said. 'He was on the ship.' She blinked. 'One of the ones who jumped off in time.'

Selena was silent for a moment, looking at the little girl who still held her hand. 'Was that when you became afraid, Natalie?'

'No,' Natalie replied, hanging her head so that her forehead almost touched her knees. 'No, I was afraid long before that.' She raised her head, but her eyes were closed. Looking at the past. 'My parents were older when they had me. My brother was already grown up.' She pressed the back of one hand to her forehead. 'They were activists – protesting nuclear testing.'

The child stood there beside Selena, listening.

'They talked about it all the time,' Natalie said. Her voice was low, harsh, her throat full of tears. 'All the time. Nuclear war, how it would destroy everyone. They had pictures of Nagasaki and Hiroshima after the bombs were dropped. There was one, I still see it in my dreams.' She paused, eyes still closed, the image looming again.

'Nightmares,' she corrected. 'It's just a shadow. Burnt into the footpath.' She shook her head, horror on her face. 'There was nothing left of the person but their shadow.'

Natalie paused so long that Selena thought she wasn't going to say anything more.

'So many pictures of these shadows. Just black shadows where there had once been people.' Natalie opened her eyes and stared at Selena, radiating pain.

'I couldn't bear it after a while. The thought of all those people reduced to nothing but shadows. I started seeing my own shadow all the time, and thinking that's all that would be left of me – just a mark on the ground, shaped like me, where I had been standing when the bomb went off.'

She hung her head again. 'Because there would be more bombs; why would countries be building and testing them if they weren't going to use them?' Natalie shook her head. 'I stopped going outside unless I was forced to. I built a blanket fort in my bedroom and played in there most of the time. I couldn't see my shadow when I was in there.' She glanced at the plastic model bear on the bedside table. 'I played with my teddy, pretending we were baking cakes, having tea parties, and that everything was all right.'

'What about school?' Selena asked.

'Oh, I had to go, of course.' Natalie nodded miserably. 'My parents moved away when I started university; they went to live in Tahiti, to take the fight to the front line, they said. The testing did a lot of long-term damage to the people there.' Natalie swallowed. 'I stayed behind, in the house where I still live.'

Natalie raised her gaze to meet Selena's. 'I tried,' she said. 'I went and got help, but all everyone said to me was that France had stopped testing their bombs, and no one was going to drop one on anyone else again.' She shook her head. 'But I don't know,' she said. 'And I don't know how to live in a world where people do such things to other people. Or even think and plan to do such things.'

She paused, then repeated the words. 'I just don't know how. I don't know how to stop thinking about it, to stop knowing about it.'

'It's paralysed you.'

'Yes,' Natalie whispered. 'It isn't even safe at home,' she said. 'But there isn't anywhere to go to get away from it. And it feels safer there. A little bit. There's no one to laugh at me when I dive and hide because a car backfires in the street and I think it's a bomb or a gun going off.'

Selena reached out and touched one of Natalie's hands, squeezing her fingers.

Natalie shook her head. 'I'm not stupid,' she said. 'I know no one has done any testing the last few years, but I still don't know...' She shook her head. 'I still don't know how to live in this world.'

'I understand,' Selena said. 'The world is a far cry from what it ought to be.'

'And I can't do what my parents and brother do – go to the heart of it and beat against it.' Natalie swallowed. 'I'm just not made of the same stuff. I just want to be safe. I want to bake cakes and muffins and be safe. I don't know how to save the world. I don't even know how to save myself.'

Her fingers tingled a little where Selena had held them. 'So, you see,' she said. 'You ought to just let me go home and back to it, because I don't know how to do anything else.' Natalie paused, forgetting that she'd asked for help. 'I'm not brave enough.'

'I'd like you to stay here for a little while longer,' Selena said.

Natalie looked at her. 'Why, though?'

'I'd like to teach you how to live,' Selena answered.

Natalie stared at her.

'You can do that?'

'Yes,' Selena answered with a smile. 'I think I can, if you're willing to try.'

Natalie's mouth was dry. She thought of Tara downstairs, humming as she pottered about the kitchen, about Clover, who had given her one of her toys.

She twisted around and picked up the bear, held it out on her palm for Selena to see.

'What does this mean?' she asked and shook her head. 'Clover gave it to me, and said it was my friend.' She closed her fingers over the animal. 'And for some reason, holding it makes me feel better.'

'That's because it is your friend,' Selena replied.

Natalie stared at the solid little bear. It stood on two legs, its face almost sweet with round ears and a long nose. Looking at it made Natalie feel warm. Safe, even.

'Bear, I think – and Clover does too, and I've no reason to disbelieve her – is your spirit kin. We've all got kin still in spirit who walk with us, who are waiting for us to walk with them.'

Natalie shook her head. 'I don't know what you mean,' she said. But she looked at the bear and wondered. 'Do you mean like God?'

'No. I mean kin. Family. A group of souls joined in relationship to ours. With a commitment to help us through the experience of being human.' Selena paused a moment. 'Which, admittedly, isn't as easy as it could be.'

Natalie shook her head. 'I don't understand.'

'That's all right,' Selena said. 'Let it come seeping in, the remembering.' She reached down to pick up the item she'd stopped in her room for and handed it to Natalie.

'What's this for?' Natalie asked, turning over the journal in her hands. She opened the front cover. It was lined, but otherwise blank. She looked at Selena.

'I'd like you to write down your dreams in it,' Selena said.

'My dreams?' Natalie frowned. 'You mean like aspirations?' She shuddered. 'I don't have those, except to bake something every day.' She trailed off. 'But that's more to steady myself than anything else.'

Selena patted Natalie's foot. 'I'm talking about the dreams you have at night, when you're sleeping.'

'I don't remember them,' Natalie lied.

Selena waited patiently. The young Natalie had vanished back to where she'd come from, but Selena thought she'd be back.

If she didn't come back, Selena would go looking for her.

Natalie was staring at the notebook, frowning. 'Why do you want me to write down my dreams?'

'It's the easiest way to communicate with your soul,' Selena said.

'My soul?'

'Yes, and your spirit kin.'

Natalie put the book down. 'I don't believe in that sort of thing.'

'May I hold your hands again?' Selena asked.

Natalie looked at her, then down at her hands. They were white knuckled, knotted together. 'What for?' she asked.

'I held them last night and it calmed you,' Selena said. 'I want to do that again.'

Natalie stared at her. 'What are you?' she whispered.

'I'm a priestess of the ancient way,' Selena answered mildly. 'My task is to keep the old ways alive, and those ways include healing.'

'Healing?' Natalie blinked. 'What, like...spiritual healing?' She shook her head. 'What sort of healing?'

'The sort that integrates body and mind and spirit,' Selena said. 'We're going to do some of it through your dreams.'

Natalie swallowed, confused, but she held out her hands tentatively, and for a moment, she thought she caught the scent of pine or cedar. She sniffed again, but it was gone.

Selena's hands, however, were warm around her, and the curious sensation of wellbeing spread over her.

'How do you do that?' she whispered.

36

Rue looked curiously at their house guest when she came downstairs that evening for dinner, trailing warily behind Selena.

Clover jumped down from her chair and scampered over to Natalie, looking up at her with a shining face. 'You come an' sit next to me,' she said, tugging on Natalie's hand.

Natalie was startled and looked down at the fair-haired child who for some reason, had decided they were friends.

'Okay,' she said. Then glanced around shyly at the others. Her vision wavered for a moment, as she realised again that she was in a new place and surrounded by people. She slid into her chair at the table and pretended to listen to Clover's chatter next to her.

Really though, she was trying not to notice that the walls and ceiling seemed to move around her. She was disoriented, that's what it was. She flinched away from them, and the voices around her pricked her flesh like needles.

In growing panic, she looked around for Selena. Where had Selena gone? Selena's hands – she needed to touch them again. She needed some of their magical calm.

But Selena was right there, sitting down also, and she glanced over at Natalie, smiling.

Natalie pulled in a gulp of air, then another, slower, forcing herself to focus on her breathing, until the walls and ceiling receded back where they belonged.

'Clover,' Rue said, shaking her head. 'Stop chattering at Natalie.' Their new guest looked like she was about to pass out at the table.

Natalie found a smile and put it on her face, shaking her head. 'No,' she said. 'She's okay.' She took another breath. 'I'm okay.'

And surprisingly, she was.

Opening her hand, Natalie turned to Clover and put the bear on the table. 'I thought you might like this back,' she said.

But Clover shook her head. 'I gived it to you.' She put a blackbird on the table next to it. 'Look,' she said. 'They can play together.'

'She gave you her bear?' Rue asked. 'That's awesome.'

'Blackbird likes to hop,' Clover said, picking up the bird and hopping it over the table.

'Natalie has decided to stay a little while with us,' Selena said, once they were all seated.

'Oh,' Tara cried, dishing up the dinner with Damien. 'That's wonderful – I learnt so much today, baking with you. I hope we can do it again, while you're here.'

Natalie ducked her head, then nodded. 'I'd like that,' she said.

'We're going to help her with her healing,' Selena continued.

Rue's eyebrows rose. 'How?' She felt a frisson of excitement – real life learning, she thought. 'This is fantastic – but how?'

Dandy, remembering the visit to the great sequoia tree, leaned forward, knowing she was going to enjoy the answer, whatever it would be.

Natalie took a deep breath and risked a look around the room. For a moment, everyone's face wavered, then they steadied, and she marvelled over how kind they all looked.

These weren't people to be afraid of. They wouldn't laugh at her.

She sat a little straighter.

'By the fact that we're all learning how to live,' Selena said. 'In a world that feels more like a battle than anything else, for a lot of the time.' She smiled at Natalie. 'We're going to learn to dig deep, stand tall, and find the real world.'

'The real world?' Rue asked.

Selena nodded. 'The one in which you fly with your albatross. Where you develop the strength to see and fly far.'

'And me,' Clover piped up. 'What I learn?'

'Hmm,' Selena said. 'That's a good question. We should ask your wizards.'

In all the excitement, she hadn't forgotten about Clover's wizards. Why, she wondered, were they so secretive?

Clover clapped her hands, then turned confidentially to Natalie. 'My wizards look like Santa Claus,' she said.

'Santa Claus?' Natalie asked, bewildered. Just when she

felt a measure of balance, sitting here with these people, they began talking of Santa Claus and wizards and flying like an albatross.

She didn't know what to make of it. She glanced at Selena, then looked back at Clover.

'We don' have Santa Claus visit, though,' Clover said. 'But they have white beards just like him.'

'Natalie doesn't have a clue what you're talking about, Clover Bee,' Rue said, then grimaced an apology at Natalie.

Damien carried steaming dishes of potatoes and vegetables to the table, followed by Tara with the rest of the dishes.

'Tuck in, everyone,' he said. 'Get it while it's hot.' He paused for a brief moment, nodded his head. 'We are blessed by this abundance and in this company.' He smiled and took his seat.

'Are you Christian?' Natalie blurted. They couldn't be, though, could they? Not the way they spoke. Of wizards and things.

Selena shook her head. 'We follow the way of spirit,' she said. 'Its way is abundance and generosity.'

Natalie watched everyone help themselves, and took a breath, turned to Clover. 'What would you like?' she asked in an effort to distract herself from her racing thoughts.

'I like the 'tatoes,' Clover said, and pursed her lips. 'An' the pie. A piece of that, please?' She looked up at Natalie, blue eyes wide.

Natalie was disarmed and put a slice of the fragrant lamb pie onto the child's plate, and then a potato. 'Is that enough?'

Clover shook her head. She held up two fingers. 'I need this many.'

'You can count?' Natalie asked, the idea delighting her for some reason. She forgot her own discomfort and beamed at Clover.

'Course I can count,' Clover said. 'I can read a li'l bit too.' She pointed over the table. 'Rue taught me.'

Natalie looked over at Rue. 'You taught her to read?'

Rue shrugged. 'It didn't take much. We just read some of her books so often she sort of just caught on, and then I, you know, wrote some words out on flashcards, and we played with those.'

A thought occurred to Natalie, and she looked from Rue to Clover and around the table, then back at Rue.

'Where are your parents?' she asked.

Rue shook her head. 'Our mum died. Dad works down south, so we live with Selena.'

'An' ev'ryone else!' Clover crowed. She turned to Natalie. 'Before that, was jus' Rue an' me.'

'Just Rue and you?' Natalie repeated.

'Yup. She looked after me ev'ry day.' Clover stuck her fork into a piece of potato and levered it to her mouth.

'I'm sorry,' Natalie said, looking over at Rue, who just shrugged in return.

'Things are better now,' Rue said. 'So, it's okay.'

AFTER DINNER, NATALIE TRIED TO MAKE HER EXCUSES AND GO back to her room. She'd made it through the meal, but most of it had been spent feeling disjointed. She wasn't used to being around so many people.

But Clover took her by her hand and dragged her to the living room. 'Can you read me a book?' she asked.

So Natalie found herself sitting on the sofa, reading a book to Clover, who curled up beside her, leaning her small warm body against Natalie. The others came in one by one, settled down each to some quiet activity, and a peace fell in the big room that had tears coming to Natalie's eyes.

She floated inside the peace and listened to her voice reading to Clover.

Maybe she was glad she wasn't going home straight away.

Natalie glanced over at Selena who sat in an armchair, reading.

Selena had said something about healing, and Natalie felt light-headed thinking about it. Clover had fallen asleep tucked up to her side, and she didn't move so as not to disturb her, just sat there thinking.

These were nice people here, she mused. What if she could have friends like this? It had been almost lovely in the kitchen with Tara and Clover earlier in the day. Their chattering didn't make her head hurt; instead, it had felt warm and friendly.

She'd forgotten what that was like. If she'd ever really known.

But they didn't know, she thought. Didn't know what the world was really like. How it could cut you and make you bleed.

How precarious it all was. They didn't know that.

Her gaze drifted down to Clover, snoring softly under her arm. And then she looked over at Rue, who sat on the floor writing in a notebook, a small frown of concentration marking her forehead.

She'd looked after Clover on her own? What did that mean? Literally looked after her on her own? Natalie wondered. She wondered what all their stories were.

How they managed.

Maybe they did know how the world was.

Could she learn too? To manage, to live in it? To be happy, even?

The thought made her tremble. What was she thinking? She coughed slightly, and on the other side of the room Selena looked up, saw her.

'Ah,' Selena said. 'Let me put Clover to bed.'

Natalie shook her head shyly. 'I'll carry her, if you show me the way.' And she eased herself out from beside Clover and picked the child up. Clover slung an arm over Natalie's shoulder and mumbled something.

Natalie followed Selena up the stairs. She laid Clover down in her bed in a pretty, cheerful yellow room and stood back, looking at Clover, then turned to Selena.

'I think I'll go to bed too,' she said. 'I feel awfully tired.'

Selena nodded, walking out of Clover's room with her, and closing the door most of the way.

'It will be tiring,' she said. 'Having to negotiate being in a different place.'

Natalie stood a moment in the hallway, clutching her hands together. 'You ah, mentioned healing.' She pressed her lips together as though the words had slipped from between them by mistake.

Selena nodded, and tucked her hand under Natalie's elbow, steering her away from Clover's door.

'It begins with you dreaming,' she answered.

'Dreaming?' Natalie was perplexed.

'Yes,' Selena answered. 'Often when we dream, we enact those things we need for our healing.'

Natalie considered this. It seemed far-fetched. 'I don't have good dreams,' she whispered.

'Even those can be useful,' Selena answered. She pushed open the door to the room Natalie was staying in and flicked on the light. Then changed her mind.

'Come upstairs with me for a few minutes, can you do that?'

'What for?' Natalie asked, but she was interested.

'I want to show you something we can do to begin your healing.'

Natalie, eyes wide, followed Selena in silence, unable to think of anything to say to that.

They went to Selena's attic room, and Natalie stood in the middle of the floor, looking around in astonishment while Selena turned on a lamp and lit a couple of candles.

'What is this place?' Natalie asked. 'Are you some sort of witch?' There was a statue of an antlered woman between the candles Selena had lit, and too many other things for her dazed eyes to take in in one glance.

'Some sort, I suppose,' Selena said. 'I am a priestess of the forest, a priestess of dreams and souls.'

Natalie shivered, but curiosity drew her forward, that and the notion that just wouldn't leave her, that she could trust this woman.

This woman with the warm hands and ready smile.

'What are we going to do?' she asked.

'You have a good imagination,' Selena replied, which wasn't a direct answer.

'Yes,' Natalie said uncertainly. 'I suppose I do, why?'

'I am positive you do,' Selena said, and gestured to one of the stools in front of the table. 'Which, depending on where it is directed, makes things easier.'

'Easier?' Natalie shook her head slightly, sitting down on the stool in front of Selena. 'It hasn't made my life easier.'

'That's because you've let it dwell on many terrible things.'

'Many terrible truths.'

'Yes,' Selena agreed. 'Unfortunately so.' She took a breath and smiled at the young woman in front of her. 'We can only comfortably confront and stand up to those sorts of truths when we have a strong foundation, practice, and spirit.'

Natalie licked her lips. She wanted to say she didn't understand, but maybe she did. Just a little. She shook her head. 'My parents only taught me there were terrible things in the world. They didn't teach me how to live with them.'

'That's because they didn't understand that you could not see things in the same way as them.' Selena gave a graceful shrug.

'They thought I'd be angry about it, like they were.' Natalie shook her head. 'But I was just frightened.'

'Well, the way to deal with that now, is to build yourself some solid ground to stand on,' Selena said. 'Your spirit will grow and strengthen from it, and you will be able to shine.'

'Shine?' Natalie glanced at the statue between the candles. It gleamed in the light, and she blinked at the antlers growing from the figure's head.

'Yes,' Selena said. 'The only way we stand to change the world we live in, is to shine, each one of us.' She tapped her chest. 'Our inner lives must become clear and calm, full of generosity and love.'

Selena sighed. 'The aggression and violence and greed you see in the world around us is a reflection of the conflict so many feel inside themselves. There is fear and the need for external power and validation, the putting down of others in order to be raised up.'

'I'm afraid,' Natalie said, and pressed a hand against her own chest. 'I'm full of fear.'

'Yes,' Selena agreed. 'But your fear has caused you to give up your natural power, rather than seeking to wrench it from others.'

'It's made me useless,' Natalie whispered. 'All I do is see the world and hide from it.' She shook her head. 'But I don't know how to do anything else.'

'Fortunately,' Selena smiled. 'Change has to come from the inside – and you're in complete control of that.'

Natalie wanted to object then, to tell Selena that she couldn't control her panic attacks. Couldn't control the way she thought. But she hesitated, because something inside her said that Selena would have an answer for that.

And if Natalie knew there was an answer, she'd have to do something about it. Follow through on it.

The pause stretched out between them, and Selena let it. She simply waited, watching the emotions flit across Natalie's face. An owl hooted from a tree outside, and Selena listened to it, drew the evening around herself like a cloak, and for a moment, there was a small owl upon her shoulder, sitting there like an old friend.

Finally, Natalie spoke. 'I am?' she asked. 'I'm in control of it?'

Selena nodded. 'Oh yes,' she said. 'But change and healing takes bravery; it takes effort and courage.'

Natalie closed her eyes.

37

NATALIE CREPT QUIETLY BACK TO HER ROOM, TWO candlesticks clutched in her hands and a box of matches in her pocket.

She closed the door behind herself, leaned against it for a moment, then walked over to the dressing table and set the candles down.

Now she had to turn out the light. For a long moment, Natalie stood nervously in the middle of the room, unable to move, wracked with indecision.

Was she going to do this? Was she really going to try this?

She tried to tell herself she could attempt it, and then quit at any time. It would be okay, if she did that. She wasn't indebted to anyone, or under any obligation to anyone to do any of this.

To try to change things. Herself.

Natalie closed her eyes, shook her head. The sun had sunk behind the hill outside her window, and she thought of her house up the road, on top of the hill. Her house that she hadn't left for a long time.

Her house, her prison.

She did have a debt to someone, she realised. She did hold an obligation.

She owed it to herself. She owed it to herself to try changing things, to find a way to stand up in the world, to shine, as Selena said.

It sounded so good.

Natalie went to the bedroom door and put her hand to the light switch to turn it off, then hesitated again.

Her legs were weak, and she held herself up with an effort. Her stomach turned over, felt queasy.

Should she?

Did she dare?

Natalie looked at her hand hovering over the light switch. And remembered her secret dream, her secret longing.

It wasn't much, she thought. Just a little shop. A cake shop. A life of sugar and icing, and making people feel better for a minute or two with her little concoctions.

Was that an okay dream?

She shook her head slightly.

It wouldn't stop the bombs being made, or tested, or new weapons being invented.

It wouldn't make any difference to that at all.

But it would make a difference to her, wouldn't it? Mightn't she shine, doing something like that?

Mightn't she be able to do something like that because she shone?

Natalie leaned her head against the door. She was tired

of thinking, she decided. Tired of thinking around and around in circles. She didn't have any answers to anything.

But maybe that was okay. Maybe all she had to do was start.

She'd end up somewhere. But only if she started.

Her fingers landed on the light switch and turned the light off.

Natalie straightened, looked around in the sudden dimness, then took a breath, drawing Selena's instructions back to mind, and went over to the dressing table and picked up the matchbox.

The match caught with the first strike, and Natalie touched the flame to each candle, then waved the match out. She put it back in the box. Set it down.

Now what? She could hear her heart pounding, and her mouth was dry.

Outside her window, the birds were singing the sun down and she stilled, closing her eyes, listening to them.

Where, she wondered? Where should she choose?

Selena had said to use her imagination to conjure a space. A clearing in the woods. A garden. A private stretch of sand.

It could be anywhere, as long as it was outside.

Natalie glanced at the picture on the wall, the cottage in the woods. She hadn't been outside in so long. She hadn't felt the caress of the wind, or heard the shuffle suck of the tide on the beach, or the rustling of leaves on their branches.

She hadn't seen any of it, for so long.

She looked again at the picture on the wall. There were animals in the woods. In those woods.

Wolves, she thought.

Bears.

Her hand went to her pocket, and she drew out Clover's model bear.

No. She shook her head. She shouldn't imagine the place in the picture. Hadn't she told Selena that was Grandmother's house, and the Big Bad Wolf was on its way?

She should choose somewhere else. Somewhere in the desert perhaps. Where there were no wolves.

Only scorpions. And snakes. Did snakes live in the desert? She didn't know. Probably.

The beach then, and she closed her eyes to see a great moon hanging over the water, sending silver shivers over the waves. Nothing could hurt her on the beach. The water nibbled at her toes, and she jerked back, looking down to see the sand covered in nipping crabs.

Not the beach then. Natalie's heart quickened, and she made herself take in a long, slow breath. She held it for a few seconds, then blew it out. Stared at the candles.

And imagined the cottage and woods in the picture. She stood outside, the lit window of the cottage just behind her, comforting, the trees tall and silent in front of her.

Natalie closed her eyes. Let herself imagine. Listened for animals. For the Big Bad Wolf.

She heard a breeze flutter the tree's leaves. Heard a bird call out and recognised the song. A tui, its call low and lovely.

There were no wolves where there were tui, she told herself, and peered into the dimness between the woods again. Something glimmered in there, and she walked toward the trees.

It was only a few steps beyond the first line of trees and Natalie's lips curved in a smile, as she stood in front of the dressing table with the two candles on it, imagining.

There was a pond, a small, perfectly circular pond, and the water reflected the moon, and the fringe of trees, and her own face when she leaned over it.

Natalie opened her eyes, tucking the imagined pond at the back of her mind. She changed into her night clothes, musing as she did on the pond she'd conjured up. There was something so peaceful about it, she thought, as she blew out the candles, picked up the bear and slid into bed.

She lay back on the pillow, listening to the small lap of water as a breeze sighed across the pond, and the trees shivered in their reflections in a sort of dance.

She held the space, just as Selena had told her to, and then she fell asleep and into it.

RUE TURNED OVER IN HER SLEEP, MUTTERED SOMETHING, THEN fell back into her dream.

She could smell salt on the air and her feet quickened upon the path. Touching a hand to her chest, she breathed the scent in deeply, and her lips turned upwards in a smile tipped with her head towards the heavens.

The newly planted stones in the circle drew her to a stop on the way along the path. They were marvellous, Bryn thought, and reached out a hand to touch the nearest. The stone vibrated under her hand.

It wasn't the largest or most magnificent of circles. She had heard, of course, of larger, more wonderful ones, but this was sufficient to their needs. For a moment, she stepped into the centre of the circle and breathed deeply, smelling the distant sea, the immediate woods, even, she thought, the stones themselves, with the scent of mountains still clinging to them.

But she had a task to perform, and drew herself away from the stone circle, bowed her head to Mother Oak, then found the path again and hurried along it.

The day was growing, and she barely needed to watch where she stepped, so familiar was she with the path. But the day was rising and she'd meant to fly with the dawn.

At last there it was, the distant sea sweeping out beneath her and she stopped, catching her breath as she looked over brightening water.

Finally, straightening, Bryn was ready. Hers was the task to see this day if that for which they hoped and prayed, that which Caelina saw in the leaping flames of the fire, was coming to pass.

For it was her wings that flew the longest, her beautiful broad wings.

She closed her eyes, now, let the late summer breeze wrap around her, and listened for the flap of great wings.

'Come to me!' she cried out, and the wind took her call and threw it out upon the ocean, and a great white and grey bird heard her and dipped his wings towards the hill where she stood.

Bryn saw him coming, even with her eyes closed, for there were other worlds in which she travelled and in which she shed her body to do so. She saw his sleek feathered body with her spirit and gloried in his flight.

Soon, she flew with him, and she saw through the eyes of the great albatross, skimmed through the air over the ocean with his broad, strong wings - wings that could fly the oceans with never a day to land for years at a time.

And this was why it was she who was rounding the great island upon which her body still stood, and crossing oceans in search of the woman the Goddess had promised to send to teach them.

She flew across a broad stretch of water, land far away from their wings, merely a shadow on the horizon, and Bryn opened her mouth and shrieked with delight, for there was almost nothing better than to fly and fly and fly without ceasing.

Then land loomed closer, foreign soil to which Bryn had never before been, and she dipped one wing to circle around in front of the cliff that rose high over the water.

Her eyes as Albatross, the Great Wanderer, were not as sharp as those of Annis, who flew with Falcon, but they were sufficient for this task. There was no mistaking the woman who stood tall upon the cliff's edge, a staff in her hand, antlers rising from her head.

Brynn circled around for another look and yes, this was her, she was certain of it - the one the Goddess had promised them. Bryn saw her lift her gaze from the boat below and look at her as she rode the air currents above cliff and cove.

Did she recognise her, Bryn wondered? Did she see the great spirit bird and the maiden who rode with him?

Bryn's feathers shivered. She flew around a third time, thinking one more look to satisfy her own curiosity, to get a good description; one more look and she could go back to the Forest House and tell the others that surely the one the Goddess had promised was on her way.

An extraordinary teacher, She had whispered to them.

Bryn went out wide over the ocean and looked down at the boat far below, taking on its cargo, waiting for the woman to make her way down to them.

Then she lifted her gaze to the woman standing on the clifftop, one hand wrapped around her staff, her cheeks coloured with swirls of blue wold, talismans hanging from cords around her neck, her dress a rich red.

Bryn swallowed. At the woman's side stood suddenly in focus a great black wolf, and Bryn wanted to peel away at the sight of him, for he too stared at her with eyes as piercing as his soul kin's.

The Priestess of the Lady raised her hand and Bryn drew in a sharp breath of salt air, for surely she was saluting her?

Bryn dipped a wing in reply, and turned her wide wings to take her back the way she had come, across the seas to the hill on which part of her still stood.

From there she would go back down to Forest House, and tell the others the news.

The one the Goddess had promised them was coming.

38

RUE SLIPPED FROM HER BED WITH THE FIRST LIGHT OF THE DAY
and pulled on her dressing gown, tucked her feet into
slippers.

She hurried out of her room, hanging onto the
remnants of her dream, and leaned over the stairs to
listen.

It was impossible to hear anything from the kitchen.
The walls were too thick, the room too far away. She stood
indecisive for a moment, fingers gripping the banister, then
turned and decided to take a chance.

She tapped on Selena's door.

'Come in.'

Rue pushed the door open and slipped into Selena's
room. It was the mirror image of her own, but more sparsely
furnished, with only bed, wardrobe, dresser, and a chair
beside the window.

'I'm sorry to disturb you, Selena,' she said in a half
whisper.

Selena turned from the dresser where she was pinning her hair up and smiled at Rue.

'It must be important,' she said.

Rue, suddenly shy, sidled further into the room and looked at Selena. Today's dress was the yellow of butter. Clover would love it.

'I had a dream,' Rue said.

Selena turned to look at her. Rue's face was still puffy from sleep under her great cloud of dark hair. The hair dye she'd used to make it black to match her choice of clothing was fading, but her natural hair colour wasn't much lighter. The colour of chocolate instead of liquorice.

'You dreamed of the priestess?' she asked.

Rue nodded, came closer to lean against the end of Selena's bed. 'Can I tell you about it?' she asked.

'Please,' Selena said. 'I would be glad if you did.'

Rue nodded, looked inward at the dream, what she remembered of it. She shook her head. 'I don't have the whole thing anymore,' she said. 'Most of it slipped away, I think, when I woke up.' She lifted her face to look at Selena.

'But what I remember is amazing - I dreamed I was a young woman, but older than I am now, and I was excited about something.' Rue smiled. 'Going flying. I was excited about going flying. About being given a task.'

Selena listened without speaking.

'I don't remember enough,' Rue continued, and she paused, frowning, trying to draw it all back to herself.

'I was following this path, around a steep hill, and I think there was something about a stone circle - just like the one you told me was at Wilde Grove, and an oak tree there that I spoke to, calling her Mother Oak. Then I went on, along this path that wound around the hill for ages, and finally I got to a clearing and I could see the ocean.'

Selena's brows rose, and she felt a frisson of something - presentiment?

Goddess, she thought. What is this? What is happening here?

For she thought she recognised the landscape in Rue's dream.

Could it be Wilde Grove?

Rue grinned suddenly, her eyes lighting up. 'Then I was flying. Out over the water. I was an albatross.'

Selena sat down in the chair by the window and took a breath. 'What happened then?' she asked.

Rue shook her head. 'It was so amazing,' she said. 'Flying!' She closed her eyes, trying to bring back the sensation. 'I flew for ages, for miles and miles across the oceans.'

She opened her mouth to tell the rest of the story, and then faltered. 'It's gone,' she said and frowned at Selena. 'I can't remember the rest of it.'

'That happens,' Selena said, hiding her disappointment. 'What do you feel about it?'

'What do you mean?'

Selena rephrased her question. 'What sort of feeling do you get about the rest of the dream? If you can't remember something, then often the emotion surrounding it gives a clue.'

Rue bent her head, thinking. 'There's just excitement,' she said. 'And the feeling that I had to do some sort of task - something really important.' She shook her head. 'I got so excited about flying that the rest just slipped away. I'm sorry. I could kick myself.'

'It's all right,' Selena said. 'What you remember is wonderful.'

Rue looked at her, suddenly shy. 'Was it her, do you think?'

'Your kindred spirit?' Selena asked. She nodded. 'I think so. I think you dreamed a scene straight out of her past.' She paused. 'Your past, for you are aspects of the same soul.'

Rue stood in the dim room at a loss for words. What had just happened seemed so enormous, so meaningful that she couldn't think of what to say next.

'What do I do now?' she whispered finally.

That was a good question, Selena thought. She would have to give this new event some very careful consideration, decide if and how it changed things.

For surely it would.

'Write what you remember down,' she said to Rue. 'More may come to you as you write it - that's often the case. Write down all your dreams from now on.'

Rue nodded. 'I will,' she promised.

Selena stood up. 'Let us go and greet this day, then,' she said.

Clover was downstairs with Tara and beamed at Rue and Selena as they entered the room.

'I waked up with the sun,' she said. 'I comin' to say hello to the day with you.'

Rue kissed her head. 'Good on you,' she said.

SELENA LOOKED AROUND IN AMAZEMENT AT HER SMALL circle. They were all there, except for Natalie, of course. But Dandy, Tara, Damien, along with Rue and Clover - they were there, sleep in their eyes, hair mussed, but there, tipping their faces towards the sky, eyes closing in appreciation of the first rays of the sun to reach them.

She lifted her own face to the light.

'Hail Gift of the World,' she said, her voice gossamer light upon the new rays. 'Hail Brigit of the Shining Face, she who beams down upon all of us, our mother, the tender of the flames of our heart and hearth.'

Selena felt the flame of her own heart brighten. 'Hail Brigit,' she repeated. 'Here we are, daughters and sons of your flame, and while we burn with your sacred fire, the life of the spirit is here with us.'

She rocked back and forth slightly where she stood. 'We shall rise and set in the rhythm of your life. We shall follow the bright path across the sky, across the seasons, across all the great cycles of humanity, and with you as our guide, we shall keep the wheel turning, and the song of your bright flame shall forever be upon our tongues.'

Rue listened to the words of Selena's prayer and glanced over to her. It was different, the things she was saying. This was not their usual morning prayer.

Was this Brigid Selena was speaking to? Rue closed her eyes, and breathed deeply of the early morning air. She would write down the prayer as near as she could remember it, and read it later to Ebony, so that they could puzzle over it together.

And perhaps, she thought with a smile, she would also ask Selena about it. For hadn't Selena promised now to teach her?

Elation rose inside her, setting her heart afire as the sun lifted over the hill above them, turning her eyelids to rose, and for a moment it seemed as though she flew with Albatross again.

SELENA PAUSED, LET HER PRAYER GO, THEN TURNED AND FACED the small shrine they'd set up in the garden. She lifted the small jug that sat there, newly filled with fresh cream, and poured some out on the grass in front of the shrine. Usually, this was Rue's job, but Selena followed the impulse that had come over her.

'Blessed Lady of the Flame,' she said. 'We make this offering to you in good faith that you will open the way and smooth the path for us. As your light throws off the darkness of the night, so too would we have it banish the dimness from our minds, so that we can see brightly the way ahead.'

She straightened. 'And my Lady of this land,' she said, not to forget the Fae people she had met and feasted with. 'This offering is for you also.'

She tipped another stream of cream from the jug.

'As you offered me your hospitality, here we return the honour. You are people of this land, and we give you our respect as is your right.'

Selena replaced the jug and turned to the circle of her new family, her new grove. She smiled at them, and the sun lit radiant halos around their heads.

'We're going to try something more, this morning,' she said. 'We're going to learn to stand grounded on this soil, in these bodies, and in balance between earth and sky.'

39

NATALIE WOKE TO FULL SUNLIGHT AND FROWNED AT IT IN consternation. How long had she slept? She rolled over in the bed and groped for her watch on the bedside table.

It was after nine.

'I slept in,' she whispered, sitting up.

Had she dreamed? She couldn't remember. For once, she couldn't remember. Which, considering her usual array of dreams, of running and ducking from the things in her nightmares, that seemed a relief.

Downstairs, Selena, Dandy, and Tara sat at the table, enjoying the tail end of the morning rush. Clover was there too and stood up on her chair to wave to Natalie.

'Good mornin'!' she hooted. 'I drawin' you a picture.'

Bemused by this, Natalie slipped into the seat next to Clover and looked at the piece of paper the girl held up.

'Gosh,' she said. 'You can draw awfully well.'

Clover nodded. 'Is your bear,' she said.

'It is.' Natalie looked at the others at the table. 'I overslept,' she apologised.

'You look well rested,' Selena answered.

'Would you like some tea?' Tara asked. 'I was about to put a new pot on.'

Natalie leapt up. 'I'll make it,' she said and blinked, then smiled uncertainly. 'Please. I'd like to.'

With a start, Natalie realised she was comfortable in the big kitchen. She was getting used to it, she supposed, looking around at it while she turned the tap on and refilled the electric jug. There were lots of houseplants in all the nooks and crannies, and Tara had some very healthy herbs growing on the windowsill. Natalie leaned over to sniff them, smelt peppermint and something else, something lemony.

'It's peppermint, lemon mint, and chocolate mint,' Tara said, coming over and pointing to each of them.

'Chocolate mint?' Natalie looked at her in disbelief.

But Tara just giggled. 'Yep. Chocolate mint – I swear I'm not lying. There are so many mint varieties.'

Natalie shook her head, looked back at the plants. 'I only use dried herbs,' she said.

'I used to, but I've been trying out growing things now,' Tara said. 'And it's so much more satisfying.'

Swallowing, Natalie nodded. It would be, she was sure, and suddenly she was mad at herself for not being able to go outside, go anywhere, do all the things she was missing out on.

She cleared her throat. 'I know a recipe for chocolate mint cupcakes,' she said. 'But it uses mint essence, of course.'

'Oh my goodness,' Tara said. 'I'm planning to make a bunch of mint extracts and you can help me, if you like.' She shook her head. 'I have a whole lot more mint growing outside, so I was going to use that.'

The electric jug boiled, then switched itself off. Natalie looked at it, then nodded. There was a lump in her throat, and she spoke carefully over it.

'I'd like that,' she said.

'It's really easy,' Tara enthused. 'I can harvest the mint outside, and you can help me with the rest.' She nodded. 'Clover and I are going to go do the grocery shopping this morning, so how about this afternoon?'

Natalie took a breath, nodded. She picked up the jug and poured the water into the teapot. 'Maybe I could try coming out into the garden with you.'

She put the jug down, unable to believe what she'd just said. What she'd suggested. Her head swam at the thought.

'Perhaps before you two do that,' Selena said from the table, 'I could teach Natalie the grounding exercises you've all just learnt.'

Natalie looked at Selena. Grounding exercises?

'Oh, that's a terrific idea,' Tara said, and smiled at Natalie. 'They're so helpful – I bet you'll find them so as well.'

'What's a grounding exercise?' Natalie asked through numb lips.

Clover jumped down onto the floor and stretched her arms up.

'We pretend to be a tree,' she said and waved her hands like the wind was blowing them. 'Stretch up,' she said. 'And out feets are the roots.' She wriggled. 'Stretch down.' She grinned at Natalie and climbed back on her chair. 'I gonna draw you bein' a tree,' she said. 'And me. I gonna be a tree too.'

'You pretend to be a tree?' Natalie said.

'Well,' Tara answered. 'There's a bit more to it than that.' She placed a hand on her diaphragm. 'It's really useful though. Selena just showed us this morning and already I can feel much better for it.'

Natalie frowned, looked at the people in the kitchen.

Dandy saw her expression and laughed. 'Yes,' she said. 'We're a bunch of kooks, for certain. But that doesn't mean we aren't on to something.'

Natalie looked at Selena. 'Grounding?'

Selena nodded. 'Part of building that strong foundation and centre we were talking about last night.'

Grounding. Natalie glanced back at Tara, then at the plants growing on the windowsill. She nodded.

'I could do it?' she asked.

'Anyone can do it,' Selena answered.

Natalie, too nervous to eat more than a slice of toast, sat at the table while the others chatted easily to each other. She was having trouble focusing on them, as though she needed to find a pair of glasses to see them properly.

She knew it wasn't her eyesight though. There was nothing wrong with her eyes. It was the inside of her head behind them where things were wrong.

First, it was like looking at everyone through the wrong end of a telescope. They seemed far away, and their voices drifted towards her as if from a great distance. She shook her head, blinked, and took a sip of tea. Everyone swam closer.

Her head buzzed.

She was going outside? Why had she said that she'd do that? She couldn't go out there, under that high, wide sky. Couldn't go out there when anything could streak through the sky, and she would be underneath it, small, unprotected, vulnerable.

Her lips were dry. She took another sip of tea.

Clover stared at her. She'd stopped drawing, and frowned at her new friend, who had read the Pooh Bear and Piglet story to her three times straight through. Hardly anyone else did that - not three times straight through.

'S'lena,' Clover said, and pointed her crayon at Natalie. 'She looks funny.'

Selena jumped up, went around to crouch beside Natalie and took her hands. 'Natalie?' she said. 'It's all right. Just concentrate on your breathing.'

Natalie locked eyes with Selena and drew in a great, trembling breath, then let it out with a whoop.

Selena shook her head. 'Slowly,' she said. 'Let's do it together.' Selena breathed in, holding Natalie's gaze, held her breath for a moment, then let it slowly out through pursed lips.

Natalie copied her.

'Did you find somewhere to imagine last night, Natalie?' Selena asked, her voice low and warm.

Natalie, not looking anywhere but at Selena, nodded.

'Was it a peaceful place?'

Natalie remembered the pond surrounded by trees, the

tui singing in the branch next to her. She breathed in again, nodded.

'That's good,' Selena said. 'Are there any trees there?'

Natalie nodded again. The wind rustled through them.

'Can you hear the breeze in their leaves?'

'Yes,' Natalie nodded. Selena was still looking at her, blue eyes deep, kind. She swallowed, took another slow breath.

'What about water?' Selena asked. 'Is there any water in your secret place?'

Natalie licked her lips. They were so dry. 'A pond,' she whispered. 'It's beautiful.'

Selena nodded. 'And the trees grow around the pond, tall and strong?'

Natalie nodded. She saw the scene at the back of her mind, stood next to the pond and hugged herself. It was daytime there this time, and the sun reflected in the water, turning it a burnished bronze, as though a fire lived underneath it.

'You can feel the sun on your shoulders?' Selena asked.

Natalie nodded. She took another breath, realised she was breathing properly now, slowly, surely.

'That's marvellous,' Selena said, and squeezed Natalie's hands. 'You're doing brilliantly.'

'There's a bird,' Natalie croaked. 'In the tree there. A tui.'

'Ah,' Selena said. 'How wonderful.' She'd been introduced to the boisterous bird with the wide vocal range as soon as she'd taken to walking through the Botanic Garden next door.

Natalie let go of Selena's hands and pulled back. 'I'm sorry,' she said.

Selena stood and put a hand on Natalie's shoulder. 'You're doing just fine.'

'Would you like another cup of tea?' Tara asked.

Natalie looked over at her. Tara had asked that as though it were the most natural thing in the world to say next. She nodded in relief.

'Yes, please,' she said. Then looked around the table. 'I was thinking about going outside.' Natalie puffed out a breath. 'I really want to, but it's overwhelming at the same time.'

Selena patted her, then went back to her seat. 'You'll get there,' she promised.

Natalie wasn't so sure, but there was a thought growing inside her that she'd like to try.

Maybe, with these people around her, she could do it.

Tara refreshed her teacup and brought over a recipe book, slipping into the chair next to her.

'So, this is the way we make the mint extract,' she said. 'It has to sit for a few weeks, to get the flavour, so we won't be cooking with it today – but I really like the idea of doing it, don't you?' Tara looked at the recipe and shook her head dreamily. 'I love the idea of cooking as many things using produce from the garden as possible.' She grinned. 'Our garden is only tiny, but it's amazing how much it's producing already.'

Tears sprang to Natalie's eyes, and she blinked them back. She knew what Tara was doing – acting normally, trying to distract her, make her feel at ease. She gave Tara a watery smile and looked at the book, focused on the words.

'Oh,' she said. 'It's so easy. I didn't realise it would be so easy.'

If only, she thought, everything could be as simple.

All the same, however, something new blossomed inside of her, and for a moment, she couldn't put a name to the sensation.

But it was hope.

After a moment, she knew it was hope.

40

Natalie waved off Clover, Tara, and Dandy as they
headed out the door to do some shopping. She turned
around to find Selena watching her, warm sympathy on her
face.

Natalie's cheeks coloured. 'I haven't been shopping for
the longest time,' she said wistfully.

Selena nodded. 'While they're gone, why don't I teach
you the grounding and centring techniques? Then perhaps
one day you'll be able to pop out of the house to go
shopping.'

'It can't be that easy, surely,' Natalie said.

'No,' Selena answered. 'But you have to put the foundations down before you can build the rest of the house.'

Natalie nodded. She supposed that was true.

'Right,' Selena said. 'Let's try it in the conservatory. That
way you can get a taste of being outside while still being
inside.'

The conservatory was a good size, and Natalie hesitated

in the doorway before stepping gingerly into the glass-walled room and looking around.

'All right?' Selena asked. Natalie had paled a little. 'Remind yourself that you're inside, that nothing is going to happen, and that you're with me.'

Natalie's voice was shaky when she answered. 'How do you know nothing is going to happen?' she asked, looking up at the glass ceiling through which she could see the sky. It was cloudy, the sky white like smoke.

'What's the worst that could happen?' Selena asked.

Natalie closed her eyes. There were many terrible scenarios that she could think of. Did Selena mean her to tell her them?

'We must live in the moment,' Selena said. 'Right now, this very moment, are you all right?'

All right sounded very relative to Natalie.

'Are you hurt?' Selena asked.

Natalie shook her head.

'Are you in danger?'

Natalie looked around, trying to focus. 'I feel like I am,' she admitted.

'What is the danger that you feel?'

'I...I don't know,' Natalie whispered. 'I feel helpless.'

Selena nodded, then smiled. 'Let me help you feel strong, then,' she said, and reached for Natalie's hand, leading her almost to the centre of the room.

Natalie's breath came faster.

'Is there anyone else by your pond?' Selena asked. 'Or is it just you and the tui there?'

'What?' Natalie looked at her in sudden confusion.

'By your pond. Who else is there?'

Natalie blinked. 'I can hear other birds,' she said.

Selena smiled. 'Do you know what sort?'

Natalie shook her head. 'Sparrows, perhaps,' she said, and she listened again. 'And the tui. He's there.' She looked over at Selena. 'Why are you having me do this?'

'You are creating a space in the worlds where your spirit is at ease.' Selena nodded. 'Now, let's ground ourselves.'

Natalie found herself nodding dumbly. She didn't know what was going on but having the vision of the pond and the birds in the back of her mind was helping. She felt as though part of herself stood there, completely okay, and it helped. It was a safe place.

'Grounding allows us to let go of energy that is upsetting and unpleasant,' Selena said. 'And centring gives us a strong place to come back to, whenever we do not feel surefooted. These practices provide the solid ground we need to stand on, if we are to walk this world and others.'

'There are others?' Natalie whispered.

'Yes,' Selena said. 'And other aspects of this one.'

Natalie's head spun. She glanced up, saw the sky again, turned her gaze quickly back to Selena and nodded. She didn't know what Selena was talking about, but she was going to try whatever this was.

Selena smiled at her. 'We're going to stand here and breathe now. Nice and slowly.'

Natalie found her breathing already slowing. She concentrated on Selena.

'Nice and slowly. In and hold it. Then out, still slowly.'

Natalie breathed in. She held the breath there for a moment, then let it out, like a deflating balloon.

'That's the way,' Selena said. 'Now, close your eyes and

focus inwards. Be inside your body and mark how it feels. Is there a tightness anywhere? Any aches and pains? Where do you feel strong?'

There had been a tightness in her chest, but Natalie discovered as she felt around it, that the breathing was lessening it, and she took another slow breath of air, feeling the tightness ease some more.

And then she remembered that she was standing under a glass ceiling, that above her draped the sky. She opened her eyes and glanced upwards, ready to cringe away.

The clouds had thinned. She could see a sheen of blue above her and let out a breath in a whoosh. It was beautiful. The sky was beautiful.

Selena watched her look at the sky. She let her stand there and stare.

Natalie shook her head. 'How can it be so beautiful?' she asked in a hoarse voice.

'This world is full of beauty,' Selena said.

But Natalie shook her head again, even as she gazed at the sky. 'It's full of people doing ugly things to each other.'

'Yes,' Selena said. 'But we must keep bringing ourselves back to this beauty. This is what we came here for.'

'Came here for?'

'As souls seeking the experience of a sunset, a river, an ocean, a touch, a laugh. We came here for joy.'

Natalie dragged her gaze away from the sky and looked at Selena. 'But there isn't any joy,' she said.

'Oh,' Selena replied. 'I think you'll find, if you look, that there's still plenty. You just have to look, and let it fill you.'

Natalie could feel the sun on the top of her head. It

warmed her, spread down her cheeks, her neck, her shoulders.

'What about the rest?' she asked.

'When you have met joy,' Selena said, 'you know how to find it again, how to radiate it, how to spread it.' She shook her head. 'Joy brings us strength, Natalie. And with that strength, we can do so much.' Selena took a breath. 'We find our way back to the world by being in the world, by knowing its depth and breadth, its spirit and its beauty.

'Now, grow roots down into the world, Natalie. Roots of light that steady you.'

Natalie breathed again, closed her eyes, felt the sun on her head, and then suddenly the light flooded through her, out her feet and down through the floor, seeking the rich soil beneath her. She stood in it, breathing, and the light and heat from the sun suffused her.

'Let all the questions and worries and difficulties seep from you into the ground under you. The earth is big and warm and kind; she will receive your energy and let you stand clear-eyed upon her. Reinvigorated. Clean.'

Natalie swayed slightly. She could feel it, could feel herself being washed clean by the light from the sun, could feel all her anxieties, her troubles, her doubts and fears being washed down into the ground.

For a moment, she almost panicked, almost groped for her fears and anxieties, gathered them back to herself, not knowing who she might be without them, not knowing how she might feel without them. She was used to them. They were her companions.

Could she give them up?

She thought of making mint extract with Tara. The feel of the sun on her shoulders, the plants against her palms.

She let the earth take her fears.

Selena watched her, watched Natalie's face grow smooth and calm. She nodded in satisfaction, then continued.

'Now we're connected,' she said. 'Now we're connected to the earth under our feet, and we can feel the light on us too. We are between earth and sky, seeking balance.'

Seeking balance. Natalie searched for it, realised she had it, clean, strung between the light of the sun and the warm soil of the earth.

'We can feel our energy,' Selena said. 'Streaming through us, all around us.' She paused, spoke again. 'Now we're going to take that energy and anchor ourselves in it.' She took a breath.

'Move your hands, cup them against your belly, the space under your breasts down to your belly button. Draw the light into your hands, then press it into yourself. This is your centre, and now, instead of flowing through you, feel your energy radiating outward from you, strong, calm, centred.'

Natalie cupped her hands. Light streamed into them, and she drew it into herself, then realised that the light was hers, and she let herself be it, radiating from her centre, and her mind was calm, clear, unworried. She breathed in, held her breath, breathed out.

Selena was quiet then, watching. Natalie's face was lit up, her eyes closed, her lips in a small, completely unselfconscious smile. Selena was glad. Natalie had a lot to deal with.

Everyone did, really.

But in amongst the trouble, the most important thing was to live.

Natalie had forgotten how – if she'd ever known.

That was changing though, Selena could see it.

Natalie opened her eyes finally and looked at Selena. 'Are we done?' she asked.

Selena nodded. 'How do you feel?'

'I...' Natalie had to stop and think about it. 'I don't know,' she said. 'Like I've just learnt how to stand up.' She winced. 'That sounds silly.'

'No,' Selena said. 'It doesn't sound silly. It sounds just right.'

Natalie nodded, looked around, saw glass all around her and began to cringe away, then glanced at Selena and pulled herself straight again. She pressed a hand to her middle, remembering the light that had streamed from there.

She could still feel it. An echo of it. Enough, though. It was pooled there inside her.

'Practice this every day,' Selena said. 'It will help. When you are frightened, or feeling vulnerable, bring yourself back to your centre. Remember that you have this strength here and use it.' She paused. 'The world will start feeling different to you.'

'Different?' Natalie wanted to ask how, but she was dazed. She had an idea that something had just changed for her, and her heart fluttered at the thought.

She pressed her hand to her middle again, and breathed in.

Changed, she thought.

For the better?

Natalie nodded.

. . .

SELENA LEFT NATALIE ENSCONCED IN THE KITCHEN, BROWSING Tara's recipe books, and climbed the stairs to her room in the attic.

It was time to go back to the Otherworld. Selena nodded and opened the door to her room. She had two reasons, she thought, and was glad that Clover was out and busy and with strict instructions to stay where she was, doing what she was doing. The last thing they needed was Clover to go so deep into trance while she was out of the house again.

Selena was glad for her long, loose dress. It was warm up in the top of the house, and she unbundled her hair around her shoulders, then retrieved the wide scarf she had come to like to use for travelling, when she was doing it during the day. She draped it over her head and around her shoulders. In a few minutes, she would sit and get comfortable, and draw the fabric over her eyes to darken the room.

But right now, she lit the candles either side of her statue of Elen of the Ways, and bent her head in prayer.

'Hear me, see me, lead me,' she said.

'I have the wind in my veins and water behind my eyes. I have fire in my heart and dirt under my nails.'

Selena took a breath. 'I am the wind, the earth, the storm, the ash. I am the cry of a child, the howl of a wolf.'

She stood straighter.

'I follow your path. Your wisdom guides me through the forest. I see your ways and I make them my ways also.'

Picking up one of Teresa's herb bundles, Selena lit the end of it and held it up so that the smoke wafted in a fragrant cloud to fill the room.

She walked in a circle, her bare feet warm against the wooden boards.

'Spirits of the east,' she said. 'It is my honour to greet you and ask you to keep sacred this space with me.' She paused, drew breath, let it out again. 'Albatross,' she called. 'You of broad wing and indefatigable flight, be with me in this space.'

Selena paused before walking to the next compass point. She was still used to calling south here, but things were back to front now.

'Spirits of the north,' she called, her mouth curving into a smile. 'Breath of fire, inspiration in my heart, keep this space with me.'

Another breath, another call. 'Spirits of the west,' Selena said. 'Those who swim in the depths and the shallows, those who straddle both. Crane, be with me, guide me. Eel, I feel your slippery strength. Keep this space with me.'

She held up the wafting smoke to the south. 'Spirits of earth,' she breathed. 'Be with me, keep this space with me. Show me your secret ways and paths.'

Selena paused, nodded. 'World above,' she cried out, holding the smoke aloft then bringing it back down. 'World below. Within, without. World to world to world.'

The smoke was scented with lavender. She breathed it in deeply, reverently, then crossed back to the table and set the small bundle in the stone pot to burn out. She took her necklace of seeds and pods and placed it around her neck, then went and lowered herself to the cushions on the rug. Already her mind was stilling, her senses expanding.

For a moment, she touched a foot in her own space between the worlds, that place she had built for herself many years ago, under Anwyn's guidance, just as she was guiding Natalie now to build hers, just as she had done the same with Morghan when it had been her time. She touched a foot there, then moved on, confident in her ability to navigate, to walk through the worlds. She had been doing so now for more years than she cared to count.

There was the path, the familiar way down into the Wildwood, and there was Hind, waiting for her. Selena bowed her head in greeting, and Hind flicked her ears, then turned and led her deeper into the green-leafed dimness.

'Yes,' Selena breathed. This was the place, the tunnel Clover had disappeared into. The tunnel from which the wizards had so unceremoniously evicted her. The slight still smarted and Selena drew breath, straightened to her full size and gazed into the dimness, breathing steadily, ready to step forward.

It was cool in the tunnel, and she walked the short way, found the doorway, put a hand to the stone, and pushed.

For a moment, there was resistance, and Selena hesitated. Was this right, she asked herself? Was she right to insist?

But the door opened, and she stepped through, blinking in the darkness.

There was nothing in here, she thought, looking around at the chamber. Had they known she was coming? Did they move somewhere else, so as to evade her?

Selena stood still, thinking hard. Who were these wizards who had Clover in their care? Who were they and what was their purpose with her?

She shook her head, because she didn't know the answer to either question.

There was a sudden light in the darkness, and Selena looked toward it, peering forward, for there was a shape in it also.

A woman stepped out into the chamber and looked kindly at Selena, long hair reddish in the magical light that seemed to emanate from her. Her face was strong, but gentle, and her hand, when it came to rest on Selena's arm, was cool and Selena shivered.

For this was Clover. This woman was Clover.

A blackbird hopped at the woman's feet, and a tumble of other animals came into the light with it. A fat bunny with sweet, furry ears, a cat, tail held high. A duckling, fuzzy with soft feathers, a swan, neck long and regal.

Selena remembered to breathe. 'Clover?' she whispered.

The woman nodded. Smiled. 'Everything is going to be all right,' she said. 'You are doing a wonderful job, and I thank you from the bottom of my heart. You are a blessing to me, and my gratitude knows no bounds.'

'You're Clover,' Selena whispered.

The woman looked steadily at her. 'In your world and lifetime, yes.'

Selena nodded slowly. Whatever she'd expected, it hadn't been this. Something was going on here, something more than she had understanding of. She found her voice again.

'How can I be of service to you?' she asked.

The woman smiled. 'You are being such already,' she said. 'You came when you were needed, and you nurture the child beautifully.' She blinked, and the animals climbed over her feet. 'Teach her what you know, do not let my light grow dim, and I am indebted to you.'

Selena shook her head. 'It is no burden,' she said. 'And I will teach her well.' She paused. 'Is there anything else I should know?'

But the woman shook her head, a hint of amusement curving her lips. 'Do not trouble yourself wondering over our purpose, Lady of the Beacons. You have your own to attend to, and it is not necessary for all curiosity to be satisfied. It is only necessary that we each follow our paths.' She paused, and the rabbit hopped over Selena's feet. 'But know that I hold you in my heart and that your love and dedication to Clover means much to me.'

The light around her dimmed, and with a last, dark-eyed look, the woman was gone back into the mists from which she had come. Selena stood a long minute, considering what had just happened, then turned, moved through the open door and back out of the tunnel into the forest.

None of her questions were answered. But nonetheless, she was satisfied. And the woman was right – it was not necessary for Selena to know every detail. It was not necessary for her to know any purpose but her own.

That, she had to follow.

A smile of sudden delight spread across her face. What a personage she had just met! How beautiful Clover's soul was, how marvellous.

All souls were marvellous, of course, but this encounter had been quite delightful, she thought. The rabbit, duckling, swan. Cat. How Clover would chortle to be told of it.

Not that Selena had any intention of sharing the encounter with Clover. Not when there was no reason to. This had been for her, she knew. A concession of sorts.

The wizards would probably have preferred it not to occur.

Selena lifted her face to the breeze that had sprung up in the trees of the Wildwood.

Now, there was one thing more to do.

41

Selena had issued the invitation, although until she got to the clearing where she usually performed such things, she wasn't completely sure that Natalie's spirit would come to her for healing.

But the woman waited for her, standing within the small ring of trees as if asleep. This was how it usually was, and Selena nodded in satisfaction.

Hind and Crane entered the circle with her.

Selena stepped close to Natalie and bowed her head in greeting. Natalie could not see her, but the greeting was still made, the respect and reverence of another soul necessary.

Natalie's spirit was studded with small black nails that went deep into her flesh. These, Selena knew, were the manifestations of Natalie's wounds, and she set carefully to pulling them out. One by one, she worked them loose, smoothing the skin they had punctured, until it was once more clear and lovely.

As she worked, a great shaggy bear lumbered into the clearing and sat watching Natalie. This was her kin, Selena knew, and nodded to the bear in greeting. She scraped away scatters of black barnacles from Natalie, and when she was done, Natalie collapsed in her arms, and Selena sank to the soft ground with her. A thick liquid poured from Natalie's head, and Selena cradled it over the ground as it did, closing her eyes, knowing that this thick run of muck were all the toxic and hurtful thoughts, all the harm and fear that Natalie suffered.

When it had dried to a trickle, Natalie sat, and Selena cleaned her face gently with a soft, damp cloth she drew forth from a pocket. Bear came to stand next to her and handed her a jar with balm made from honey in it, and Selena took it and smoothed it over Natalie's skin.

This would only be the beginning of Natalie's healing, Selena knew, but it would help it greatly. Sometimes the world grew great crusts and inflicted great wounds on a person, and they walked around with these. Clearing them away was a job Selena could do well, and it would give Natalie a head start.

She sat back and looked Natalie over. Natalie lay now as if asleep, her skin golden and soft, clear of the dark nails and wounds.

There was one more thing to do, and Selena got to her feet, entrusting Natalie to the care of her bear, nodding her gratitude for his presence.

She walked to the edge of the clearing and lifted her face to the breeze, listening to it a moment, spreading her arms wide so that her heart was opened.

Then she followed the call of the wind, followed it

back through the trees, Hind at her side, Crane flying overhead, great feather-fringed wings outspread and graceful. Selena retraced her steps through the Wildwood and into the house where Natalie had grown up and still lived.

This was the Otherworld version of the house, and the door opened easily to Selena's touch, and she listened for a moment, then walked through to the bedroom with the blanket fort in it.

'Natalie,' she called softly. 'Are you still here?'

Hind nosed at the opening to the tent, and Crane appeared in the room as well, tucking his wings snugly back at his sides. Selena drew the blanket flap gently open and got down on her knees.

'Hello love,' she said. 'Do you remember me?'

The girl in the tent nodded, inched forward. 'I played with your friend,' she said.

'Did you?' Selena smiled. 'I think she told me that.'

Little Natalie nodded. 'It was fun. She's still a baby but we played with the bear.'

Selena's smile widened. 'Bear is definitely a friend of yours.' She knew the girl was talking about the same bear she'd just left in the clearing. It was a sweet thing that it had shown up as a cub to play.

'I think it's time to come home now,' Selena said.

Natalie's smile turned to a frown, and she shook her head. 'I don't think so,' she said and looked back at the nest she'd made. 'It's not safe out there.'

'It's time for you to come back and be with Natalie,' Selena said. 'She's grown up now, and she needs you to be with her so that she can move on and find joy in her life.'

The child stared at Selena. 'How can you be happy when you're in danger all the time?'

Selena shook her head. 'You're not in danger all the time,' she said. 'There is plenty of time to laugh and dance and play, and then to be strong and sure when necessary.'

'I don't like it out there,' little Natalie said. 'It's a scary place.' She lowered her head, the frown on her face furrowing her brow. Then she looked at Selena. 'We can play?' she asked. 'And go outside and be safe?'

'Natalie is working on just that,' Selena said. 'But she needs your strength too.'

The child shook her head. 'I'm not strong,' she said. 'I keep imagining all these bad things happening and it makes me scared.' She blinked at Selena. 'Then I have to hide.'

Selena nodded in understanding. 'Your imagination can be used to imagine good things as well, though,' she said.

'But the bad things are real.'

'So are the good and beautiful things. There are not just bad things in the world, and we need more of us to see the good and the beauty and inspire others to do the same. That makes us all stronger.'

Little Natalie looked at Selena for a long time, and Selena knelt there, letting her.

Finally, little Natalie nodded. 'What do I have to do?' she asked, her voice barely above a whisper.

'You just have to come with me. I shall take you to your grown-up self, so that you can be together.' Selena stood up and held out her hand.

Natalie shimmied out of the tent, then looked back at it. 'Wait,' she said. 'Can I bring my teddy?'

Selena remembered the small brown bear, his fur

ragged with love, and nodded. 'Yes,' she said. 'By all means, we need to bring your bear.'

Natalie looked at her, eyes wide, then reached back into the tent and got her bear. She tucked him under her arm and reached for Selena's hand.

'Ready?' Selena asked.

The little girl nodded.

Selena retraced her steps, the little girl looking all around in wonder beside her.

'What is this place?' she whispered in awe, gaze fixed on Crane flying high overhead.

'This is the Otherworld,' Selena said. 'It's a world of spirit.'

Little Natalie shook her head, not understanding, but she marvelled at the trees and smiled at the birds she could hear in them.

Then she stopped walking.

'What is it?' Selena asked.

'There's something over there,' little Natalie said, pointing a finger between the trees.

Selena looked, then relaxed. 'He's a friend,' she said. 'A very good friend of yours.'

Natalie and Selena watched transfixed as the shadow came closer, gained fur and a long snout, round ears, and bright brown eyes.

Natalie looked up at Selena. 'He's so big. Is he going to eat us?'

Selena shook her head. 'He's come to protect you,' she said.

The girl's eyes widened, and she let go of Selena's hand and grasped her old brown teddy bear, holding him up in front of her.

Bear dropped to four paws and walked up to Natalie. He nosed at the teddy, then stood still and gazed at the child.

Natalie glanced up at Selena. 'Can I pat him?' she asked.

'Yes,' Selena said. 'I think you can.'

The bear lowered his great head and Natalie put a tentative hand out, touched his fur, then gasped.

'It's so thick and soft,' she said, and stroked the bear's head. She touched his snout in wonder, then moved a little and ran her hand down his neck. 'He's so big and strong,' she said. She looked over at Selena again. 'He's really my friend?'

'For all time,' Selena answered.

Natalie nodded. 'Hello Bear,' she whispered. 'I'm glad you're my friend.'

The bear moved his head, then stood up on his hind legs and Natalie stared up at him in surprise before he swung her up into his arms.

'I think he wants to carry you the rest of the way,' Selena said, shaking her head in wonder.

Natalie looked down at her with startled eyes, then looped her arms around the bear's neck and rested her head against his shoulder in a gesture of trust that disarmed Selena completely.

Bear carried Natalie the last small distance to the clearing, then knelt in front of the grown Natalie and set the child down.

Little Natalie kissed him on his head, her teddy tucked back under her arm. She looked resolutely at her grown self, who opened her arms to her.

A moment later, the child was gone, back to herself where she belonged. Selena closed her eyes.

'Thank you, my lady, my kin,' she said. 'For the gift of bringing healing.'

She let out her breath, watched as Bear escorted Natalie from the clearing, leaving Selena there with Hind and Crane and the rustling of the wind in the leaves.

NATALIE PUT THE RECIPE BOOK DOWN AND LIFTED HER HEAD. The house was quiet, and she listened to it for a moment, feeling its calm air of peace. Everyone but Selena was out, and Selena was upstairs and had asked not to be disturbed.

Natalie rose from the chair at the table and tiptoed quietly to the back door. There was a square of frosted glass in it, and she peered through it, saw the world outside blurred and distorted, then touched the doorknob.

The last time she'd done this, she thought, she'd gone outside and had a panic attack.

And seen the two men, who had watched her, then come back for her.

But they wouldn't be out there now. The police had both in custody. They'd told her so when they came for her statement.

Natalie pressed her other hand to her chest, drew in a deep, slow breath, and remembered what Selena had just taught her.

'Centred,' she whispered. 'Not in my head, but here, where I am strong.' She tapped her hand against her ribs, below her heart.

She closed her eyes, because her head swam. Standing

there, one hand on the door, the other pressed against the bottom of her rib cage, she concentrated on moving her focus from her head to her centre.

She steadied. Stood there longer, continued the deep, slow breaths.

Her back straightened. She twisted the doorknob, opened the door, and stood on the ledge. Neither fully inside, nor fully outside.

She did not teeter there, but stood breathing, hand pressed to her middle, back straight, breathing coming easier. She let herself look around.

There was a driveway that spread out into a turnaround area. And a path that led down the side of the house and around to the back. Natalie looked down that way and wanted to go there.

Suddenly, she remembered the old teddy bear she had used to carry everywhere with her when she was a child. The thought startled her, and she stopped a moment to think about it.

She couldn't remember what had happened to the bear, but her lips curved in a smile remembering him. She had used to tell that bear everything. All her worries. All her secrets.

Still smiling, she reached into her pocket and pulled out Clover's model bear. It tucked snugly into the palm of her hand, and she looked at it.

'Want to come with me on an adventure?' she asked.

Her fingers curled around the figure, and she looked back outside, then stepped onto the path. Her free hand groped out to steady herself against the wall. The stone was warm from the sun, gritty under her fingers.

'We're going on a bear hunt,' she sang under her breath. 'We're going to catch a big one.' The book had come out when she was older, but she still remembered it.

'We're not scared,' she sang, and came to the corner.

'We're not scared,' she repeated, breathing the words.

42

'NAT'LIE!' CLOVER LEAPT AWAY AS SOON AS TARA HAD GOT her out of her car seat. She took off around the side of the house to the garden.

Natalie? Tara straightened, then followed.

'Nat'lie,' Clover said. 'You in the garden!'

'Goodness,' Tara said. 'So you are.'

Natalie looked up at them both and managed a smile. It was somewhat shaky, but it was a smile, nonetheless.

'I wanted to see it,' she said. 'Your talk of it this morning made me want to see it.'

Clover climbed up on the garden seat beside her and turned around so that her legs swung above the ground. 'You got bear with you,' she said and nodded. 'Bear's keepin' you safe.'

Tara came over and shook her head. 'Are you doing all right?' she asked.

Natalie looked down at her hand and opened it. The bear lay still in her palm. She looked at it for a moment, then gazed up at Tara. 'I am,' she said. 'I'm really pretty good.'

'Well,' Tara answered, beaming. 'How about I grab us a drink and join you before I make lunch?'

Natalie looked out across the small garden and nodded. 'I'd like that,' she said. 'And I'll help with lunch.'

'Can we make cake?' Clover asked. 'A honey cake for bear?' She leaned against Natalie. 'Bears like honey,' she said in a dreamy voice.

'A honey cake,' Natalie said, and blew out a slow breath. She'd not been out here long, and she wasn't going to lie – it was hard. But she was here. She was doing it, even if her other hand was holding grimly onto the seat.

As long as she kept her...energy...out of her head and down in her middle, she was all right.

Managing it, anyway.

Clover was gazing up at her, and Natalie looked into the bright blue eyes, wondering what they were seeing.

'You got your little girl with you,' Clover said.

Natalie was taken aback. 'What little girl?'

Clover shook her head. 'You know,' she said, and looked back out over the garden. 'The one that slept in the tent.'

Natalie stilled, and suddenly her mouth was dry. 'How do you know about that?'

Clover shrugged, slid down from the bench and went over to the tiny pond. 'Dunno,' she said. 'Just do.' She smiled at the pond. 'Have you seen our fishies?'

Natalie had closed her eyes, trying to keep her fragile equilibrium. She shook her head. 'No,' she said faintly.

'Are you all right?' Tara asked and sat down next to Natalie. 'I can help you back inside if you need.'

Natalie shook her head. She wasn't ready to give up yet. 'How,' she asked, then stopped and tried again. 'How does Clover know the things she does?'

'Oh.' Tara handed Natalie a glass of lemonade. 'Has she said something?'

'She hasn't really stopped saying things.' Natalie took the glass with a hand that shook.

But she was sitting outside in the sunshine. That was a victory.

It felt astonishing.

'You should have heard what Clover said to one of the mothers at the playgroup I tried taking her to last week,' Tara sighed. 'I'm getting my qualifications to look after kids at home here, so we don't have to go to these things and have this happen. But I thought we'd be all right, once or twice, you know?'

Natalie didn't know. Not really. 'What did she say?'

'She told this woman that she was going to win Lotto.'

Natalie raised her eyebrows, forgetting for a moment all about being outside. 'But that's all right, surely?' She shook her head. 'How does she know these things?'

Tara looked over at Clover, who was sprawled out on the ground watching the goldfish they'd bought for the small pond.

'I don't know,' she said. 'I have almost no idea how she knows these things. It's like she's still connected to...I don't know. The unseen part of things, I guess. I'm no expert – I'm just starting out with all this, like you.'

Like you. Natalie heard Tara's words, and a flush came over her. For the first time in so long, she didn't feel alone.

Natalie looked over at the child at the pond. The sun

made her hair shine gold, and Clover was talking softly to the goldfish, telling them some sort of story. Natalie looked down at the bear still gripped in her hand, then looked back at Tara.

'What happened?' she asked.

Tara sighed. 'You'd think at least she didn't tell the mother that her husband was cheating on her, or something, right?' She shook her head. 'But it turns out that saying she was going to win a big prize with Lotto was just as bad.'

'How so?'

'Five minutes after saying it, there was a crowd of women around us, all wanting to know if they could win something too, if Clover could tell them the winning numbers.' Tara shuddered. 'It was horrible. They were like a sudden flock of vultures, all wanting a piece of her.'

'I'm surprised they believed Clover.'

'I was too,' Tara said. 'But they did.' She shook her head. It had been a weird and uncomfortable situation. 'I decided not to go back again, after that, and just wait instead until we can run our own little playgroup here. Then at least Clover won't have the opportunity to say anything to adults other than us.'

'Us?'

'Yeah. Us. The ones who know about her.'

Natalie nodded and looked down into her lap, absurdly pleased to be included. She'd never been included in anything before.

She sipped her drink.

'Hey,' Tara said. 'Do you think you might want to come back out here after lunch? We could harvest some of the mint that's growing like crazy over there and make those extracts.'

Natalie looked over at the boxed garden beds, picking out the mint easily. She judged uneasily how far away it was from the back wall of the house.

'I'd like to try,' she said around the lump in her throat. 'If it gets too much for me, I could sit here while you do it.'

'That sounds perfect,' Tara said, and she meant it.

'An' we gotta make a honey cake for Bear,' Clover called out, looking up at them.

Tara raised her eyebrows. 'A honey cake for bear?'

Clover got up and dusted herself off. 'Yeah,' she said. 'Nat'lie's Bear.' She put her hands on Natalie's knees and looked up into her face. 'He likes honey, doesn't he?'

Natalie didn't know what to say. She nodded, cleared her throat. 'I guess so,' she said. 'Bears like honey, right?'

Clover nodded emphatically. 'Right. Bears eat lotsa honey.' It was Winnie the Pooh's favourite food in the whole world.

Selena joined them for lunch, and there was a last minute kerfuffle at the door, and Damien blew in on the breeze.

'I'm not too late, am I?' he asked, standing there rubbing his hands together. He looked over at Tara. 'There's not a place in the city that does better than the spread you put on.'

Tara laughed and shook her head. 'Well, you're in for a disappointment today, then. There are only sandwiches and cake.'

Damien nodded in satisfaction. 'Sandwiches made with bread fresh from the oven this morning – nice and crusty and tasty, and home-made cake which is always the best sort.' He went off whistling to wash his hands. Came back and winked at Clover and Natalie as he sat down.

'You know,' he said, 'I had the strangest dream last night.'

Selena smiled. Damien had taken her instructions about his dreams to heart. It would pay to listen. 'Can you tell us about it?' she asked.

Damien nodded as he expertly built his sandwich. 'Dreamed I was back at home with my mum and gran.' He shook his head. 'I wasn't a kid, I was, you know, the same age I am now.' He stopped talking to concentrate a moment on cutting his enormous sandwich in half.

Natalie only half-listened. She was nibbling at her food, still fizzing inside from the victory of the morning. She had gone outside!

'What happened in your dream, Damien?' Selena asked.

'Right.' Damien looked at his sandwich and nodded. 'So, I was there with Mum and Gran and a bunch of others, like it was for a tangi or something.'

'Tangi?' Selena was unfamiliar with the word. She'd learnt a few in the short time she'd been sharing a house with Damien – that *kai* meant food, for instance, and *whānau* was family.

Damien frowned. 'Funeral,' he said. Then shook his head. 'Dunno whose it was, though. Could have been anyone. I might not have even known them, although I felt like I did.'

Selena waited while he thought it through.

405

Finally, Damien drew in a breath. 'So, I was there, and me and Mum and Gran, we were standing on the riverbank, right? Just standing there watching the water flow.' He shook his head. 'I don't know what that was about, just standing watching the water go by. Weird.' He picked up half his sandwich and shrugged. 'I don't know, right? It was just really clear. Watching the river flow.'

'I like that dream a lot,' Selena said. 'Dreams that have such large elemental symbols like your river, are particularly interesting.'

Damien had taken a bite of his sandwich, but he shook his head.

Tara asked for him. 'What does dreaming of a river mean?'

Damien swallowed. 'It's a real river,' he said. 'Plays a big part in the life of my people.' He looked at his sandwich. 'Rivers are people,' he said. 'That's how we see them.'

'Rivers are people,' Selena answered, smiling. 'Everything in the land has its own sovereignty.'

'But you said the river was also an elemental symbol?' Tara asked.

'The thing with dreams,' Selena said. 'Is that they have layers of meaning.' She nodded at Damien. 'So, your dreaming of your family, of being home for a funeral – all those are things to look at. But the river, the focus of everyone's attention – look into the stories of the river, see which strike you. And water traditionally has to do with the emotional life and being of the heart.'

Damien nodded. 'Being of the heart. My gran would agree with you.' He smiled. 'I'll write it down,' he said. 'See what comes to me.' He put the sandwich down. 'I've been thinking about going home for a visit. Maybe I should make actual plans.'

Natalie sat silently at the table, listening to the conversation. She'd never heard one like it. Was this how other people lived?

She didn't think so. This seemed too unusual. Talking about dreams over lunch. She glanced over at Clover, who was concentrating on folding her piece of cheese in half.

Then there was Clover.

Clover was very different. She knew things. Could see things.

Natalie cleared her throat, looked over at Selena. 'I went outside,' she said.

Selena's face broke into a wide smile. 'You did? But that's marvellous.'

'She was sitting outside soaking up the sun when we got home,' Tara said.

Natalie nodded and didn't add that she was sitting there because she hadn't trusted herself to go further, not even to turn around and go back inside. But it had been extraordinary enough for the first time.

She puffed out a breath. 'It was the centring exercise you taught me that helped.'

Selena nodded. 'Yes,' she said. 'Our energy comes from our centre. And if we can live from here...' She tapped her chest over her heart. 'If we can live from our hearts, instead of always being in our heads, we can work miracles.'

Natalie nodded slowly and unconsciously touched her own middle. She took a breath and let it out slowly, moving something – energy? Awareness? She didn't know how to describe it, but she relaxed on her exhale and became centred.

'Heart-centred,' Selena said, and smiled.

The noise dropped out of Natalie's head, and she felt surrounded by calm.

'Is it this easy?' she asked, her voice a half-whisper.

'It is this easy,' Selena agreed. 'But staying in our hearts is the more difficult part. We must keep remembering, keep drawing ourselves back there. We are in the habit of being up inside our heads and not even realising that's where we are.' She looked around the table. 'We're an upside-down lot, really. We get everything back to front – I believe that happened a long time ago, when values changed away from being close to nature and sharing the world with those others who lived alongside us.'

'Those others?' Damien interrupted.

Selena nodded. 'The animals, the trees.' She raised her eyebrows. 'The rivers.'

'What do you mean by upside-down, though?' Natalie asked, her lunch forgotten in front of her.

'I mean a lot of things, I think,' Selena said with a laugh. 'But mostly we have come to accept a broad state of boredom and depression with the world as normal, when really the world is a startling and vibrant place. We have just forgotten how to see it as such. The world is marvellously alive, beautiful, fulfilling.' She touched her heart again. 'And when we move through it as heart-centred people, that's when we see this. When we're in our heads too much, we too easily become overwhelmed, and believe that life has no meaning.' Selena shook her own head. 'That's when we start living upside-down. We must learn to notice how beautiful the world is.'

'But it's not,' Natalie answered. 'It's full of people who hurt and destroy.'

'Yes,' Selena said sadly. 'It is. We need widespread change, as a species. Sometimes I want to fall into despair, thinking over our history on this planet.'

'How don't you?' Tara asked. 'Other than turning away from it and not thinking about it?'

'I tend and grow my spirit into strength,' Selena said. 'I support others to do the same. It is a slow revolution, perhaps,' she said with a smile.

'But it is the one that will overcome.'

43

RUE WAITED UNDER THE FRINGE OF THE WILLOW TREE, staring at Ebony's makeshift shrine and shifting from foot to foot.

There was a rustling and the willow's tender branches and long leaves parted like a green curtain.

'Here you are,' Rue said. 'What took so long?'

Ebony shook her head, dropped her bag to the ground and reached into one of its pockets. She pulled out two pikelets stuck together with butter and peeled them apart.

'For you, Athena, strength of my head and heart.' She put one of the drop scones down on the ground in front of wide flat stone on which she'd drawn a wide-eyed owl, then paused for a moment with her eyes closed, before standing up and looking over at Rue.

'It's been a shit morning,' she said, and glanced at the pikelet still in her hand, shrugged, and took a bite.

'What's happened?' Rue asked, sitting down on the grass

and gazing at her friend. Ebony looked uncharacteristically fed up.

Ebony threw herself on the ground, lay back, and popped the rest of the pikelet in her mouth, chewing while she thought.

'I'm sick of it here, I guess,' she said finally. 'I mean – what's the point of us, or me at least, being here day after day, learning to get up when a bell rings, sit down when a bell rings, go outside at the sound of another bell, and so on and on and on?'

She shook her head. 'I've been thinking about that conversation we had, you know? When you asked us what we all wanted to do, and how we wanted to live?'

Rue nodded. 'I remember,' she said. 'You wanted to be a ghost hunter, help lost spirits cross over.'

'Not wanted,' Ebony said. 'Want to. I want to.' She sat up and hugged her knees. 'Only, am I going to learn anything useful for that here in this place?'

She answered her own question. 'No, I am not.'

'I don't think there's any school that teaches the things you want to learn to do that,' Rue said.

Ebony turned her head to look at Rue. 'No,' she said. 'Or maybe not, anyway. Not schools.' She groaned. 'I'm just sick of this place.'

'Did something happen?'

Ebony shook her head and heaved a great sigh. 'Nah,' she said. 'It's just boring and pointless here, is all.'

Rue nodded. 'We don't have any choice about it, though,' she said. 'And hey – at least we get to see each other every day. There's that, right?'

Ebony's face lit up at last and she laughed. 'Yeah,' she said. 'There's that.'

'Good,' Rue told her. 'Because I have some things for us.'

'You do?'

Rue reached for her backpack and drew out her notebook. Her Book Of Ways.

'Selena said a new prayer this morning,' she said, deciding she'd begin with that – it would be bound to cheer Ebony up. Rue gave a slow, humorous smile. 'I wrote it down in here during English.'

Ebony stared at her, then burst out laughing. She held out her hand and Rue gave her the book, open at the page where she'd transcribed the prayer as best as she could remember it.

'This is different,' Ebony said, and shook her head. 'Since when has she prayed to Brigid?'

'She's mentioned her a couple times, but not like this.'

'Why do you have Brigit in brackets after the name?'

Rue looked at the page. 'Because I'm not completely sure whether she said Brigit or Brigid. And I didn't have time to ask her about it.'

'She's speaking to the goddess like she's a sun deity,' Ebony said, her brow furrowed in concentration. 'This is really interesting.'

'Isn't it, though?' Rue took the book back and gazed down at the prayer. 'Do you want to copy it into your Book Of Ways?'

Ebony got her notebook out of her bag and turned it to a fresh page. 'How do we find out about this Brigit, and whether she's Brigid, and so on?' she asked.

'You're coming around on Saturday, right?' Rue said. 'We

can ask her then, if I don't beforehand.' She wrinkled her nose. 'I wish the books from the library were more interesting.'

'I'll look it up on my computer,' Ebony said. 'See if I can find anything else.'

Rue nodded. There was still no computer at her house, which seemed a giant shame.

'Selena should teach us fulltime,' Ebony grumbled as she wrote in her book. 'That would be the best thing ever.'

'That reminds me of my dream,' Rue said, eyes widening. She shook her head. 'That's the other thing I wanted to tell you – about my dream.'

Ebony paused. 'What about it?'

'I dreamed I was her – the woman from my past life.' Rue shook her head. 'I'm sure it was her. In my dream, it was like I was her again.' She looked expectantly at Ebony. 'And in my dream, she – I – lived in this community of priestesses.'

'That is so cool,' Ebony said, shaking her head slowly. 'Why aren't there still places like that? I don't understand it.' She sighed. 'I wish I could dream like that.'

'Maybe you can,' Rue answered. 'Maybe you already are, and just don't remember it.'

'I think I'd remember that.'

Rue shrugged. 'Start writing your dreams down, anyway.'

'Yeah,' Ebony said. 'I think I will. So, what happened in your dream?' She grinned. 'Stick anyone with a sharp stick?'

Rue sniggered, then shook her head. 'No. I was walking along this path, right? And it wound through a forest, and then there was this stone circle.'

Ebony listened, pen in her hand, the prayer forgotten for a moment.

'The stones were new,' Rue said, and sat back to wait for Ebony's reaction.

'New?'

'They'd just been erected, I mean.'

Ebony gaped at her. 'What?' She shook her head slowly. 'When was this, then?'

Rue shrugged, but she answered. 'Remember how the board spelled out 2500 BC? I reckon I'm dreaming about that one, or sometime way back like that.'

'I wish we were learning this sort of history in class,' Ebony said. 'Instead of just talking about all the wars of the last century instead. If we were talking about this – I might be interested.'

'Yeah.' Rue nodded in agreement, plucked up a stem of grass and rubbed it between her fingers. It was cool under the willow, and maybe that was why she suddenly shivered.

'I don't recall the whole dream now,' she said. 'But I followed this path around the side of a steep hill until I could see the sea.' She frowned in concentration, trying to remember. 'I – she had some sort of task to do.'

Rue relaxed and grinned. 'Which involved flying.'

'Nah,' Ebony said. 'They didn't know how to fly back then.'

'As Albatross,' Rue finished.

'Albatross?'

She nodded. 'Oh my god it was amazing. I called Albatross to me, and he came and took me up into the sky and then I was him. I was a bird, and we flew for hours over the ocean.'

She touched her heart as though she'd still be able to feel it beating as fast as a bird's.

'That sounds fantastic,' Ebony enthused. 'What wouldn't I give to be able to fly as a bird?' She thought about that for a while, then changed track. 'What was the task, though?'

Rue frowned. 'That's the bit I can't remember.' She shook her head. 'It's just a blank now. I thought I might remember more of it when I wrote it down. Selena said that sometimes happens.' She shrugged. 'But it's gone. There's just the flying out across the ocean.'

'Maybe you'll dream it again,' Ebony said. She sniffed. 'What era was it 2500 years ago?'

'4500 years ago,' Rue corrected. 'And I've no idea.'

'We should find out.'

Rue flicked the blade of grass away. 'There's not going to be anything in the school library about it,' she said. 'They have a pretty crappy selection of books.'

'True,' Ebony agreed. She picked up her pen again, then looked at Rue. 'What about the encyclopaedias though? Shouldn't they at least have something to say?'

'Or the computers,' Rue added. 'We could look it up online.'

'We'll never get a turn,' Ebony sighed. 'But how about I finish writing this down, and then we go check out the encyclopaedia? I can look it up on the computer when I get home.'

'Do you have a printer?' Rue asked.

Ebony nodded. 'Mum keeps printing out screeds of stuff about her horoscopes.'

'Print out for me whatever you find, okay?'

'You can count on it,' Ebony said. She picked up her pen again, then grinned over at Rue.

'What?' Rue asked.

'This is awesome,' Ebony said.

Rue grinned back. 'I know.'

Her eyes widened suddenly. 'I can't believe it,' she said. 'I almost forgot.' She shook her head. 'Selena taught us this new thing this morning as well. She called it grounding, I think.'

'Will you teach it to me?' Ebony asked. 'I want to learn it too.'

Rue nodded. 'Yep. Selena said it's one of the foundational practices of...' She stumbled.

'Of what?' Ebony asked.

Rue raised her eyebrows. 'Of walking between the worlds.'

They looked at each other, excitement rising.

Despite everything, they both thought, the world seemed marvellous.

Suddenly full of possibility.

44

Natalie went to her room that night exhausted. She closed the door behind her and sagged against it, looking out the window at the waning light. The seasons were turning, she thought. Summer coming to an end.

She liked winter, usually. Summer made her feel guilty that she couldn't go outside, couldn't get out and weed the garden, or go to the beach. In winter, who wanted to go out anyway? Winter let her lie to herself that she was justified in hiding away under a blanket with a book or on the couch watching a movie.

Her gaze shifted to the candles Selena had given to her, and she pulled herself upright and walked over to them, turning to glance at the picture on the wall.

The cottage, one window lit, as though a beacon for whoever was on their way. The trees around it didn't look as menacing as she'd thought they had the first time she'd seen it. Now she looked at them and remembered the path through them that led to the pond.

Thinking about the pond made Natalie smile – Clover had been so cute with her little pond in the garden outside, and the three or four fish in it.

Natalie had finally walked over to it on wobbly legs and looked in, Clover pointing at the fish and telling her their names. Natalie shook her head – she'd been outside. How had that happened? How had she managed to stand there, the sun shining on the top of her head, and look at the tiny round pond?

It seemed a miracle.

Natalie picked up the box of matches and set a flame to the wicks of the candles. It had been a miracle, she decided. She'd been outside not just once either, but twice, going back out in the afternoon with Tara and Clover, where she'd helped pick the mint.

It had been glorious.

Still terrifying, and she'd shrank back at every loud noise, but it had been glorious.

And whenever she'd felt wobbly or close to panic, she'd dragged her awareness down to her heart, standing there for a moment, eyes closed, doing as Selena had shown her.

Every time she'd done it, she'd felt stronger. Just a little bit.

Enough to begin with.

At one point, she'd stood up, arms full of fragrant spearmint, and looked up at the sky. It was a beautiful day, she thought. She gazed back down at the herbs in her arms, and they were such a bright, perfect green that their beauty stole her breath away and she gasped. She could see every little striation on the leaves, and their scent filled her lungs. When she lifted her head and looked around, everything was beautiful. The sky with its deep clear blue, Clover with her wide smile. The garden, profuse with flowers of so many colours that Natalie blinked at them, swaying slightly.

Tara had asked her then if she was all right, and Natalie couldn't answer, couldn't speak, could only shake her head.

The world was so alive, she thought.

She wanted to be part of it.

Now, in her room, she gazed back at the candles then closed her eyes.

'Thank you,' she whispered, although she didn't know to whom she was speaking. Perhaps she was just thanking herself, for being brave enough, or Selena, for giving her the key, or the world itself, so broad and deep it dazzled her mind.

Natalie took a slow breath. She glanced at the picture again. She'd used that too, when she was outside. She'd drawn the trees around her, imagined part of herself standing by the pond, breathing in the calm, the peace.

It had helped. It had really helped.

She changed for bed by the candlelight, imagining as she did that the trees from the picture were all around her. The walls were trees, and there was a path through them that she could walk if she wished, and it would lead to a lovely wide pond.

When she blew out the candles and climbed into the bed, she was calm, lulled by the inward vision of the pond, its water silvered again by the moon.

The bed was warm and comfortable, and Natalie lay back, head cushioned on the pillow, eyes closed. She was looking at the scene Selena had asked her to build; she was walking through it.

There were reeds growing through patches of the water, she saw, kneeling on the bank, the grass tickling the backs of her bare legs. The moon, when she leaned out over the water, was a great silver coin that seemed to float just under the gently rippling surface.

Natalie slipped into the water. It was cool, and somehow fizzy, like bathing in champagne.

She swam out to the middle of the pond and floated there, looking up at the tree's branches and the moon, elated. The water lapped around her, cushioning her, washing all her troubles away.

She fell asleep, lying in the cool clear water of the pond, soothed by the sighing of the trees.

And when she dreamed, she was still at the pool, for in her dreams, it was a real place. There was a noise in amongst the trees and Natalie lifted her head and looked over in the direction where she'd heard it.

A young girl stood there, a teddy bear tucked against her chest with one arm.

Natalie stood up in the pond, water streaming from her, and she peered at the figure.

'Who's there?' she asked.

The trees whispered more loudly, then began a low, humming chant.

'Hello?' Natalie said, staring at the figure. The girl looked familiar. Natalie waded to the bank and drew herself out of the water. Her skin sang and her heart thumped steadily, strongly. She pressed her hands against her ribs, under her breasts.

'I know you,' she said, and tears sprang to her eyes as she looked at the child.

The girl stared steadily back.

'You're me,' Natalie said, falling to her knees and putting out her hands. She hesitated a moment, then touched the girl's cheeks. Natalie shook her head in wonder. 'Where have you been?' she whispered.

The girl shook her head. 'I stayed in the tent,' she whispered.

Natalie gasped, covered her mouth with a hand and shook her head at the child. 'I know,' she said, then dropped her hand and reached for the girl again. 'I'm sorry. think I've been stuck too.' She stroked her hair – such lovely thick hair, she'd had. Then looked at the bear.

'You've still got him.'

Her younger self held up their teddy bear. Natalie took him and touched his beloved face, his ears, his little button nose.

'I can't believe you still have him. We took him every-where with us.'

Little Natalie nodded. Then turned her head at the sound of twigs breaking in the forest. 'Shh,' she said, and smiled at Natalie. 'He's coming.'

Natalie looked into the darkness between the trees. 'Who's coming?'

But her eight-year-old self just shook her head and held the teddy bear up to look between the trees.

Natalie stood up. She could hear whatever it was now. It moved through the woods, its footsteps heavy, ponderous. She folded her arms across her chest, her heart beating too quickly. Glanced again at the girl.

But the girl was smiling, almost laughing, and turned,

bouncing on her toes, to look at Natalie. 'Here he comes,' she said.

'Here who comes?'

'Bear,' Little Natalie said. 'Here comes Bear.'

Natalie shrank back. A bear was coming? She looked behind her, but the pond was there. If she took a step backwards, she would be in the water.

A dark shadow appeared between the nearest trees, then condensed into the figure of an upright bear. Natalie stared at it, horrified.

'Run!' she cried, and snatched at her younger self, looking desperately around for somewhere to go.

She'd been right, she thought, when she'd told Selena that the Big Bad Wolf was in this forest – only it wasn't the Big Bad Wolf, it was the Big Bad Bear. How had she gotten that wrong?

But the little girl wasn't coming with her. She was laughing instead, twisting out of Natalie's grip, and walking up to the bear.

Natalie yelped, tried to scream at her, but her voice froze in her throat, and she fell to her knees, plastering her hands over her face.

She waited for a long, long time, for the scrape and gouge of the bear's claws. For the sound of him breaking the girl's bones, chewing on them, sucking out the marrow.

Fingers grasped hers and tugged them from her face. Little Natalie squatted in front of her, her eyes only inches away. Natalie blinked at her.

'He's our friend,' Little Natalie said. 'Look.'

Natalie turned her head, looked.

The bear sat placidly, staring back at her. His dark fur was thick, his snout long, black nose twitching.

Little Natalie left her there and went over to the bear, tucked herself under his shoulder, so that his great, heart-shaped head was next to hers.

'He's our friend, look,' she said.

'He's come to tell us we can't be afraid anymore, not when we have him with us.'

NATALIE WOKE IN THE MORNING AND ROLLED OVER IN THE BED to look at the picture on the wall. There was the cottage, and there were the trees. All that was missing was the pond.

And the bear.

She sat up and groped for the notebook Selena had given her, and found the pen, then wrote it all down.

The pond – swimming in that beautiful innervating water, and then herself. Finding herself.

And the bear.

She closed the book and sat there staring at nothing for a long minute, her mind dazed.

What did it all mean?

At breakfast, she sidled into the chair next to Selena.

'I dreamed of a bear,' she said. 'And of myself when I was a girl.'

Clover, who was sitting on Selena's lap, clapped her hands in delight. 'You foun' Bear,' she said. 'An' little you.' She nodded. 'I played with 'em. Bear pr'tended to be a baby.' She squirmed around and looked up at Selena. 'Wha's a baby bear called?'

'It's a cub,' Selena said. Then looked at Natalie. 'This is

your healing,' she said, with a smile. 'Finding those parts of you that were lost, that need nurturing and reassuring.'

'Me when I was a child, you mean?' Natalie asked, aware that everyone else at the table was listening, but not caring. This was too important. She felt on the verge of something here.

Something that would take her to a new place, or it would make the old safe. She wasn't sure which, only that she strained to know.

'Yes,' Selena answered. 'You've found a part of you that was stuck, and now you're whole again. And you've found one of your kin, who will be with you always, lending his great strength and courage.'

'Gotta give him some honey,,' Clover said. She nodded with great seriousness. 'Bears love honey.'

'But it was just a dream,' Natalie said. 'And the place with the trees and the pond – that was just imaginary.'

Selena guessed the place with the trees and the pond was the scene that she had asked Natalie to imagine, a safe place between the worlds that would be hers to steady herself in, and from which she could venture forth.

'There are some forms of imagining that are actually doing magic,' she said. 'And as for dreams, sometimes they are our souls talking to us. And our kin greeting us.'

Natalie sat back, her head swimming. She placed her hands on the table and looked at the lines on her palms. Somewhere, she realised, those lines had swerved way off track.

But a thought occurred to her.

Perhaps, just perhaps, this was them finding the path again.

45

'EB'NY!' CLOVER FLEW DOWN THE DRIVEWAY TOWARDS THE three girls. She'd been waiting for them to arrive.

So had Rue, and she walked behind Clover, grinning.

'Clover Bee!' Ebony knelt down, caught Clover as she barrelled into her, and picked her up, spun her around. 'How ya doin'?'

Clover, set back on the ground, beamed back up at her. 'I doin' good,' she said. 'We makin' staffs today?'

'That's the plan.' Ebony looked up as Rue reached them. 'Hey there. Looking good.'

Rue smoothed down the skirts of her dress. She'd just finished it the night before. 'You like?' she asked.

'I do,' Sophie said. 'And I love the colour.'

Rue nodded, fingering the blue dress, very similar to the ones Selena sometimes wore. 'Trying something new.'

She looked up and smiled at Sophie, then realised her friend was carrying a good long stick. 'Whoa,' she said. 'You brought that on the bus with you?'

'Much to the consternation of the driver,' Ebony answered, reaching down to tickle Clover. 'We had to stash it behind his seat before he'd let us on with it.'

'Well,' Rue said, raising her eyebrows and looking at her friends. 'They can be a kind of a weapon, I guess.' She cleared her throat. 'In a pinch.'

They gazed at each other, remembering what had happened the week before, then shook it off and grinned, glad the guys had been caught and weren't going to be a problem to anyone for some time.

Clover tugged on Ebony's hand. 'Wanna meet you my other frien',' she said.

Ebony closed one eye and squinted at the child. 'Wha?'

'Come roun' here,' Clover said. 'Meet Nat'lie.'

Ebony raised her eyebrows to Rue, who just shrugged.

'Nat'lie!' Clover pulled Ebony around the back of the house, and the rest of the girls followed her. 'Meet my frien's.'

Natalie, pale and tired, looked up from where she sat, her back pressed against the wall of the house.

'Hey,' Ebony said. 'You're outside. That's cool.'

Rue grimaced. 'Sorry, Natalie,' she said, and nudged Ebony with her elbow. 'I sorta said you were staying with us a while.'

Natalie nodded. 'It's okay.' She took a breath, still a little shuddery but that was all right, because yes, she was outside.

Which was a very fine thing.

She looked at Clover, who stood swinging the hand of one of the girls. 'These are your friends?' she asked her.

'Yep,' Clover said, and bounced a little. 'This is Eb'ny, and this is Sophie, and this is Suze.'

'She dragged us around,' Suze said. 'Sorry if we're interrupting you.'

'You're not,' Natalie said.

'Eb'ny has an el'phant frien',' Clover confided. 'An' Suze has a bird with feets like this.' Clover dropped Ebony's hand and turned her hands into claws. 'They got big nails.'

'Claws?' Natalie asked and looked at the girl called Suze. 'What sort of bird?' She heard herself asking the question and felt a moment's consternation that she sounded like she was taking any of this seriously.

Then she realised she was, and she did. Take it seriously. It was difficult not to, now that she'd met Selena.

'Don't look at me,' Suze said. 'This is the first I've heard of it.' She broke into a sunny smile. 'I've got a bird with big claws? That's pretty cool.'

'What about Sophie?' Ebony asked, looking at Clover. 'Who is her friend?'

Clover giggled. 'Sophie has a white piggy.'

'What!' Sophie shook her head. 'A pig?'

Selena came around the corner. 'The sow is sacred to Cerridwen,' she said.

'Who's Cerridwen?' Rue asked.

Selena patted Clover on the head and sat down in one of the patio chairs. 'Cerridwen is the Welsh goddess of rebirth, transformation, and inspiration.'

'And she walks around with a pig?' Sophie looked doubtful.

'Indeed,' Selena said placidly. 'I would relish the association, if I were you.'

'Well,' Sophie said. 'Inspiration? I guess I like that, since I've sort of decided I want to go around the world studying folktales and their history.' She blushed slightly. 'Then write about them.'

'When did you come up with that, Sophie?' Ebony asked. 'That's really specific.'

Sophie shrugged. 'Since we went to the library the other day, and I got some books out on folktales and mythology – it's like I can't get enough of it. Talk about fascinating.'

'Your kin will serve you perfectly, then,' Selena said, and looked over at Suze. 'Did I hear Clover say you had kin too?'

'She said I had a bird with big claws,' Suze replied.

Selena nodded, glanced over at Natalie, and back at Suze. 'Yes,' she said. 'I can see that.'

'You can see what sort of bird it is?' Rue asked.

'An osprey, I think,' Selena answered. 'Yes. Osprey.'

'I've never heard of that,' Suze said. 'What sort of bird is it?'

'It's a bird of prey usually found fishing in wetlands and lochs.' Selena smiled. 'Very impressive bird – and Rue told me you have plans of becoming a doctor?'

Suze coloured slightly and nodded. 'If I get good enough grades, and all that.'

'Osprey will be a great help in your chosen career.' Selena smiled at Suze. 'Osprey see extremely well to fish, and they are birds that inhabit liminal areas between water and land, and doctors work between life and death, so you are well-suited.'

Suze looked rather dazed.

Rue shook her head. 'How do you know what sort of bird Suze has as her spirit kin?'

'I see it,' Selena said, and lifted a hand to touch her temple. 'In my mind. Just a flash.'

'Wow,' Ebony said. 'Wish I could do that.'

'Well, you can if you walk the path between the worlds.' Selena smiled at her.

Natalie leaned forward slightly. She'd been following the conversation with fascination, despite still not knowing what she thought of it all. 'What do you mean between the worlds?'

'That's a good question,' Selena replied. 'I mean straddling the material world and the spirit world. They're joined, but we've mostly forgotten how to see that of the spirit.' She looked at Natalie. 'When you imagine and build that place of yours in the woods, Natalie – the cottage and the trees and the pond – it becomes a doorway to the world of spirit. A safe place where you can become all that you really are.'

Natalie swallowed and nodded. She didn't really understand any of this, but there was no denying that it was doing something to her. After all, here she was outside. Not diving for cover, not scanning the sky for incoming threats, but sitting in the sunshine. She still felt raw, and vulnerable, and she'd begun dreaming again of bombs and blasts, but still, she was sitting outside in the sunshine.

Selena looked over at the group of girls. 'Are you ready, then?' she asked.

'Yes please and thank you,' Ebony answered, and Clover looked up at her and giggled.

'Right then, girls,' Selena said, getting up. 'Let's go learn how to make our sticks into real pieces of magic.'

She paused and looked back at Natalie. 'Would you like to join us?'

'I don't have a stick,' Natalie said.

'I have some spare,' Rue said. 'I've collected quite a few on my walks with Clover.' She shrugged and smiled shyly. 'I kept seeing good ones, you know?'

'I got a short stick,' Clover said, nodding. 'You can have one too, Nat'lie.'

Natalie shook her head. She thought she might do some baking that afternoon. 'I don't even know what you use a staff for.'

Ebony laughed. 'Nor do we, but I'm really looking forward to finding out!'

SELENA LED THE PROCESSION OF GIRLS UPSTAIRS TO THE second attic room, where she'd set up a table and the tools needed for them to make their magical objects.

'I've blessed and cleared this space,' she said, letting them into the room. 'We are doing magical work, so this is an important part of it.'

The girls looked at each other, a hush falling over them, and they stepped into the room, and saw that Selena had arranged cushions enough for all of them in a circle on the floor.

Selena smiled at them. 'Now,' she said. 'Because all outer work is really inner work, we are going to begin by blessing and clearing ourselves also.'

Rue's eyes widened. This was even better than she'd thought it would be, and they were only just beginning.

'Arrange yourselves in a circle, girls,' Selena said, and

gestured to Clover. 'You can come and stand next to me, if you like.'

Clover dashed over with a big smile on her face. 'We gonna be trees?' she asked.

'Yes,' Selena said. 'Something like that.' She took a breath and blew it out. 'We begin with our breathing,' she said. 'Slow breaths in, hold them for the count of four, then let them out just as slowly.'

'What does this do?' Rue asked, deeply curious about everything Selena was telling them.

And they had barely got started.

'This breathing exercise brings us calmly to centre in our bodies. It makes us mindful of the moment we are in, and holds us there. The mind cannot easily wander when we breathe this way, when we focus on the sensation of our breath.'

The girls began, even Clover, who reached out a hand to hold Selena's. Selena grasped it in her own, not wanting Clover to fly off into trance. She would anchor her here in the room.

'As we breathe slowly in and out,' Selena said, 'we imagine a ball of light glowing in front of us.' She paused, then continued. 'If you like, you can hold your hands out, palms cupped, holding this ball of light.'

Rue held her hands out, cupped in front of her chest. She had her eyes closed, concentrating on her breathing, on the ball of light that fit snugly within the bowl of her palms.

Selena glanced down at Clover, then watched the young child for a moment. She'd expected that Clover would fidget and squirm during these exercises, but instead, she was calm, standing straight, breathing quietly, as though she were much older and had been doing this all her life. Selena could almost see the ball of light in her hands.

'Now,' she continued. 'On an inward breath, I want you to draw the light into your body. The light fills you, lightens you, brightens you, and on your exhale, I want you to let the light shine outwards from you.'

Rue drew the light inside herself and held it there for a long moment. She felt it inside her blood, organs, even her bones. The light was white, bright, and she thought that if she opened her eyes and looked inside herself, she might be blinded by it.

She breathed out, and let the light free, so that it shone from her, as though she were a star.

'We are blessed,' Selena said. 'We are blessed creatures of light and heat and love. We are joy and bone and eyes that see far, hearts that echo the beat of the worlds. We are here, and we are full of our purpose, and we are blessed.'

She looked around at each shining face in the room and smiled.

'Let your eyes open again,' she said, 'and come back to the room we are in, knowing still that you have this light within you, that it is always there, the bright shine of your own soul.'

Rue blinked, licked her lips, looked around at her friends. Their faces glowed as they smiled at each other.

'That was awesome,' Ebony said, and shook herself. 'I feel amazing – is that something we should do, like, regularly?'

Selena nodded. 'You can do it whenever you like. Daily is good – use that light not only to bring yourself back to balance, but to burn away troubles and cares.'

'I have quite a few of those,' Sophie said. 'Will it really help?'

'It will,' Selena told her. 'It will aid you in dealing with them by making you feel stronger, and surer in your skin.'

Sophie nodded, pleased, deciding to practice it every night.

'Are you still being troubled by the spirit in your house?' Selena shook her head. 'I'm sorry I've been too busy this last week to come over.'

'That's okay,' Sophie said in a hurry. 'She's still there, though. I still smell her sometimes, and I often feel like someone – her, I guess – is watching me in my room.' She squirmed a little at the thought. 'It's really uncomfortable.'

Selena nodded. 'I will come over tomorrow. Will your parents be home?'

Sophie cleared her throat, looked uncomfortably around the room. 'Um. We go to church in the morning, but after that we will be.' She winced. 'You couldn't come around and do it when my parents are out, could you?'

'I don't think so,' Selena said.

Sophie nodded, but she really wasn't sure how her parents were going to react to Selena coming to see them about a ghost in their house.

'Will it take long?' Ebony asked. 'I mean...' She hesitated, looking for a way to rephase that. 'I mean, is it a big deal to help a spirit cross over?'

'Not usually,' Selena said, and smiled.

'I want to be there,' Ebony said, determined to get that in there. 'I don't want to be a doctor or a writer or whatever. I want to help spirits cross over when they get stuck.' She blinked her fair eyelashes.

Selena could see that Ebony was serious. She nodded. 'I'll get Rue to let you know when we're going to Sophie's house, then.'

Ebony's eyes widened. 'Wow,' she said fervently. 'Thank you so much.'

She looked over at Rue, eyes shining, shook her head.

'I am so glad I met you all.'

46

'So,' Selena said. 'A staff is a magical tool, and like all magical tools, its purpose is to provide focus for the practitioner's will.'

'Practitioner?' Rue asked.

Selena nodded. 'Witch, shaman, wizard, magician.' She smiled down at Clover. 'Priestess of the Ancient Way.' She transferred her smile to Rue.

Rue felt her heart flutter, a butterfly inside her chest.

Selena continued the small lesson. 'Really, it is possible to do magic with no tools at all other than your mind and your intention. But the making and consecrating of tools helps hone that focus, and the tool holds the...' She groped for the right word. 'Let's just say it holds within it the focus and purpose you gave it, so that it makes it easier for you to go where you need go and do what you need to do.'

'My mother would kill me if she knew I was here doing this,' Suze said.

'We are not going to tell her,' Ebony said seriously.

Selena looked over at Suze. This was something that had escaped her attention – that the parents of these girls would not want them here doing this.

'We're Catholic,' Suze said apologetically.

'Ah.' Selena was nonplussed. She didn't like the thought of going behind anyone's back, teaching these things.

And yet, the girls were here, and she had told them she would show them this. Perhaps, she hoped, it was the flow of their purpose that had brought them to this room.

'Right,' she said. 'Well. Let's prepare the wood anyway, shall we?' She looked over at Clover. 'I will do yours,' she said. 'We're going to cut off the bark, then smooth and oil the wood.'

'With what looks like a giant potato peeler,' Ebony said, sitting down on her cushion and picking up the tool.

Selena laughed. 'These are actually very old wood-working hand tools,' she said. 'They were what was once used to shape the spokes for carriage and wagon wheels.'

Rue looked at her potato peeler with renewed respect. 'How do you use them?' she asked.

Selena laughed. 'Like a giant potato peeler.'

Dandy came in while the group was scraping the bark off their sticks and claimed a cushion. 'You don't mind if I join you, do you?' she asked.

'Not at all,' Selena said. 'We are making staves.'

She bent back to the task of slicing the bark from the short length that would be Clover's.

'I'm having one like my wizard's,' Clover told Dandy. 'I not 'llowed to use the 'tato peeler, though.'

Dandy's eyebrows rose and she smiled at the name Clover had said for the tool Selena was deftly using. And the other girls had them also, wielding them not quite so deftly, but effectively nonetheless.

'Exactly how many wizards do you have, Clover?' she asked.

Clover looked at her fingers and counted. She held some up. 'Seven,' she said.

'Goodness,' Dandy said, and looked at Selena. 'What do you know about these fellas?'

Selena shook her head. 'Only that they are very protective of Clover, and that they are unwilling to share whatever purpose they follow.'

Rue listened as she peeled the bark from her stick. 'Do the rest of us have wizards?' she asked, not sure whether she hoped the answer would be yes or no.

'Our kin are varied,' Selena said, smoothing a hand over the short stout branch that Rue had picked with Clover. 'Sometimes they are wizards.' She smiled at Clover and gave her the denuded stick to hold. 'Sometimes they are angels, or Fae, or Gods or Goddesses, and sometimes they don't have recognisable bodies at all.'

'What are they if they don't have bodies, then?' Ebony asked.

'Beings of light, perhaps,' Selena said. 'Often too, some of our kin will be our ancestors. Family bonds can continue within and between lifetimes, and sometimes the kin that guide us are related to us in the lives we have lived. From the same soul family.'

'What's a soul family?' Suze asked.

'Our souls form bonds, just as we do here,' Selena said. 'Groups, based on all sorts of things, I imagine. Purpose, traits, desires.' She smiled. 'Are we ready to sand our staves now?'

They inspected their handiwork and reached for the sandpaper.

'Are we going to use the wood burner thing?' Suze asked.

'If you wish to,' Selena said.

'But I don't know what to put on my staff,' Rue said. 'I don't know any Ogham or whatever.'

'I'm sure Selena will translate a short line or two for you,' Dandy said. She'd taken Clover's staff and was sanding it, enjoying herself.

'Yes,' Selena said. 'And there are a range of symbols that can be used appropriately.'

'I want to dedicate my staff to Athena,' Ebony said. 'What should I put on mine?'

'An olive branch,' Selena suggested. 'Or an owl.'

Ebony nodded. 'Don't know if I could draw an owl, but I could sort of twine an olive branch around it for sure.'

Sophie cleared her throat. 'Could I put a rose on mine?' She looked uncertainly at Selena. 'For Mary, Mother of God?'

Selena smiled back at her. 'Yes,' she said gently. 'You may certainly do that.'

Rue looked at her staff. It was coming along nicely. The wood was a light golden brown and felt good underneath her hand. What should she put on hers, she wondered?

'I don't know what to put on mine,' she confessed. She wanted it to be something really meaningful. 'I'll have to think about it.'

'Or dream about it,' Selena suggested. 'Sleep with the

intention of the right symbol being revealed to you in your dreams.'

Rue blinked. 'You can do that?'

Both Dandy and Selena nodded. 'Dreams,' Selena said, 'answer our questions very well, if we put them to ourselves with proper reflection.'

'Proper reflection?' Ebony asked.

'Indeed,' Selena answered. 'A seriously considered question, deliberated on, and the response to which you are determined to act upon, will be answered in your dreams.'

'There's even a term for it,' Dandy added. 'It's called dream incubation.'

'Wow,' Ebony said, shaking her head. 'This is the sort of education I've been hanging out for.'

'Right,' Selena said, standing up, then realising when Dandy handed Clover's staff to her that it was so short that it wouldn't touch the ground. She would just have to imagine that it did. She smiled around at the earnest faces looking towards her.

'Before we come to decorating our staves, I think we'll dedicate them. Perhaps after doing that, it will be easier to decide what we want them to look like.' She paused. 'It is of course, entirely okay to leave yours as bare wood. The power of this tool is not so much in the way it looks – although aesthetics are always pleasing – but in the way we tune it to our needs.'

The girls stared at her, rapt.

Dandy leaned back on her cushion, enjoying herself immensely.

'When I use my staff, it is in two ways,' Selena explained, then thought for a moment. 'I am speaking personally here about my own practice, which is all I am able to speak clearly of.' She smiled widely.

'Firstly, it is a symbol of my authority.'

'We don't have any authority,' Rue broke in, shaking her head, holding her length of smooth oak.

'You have sovereignty,' Selena said. 'Authority will come as you grow into your responsibilities.'

She looked at the girls' confused faces and shook her head. 'You have the sovereignty of your own flesh and spirit and purpose,' she said, 'and that will be sufficient for now.'

She was relieved to see them nod at her.

'Good.' She smiled again. 'My staff, when I plant it upon the ground, also marks my place in the worlds. It gives me the centre point around which the Wheel turns.'

'The Wheel?' Dandy asked, thinking elaboration on this point might be helpful.

'The natural cycle and patterns of the worlds,' Selena explained.

Dandy nodded.

'The staff pinpoints me in that cycle and holds me in balance between the worlds – the three parts of the Otherworld, the Upper, Middle, and Lower, and also between Sky, Earth, and Sea in this one. It helps me know where exactly I am.' She drew breath. 'I plant my staff upon the ground and hold the worlds within me.'

She glanced at Clover, who had crawled onto a cushion and fallen asleep in the warmth of the attic room.

Everyone else, however, was wide awake and gazing at her.

'So that is what we are going to imbue our staves with –

we are going to give them their purpose, to mark our place in the worlds.'

Selena shook her head slightly, thinking perhaps she should have begun with something easier, but she straightened, carried on.

'How do we do that?' Rue asked.

'By using our imaginations,' Selena answered.

'Our imaginations?' Suze looked dubious. 'I thought this was something real?'

'The imagination is our initial gateway to this work,' Selena answered.

'Okay,' Suze said. She still wasn't sure. It sounded too easy, somehow. She'd thought there would be...incantations, perhaps, mumblings of secret spells.

Selena nodded. 'Generally, when we start out on this journey...' She looked at Dandy, then back to the teenagers. 'We first begin with building an altar, and making tools to represent the four elements, and then work our way up to such things as staves.'

'Why aren't we doing it like that, then?' Ebony asked.

'Because I'm throwing you in the deep end,' Selena laughed. 'And because of the way I use my staff – it's something I'd really like for you to learn, and this seems a grand way to do it.'

'What is it that you really want us to learn?' Rue asked. She held her staff across her lap, the length of wood warm under her touch.

'How big the world is.'

Suze shook her head. 'We already know how big the world is,' she said. 'And sometimes, that's a bit intimidating.'

'That's because you're seeing the world in only one way,'

Selena told her, gesturing to the girls to stand. 'You're seeing the material side of it, which is competitive, challenging, and often lonely. What I want most for you to realise, is that the world is a place of spirit also, and you are never alone in it.'

Rue stood, feeling a trembling of excitement inside. She put both hands on her staff and planted the end upon the ground in front of her. The simple act of standing with her staff had her shaking her head.

'I feel like I've done this before,' she said. 'Like, I don't know, a long time ago.'

'I'm sure you have,' Selena said. She looked at the rest of the girls. 'You probably all have. And even if you can't remember, consciously, your spirit knows.'

She passed Clover's short staff to Dandy. 'If you'll excuse me a moment,' she said to them all. 'I'm just going to pop next door and retrieve my own staff so we can do this next part together.'

The girls looked at each other when Selena slipped out the door.

'Are you two okay with this?' Rue asked Suze and Sophie.

Both of them nodded.

'It's exciting,' Suze said. 'I never believed in all Ebony's stuff.' She glanced at her cousin. 'No offence, Ebony.'

Ebony grinned at her. 'None taken.'

Suze nodded, looked at Sophie. 'But this feels like I'm learning about something important and helpful.' She shrugged. 'It's hard to describe. Besides, it's fun, right?'

Sophie nodded.

Selena came back into the room, carrying her own staff. 'Are we ready?' she asked.

There were nods all around the room. Clover still lay tucked up asleep on her cushion, but all the rest were wide awake and ready.

'This is how we're going to do it,' Selena said, quite enjoying herself. 'Plant your staff solidly on the floor in front of you – just as Rue has done – and hold it like so.' Selena gripped her staff loosely in both hands.

'Close your eyes. Use your imagination. See or feel yourselves standing where you are, high up in this room under the roof of this house.'

She watched as everyone obediently closed their eyes and nodded to herself.

'Feel the rooms underneath you,' she continued. 'Feel the sky above you. Spread out in your imagination and feel the land outside the house. Over the road are the great trees in the Botanic Garden. The road winds up the hill.'

She blinked, breathing slowly, her voice hypnotic.

'The land spreads out around us. We stand at this point within it. We can see the ocean in the distance, and beyond that is more land that we could see, if we just stretched out a little farther.'

Rue could see the ocean, thought for a moment that she could almost hear it, and for another moment, she was riding above its waves on Albatross's wings. Then she stood once more in the warm room at the top of the house where she lived.

But around her was still the rest of the house, and the world outside. She could feel it.

'Hold onto your staff,' Selena said. 'Feel the wood of it

under your hands even while you are looking at the trees outside, hearing the birds cry out over the ocean as they dive for fish. '

Selena drew breath. 'This is where we are,' she said. The world moves around us. We are part of it. We see its cycles; we see it tilt and spin and we are part of it. We stand here. This is where we stand, our staff anchors us.'

She paused. 'Our staff anchors us.'

47

DAMIEN BLEW INTO THE KITCHEN ON A BREATH OF LATE summer air. He closed the door behind him and grinned at Natalie sitting at the table.

His smile faded a moment later, and he inched toward her.

'Hey,' he said, slipping into the chair beside her and peering at her, concern wrinkling his face. 'Are you all right?'

Natalie looked at him. Her eyes were wet with tears, and she sniffed, dug around in her pocket for a tissue and wiped her nose, shaking her head.

'I'm sorry,' she said. 'You must think I'm a terrible mess.'

Damien shook his head. Natalie, her hair a dark cloud wreathing her head, her eyes so large and sad, tugged on his heart and he felt suddenly protective of her.

'Why are you crying?' he asked, then glanced around the kitchen. Where was everyone else, he wondered? Why was Natalie left here to sit at the table by herself and cry?

Natalie sniffed again, catching his quick look around the room. 'Everyone's home,' she said. 'They're just busy.' She looked over at the stove. 'I thought I'd come quietly in here and do some baking.'

'I like that idea,' Damien said, smiling widely at her. 'You're an amazing baker.' He shook his head then. 'So why the tears?'

Natalie lowered her head at the question and squeezed her eyes shut for a moment as fresh tears threatened to flow. She mopped at her face with the tissue.

'I am a mess,' she said. Then pushed the book she'd been reading over to Damien and pointed to it.

'This is what I want,' she said. 'I want it so much and yet...' She shook her head again. 'I don't know. I feel so stupid that I don't have my life like this already.'

Damien pulled the book closer and frowned at the page Natalie had stabbed at with her finger. It was one of Tara's kitchen witchery books. He raised an eyebrow at Natalie.

Her face crumpled in pain. 'Read that page,' she said.

He nodded and turned back to the book, skimming the page. 'I don't get it,' he said after a minute. 'She's just talking about roses.'

Natalie covered her face with her hands, took a great shuddering breath, and nodded.

Damien looked back at the book, skimmed a little more. 'You can do a lot with roses,' he said, surprised. 'Who knew?'

'I didn't,' Natalie said. 'But now I do. Now I know I can make rose vinegar, and rose water for a skin toner, and a rose rinse for my hair.'

Damien looked at her hair. 'You have very nice hair,' he

said, still wondering what was going on. He cleared his throat. 'I bet a rose rinse would smell wonderful.'

He looked back at the book.

Natalie shook her head, sniffing again. 'It says I could bake biscuits with rose petals, and make jam, or even wine.' Her voice was rising. 'I could crystallise them for cake decorations or put them in my bath.' Her face crumpled again and her next words were barely more than a whisper. 'All the things I can do with roses.'

Damien looked at her. 'Do you want to do all that sort of stuff?' He turned the cover of the book over and read the title. 'Do you want to be a hearth witch?'

Natalie pressed her palms to her cheeks and nodded. 'I want my home to be like that,' she said. 'Full of wonderful potions and things I've made.' She blinked, looking over at Tara's herbs and nodded at them. 'Full of herbs growing in pretty pots.'

The words tumbled from her mouth. 'I want roses growing in my garden, and a little salad garden, and I want to grow...' she groped around for all the things. 'Courgettes and carrots and strawberries, so that I can get the ingredients for my cakes straight from my garden.' She trailed off. 'Or some of them, at least.'

Damien was shaking his head. 'But you can do all that, can't you? It's just a garden.'

Natalie's look was anguished. 'You don't understand!'

'No,' Damien said gently. 'I don't. But I want to. Can you explain it to me?' He wondered if he should go and fetch Selena or Dandy but reached out and touched Natalie's hand for a moment instead. 'Tell me,' he said. 'Help me understand.'

She looked at him, teary-eyed, and drew in a watery breath. 'It's too late, you see,' she said. 'I've wasted all these years being too afraid to do any of it.' She swallowed. 'There used to be a nice garden at my house, but I let it get overgrown. The rose bush hasn't been pruned for years. I've destroyed it all,' she said.

Damien gazed at her for a long moment.

'I'm useless,' Natalie said. 'I wrecked it and now I have to live with it like that.'

'No, you don't,' Damien said. 'You're not useless.'

'I've been useless for years.'

'I don't agree,' Damien said. 'You taught yourself to be an amazing baker, didn't you? And you managed despite some really tough things going on. That doesn't smack of useless to me.'

Natalie closed her eyes. The lids were puffy from crying.

'I wasted all that time,' she said.

'But you don't have to waste today, or tomorrow,' Damien answered. He straightened. 'Listen,' he said. 'I'll help you with your garden.'

She opened her eyes and looked at him. 'What do you mean?' she asked, her voice cracking.

Damien shrugged. 'I'll clear it out and dig it over. You want roses? We can go get roses. We can go get everything you need – vegetables to plant, herbs, whatever you like.' His voice softened. 'You can start again with all of it.'

Natalie dipped her head and thought about that. Could she start all over?

She'd been going outside every day. Just into the garden, and onto the driveway. Yesterday, she'd pushed herself and made it all the way down to the street. Clover had come with her, tugging on her hand, wanting to show her the stone lion she said was hers. She'd made it right down to the end of the driveway and laid her hand on the strong back of Clover's stone lion.

She shook her head. 'But I've made such a mess of everything,' she whispered.

'That's okay, though,' Damien answered. 'I think you can forgive yourself for that.'

Forgive herself? Natalie shivered at the thought. How did she do that when she felt so stupid, so foolish and mad at herself for being so weak that she couldn't even go outside her own house for months on end?

She didn't deserve to be forgiven. Not even by herself.

Did she?

Damien nodded earnestly at her. 'Living with Selena has taught me a lot of things,' he said. 'And one of them is that whatever you did yesterday doesn't have to be what you do today or tomorrow.'

'I don't know how to make that shift,' Natalie admitted.

Damien shrugged. 'I think you just stop beating yourself up over being a screwup – that's what I'm trying, anyway. Just letting all the mistakes I've made rest, and I'm choosing differently. I guess that's what I mean about forgiving yourself. Beating yourself up over stuff doesn't help but forgiving yourself does. It changes everything. It gives you space to try something new.'

He blew out a breath. Shook his head. 'I'll tell you what – let's go buy a rosebush.'

Natalie looked at him, startled. 'What?'

'What colour roses do you like best?'

She blinked. 'Um. I don't know. Pink, I guess.'

'Excellent,' Damien said, pushing back from the table and standing up. He held out his hand. 'Let's go find the most beautiful pink rosebush there is, and then take it to your place and plant it. It can be the beginning of your new life.'

Natalie gazed up at him, looked at his outstretched hand. Go get a rosebush?

She couldn't possibly do that.

Could she?

She looked down at Tara's book and read a couple of sentences and felt the intense tug of the words again.

That was what she wanted her life to be like. She wanted it more than anything.

Was it really okay to forgive herself for everything she felt as though she'd failed at, and just move on, start over?

Natalie touched her hand to her middle, taking a deep breath, and she nodded.

She could do it, she thought, if she kept calm, centred. She could build something.

And it might as well begin with a pink rosebush.

The tears were back in her eyes again, but this time she smiled through them and reached up, grasping Damien's outstretched hand.

'Hey,' Damien said, opening the car door to see Natalie staring wide-eyed at her house. 'You've done brilliantly all afternoon – this is the easy part.'

She transferred her gaze to him and made herself nod. She could do this bit.

'It's just the first time I've been back since, you know.'

'I know,' Damien said. 'But we'll do it just like we got along at the garden centre, okay? Slowly, and together.' He winked. 'Just breathe, right?'

Right. Breathe. She smiled weakly up at Damien. 'I really did it, didn't I?'

'You really did. Out and about, hitting the shops, buying up the place.'

Natalie coughed out a laugh. 'All right, then,' she said, and grasped his hand, hauled herself out of the car.

She stood on the footpath in front of her house, Damien's hand held tightly in hers, and she looked at her house.

'It looks so sad,' she said, hunching her shoulders.

'Needs a couple weekends' work, that's all,' Damien said. 'We can have it spruced up and tidy in no time.'

He was already planning to bring the lawnmower over the next day.

'Ready?' he asked. The rosebush was tucked under his other arm. 'Gotta get this baby's new home picked out.'

Natalie nodded. 'I want it where I can see it out the kitchen window.'

'Sounds like a fantastic plan.'

Natalie stepped forward and pushed the gate open. The hinges screeched. She'd have to get some oil for it, she decided.

They walked down the path, Natalie taking deep, slow breaths, trying not to think about the last time she'd walked down here, the way the world had spun and made her dizzy, her hands flailing, grasping at the house for support.

This time, she walked properly. Slowly and carefully, her hand back in Damien's, but she was upright and not panicking, feeling the strength and light radiating out from her centre, and her heart.

'You're smiling,' Damien told her.

She flicked a glance at him. 'I'm doing it,' she said. 'I'm really doing this.'

'Yep,' he agreed. 'No mistaking it. You're doing it like a pro.'

She reached the back door and pulled the keys out of her pocket. Slotted the right one in the lock and twisted it.

'Wait,' Damien said.

Natalie froze, looked at him.

He grinned at her and thrust the rose into her arms.

'Make it meaningful,' he said, nodding at the rosebush. 'Here you are, entering your house with your first new rose, on the first day of the rest of your beautiful life.' He tilted his head slightly.

'May it be rich and full and scented with roses and sugar.'

Natalie looked at him, then at the plant in her arms. It had two roses already in bloom on it and she bent her head to put her nose delicately to one of the blooms.

It was fragrant, perfect.

She nodded. Opened the door.

Roses and sugar, she thought. That needed to be a sign over the door.

Maybe it could be the name of her shop one day.

Natalie stepped inside, looked around at the house, felt it close in on her. Her face fell and she looked back at Damien.

'Maybe this wasn't such a good idea,' she said.

Damien raised his eyebrows in a question and Natalie hugged the plant to her.

'It's full of my old life,' she said, looking back at the house. 'I can feel it – all my fears, like they're clinging to the walls.'

'I get it,' Damien said, and his face bloomed into a grin again. 'We'll just have to clean it out.'

Natalie was confused. 'Clean it out? You mean scrub it down, or something.'

'Or something,' Damien answered. 'I've learnt a few things from Selena in the last months, and I did not come empty-handed to this party.'

'This party?' Natalie still stood just inside the door, frowning at him.

Damien shrugged. 'Figure of speech – although you know what? A little music while we work wouldn't go amiss.'

'Music?'

'Yeah. You have a radio or something?'

Natalie nodded. 'I have a little one in the kitchen.' She coloured slightly. 'Sometimes I turn it on just to hear another's person's voice.'

'Well,' Damien said. 'How about taking that rose inside with you, putting on some music, and I'll be back in one minute, okay?'

Natalie looked alarmed, but Damien just grinned at her one more time, then turned and took off back down the path out of sight around the side of the house.

Telling herself that he was just getting the rest of her purchases out of the car, Natalie took a deep breath, turned, and stepped into her kitchen, the place that had always been at the centre of her house, and of her heart.

She set the rose down on the kitchen bench and looked at the curtained window, staring at it as she vacillated.

Then, with a hand that trembled slightly, Natalie reached out and pulled the curtain aside. There was the back garden, still overgrown, and there was the garage.

Behind which no one lurked.

The sun shone down through the branches of the kōwhai tree at the back fence, and she leaned closer over the counter to see a tui upside down in one of the tree's branches, sucking nectar from a bright yellow flower.

Natalie took a breath. Then another. Closed her eyes.

And made a wish.

Roses and sugar.

48

'HEY,' DAMIEN SAID. 'ARE YOU OKAY?'

Natalie opened her eyes, but part of her, tucked into the back of her mind remained at the cottage in the woods, walking down to gaze at the beauty of the pond.

She nodded, then smiled. 'Do you think I might put a tiny pond into the back garden?'

Damien thought about it for two seconds and nodded. 'Heck yeah,' he said. 'Can do that in an afternoon.'

Natalie's gaze went to the items he was carrying. 'I thought she was for your house, for Tara,' she said in surprise.

Damien looked around the room, settled on a small corner shelf above the counter. He took the bowl that sat there down, and placed the small, serene statue there instead.

'I let you think that,' he said, standing back and nodding at the tableau. 'But it is my gift to you – your very own kitchen goddess to look over you as you make magic in this room.

Natalie gazed at him, speechless, then turned to look at the statue.

'She's holding a pinecone,' Natalie said, looking at the figure draped in Grecian folds, with flowers in her hair and a large pinecone in her hand. 'I don't know why that makes me so happy, but it does.'

She blinked, shook her head. 'I wonder who she is?'

'She's the spirit of your kitchen,' Damien said. 'Now, let's get this show on the road, shall we?'

Natalie turned back, stepped towards him, and kissed him suddenly on the cheek.

'Thank you,' she said. 'Thank you so much – you've just done the kindest thing I've ever experienced.'

Damien blinked, feeling the warmth grow in his cheek where her lips had pressed.

'You're ah, welcome,' he said, lost momentarily for words.

They looked at each other, smiling, then Natalie turned away and gazed at her new kitchen deity. She clasped her hands in front of her heart, then looked back at Damien.

'What else do you have?' she asked.

'One of Teresa's herb bundles,' he said, passing it to Natalie.

'Who is Teresa?'

'She's an old friend of Selena's, from back in the UK. She stayed with us for a few weeks over Solstice.'

'Solstice?' Natalie sniffed the bundle, handling it gently. It was a glorious mix of dried herbs, tied with green, braided thread.

Damien shrugged. 'Solstice instead of Christmas. We celebrated the longest day. It's sort of Selena's thing, and I gotta say, it was a lot more meaningful than Santa.'

'This smells wonderful,' Natalie said, passing the bundle back. 'But what is it for?'

'We're going to use it to cleanse your house.' Damien dug in his pocket for a lighter. He'd used to be a smoker, a few years back, but while he'd quit the cigarettes, he'd never quite got around to not carrying a lighter.

They were too useful.

He lit the end of the herb bundle and waited until it had caught properly, then blew the flame out so that it sent fragrant smoke into the air.

'This smoke cleanses as it fills the room.'

'Cleanses?'

'Clears the energy. Selena and Teresa and Dandy did it at our place before we moved in.' He smiled at Natalie. 'I don't know if you've noticed this, but our house has a really nice, calm atmosphere, which is a miracle considering Selena bought the place from a guy who had turned into a bit of a hoarder before he died.'

Natalie's eyes widened a fraction. 'Your house is so warm and welcoming.'

Damien nodded and held up the still-smoking herbs. 'Partly because of this,' he said. 'Shall we?'

Swallowing, Natalie let herself nod. She'd never done anything like this before, but so far, everything that Selena had taught her to do had helped – wasn't she now going outside?

Hadn't she just been in a car, gone to some shops?'

She took a breath, nodded again.

Damien gazed at her, watching her thoughts play across her face. 'Okay,' he said softly. 'Let's make this place your new home.'

He turned and led the way into the living room, figuring to start there. Natalie followed him.

Then turned back. 'Wait,' she said, and hurried back to the kitchen, picked up the small statue from the shelf, and came back.

She shook her head when he looked at her with it. 'I don't know,' she said. 'It just feels right.'

'I'm good with that,' Damien said and grinned at her before walking across the room and holding the herb bundle up near the ceiling so that the smoke drifted up into the corner of the room.

'I don't know all the fancy words like Selena does,' he said apologetically.

Natalie shook her head wordlessly.

Damien turned back to the drift of smoke, took a breath, and said the ones that came to him.

'Let all the shadows, the fears, failures, and wounds be cleared,' he said. 'This is a new day, and a new dream.'

He moved around the room, letting the smoke waft everywhere, stirring the energy, breaking it up and clearing it away.

Natalie followed him, breathing in the scented smoke and when they moved on to a new room, and Damien held out the herb bundle to her, she froze, staring at him with wide eyes.

He smiled back at her. 'You can do it,' he said.

'But I don't know what to do.'

'Exactly what I have been,' Damien replied. 'Imagine

the smoke clearing all the old energy that's collected in the corners and near the ceiling and under the bed.' He grinned at her, nodded. 'Have a go. It's empowering.'

'Will it work if I do it?' Natalie asked, hesitantly taking the smoking herbs from him.

'It will work if you intend it to.'

Natalie looked at him, then she nodded, stepping into her bedroom and held the herb bundle up so that the smoke drifted towards the ceiling.

'This whole place needs a paint,' she said, noticing how yellowed the ceiling was.

'I'm sure we can arrange that,' Damien said from his place in the doorway.

Natalie glanced back at him. 'You're already doing enough,' she said. 'All of you are.'

But Damien just shrugged. 'We help each other out. That's just how it goes.'

Natalie didn't know what to say to that, so she turned back to the task in hand and drew breath, wondering what to do, to say.

But the vision of the cottage in the woods came to her, tucked away in the trees behind the shining pool, and she knew suddenly that this was what she wanted her home to feel like.

A sanctuary instead of a prison.

A joy instead of a dimness.

She thought of Tara's book, of the woman who wrote it making so many things from rose petals.

She thought of the new rosebush sitting on her kitchen bench. Its flowers were a light blush of pink, and she sighed slightly thinking of the variety's name. New Dawn.

This could be a new dawn for her if she chose it.

Natalie straightened. She was choosing it. She'd been crying silently out for it for a long time, and now she was stepping forward into it.

Her new dawn.

'I clear this room,' she said, her voice growing stronger with each word. 'Of all my own worries, and fears.' She fell silent a moment, then spoke again. 'Not because there is nothing to fear, not because there aren't things I'm afraid of in this world, but because I'm standing straight and learning to be strong.'

She looked over at Damien, and he nodded.

'Keep going,' he said softly.

She smiled back at him and took another breath. Moved around the room, letting the smoke trail behind her, imagining it permeating all the nooks and crannies of the room, cleaning and clearing as it drifted with the smell of rosemary and thyme.

Perhaps she was imagining it, she thought, but the room felt lighter, looked brighter. She pulled the curtains open and looked outside.

My house, she thought.

My garden.

My sanctuary, not my prison.

Could she do it, she wondered? Turn it from one to the other?

With Damien, she walked to the next room, thinking that perhaps after all she could.

They circled around the whole house, Natalie with the statue tucked against her as though watching, let the smoke seep into the corners of each room, imagining as she did so that it was clearing away her old fears, leaving the space bright and open for her fill with something different. Something more vibrant.

Life. Living. Love.

They reached the kitchen again, and Natalie placed the statue back on the shelf, stood back and looked at it, then nodded, took a deep breath, and let it out in a cleansing sigh. She held up the herb bundle, still smoking, and drew the smoke around the room, then stood for a minute back in front of the statue.

She hesitated, then followed her impulse, and drew the bundle closer to herself, letting the smoke cover her, and she twirled it all around herself, closing her eyes as she did so, imagining that she too was being cleansed by the smoke.

Natalie nodded, gave the herb bundle back to Damien.

'I'm done,' she said.

He took it and nodded. Found a mug and dropped the herbs in there to smoulder out.

'One more thing,' he said.

Natalie looked at him, frowning, but he shook his head.

'Just a blessing,' he said. 'I remembered it while we were going around the house.' He cleared his throat, reached for Natalie's hand and held it lightly, lifting their hands together.

'Whāia te iti kahurangi, ki te tuohu koutou me he maunga teitei,' he said.

Then he smiled and let go of her hand.

'Pursue that which is most precious,' he translated. 'If you should bow down, let it only be to a lofty mountain.'

Natalie shook her head. 'That's beautiful,' she said wonderingly. 'Pursue that which is most precious.'

She pondered the words, trying to imagine herself into a new life where she was brave enough to pursue anything.

But hadn't she taken the first steps towards that already? She nodded and looked over at Damien.

'Shall we pick a spot to plant my rose?' she asked.

Damien threw back his head and laughed with a sudden joy. He grinned at Natalie.

'Let's plan the whole garden,' he said. 'Pond and all.'

Natalie looked toward the back door, imagined herself outside, looking around her garden, planning where things ought to go.

And then making it happen.

She nodded. 'Yes,' she said. 'Let's do that.'

49

DAMIEN PULLED IN CLOSE TO THE KERB AND TURNED IN HIS
seat to look at Selena. 'I'll wait here for as long as it takes,
okay?'

'Rue can text you when we're done, if you want to go and
do something else,' Selena replied.

But Damien shook his head. 'Nah,' he said. 'I'm good.
I'm gonna listen to my CDs. Get a bit of practice in.' He'd
begun learning Māori recently, determined to one day be
fluent in what should have been his native tongue.

Selena nodded, looked at Rue, a smile on her face. 'Shall
we, then?'

Rue nodded and stepped out of the car, looking appre-
hensively towards Sophie's house. 'Ebony said she'd meet us
here,' she said to Selena. 'That's okay, right?'

Selena laughed. 'I doubt a herd of elephants could keep
Ebony away from this.'

Sophie's front door opened, and Ebony thrust her head

out, saw Rue and Selena and grinned widely. She hurried down the path.

'You're here!'

Rue nodded at her friend, but she was apprehensive, rubbing her palms against the cotton of her dress and trying not to take great gulping breaths. She glanced at Selena.

'Is this going to be all right?' she asked.

Selena looked at her in surprise. 'I would imagine so, why?' she asked.

'I just hope Sophie's parents are nice,' Rue said.

Ebony shook her head. 'They're humouring us,' she said. Then shrugged. 'But that's enough, right?' She winced, then squinted at Selena. 'They've got Father Joseph in there, though.'

Rue was immediately alarmed. 'Father Joseph? Who's he?'

'Their parish priest.'

Rue looked at Selena. 'What do we do now?'

Selena shook her head, smiled at Rue. 'We go inside,' she said, and stepped along the path to the front door.

Ebony flung and arm around Rue and steered her towards the house as well. 'Don't worry,' she said. 'I'll bet Selena can run rings around any priest.'

Rue nodded. 'I just wanted it to go smoothly.'

'It was never going to happen that way once Selena insisted on talking to Sophie's parents about it.'

Rue groaned.

Ebony laughed, patted her on the shoulder. 'Come on. I want front row seats to this.'

They stepped into the house, in which all the lights were

on. The day had dawned overcast and damp, the southerly wind bringing a summer's-end chill to the air.

Rue expected they'd all go down to the kitchen, but Ebony led them instead into the living room, which Rue had never done more than peek into before. Sophie and Suze sat on the couch looking grim. They perked up a little at the sight of Rue and got up to sidle over to them.

'My parents are not too happy about this,' Sophie said. 'For starters, they don't believe the house is haunted, and they certainly don't believe in bringing some flaky woman into the house to help the spirit cross over.'

Sophie sighed.

'Selena's not some flaky woman,' Rue said. They were talking in low voices, away from the cluster of adults.

'You and I know that,' Sophie said. 'But good luck convincing my parents.' She bared her teeth for a moment. 'Which is why good ol' Father Joseph has entered the scene.'

'Don't you like him?' Rue asked, looking sideways at the man in the black cassock. He was younger than Rue expected, and actually quite handsome.

'We'd like him better if we didn't have to confess our sins to him every month.' Suze shook her head. 'It's a running joke in our school that all our imaginary sins are committed with him. Awkward!'

Rue looked around. Selena was in a tight huddle with Sophie's parents and the priest. 'What's going to happen, do you think?'

Suze shrugged her slim shoulders. 'Let's go eavesdrop, shall we?'

Ebony looked at her in admiration. 'A suggestion straight out of my own mouth.'

Suze snorted. 'Blood runs thick after all.'

They inched closer to Selena, Father Joseph, and Sophie's parents.

Her mother caught sight of them, as if remembering suddenly that they were there. She shook her head at them and made a shooing motion in her daughter's direction.

'You lot can go and wait in the kitchen,' she said. 'Off you go.'

Rue tried to catch Selena's eye, but she was deep in discussion with the priest and didn't look up. With a sigh, Rue trailed out of the room with the others.

'Well, that was a bust,' Ebony said. 'We're not even part of it, banished back here.'

'Could have been worse,' Sophie said. 'My brothers were packed off to Grandma's house for the day. Wow, were they annoyed about that – and they don't even believe in the ghost.'

'They believe in you getting into trouble,' Suze said.

'Yep.'

They stood silently for a moment, looking across the hallway into the living room, until Sophie's mother closed the door, and they could see nothing.

'Well,' Ebony said, going morosely over to the kitchen table and planting herself on a seat. 'Bugger.'

Rue looked at the closed door a moment longer, then shook her head. 'Selena said we could be part of it – watch, at least. She's not going to go back on her word.'

'If she gets a chance to do anything,' Sophie said, joining Ebony at the table.

She looked at Rue. 'I told my father that my staff was

just something fun we made, not a real magical tool, and he still looked sideways at me.'

Ebony laughed. 'My mother asked if I wanted a crystal to put on the top of mine.'

'Did you say yes?' Suze asked.

'She offered me this great hunk of amethyst, but I kind of like mine as it is,' Ebony said with a shrug. 'Have you guys been using yours?'

'For what?' Suze asked.

Ebony's eyes widened at her cousin. 'For standing strong on the ground and proclaiming allegiance to the goddess, of course.'

Suze stared back at her. 'No,' she said, deadpan. 'Not quite for that.' Then she relaxed and drooped sideways over the table and looked at Rue instead. 'I have been using it though – just sort of standing there and going through the light thing that Selena taught us?' She shook her head. 'It's kind of weird right? I swear that my staff has this sort of... feeling to it.'

Rue nodded. 'Mine too,' she said. 'Like it's really something.'

'I agree,' Ebony said, and Sophie nodded too. 'What Selena had us do, all that imagining, was pretty simple, and yet...' She shrugged. 'It made it magic.'

The living room door opened then, and Selena came out, seeing the girls in the kitchen and smiling.

Rue straightened. 'What's happening?' she asked.

Selena looked over at Sophie. 'Your parents have agreed to let me help the spirit.'

Sophie's eyes widened in surprise. 'They actually believe you.'

Selena shook her head, but she was still smiling. 'I don't think we could go that far, but they're willing to do it for the sake of your peace of mind.'

'Mine?' Sophie asked and shook her head. 'Wow.' She frowned. 'What about Father Joseph? What's he going to do?'

'Ah,' Selena said. 'Father Joseph and I have come to an agreement. He will bless the room – the whole house, actually, and I will do...my thing.'

Rue shifted on her feet. 'He's backing you in this?'

Selena looked at her. 'You have to understand the Catholic Church's basic stance on spirits,' she said.

'I didn't know they had one,' Suze blurted.

'It is acknowledged that spirits of the dead can appear to the living to ask for prayers – help, essentially, or to provide inspiration,' Selena explained. 'And these are the only terms on which it is all right to interact with spirits.'

'And Sophie's ghost is asking for help?' Rue said.

Selena nodded. 'We can say so, yes.' She paused. 'If we knew more about the spirit that is uneasy in this house,' Selena said. 'A name, maybe, a history, then Father Joseph would say the prayers of the dead, perhaps hold a mass so that they might go to their rest.'

'Does that work?' Ebony asked, looking sceptical.

'I would imagine so,' Selena said. She smiled. 'At least some of the time.' She clasped her hands together. 'Shall we proceed, then?'

Ebony got up from the table so suddenly that her chair scraped along the floor and fell backwards. 'We can take part?' She ignored the chair.

'You can watch,' Selena said. 'I will try to let you know what I'm doing.'

Ebony grinned from ear to ear. 'Count me in,' she said. 'Oh, heck yeah.'

Selena nodded and turned, walking past the open door to the living room where Sophie's parents stood, looking serious and not at all happy.

'Sophie,' her mother called. 'Stay in here with us, please.'

'But Mum!'

Sophie's mother shook her head and Sophie groaned, but dutifully joined her parents.

'You too, I think, Suze. Your parents wouldn't want you involved with this.'

Suze exchanged a look with Rue and Ebony, shrugged, and went to sit down on the couch with Sophie.

'Just us heathens, then,' Ebony said brightly, and hurried after Selena, Rue on her heels.

Father Joseph was in Sophie's bedroom, a tall figure in black who smiled at them in the doorway as they clustered beside Selena before turning back to his prayers. He flicked holy water at the walls in each direction, and Rue watched, wanting to ask Selena if what he was doing would help.

But it didn't feel right to interrupt. Instead, she followed Selena into the bedroom, and sat down on the side of the bed with Ebony when Selena gestured for them to do so.

Selena used the time while the priest blessed the room to centre herself and slip partway into the trance that would allow her to see the restless spirit, and then communicate with her.

Her breathing slowed and the room expanded around her. She could feel the length and breadth of the world outside the room, outside the house, could feel the spirit of it unfolding.

And here in the house...

She looked around, using her inner vision to see.

The priest's prayers floated on the air, delicate webs of benedictions.

He turned and nodded at her. 'I shall bless the rest of the house now,' he said, then smiled at the girls sitting on the bed. 'And all its occupants.'

'Thank you, Father,' Selena said and waited for him to leave.

'Is she here?' Ebony asked. 'Is the spirit here?'

There was movement in the shadows and Selena waited a moment, watching, letting herself feel the spirit's presence, its history, her story.

For Sophie was right, it was a woman.

'Oh wow,' Ebony whispered and looked at Rue. 'Can you smell that? I can totally smell that.'

It was perfume. Floral and heady, a summer garden on a balmy day.

Rue nodded, heart suddenly in her throat, and she looked up at Selena who had moved into the centre of the room, standing there with her eyes closed, head slightly upturned.

'Selena?' she asked, getting up. 'We can smell perfume.'

Selena nodded, hearing Rue's voice. She found her own, remembering that she had promised the girls that she would tell them what she was doing.

'She's here,' she said, taking another deep, slow breath.

Rue glanced out into the hallway, then pushed the door almost closed.

'In the room?' Ebony asked.

Selena nodded. 'Close your eyes,' she said. 'Be still, breathe slowly, open your senses.'

Rue and Ebony looked at each other for a moment, then closed their eyes. Rue felt the hairs on her arms stand up under the cloth of her sleeves, and she took a deep breath, remembering Selena's lesson in the attic the day they made their staves, and all the grounding and centring she'd had them do every morning, and the talk about dreams in the evenings.

She'd taught Ebony these things too, during their free time at lunch at school, standing under the generous green fringe of the willow tree.

'Ah, she has a sad story,' Selena said. She pressed a hand to her chest. 'I see a lot of waiting.' She shifted on her feet and looked into the dimness of the past. A light, scented breeze lifted the hair from her neck.

'She lost someone out at sea, I think,' Selena said, remembering to speak out loud for the girls' sakes.

'Out at sea?' Rue asked, feeling a great, sad longing well up around her. She swallowed, tried to shake the sensation away.

Selena had opened her eyes, and now she looked over at Rue. 'She's coming too close to you, Rue, tell her to stand back.'

Rue's mouth was dry, even as her eyes filled with tears. She shook her head, took a trembling breath.

'Stand back,' she said. 'You have to stand back.'

The atmosphere lightened, and Rue gulped great lungfuls of air. She looked at Ebony, then Selena. 'What happened?'

Selena touched her lightly on the shoulder, her touch steadying, reassuring.

'Sometimes spirits come a little too close,' she said. 'To the point that some of them will try to overshadow you.'

Rue was alarmed.

'Overshadow you?' Ebony asked. 'What, you mean, like possess you?'

Selena tipped her head to the side. 'Yes.'

'Okay,' Ebony nodded, looked over at Rue and grinned, then turned back to Selena. 'You can teach me to see or sense spirits like you can? I need to learn this.'

A moment's contemplation, and Selena nodded. 'If that is what you want.'

'More than anything,' Ebony said. 'Now, where were we? What's her sad story?'

'Her husband, or someone like that, I think?' Rue said. 'Never came back from sea?'

Ebony closed her eyes, remembered the way Selena had told them to relax and expand their senses when they were doing the thing with the staves.

'Boyfriend,' Ebony said, the idea coming to her as if from out of a mist. Then she shook her head, her eyes closed, concentrating. 'No; fiancé. Jeez, that's sad. She never you know, got over it and moved on.'

Excitement washed through Ebony. She couldn't see the spirit, or at least, not with her eyes. It was more a feeling, impressions coming to her.

She was really doing it.

Selena nodded. 'Now, let's see if she'd like to move on.'

She closed her eyes again, found the woman easily, standing in the middle of the room, looking around as though lost.

'It's all right,' she said to her. 'He's gone, but you can see him again; no one is gone forever. I think it's time.' She spoke to Rue and Ebony. 'I want you to fill the room with light,' she said. 'Bathe it in light.'

Inside Rue, everything glowed in a wash of golden light. Ebony too, turned on the light inside her and smiled. She could feel the spirit's presence, looking around, looking for something.

'Someone's come to meet you,' Selena said softly. 'It's him, look, can you see him?'

She saw the woman's spirit turn to the doorway, now lit brightly, and put her hands to her mouth at the sight of the man come to find her, to greet her.

To help her pass over.

'She's going,' Rue said softly.

They watched her step through the doorway, her loved one's arms around her now, both of them agleam with light, heads bent towards each other.

Ebony opened her eyes. 'That was amazing,' she said, and her eyes grew wider. 'I did it? Holy cow, I saw her – or felt her – or whatever.'

'You did more than that,' Selena replied. 'Both of you helped her move on. You're naturals at this.'

'Wow.' Ebony grinned. 'Where do we find another haunted house?' She shook her head, delirious with joy.

'I could do this all day long!'

50

It was Natalie's first time alone at her house since the night the man had tried to break in.

The night she'd met Selena.

And the others of course. All of them.

The sun was just setting, and she could still hear Damien's car driving down the road, heading back down the hill to Selena's house.

She touched the mobile phone in her pocket, wanting for a moment to pull it out, flip the lid on it and push the numbers that would have Damien turning around to come back and get her.

But she closed her eyes instead, drawing in a deep breath, and steadying herself where she stood, remembering Selena's lessons and drawing around her the trees of her special place.

When she opened her eyes again, she was able to nod.

'It's going to be all right,' she said out loud.

To prove it, she stepped into the back garden from her perch on the doorstep.

It was transformed. Natalie walked over to the rose bush Damien had planted for her, touched her fingers to the soft petals of a flower, then bent and inhaled its delicate fragrance. She stood and looked around the rest of the garden.

It was barely recognisable. Gone were all the weeds, and the overlong grass. Instead, there were three small, square vegetable beds, planted already with seedlings hardy enough to withstand the coming winter. Damien had fashioned cloches to go over them, hinged to the wooden bed edging on one side so that she could lift them to water her new plants.

In summer, he'd said, they could easily remove them altogether.

Natalie shook her head in wonder. Then smiled at the birdbath.

It was a present from Selena and everyone else – as though the rest of this had not been, all their hard work outside in the garden, and inside the house too. The circular bath was tiled in brilliant blue, and it stood on a plinth like a roman column. Natalie adored it.

She dipped her finger into the water then impulsively touched her forehead, as though blessing herself.

Perhaps that was exactly what she was doing.

'Sugar and roses,' she murmured.

Back inside, the house had undergone its own transformation. It smelled of fresh paint. Everyone, right down to Clover, had come around for four evenings straight, and painted the rooms. Natalie stood in the kitchen, a hand over her mouth.

The kitchen, a soft mint green now, still needed a last coat of paint, but she wanted to do that herself. Here, she'd decided, she would work on her recipes. Perfect them. Learn to make all the things from roses.

She glanced at the lettered sign Damien had made for her and her heart filled with gratitude and love for her new friends. The sign was perfect.

Sugar & Roses.

The house was very quiet. Natalie stood in the kitchen, missing Tara and Damien's company. She wasn't there to read Clover her bedtime story, or listen to the conversations between Selena, Dandy, and Rue.

She patted the new phone in her pocket and thought about calling to ask if she could spend another night with them. No one would mind, she was sure.

But after a moment, Natalie shook her head and made for the pot of paint, instead, pulling her hair back and tying a bandanna over it. She already had a streak of mint paint in her hair.

This is what she'd do, she decided. The last coat of paint in the kitchen, and then tomorrow, when it was dry, she could put everything back on the shelves, and arrange the new pots of herbs, and put up her new sign.

Sugar & Roses.

That was what the future held, she thought, dipping her roller in the paint. Friends, and purpose, and whatever else, she decided, whatever else came along, she would stand up as straight as she could, and spread her little bit of love in the world.

. . .

SHE WENT TO BED THAT NIGHT UNDER THE DARK SKY OF A waning moon, stepping into her bedroom with a trepidation that faded away when she realised how differently her room looked. She could, she thought, be in another house altogether than the one in which she'd lived all her life.

The room was freshly painted, and someone – Tara, most likely – had set a vase of bright late summer flowers on the dresser.

And the candlesticks were there. The ones she'd been using at Selena's house.

That, Natalie decided, was the work of Selena herself. Between them stood the bear Clover had given her.

Natalie hugged herself. Everyone had been so kind to her. They'd drawn her into their close-knit group as though that were the most natural thing in the world, and Natalie took a deep, watery breath just thinking of it.

'It's going to be all right,' she said out loud, and stepped into the room, crossing the floor to reach for the box of matches.

She lit the candles, touched a light finger to the bear, and closed her eyes, swallowing, drawing the trees of her small grove around her, looking at the warm, lit window of the cottage and thinking now that it could be her house, safe and secure, a little sugar and roses cottage.

'We believe in generosity and abundance,' Natalie whispered, repeating the words that Selena had once said to her. They seemed somehow to open up the world, and she stood straighter, seeing the beauty that was still in the world, no matter how painful and confused parts of it were still.

Leaving the candles burning, Natalie sat on the bed with her dream journal. She'd filled a good bit of it now, writing down her dreams, facing, with Selena's support, the recurring sights of bombs, missiles, and greasy shadows burnt upon the ground.

This was her history, she thought. This was the way she'd seen the world for so long that she'd lost sight of there being anything else in it.

But there were other things. Selena had taken her by the hand and shown her.

There was the laughter of a small girl who had sat in a chair outside Natalie's room waiting for her to get up in the mornings. There was Damien's strong back as he bent over his spade, turning over the soil for a new garden.

Natalie touched her head. There was the streak of mint green paint in her hair.

She turned through the pages in her journal, until she looked at the next blank one.

There was possibility, she thought. A blank page on which to write whatever came.

Setting the notebook back by the bed, Natalie got changed, blew out the candles, and slipped into bed. For a long while, she lay there, aware that she was alone in the house and listening to the sounds it made, settling into the darkness.

The phone was on her bedside table and that comforted her. Not that she would use it, she thought, just that there was someone to call if necessary. People who would care and who would come if she needed.

Not feeling alone changed so much.

Not feeling weak and stupid changed even more.

Natalie closed her eyes, fell asleep.

Slipped into a dream.

There was a missile coming. Natalie ducked her head and ran with the panicking crowd as it heaved down the street one way, then turned and bucked against the tide, rushing in the other direction.

There was a missile coming, a bomb riding on its back, and everyone knew it. The end of the world was on its way, and Natalie felt the sweat bloom cold with fear on her skin. She knew why the missile was coming – her world had sent five of their own, snub-nosed, white with painted black stripes, off to another, feared world.

And now, that faraway world was sending one in return, giant, bigger than the five, bigger than five and two more.

The crowd heaved again and suddenly Natalie was washed up upon the concrete shore of a parking building, one that stood open to the clear, beautiful sky, through which a missile would soon tear. She stood near the entrance and closed her eyes for a moment, then blinked at the sight of a woman gesturing to her from within the parking building.

She shook her head, knowing, in the way of dreams, that this woman wanted her to come up to the top floor with her.

The roof, Natalie thought.

Yes, the other woman said, coming forward and touching Natalie on the arm.

The roof. To watch the missile come.

The woman smiled at her with Selena's eyes, then turned, running lightly across to the stairwell.

Natalie followed her. Up the stairs. Right out onto the roof.

The sky was brilliant, the clearest, most perfect blue Natalie had ever seen.

She stood, looking at it, shaking in fear.

The woman with Selena's eyes smiled at her again. 'It won't be long,' she said.

Natalie shook her head. 'But I'm afraid.'

The whole world was afraid, she thought. Below them, on the streets, people screamed and ran this way, then that.

'Put this on,' the woman said to her, and Natalie looked at the bomber jacket she held out.

It was made from bear fur. In the way of dreams, she knew this.

Natalie touched the spiky fur, then slipped the jacket on and followed the woman out across the roof and over to the edge where the woman turned and looked at her again, her face lit up with excitement.

The woman with Selena's eyes tilted her head to the sky and spread out her arms to it.

As if to embrace what was coming. A missile from another world.

A message from another world.

Natalie, the bear pelt heavy on her shoulders, looked into the sky and saw the missile at last. It was huge, growing larger by the second. She stood mesmerised by it.

It was larger than she'd ever feared it would be.

Bearing down upon the only world she'd known.

Soon, everything would end.

Everything would change.

At the last moment, Natalie flung out her arms.

The bomb exploded in the air above her. The world around her filled with bright, clean light that enveloped everything and everyone.

All Natalie could see was the light.

It was the most beautiful thing she'd ever known.

51

'THOSE KIDS ARE AS EXCITED AS IF IT'S CHRISTMAS IN THERE,' Dandy said, stepping out into the small garden and finding Selena there. 'It's even better though, since Christmas is only once a year, and this now happens – how many times?'

Selena turned and smiled at her friend. 'Eight,' she said.

'Eight.' Dandy grinned. 'Oh, the riches of this world.' She looked over more closely at Selena. 'Are you all right?' she asked. 'What are you doing out here?'

'I am well, thank you,' Selena said, but she sighed. 'I'm thinking about Wilde Grove, I'm afraid, how while I am sleeping tonight, they will dance at the standing stones and celebrate the arrival of spring, when we are only beginning our seeding for it.'

Dandy nodded. 'It must be strange,' she said. 'Knowing it is all carrying on without you.'

'Morghan is doing well,' Selena said. 'I called her very early this morning.'

'I know you write to her.'

'Yes.' She glanced sideways at Dandy. 'May I confide in you?'

Dandy's eyes widened. 'Of course you may. I would be honoured if you did.'

Selena smiled faintly, then reached out and clasped Dandy's hand for a moment before letting go and tucking her arms crossed back over her chest. She was dressed in russet brown this morning, the colour of autumn, and the felt leaves that Rue had made were entwined in her loose hair, ready for the day.

'Rue told me a dream she had,' Selena said after a pause. 'I believe it was a past life dream.'

'Goodness,' Dandy said. 'The same lifetime that...helped her with those two men?'

'Probably,' Selena answered. She watched a lone yellow leaf fall spiralling to the ground from its branch. Most of the trees she could see were deciduous and hung as tightly to their leaves as ever.

'What about this dream, then?' Dandy prompted.

'It was set in Wilde Grove.'

Dandy frowned. 'What do you mean?'

'I recognised the landscape,' Selena said, turning now to look at Dandy. 'This life of hers was lived at Wilde Grove, or whatever it was called back then.'

Dandy was silent, trying to take in the implications of this. She shook her head. 'What does it mean?' she asked.

'I don't know,' Selena admitted. 'I've been trying my hardest to fathom what could be going on here, and it won't leave my mind.'

'What does Morghan say about it – I assume that you've told her?'

Selena nodded. 'That's mostly why I called her, but she has as little an idea as I do.'

Dandy looked back at the house. Rue was inside with her girlfriends, decorating for the autumn equinox and their celebration later that day.

'Has she had more dreams like that?'

'No,' Selena said. 'Not that she's remembered.'

'So, what, if anything, do we do about it?'

Selena didn't answer for so long that Dandy turned and stared at her.

'You already know what you want to do, don't you?'

Selena nodded, pressed her lips together, then nodded again. 'I'm going to take her to Wilde Grove.'

Dandy thought she'd probably known this was coming. 'Just Rue?'

'Likely Clover too,' Selena said. 'But someone will have to come with us, to take care of Clover.'

'Tara will do that,' Dandy said. 'In fact, I doubt she'd let you take Clover without her along as well.'

Selena smiled. 'You're probably right.'

'I know I'm right,' Dandy said. 'When?' she asked. 'For how long?'

'I don't know,' Selena said. 'Soon, I think, and I imagine it won't be able to be for longer than a few months.'

They were both silent then, thinking about it.

'Just when we were all settling in,' Dandy said at last.

THEIR AUTUMN EQUINOX CELEBRATION WASN'T DUE TO BEGIN for a while yet when Selena sought out Damien and tapped him on the shoulder. He turned to her with a beaming face.

'Do you have a spare hour?' she asked.

Damien nodded. 'Of course.' For Selena, he had all the time she needed, despite the fact that he was enjoying himself getting things ready in the kitchen with Tara and Natalie. 'Do you want me to take you somewhere?'

Selena nodded. 'Please.'

'I'll get my keys.'

Selena looked around at the hustle and bustle going on inside the house, smiled at the chatter, then slipped out of the room and went upstairs. She fetched her staff and came back down, going out by the front door, hoping to slip away unnoticed.

Damien was already at the car.

'Where to?' he asked as they waited to turn out of the driveway.

'I'd like to go to the beach, please,' Selena said.

Damien nodded, but he eyed her staff. 'Which one?'

Selena thought about it a moment. 'The one you think will have the least people.'

'Gotcha.' Damien turned the car towards the coast. 'Going to rain later,' he said. 'Good thing we're heading out now.'

But Selena just nodded and subsided against her seat.

The wind was up when they reached the beach, and Selena was glad.

'Scrabble up over the sand dune, or walk around by the creek?' Damien asked.

Selena smiled at him and turned to walk through the bush beside the creek.

The beach was deserted when they got there, and Damien fell discreetly behind while Selena strode forth around the great sand dune until the beach spread out either side of her, met at each end by rocky peninsulas.

This beach, she thought, looking out over the Pacific, had the most peculiar feeling to it. A lonely place, never quite adapting to the people who walked its length, ignoring them instead. Here, the birds and sea lions belonged. That was all.

The wind was fierce out of the protection of the dunes. It blew Selena's hair back and pressed her dress against her. She walked out close to the water line and planted her staff in the sand, placing both her hands on it and closing her eyes.

A seagull shrieked as it rode the air currents overhead, blown forward faster than it could ever fly, then spinning around to go back for more.

The wind rushed up to Selena, and after a moment, she changed her stance, holding her staff with one hand and stepping to the side, spreading her arms so that her heart was bared to the wind.

'Tell me,' she whispered. 'Show me.'

The wind laughed and whipped her words away, tossed them out upon the waves.

'Blessed Mother of the World,' Selena murmured. 'Blessed earth, sea, sky.'

The wind pummelled at her again.

'This is the day when we are held suspended in brief balance, before the Wheel tips and turns again. For this moment, my in-breath is as long as my out-breath.'

Selena breathed in, then out. Salt coated her tongue. She opened her eyes and looked out at the great stretch of water. She could not see the horizon. Sky met water in a haze of green and grey.

She closed her eyes again and felt the spin of the world around her. The wind swept itself up against her, wound around her, and with it, came the memories.

Not hers, Selena knew.

They came in snatches, and she tried to grasp hold of them, draw them closer, for examination, but the wind tugged them away again, and she became patient, waited for them to be revealed.

The wind brought Selena a different scent. Instead of salt, there was soil. Trees, not sand.

She was in the woods of Wilde Grove.

There was a young woman in a woad-blue dress, and Selena recognised her immediately, for she'd glimpsed this life of Rue's before.

And there behind her, between the trees, large and pale, the colour of the moon, rose a great dragon, spreading its wings and lowering its head so that it looked over the priestess's shoulder directly at Selena.

Selena stilled and time seemed to stretch out, her heartbeat low and slow in her chest as she stared at this vision.

They gazed at each other, eyes unblinking, and Selena saw every detail of the great white dragon, its scales and feathers, its ridged brow over large eyes the colours of the labradorite stone, iridescent and changing in front of her. Horns rose from its head, and she watched its breath, misty in the damp air, stir the hair of the young woman standing in front of it.

Then the dragon moved, graceful and swift despite its

size, launching itself upwards, between the trees and away into the sky out of sight.

The priestess in blue watched Selena a heartbeat longer, and then she turned and ran, swift as a deer, out of Selena's sight and vision.

Selena blinked her eyes open and stared out at the water. The tide had inched further up the beach toward her while she'd stood in trance, reaching out and reaching back, reading the memories the wind carried around and around the worlds. Now it wet her toes and she stepped back, shaking her head.

What was the meaning of it all, she wondered?

Clover and her wizards, Rue and her ancient life at the Grove.

For there would be a meaning, Selena thought.

And with the meaning, would come a task.

And a calling.

THE WIND HAD FOLLOWED SELENA BACK FROM THE BEACH AND bustled importantly about now as she stood in a loose circle with the others of her household.

She gazed around at them.

Her beacons, she thought.

The group had swelled since the Season of First Fruits back in February. Now they had Natalie amongst them, who stood outside under the lowering dome of the sky, her body tall and straight, the tension inside her revealed only in a slight tightening around mouth, eyes.

And there were Rue's friends, each one arrayed in a robe Rue had sewed for them, more felt leaves tied into their hair.

Selena closed her eyes briefly, for the image of a great dragon rose up in her mind behind Rue, who wore an indigo dress.

Damien stepped forward and lit the fire in the brazier, and Selena watched it crackle to life, clearing her mind of everything except their gathered purpose and the small flickers of growing flames.

She stepped forward. The fire, leaping to life, warmed her cheeks.

'May there be peace in the east,' she said.

'May there be peace in the south.' Her voice rose with the wind.

'May there be peace in the west.

'May there be peace in the north.'

She looked around her circle of friends. Thought of Morghan waking later and rising to dance around the stone circle, leading her small grove in the same prayers.

'May the peace of this season be upon us and upon all with whom we share this world.' Selena breathed slowly out.

'Here we are,' she said. 'At the balance of the season, the very moment before we breathe in, turn towards our hearths, and begin the growing of the seeds we plant at this celebration.'

She let her words settle upon the air, the wind withdrawing, leaving them floating.

'This is the time when the last harvest is gathered, and we turn instead to the great mystery of the worlds, the time when the Goddess takes into her womb the new seed and withdraws to nurture it until ready to birth the world to renewal at spring's touch. The seasons turn, the Wheel spins, and we follow the path of the Goddess, each of us nurturing inside us that which is precious, that which we desire to grow, to birth in our lives and the life of the world in which we live.'

She closed her eyes.

'May there be peace in the world,' Damien said. 'Whāia te iti kahurangi.' He smiled briefly at Natalie. 'Follow that which is most precious.'

Natalie smiled back at him.

Rue took a breath. Her voice, when she spoke, barely shook.

'May we be blessed and kept in peace.'

Clover hopped on one foot. 'Dragon flyin' behind ya,' she said.

Selena looked at her, breath held in her lungs, but Clover just smiled happily, and Rue looked startled, but she didn't say anything, unwilling perhaps to interrupt things.

Selena let herself breath again. Then nodded to Damien.

He stepped forward and picked up a coal shovel and dug it delicately into the fire until a small piece of burning wood was balanced upon it.

'We take this fire,' Selena said, 'lit under the last breath of the sun, and carry it inside to our hearth, there to burn until spring's touch is once more upon the earth.'

They turned as a group then and followed Damien inside as he carried the burning wood.

The fireplace in the kitchen had been carefully cleaned and set with pinecones, and strips of eucalyptus bark collected from the ground around the grove of the trees in the Botanic Garden. It was ready to light, and Damien tipped the burning ember carefully into the prepared grate and stood back to watch the flames catch.

'It's going!' Clover squealed, and then everyone was chattering and laughing.

Rue sidled over to her sister and bent down. 'What did you mean about a dragon?' she asked.

Clover shrugged. 'Dunno,' she said. 'Just saw one behind ya.' She nodded. 'Was white.'

'But dragons aren't real,' Rue said.

Clover looked horrified. 'But I saw it.'

'Okay.' Rue stood up, as mystified as before.

There was one more thing to do before they sat down to feast together at the table that groaned with dishes. Selena cleared her throat, and everyone gathered around again.

'Beside our hearth is a pot in which we will store our seeds for the coming cold season,' she said.

She and Dandy had come up with this simple ritual, and she smiled now, knowing that sometimes the simplest things were the most effective.

And that while this wasn't Wilde Grove, magic still lived.

'We have each prepared the seeds of that which we want to nurture over the coming season,' she continued. 'And these we will put in the pot, placed by the warmth of our hearth, as a symbol of what we will grow over the next months, just as the Mother of the Worlds grows our land back to life.'

Natalie picked up her small package from the table and held it in both hands. She'd given a great deal of thought to what she wanted to put in the big terracotta pot along with everyone else's seeds.

In the end, she'd wrapped up the dried petals from the

last rose of the bush growing in her garden, actual seeds for a smattering of plants, and a tiny stuffed bear she'd sewn from a scrap of fabric.

She wanted to grow a whole life, she thought, placing her small package inside the pot.

Sugar and seeds and roses, all under the protection of Bear, whose strength could help her face anything, even that which she feared the most.

She backed away from the earthen pot, her parcel deposited, her cheeks flaming. She smiled self-consciously, then more easily, as Selena reached out and took her hand, held it for a second, as though in blessing.

Then, when all the small packages of seeds and wishes and promises were put in the pot, they stepped back from the hearth and sang the words Selena had taught them.

Round and round the Wheel is turning.
In and out the web is woven.
Here I am. Here I am.
I sing the song of the worlds.

PRAYER OF THE WILDWOOD

Here is the path I seek, Elen, Lady Of
    The Ways,
It is your flame I tend, Brigid Of The
    Hearth.
I walk the path with my heart and
    head on fire,
bright with the beauty of the soul.

I am a spoke on the wheel.
I am the singer and spinner of worlds.
I am one bright soul among many
and I would sing us into harmony,
world to world to world.

ABOUT THE AUTHOR

Katherine has been walking the Pagan path for thirty years, with her first book published in her home country of New Zealand while in her twenties, on the subject of dreams. She spent several years writing and teaching about dreamwork and working as a psychic before turning to novel-writing, studying creative writing at university while raising her children and facing chronic illness.

Since then, she has published more than twenty long and short novels. She writes under various pen names in more than one genre.

Now, with the Wilde Grove series, she is writing close to her heart about what she loves best. She is a Spiritworker and polytheistic Pagan.

Katherine lives in the South Island of New Zealand with her wife Valerie. She is a mother and grandmother.

Printed in Great Britain
by Amazon

84685951R00287